Etienne van Heerden

Following a career as an attorney and then in advertising, Etienne van Heerden moved to academia. He has taught at the Universities of Zululand and Rhodes, South Africa, and regularly teaches at universities abroad. He has been Writer in Residence at the Universities of Leiden, Antwerp and Iowa, USA, and is currently Professor of Literature at the University of Cape Town. He is the author of collections of poetry and short stories and several previous novels, including *Ancestral Voices*, which won the CNA Literary Award and the Hertzog Prize. He has also won the M-Net Book Prize (South Africa's most high-profile prize for fiction) and the WA Hofmeyr Prize for *The Long Silence of Mario Salviati*, and his work has been translated into nine languages.

Also by Etienne van Heerden

Ancestral Voices
Mad Dog and Other Stories
Casspirs and Camparis
Leap Year
Kikuyu

The Long Silence of Mario Salviati

Etienne van Heerden

Translated by Catherine Knox

SCEPTRE

Copyright © 2002 Etienne van Heerden
Translation © 2002 Catherine Knox, Etienne van Heerden and
Isobel Dixon

First published in Great Britain in 2002 by Hodder and Stoughton
A division of Hodder Headline

The right of Etienne van Heerden to be identified as the Author
of the Work has been asserted by him in accordance with
the Copyright, Designs and Patents Act 1988.

A Sceptre Book

2 4 6 8 10 9 7 5 3 1

A CIP catalogue record for this title is available
from the British Library

ISBN 0 340 81999 5

Typeset in Sabon by Palimpsest Book Production Limited,
Polmont, Stirlingshire
Printed and bound in Great Britain by
Clays Ltd, St Ives plc

Hodder and Stoughton
A division of Hodder Headline
338 Euston Road
London NW1 3BH

To Kaia

The Yearsonend

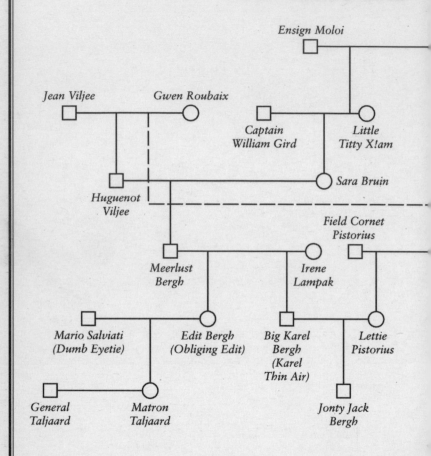

Blood Tree

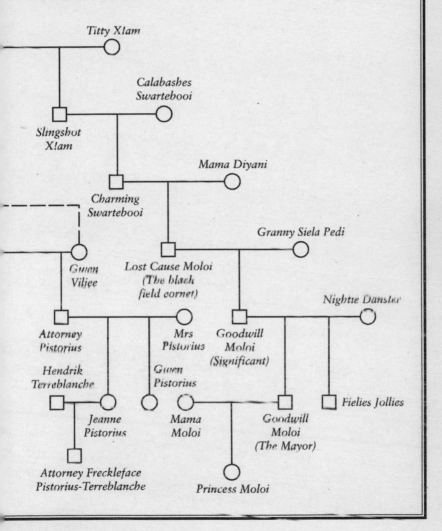

Prologue

In time, their eyes grew accustomed to the darkness as they crowded together at the mouth of the cave. The carriage seemed to shimmer up out of the depths.

Then the past rammed into their chests and they reeled back, because it seemed as though the black carriage had begun to move, to bear down on them. But it was just an illusion. The dust was beginning to settle and the onlookers' pupils dilated as they peered into the darkness.

The carriage was an apparition; a ghost carriage glinting with the swarms of fireflies that kept vigil over it. Removed for so long from the ravages of light and the touch of human hands, it had been almost perfectly preserved. A stalactite had dripped down right onto the carriage roof and stalagmites had reached up from the cave floor to anchor it from below. The earth reaching out her fingers to protect the improbable carriage.

A white skeleton sat on the driver's bench. He was still dressed and you could tell from their bones that the six horses had died in harness. Ostrich feathers on the crowns of their skulls stirred in the light breeze.

Ingi Friedländer pressed forward to get a better view. A half-smoked cigar was still gripped between the fingers of the skeleton's left hand. The other bony hand clasped a parchment. It was ancient and brittle and yellowed, and fireflies glistened on its edges.

The third map, everyone thought.

Part One

Lightning Water

When Jonty Jack pushed open the door of his cottage in the gorge above the little town of Yearsonend one morning, and the smell of damp ferns and old wood shavings rose in his nostrils, he found the sculpture standing there, just as though . . . 'God's my witness,' said Jonty Jack, 'just as though it had sprouted from the ground overnight.'

Whenever he told the story in the months after the sculpture's apparition, Jonty became positively maudlin. 'The Staggering Merman pushed his head up through the wood shavings and bark and dagga butts; that fish-man, he came staggering into the world . . .'

In spite of the national renown the sculpture earned for Jonty Jack, he continued to insist that the image of the Staggering Merman was not the work of his own hand. No one believed him; there was a hunger for artists with god-like gifts here in this new republic, in the last year of the twentieth century. 'For heaven's sake,' Jonty was to exclaim later to Ingi Friedländer, 'I'm only a woodworker, a carver, a layabout and a cynic. I don't have the talent for a sculpture like this – I'm too limited for that, I swear to God.'

This is what he told Ingi Friedländer when she arrived in Yearsonend to buy the sculpture on behalf of the National Gallery in Cape Town, the special collection destined for the Houses of Parliament.

Jonty recounted how he'd emerged from his cottage one morning, still slightly hung over from the previous night's boozing, and there stood the fish thing, taller than a man, his body curved like a dolphin leaping from the waves, or like a swan flapping up from the water, that moment just before it's airborne, feet still in the water, but the body already gloriously in the air. But along with this exuberance – and Jonty had noticed this at once – the sculpture was imbued with a deep sadness.

That first morning, Jonty had walked slowly up to the sculpture. He wanted to touch it, but something restrained him. At the front, the dolphin lines were clearly recognisable, but if you walked round, they became the contours of a shark; and sombre markings at the back suggested that, in rising, the sculpture was already predicting its own downfall. There were lines that suggested a folded wing or, on closer examination, a man's sinewy thigh.

The sculpture was neatly finished off. This was no amateur piece. It was definitely much more accomplished than the selection of half-finished figures lying around his small house. That man with the grand ostrich-plumed hat, leaning against the fowl-run over there, for instance. The figure was supposed to say something deft and humorous about self-confidence and machismo but, alas, probably owing to the wrong choice of wood and a blunt chisel, he swaggered on only one leg. And then the angel figure lying at the back door with half its face splintered off where a fault in the wood had given way under the chisel's blow – almost as though the devil had taken a bite out of the angel-man's cheek. And that young boy in shorts with the missing right hand . . .

My crippled lambs, Jonty often murmured. But he realised at first glance that the fish-man was the embodiment of art at its finest. It's a message to me, he decided, a message about what can be created, about what one should strive for. He sniffed the sculpture and he could smell the cinnamon and sulphur odour of the Creator's touch. And, right there and then, Jonty fell to his knees and gave the fish sculpture a name.

The Staggering Merman, he called it, starting an argument in Yearsonend: 'But the fish thing is rising; he's flying up from the water. What's this stagger business of yours, Jonty?' Others maintained: 'You haven't seen a man stop a bullet in his chest yet. Then you'd understand what it is to stagger.'

But Jonty stood his ground: the fish-man rose up, yes, but he was staggering at the same time. 'That's what life's about,' he would often expound afterwards in the pub. 'When you think you're moving forward, in truth you're actually staggering back into the past again.'

And when he was completely drunk, he'd fall to testifying all over again. The fish-man was not the work of his hand: it had just materialised one morning, standing there complete, shining in the morning sun, wet with dew, while wisps of mist still hovered about the arum lilies that thrust their way up through the wood shavings. The sculpture was still steaming, Jonty would declare after his fourth brandy, from the Creator's warm hands, like a newborn calf that has tumbled, hot and slippery, from its mother's hindquarters.

Laughter echoed round the bar. 'Staggering Jonty', the drinkers called him – cautiously because they couldn't understand why a rich man like Jonty should seclude himself in a small house up there in the Cave Gorge. Once it was common knowledge that he'd rejected Ingi Friedländer's offer on behalf of the National Gallery, people whispered as he ambled past, dreamy from the marijuana he grew in the ravine behind his house, 'There goes the Staggering Merman. He plants dagga seeds in his garden and sculptures come up.'

And eventually they even started saying to his face, 'Hey, Staggering Merman, are the sculptures still sprouting in your backyard?'

The Yearsonenders had great fun teasing Jonty – actually more than fun: it was a relief. Because the deeds and misdeeds of the two families from which Jonty sprang – the Berghs and the Pistoriuses – were entwined in the tragic history of this remote town. To have a Bergh who was now clearly going round the bend provided comic relief for a community that had always believed it was the Berghs and the Pistoriuses who kept the great secret that trapped their town in the past close to their chests, carrying it with them always.

And people whispered behind their hands, 'If only he'd conjure up the lost gold from underground instead of sculptures.' But the silences and fears of years prevented them saying these things directly to the sculptor with the red ponytail.

2

'Schizophrenic,' whispered a colleague in Ingi Friedländer's ear, as she prepared for the long journey to Yearsonend.

The reference was to Jonty Jack, the artist about whom so little was known. But she combed her fingers through her long corn-gold hair, turned her Florentine profile to the man and declared, 'Art without madness isn't worth the bother. Just look at all the politically correct canvases on these walls. On the eve of the new millennium we need a few stoned madmen to paint for us . . .'

Annoyed, Ingi tidied her desk and filed sheaves of documents: columns of figures detailing the expense of entertaining ministers and their officials who'd stand about with their shiny ties and cocktails before yet another boring exhibition; the estimates for repairing the roof, which always sprang a leak in the heavy winter storms, when gusts blew across Table Mountain and wind and rain shook the museum; the endless correspondence with artists who were furious that their work did not hang in the National Collection.

It was a relief to walk out through the museum doors, over the square with its formal lawns, past the fountain sparkling in the morning sun, through the scrabbling, flapping pigeons and playing children, to her yellow Peugeot station wagon, its trailer already hitched.

The Minister's smiling request had been that she bring 'rainbow art' back to the museum – 'to celebrate the wonders of freedom' – but there were no rainbows on the long road undertaken by Ingi Friedländer, who was somewhat inexperienced for her job; perhaps too young, perhaps too cynical. Overloaded minibuses wove recklessly through the traffic leaving the city. Sheep and goats grazed on the verge and vehicles careered past, perilously close to their grazing heads.

But eventually the traffic thinned. She left the hubbub of the city. Like a fist slowly relaxing, opening, the landscape unfolded about her. The stress of urban life drained from her body – the perpetual threat of armed robbery, hijacking, and corruption. Colours shifted subtly in the vineyards against the slopes; the wind swept over the fynbos plains; a flock of birds wheeled slowly in front of the car.

She stopped once to buy a bunch of grapes at a roadside fruit stall; took the first grape between thumb and forefinger, sniffed it, then bit it slowly, contemplatively, in half.

The trailer was packed high with foam rubber and blankets to cushion the famous sculpture, which hardly anyone had seen but which already occupied a special place in the imagination of every art expert.

And when they learned in the Cape that the sculpture was called the Staggering Merman, interest would increase exponentially. Museums almost always bought works on hearsay; desperate to capture the new spirit of now, desperate to remain relevant in the context of merciless cuts in government culture budgets.

As she left the winelands and the endless plains of the Karoo opened out around her, Ingi Friedländer began to sing. She wound down the windows and saw herself as though from afar: a young woman, in her late twenties, of average height with brown eyes and with her blonde hair streaming out in the wind, at the wheel of a slightly dated, shocking yellow Peugeot station wagon, driving through a landscape where, far away, the rock strata against the hills seemed like brown waves, in perpetual motion, surging and restless.

A hundred metres from the vehicle, a herd of springbok took to their heels, bounding into the air, leaping like ballerinas.

3

With George Gershwin's 'Summertime' floating from the cassette player, Ingi Friedländer swung off the tarred road. She'd been warned that the gravel road to Yearsonend might be rough, but no warning could have prepared her for the stretch of road she had to tackle now. Heavy buses had churned deep tracks into every bend and in other places the hard, compacted gravel gleamed as though it had been tarred. Then there were stretches where the surface was loose and sandy, ridged with juddering corrugations under the layer of fine dust. The trailer – specially elongated for the museum's purposes – bounced hazardously from side to side.

Ingi stopped at one point to make sure that the trailer hitch was holding, switching off the Gershwin for the time being. The veld stretched out around her. Where she expected to see the line of the horizon, a scarcely visible, shimmering outline slowly danced.

She tied up her hair because whenever she had to tread hard on the brake as she hit a particularly bad patch, the boiling dust behind the car caught up with her. Her nose was already running from the fine powder that filtered down over the steering-wheel and dashboard.

Cicadas shrilled and the wind sighed round her. The highway was far behind; the city further still. Her mind returned to Jonty Jack and his sculpture. Rumours had reached the museum that the sculptor had turned down generous offers from other collections on principle.

She watched a falcon hovering over the plains like a scrap of fluttering fabric. She could no longer endure the internal politics at the museum – it was time to break away. She had to make a change and this mission was a way out – seeking out Jonty Jack in Yearsonend, evaluating his work, and then, if it was as exceptional as rumour claimed, buying the sculpture.

She got back into the car and took a swig from her water bottle before driving on. What's the rush, Ingi? she asked herself. You're caught in timelessness itself here. No one gives a damn whether you arrive tomorrow or the day after.

The thought made her relax; she slowed down and flicked the cassette on again, singing along as the vehicle nosed its way into the dry wind. The falcon tracked her passage for some way, through tight corners and river fords, which forced her to creep along. The bird hung fluttering over the vehicle, then abruptly veered off in search of prey.

She'd spread a sketched map open on the passenger seat beside her. A colleague who frequented remote mountain-bike trails had explained that the Yearsonend road turned off from the gravel one she was travelling on now. This turn-off was hardly ever marked on maps, her colleague had said, so now Ingi followed his directions.

After an incline, you suddenly realised you were on the plateau of an escarpment and were now really heading into the open, where subtle blues and grey-beige melted away into buff. The turn-off to a side road lay unexpectedly near a thorn tree, the route careening off on to the plain, ducking through a rut marked by the wreck of an old car. Then, as though the road gained courage, it broadened and levelled out. Low dykes here and there to limit flood damage, and then an old milestone on which the barely legible numerals 68 were carved.

'When you see 68,' Ingi's mountain-biking colleague had told her, 'you have to realise that milestone is a bluff, so take a sip of water and pray for deliverance: the worst is yet to come. You'll yearn for the N1 . . .'

But it wasn't so bad after all. The road had obviously been graded recently and Ingi was able to loosen her hair again and let the wind blow through it. The road stretched dead straight ahead, bordered with low bushes. Now and then she made out a lonely farmstead with curtains drawn against the sun, or with black holes in the walls where wind and weather had forced the windows from their frames.

Unexpectedly, almost ominously, the huge mountain reared up in the distance: dark, brooding, anomalous.

Mount Improbable, her colleague had told her. Without warning, an apparition in the nothingness on that windblown plain, a massif, as though a gigantic chunk of the Boland had torn loose from the Hex river range and absconded, to crouch here in the hinterland, grim and obdurate. 'And a mountain,' her colleague had murmured, 'of many mysteries.'

As she drove closer, Ingi observed the way the mountain changed in form and appearance, as mountains do when you draw nearer. One moment it looked dangerous and shrouded in shadows; the next, after thorn trees screened it from view as she negotiated a ford, it was gleaming silvery in the sun with triumphant rocky peaks lording it over the plains.

Then, the cold shadow of Mount Improbable fell over her and the surface of the road grew slippery as silk, the dust floated up like talcum powder and the texture of the earth and the veld changed. She increased her speed, enjoying the smooth hum of her Peugeot's tyres on the road. At the foot of the mountain she came upon a fence and a parched, dying orchard – pears, she wondered, or peaches? They stood there, gnarled, and a grey stone furrow with rusted sluice gates ran beside the desiccated plot.

Then another fence, this time enclosing a lucerne field, and the first dwelling: a Cape Dutch cottage with snowy whitewashed walls, a curved gable and shuttered windows. A rectangular stone pond lay behind the house, a windmill turned in the breeze, and a man looked up and gazed after her for a long time, she noted in her rear-view mirror.

At first she wasn't sure whether she'd entered the town or only a group of smallholdings, but as she progressed, the houses stood closer together, with cultivated fields stretching out behind them. Ingi looked at orchards and lucerne fields, workers who unbent from their spades to watch her, arms akimbo. Now the houses stood side by side, fronting on the street; dwellings with pleasingly clean lines and no ornamentation.

She pulled up beside an old woman carrying a bucket.

'Good-day,' said Ingi. 'I'm looking for lodgings.' The woman stared at her uncomprehendingly. Ingi noted the brown teeth behind the wind-chapped lips, the scarf tied tightly over the forehead. 'A room, perhaps?' she tried again. But the woman simply stared and Ingi couldn't decide whether it was bitterness or stupidity that gazed at her so intently. 'A guest-house?' she prompted.

'Ask over there at the Baas Dealer,' said the woman, raising her shoulders as though to shrug off Ingi's unusual request, then stumping off. Ingi drove on slowly. There was a small police station behind a wire fence. A convict was busy with a rake in the neatly laid-out rose garden.

She drove on, past a house with an antique sign that announced in copperplate: *Pistorius Attorneys: Criminal, Conveyancing, Estates, Water Rights*. Then there was a general store with people lounging on the veranda, staring at her curiously, and even one who jumped up and ran inside, then came back with a man in a white apron. He was evidently the 'Baas Dealer' and he waited on the veranda, his hands on his hips and his apron draped comically over his paunch. The sun was in his eyes so he had to squint at Ingi, who took her time getting out of the car, smoothing her hair, taking off her sunglasses and looking around her.

She felt self-conscious as she locked the car. They watched every movement. It was obviously unnecessary to lock it here, she thought, and this city habit would probably be interpreted as a sign of distrust. But when she turned to the storekeeper and the people sitting on the veranda, she said, 'Good-day,' in her friendliest voice.

The man in the apron continued to stare at her without so much as a word of greeting, but he didn't seem unfriendly. Then he raised his hand in a kind of salute and came down the steps. She put out a hand. 'Friedländer. Ingi.'

'Good-day,' he answered, and she wanted to ask: Do you always welcome strangers like this? But she thought better of it.

'I'm looking for lodgings.'

The man rubbed his jaw. 'You're from Cape Town?' he asked cautiously. Ingi nodded. 'Tourist?'

She shook her head. 'No. Business.' She looked round again. Some of the children who'd been sitting in the shade of the veranda roof had drawn closer. They were listening inquisitively.

She noted the way the storekeeper's eyebrows shot up at the word 'business'. He was on the point of asking her what her business was, she saw, but then decided against it.

'There isn't a hotel here, Missy. You'd better drive through to the next town. There's a Protea hotel there – they've got a lounge and a breakfast room.'

'I have to stay here for a while.' This exchange in front of such an avid audience was making Ingi profoundly uncomfortable.

'Missy?'

He looked questioningly at her and for a moment she was nonplussed. Then she realised he hadn't caught her name. 'Friedländer,' she smiled.

'Miss 'Länder,' he continued, 'the best thing is to rent the stonecutter's cottage from the Munis. How long do you have to stay?'

'Stonecutter?' Ingi squinted questioningly into the sun. 'Munis?'

The storekeeper wiped his hands on his apron. 'Wouldn't you enjoy a cold drink, with the establishment's compliments?' he asked, and led the way up the steps, into the dim interior of the shop. He handed Ingi a can of Coke and explained, 'The Municipality – we call it the Munis – rents a house to visitors. It might suit you. If there aren't any hunters or prospectors.'

'Prospectors?'

'The farmers are having a hard time and the new thing, these days, is game farms. People come to shoot kudu.'

'And the prospectors?'

He shrugged and avoided meeting her eyes. 'Oh, Miss 'Länder, you know how it is with the wagon of gold . . .'

The Coke was deliciously cold in Ingi's throat. 'The wagon of gold?'

He didn't answer, and went off to attend to a customer waiting at the cash register. People were crowded in the doorway watching Ingi. 'You obviously don't see many strangers round here,' she observed drily, when he came back.

'The ostrich-feather boom is over,' he said, 'and the gold still eludes us.'

'Gold?' Ingi choked on her Coke, but he led her by the elbow back on to the veranda and pointed down the street. 'Past Blood Tree, down there, then round the corner, then a bit of a bend, and it's just a little way on. '

'Accommodation?' asked Ingi.

'Yes.' The storekeeper's breath smelt of mutton and roast potatoes.

She walked down the steps, blinded by the bright sunlight, and got back into the car. In the rear-view mirror she saw the storekeeper, the veranda sitters still craning inquisitively after her, and the old woman with the water bucket coming round the corner and trudging slowly up the street.

She found the pepper tree with its great broad branches, its bark and tissue bulging over the fence beside it, and gazed in wonderment at the melding of barbed-wire fence and tree flesh. 'The Blood Tree,' she murmured.

Then she drove slowly in first gear round the corner with a stone wall and there were the municipal offices, all unpainted cement and functional lines, with a plaster rising sun over the door.

Ingi parked under the thorn tree and got out, slow and sweaty. She locked the car and drew a deep breath. I was crazy, she thought, to come this far without arranging accommodation in advance. But someone had told her: There's neither a hotel nor a guest-house and you'll have to find lodging when you get there – people in the Karoo are famous for their hospitality. Just go, there'll be a bed and a meal somewhere.

And now she'd been delivered into the hands of bureaucrats: the last thing she wanted. She followed the concrete path between the little flowerbeds and into the air conditioned building with its low ceiling and pot plants. Built in the late seventies, or early eighties, she thought, when these clinical administration offices were constructed all over the country.

The young receptionist could barely speak English – her Afrikaans would have been much more fluent, if she'd only cared to use it, Ingi suspected. 'No, I realise there's no hotel. Anything, you know, a cottage or any . . .'

The word 'cottage' struck a spark and the heavily made-up eyes looked up from the papers before her. 'Oh, we have a tourist cottage. But no breakfast included.'

'God forbid,' responded Ingi, 'that breakfast should rule our lives.'

Ingi rented the cottage for a nominal fee – 'Florentine Cottage', according to the photocopied A4 sheet the receptionist gave her. She would, she confirmed with an irritable signature, organise her own breakfast.

Then she waited impatiently. After a search and a debate in a back room, the receptionist reappeared with a key. Ingi could only occupy the cottage for seven days; after that it was booked for three weeks for an American hunting party. 'For the hides, the photographs and the horns,' as the receptionist put it.

After extensive explanations about the location of Florentine Cottage, Ingi got back into her car. Florentine, she thought, could you believe it? Florence in the old Karoo.

She drove slowly back round the stone-wall corner and past Blood Tree once again.

She was immediately struck by a man who was walking past the general store. He made his way down the middle of the road as though he didn't expect any traffic. She couldn't tell his age, but he had a strong, fit body under his faded red vest. He wore his red hair in a ponytail and Ingi couldn't help noticing the strong hands and forearms. Yes: it was he, without a doubt – she'd heard tell of his red hair. She overtook him, tempted to stop and ask: 'Are you Jonty Jack?'

But she thought better of it and watched as he walked on through the dust behind her car as though he hadn't noticed the unusual sight, in this remote village, of a visiting vehicle with a young woman at the wheel.

'Good-day,' murmured Ingi as she drove on, still watching him in the rear-view mirror. 'Good-day to you, Jonty Jack. I am Ingi. Ingi Friedländer from the National Gallery. '

4

Like all the towns and hamlets in the Great Karoo or on the edge of the plains, where shrubveld runs into bergveld or sourveld, Yearsonend had a troubled past.

The San were here first, as they had been on the sweetveld of so many other bends in the river or armpits of the mountain in this part of the world. They'd occupied the cave on the mountain and they'd left their paintings on the walls for coming generations to puzzle over in wonderment.

Khoi tribes had also driven their herds through here and camped on the sandy banks of the river. And it was here, close to the spot where the pub now stood – the pub where Jonty Jack liked to testify that the sculpture was not the work of his own hand – that a British captain, the young explorer William Gird, reined in his horse. He gestured to his guide, who also served as groom and interpreter, to keep quiet.

The captain – ancestor of the man whose skeleton Ingi would stare at in the cave one day – gazed in amazement at the first giraffe he'd ever cast eyes on. The young Briton, fresh from colonial India where he'd been decorated for bravery, slid silently to the ground. His guide, Slingshot X!am, pulled the pack mule closer, gently, so as not to disturb the elegant creature with the tiny head, browsing on the topmost crown of a tree.

Gingerly, the guide folded out the table and placed the canvas chair beside it. He unpacked the ink bottles and placed the two sharp-nibbed drawing pens to the left, for the captain was left-handed. A white bird alighted on the giraffe's hump and pecked unhurriedly at the ticks feeding there. Gird removed his jacket and handed it to the guide, then rolled up his sleeves and sat stiffly at the table.

The cicadas shrilled, the smell of dry grass filled his nostrils, and the captain sweated in the sun as he drew the giraffe with careful strokes. He uncapped the paint bottles and mixed the precise colour for the blotches on the animal's hide. He wanted to capture the markings, the lines of neck and back, the combination of elegance and boyish clumsiness. In time the smell of wet paint mingled with the smell of the earth, dry grass, dung and soil.

When he was done, the captain blew the paint dry carefully and showed the picture to the guide, who nodded approvingly. Earlier, he had waited outside the mouth of the cave while Captain Gird crept down beside the walls, touching the Bushman paintings with hungry fingertips as though he wanted to steal them from the rocks. Now the captain was making his own painting in brighter colours; more realistic than the San's, the guide observed, as he craned his neck to follow the movements of the paintbrush. It was to show the people overseas what the creature looked like, the captain explained.

Slingshot X!am stowed the dry painting in the pigskin saddlebag along with the other paintings of elephant, lion, buffalo. Without waiting for Captain Gird to ask him, he pulled the rifle out of the gun bag hanging against the shoulder of the captain's horse, loaded it and handed it to him. Still seated at the table, his fingers still sticky and yellow with paint, the captain calmly took aim.

When the shot rang out, the giraffe swung his small head round in surprise, leaves fell from his mouth, and his improbably long legs caved in. But even in its dying, grace overcame clumsiness, as the body crashed through the tree on which he had browsed and the long neck swept down like a falling branch. Fascinated, the captain watched the small head travel a great distance before it hit the ground with a crack like a whiplash.

The captain sat and waited until the dust settled and the last tremors left the body. The guide fetched a pencil, a notebook and measuring tape from the mule's saddlebag and handed them to the captain. Gird stepped up closer, studying the giraffe, stroking the hide, counting the markings on the neck and feeling the horns. He sniffed the animal's hide then made careful notes under the heading 'Giraffe'. The measurements took some time, for the captain insisted on double-checking the distance between hoof and knee, knee and groin, between shoulder and neck, between chest and head. The neck particularly interested the captain. He tried to count the neck vertebrae, digging into the skin with his fingers.

Finally the captain and Slingshot X!am rode away, leaving the dead animal to the vultures that had already alighted in the surrounding trees.

But the captain would return years later, for his paintings earned him great fame in London and Paris, and, as the whole Empire read in the papers, this particular portrayal of the giraffe would be bought by the King himself and hang in his study in Buckingham Palace. In gratitude for the honour, Captain Gird returned with the same guide to the stream, the sandbank, the cave and the mountain, so improbably high here on the flat landscape, and to his surprise he found, when he loosened the soil between a tuft of grass and an anthill with the toe of his boot, the remains of bones, a scrap of hide with bristles still showing, still attached to a vertebra and cured hard by the elements – unmistakably the remains of the beautiful creature he'd so cold-bloodedly sat and sketched.

The acknowledgement of cold-bloodedness had only come later to the captain, once he was back in London. By then the King had bought his painting so he was famous, but his wife had left him due to his gnawing passion for exploring far-off lands. That made him decide to return to Africa, to retrace his old trails and reassess his life.

I will return to that improbable mountain, he thought, to that small valley with the river and the cave, the great boulders and the empty winds that blow there.

Captain Gird decided to pitch camp beside the remains of the giraffe. He remained there from full moon to full moon. Later a group of itinerant Khoi erected their shelters on the opposite bank of the river. They bartered sheep for the little hand mirrors, beads and a bottle of brandy that Gird's groaning mule had borne all this way.

Later that night, they came and stole back the animals and the next morning, when the captain and the guide crossed over to their camp, they feigned ignorance and innocence. The captain, who'd envisaged the sheep he'd purchased as the beginning of a farming enterprise, recognised the very same animals back in the Khoi-Khoi flock.

He lost his temper and ordered Slingshot X!am to snatch the mirrors from the women and children. The guide obeyed and things got ugly. A shot was fired, knobkerries were brandished, and the captain and his guide had to beat a hasty retreat through the shallow stream back to their camp, leaving drops of blood dispersing slowly in the water.

It was never reported how many people died, but the sun sank sadly on the place that would be known one day as Yearsonend. An insignificant incident, but it set a precedent and, from then on, this valley and its mountain would always be a place of misunderstanding and death – 'A hotbed of avarice and suspicion,' as Jonty Jack explained it to Ingi Friedländer shortly after the arrival of the yellow station wagon at his little house in Cave Gorge.

5

Ingi found the municipal cottage easily. It stood on the outskirts of town, close to the mountain, and, from the back door, her eye followed the slopes of a densely forested gorge up to the summit where a couple of eagles circled Mount Improbable's cliff-faces.

She left the car on the shady side of the house. She couldn't resist stroking the immaculate masonry with her fingertips – the hairlines where stone met stone. 'The stonecutter': she recalled the words the storekeeper had used. And she thought: A cottage like this deserves preservation status. I wonder when it was built and whether the National Monuments Commission . . . ? But then she brushed her hand over her eyes. You're here on a specific mission, Ingi, she scolded herself. You aren't here to fantasise about stonecutters and prospectors and Blood Trees, you're here to buy a sculpture from that fellow with the ponytail then take it back to Cape Town.

After hovering for a while at the entrance near a wooden bench, polished to a shine by years of use, she pushed open the door. It, too, had obviously been made with care by someone who knew his craft. Inside, she was struck by a cold smell that seemed to come from the bowels of the earth. It was cool and dim here. Yes, it smelt like a mountain cave, she thought – a house that belonged to this earth and that mountain. When her eyes grew accustomed to the dimness, she unlatched the shutters and pushed them open, letting the light stream in.

She looked around her. The walls were plastered inside and the low, almost too low, ceiling was made of reeds. The room she stood in was a kitchen and living room combined, with a great hearth containing an old wood stove. Stone ledges were built into the wall on either side of the stove, so that in winter one could sit and eat right up against the warmth. A broad beam, as thick as a man's trunk, had been built into the stonework above the hearth. There were small windows on either side of the stove, dulled by years of broiling stove heat inside and the iciness of winter nights without.

The floor was stone too, Ingi noticed, with a couple of springbok hides and a worn old zebra skin spread out in the sitting corner. There was a small bathroom with an old-fashioned bath and taps. Just the bare essentials, she noted, with satisfaction. Frugal and stripped down, scrubbed clean, with a simplicity that promised peace. The furniture in the two bedrooms was just as simple: a pair of decorative porcelain jugs standing in the white washbasins was the only indulgence.

Ingi studied the black and white photographs above the fireplace. In the centre hung a large black-framed picture, so faded that she had to look closely to make out the faces. There stood a stocky man dressed in khaki. His shorts came almost to his knees, and the calf muscles were striking, as were the large hands. But a reflection – or perhaps a processing problem in the darkroom – hid his features. She could only make out something of an unusually large nose, and hair combed back. The woman next to him was far from exceptional; lumpen and camera-shy, her face was obscured too.

The builder of Florentine Cottage, Ingi read in the caption to the photograph, *Mr Mario Salviati, Italian stonecutter of repute, alongside his wife, Edit, singer of opera arias.*

The photograph beside it showed a station platform with a long train and young men in threadbare uniforms leaning out of the windows. A crowd had gathered on the platform and two mounted policemen stood by, their horses' ears pricked. *The Italian Prisoners of War from Zonderwater Prison arrive at Yearsonend.*

Ingi gazed at the two photographs. The glass was flyblown. Suddenly she shivered: a cold draught had swept through the room. Rubbing her forearms, she went out into the sun to fetch her luggage from the car. She stood irresolute for a moment, before choosing the slightly smaller bedroom, the one with only one bed. She moved the ornate porcelain jug to the other room, but kept the simple white basin on her chest of drawers.

After hanging up her clothes, she unhitched the trailer. Jonty Jack would have noticed the trailer, she thought, and might wonder about it. So she hitched it up again and drove it round to the other side of the house where it would be out of sight.

Back in the cottage she carefully wiped the fly-spots from the glass over the photographs. She studied the figures: the stone-cutter, Mario Salviati, and his wife; the smartly-dressed people on the platform, women with ostrich-plumed hats, men wearing waistcoats, and the faces of the prisoners – some eager and jovial, here and there sombre, depressed. A couple had their eyes closed: the camera had clicked at the wrong moment. And something Ingi couldn't quite make out was sitting on the locomotive, up on the water tank. Another faded patch, a dullness obscuring the reality.

She turned away, picked up her rucksack from the bed and swung it over her shoulders. She pulled the cottage door shut behind her, locked it carefully, double-checking that the latch held, and went out through the front gate. Across the road lay the forested gorge; behind the concertina gate among the trees a well-trodden footpath and a faint double-track both disappeared upwards to the mountain. Ingi wanted to take the footpath, for the mountain beckoned, but she turned instead towards the town.

Furrows ran along beside the streets, she noticed, and there were neatly cemented weirs at every corner. Masonry sluice gates led the water into back gardens and smallholdings and she recognised the hand that had built the cottage in the neat, overly sturdy work.

Eventually the rhythm of her limbs calmed Ingi. She'd been disturbed, she thought at first, by the old woman with the intense gaze and the shoulder drooping under the weight of her bucket, the suffocating curiosity on the store veranda, and the way the man she suspected was Jonty Jack hadn't shown he'd noticed her by so much as a flicker.

But now she realised it wasn't all that. She had been moved by the old woman with the bucket, yes, but more by the fragrance of stone and behind it, like a memory, the smell of cool water. The cottage is like a work of art to me, Ingi realised, and I have walked right into its belly. I'm expected to sleep there tonight. It will be strange trying to fall asleep inside a stone sculpture. Something about it makes me feel uneasy.

And the faces of those young men hanging out of the train windows in the photograph; and the dim figure – something on the locomotive that didn't cast a shadow; the absurd plumed hats and the self-satisfied men waiting on the platform . . . What exactly had unsettled her?

Not knowing, she walked on. Workers in the fields straightened from their implements as she passed. A town full of people who stare at you, thought Ingi; people who are obviously curious about visitors from the outside world. In a way the inquisitive glances seemed to stroke her as they slid over her skin, along with the sun, down her arms and over her legs. They took it all in, she knew: the sunglasses, the Walkman headphones, her lace-up boots. And they recognised her as a stranger from far away.

As she strode along, revelling in the wind in her hair, breathing in the smells of weeds and lucerne, as well as a distant smell of dust and Karoo-veld, she wondered where Jonty Jack's studio was. What would his workplace look like? In her time at the museum

– could it be two years already? – she'd visited a number of artists' studios. It was always fascinating to compare the practical necessities of light and space and materials with the idiosyncrasies of the particular artist's world.

Yearsonend had a specific fragrance, she discovered. Situated here against the mountain, a whiff of dry Karoo mingled with the more sultry, slightly bosky aromas of mountain slope and gorge; of rock-rabbits' pee against cliffs and another smell that Ingi couldn't place. She liked to put her nose close to a sculpture and sniff it. The smell of rubber and steel, of wood and cast iron and plastic – it was part of the work, she always said.

Yes, Jonty Jack, she thought, I will sniff you out; my nose will lead me to your lair. She never doubted her ability to buy the piece; she'd never experienced that kind of failure; in all her undertakings, in and around Cape Town, no artist had ever turned her down. Initially they were often tough and stubborn, playing at being remote and enigmatic. No one wanted to seem too eager to exchange a work for money. But gradually, after repeated visits and conversations during which trust was nurtured, they gave in. Then the final negotiations slipped through and the deal was concluded with surprising speed. But first the artist had to feel he or she could afford to give in. It was like love, Ingi thought cynically – all the avoidances and retreats that were so much part of the initial seduction.

She went to sit against the fence in the shade. The tree's flesh congealed like candlewax around the corner post and wire to which it was welded. Ingi dug the water bottle out of her rucksack and took a deep draught. Drops of water ran from her bottom lip down between her breasts. Then she saw the old woman with the bucket struggling along. The headscarf seemed to be pulled down lower than ever over her eyes. She watched her approach on her dusty bare feet. From where Ingi sat in the shade, she decided the woman wouldn't be able to see her. She didn't want to startle her, so she began to fidget with her rucksack to draw the attention of those dull eyes.

The woman came as far as Blood Tree, put down the bucket of

water, and pushed her headscarf further up on her forehead. The way she looked at Ingi was more intelligent than the suspicious glance of earlier had suggested.

'There at the Baas Dealer's they're saying the missy is looking for the gold pounds.'

Taken completely by surprise, Ingi stuttered, 'Gold . . . ?'

The old woman nodded. 'That's it. The pounds.'

Ingi shook her head, bewildered. 'No,' she said. 'It must be a misunderstanding. I'm here on other business.'

The old woman's eyes narrowed again and she tugged the headscarf down to her eyebrows. 'At the shop they're saying—'

'Well, they're wrong!' Ingi interrupted, then realised immediately that she had spoken too quickly; she should hear the woman out. But it was too late, because the woman picked up the bucket and fixed her eyes on the dusty road ahead. 'I . . .' said Ingi.

But the woman set off. Ingi gazed after her: the thin calves, the heels, the water splashing from the bucket and disappearing into the dust.

'Where's Jonty Jack's house?' Ingi called after her, more to explain the real reason for her visit than to get an answer.

The woman stopped, put down the bucket again and turned. She gestured with her head while her arms hung limp at her sides. 'Up the kloof,' she said, 'There, near the stonecutter's house, there's a concertina gate. Through that, up, up. As far as the arum lilies.'

'Can I walk or must I drive?' called Ingi. She was on her feet now.

'Drive. Walk and you'll be turned back.'

'By whom?'

'The woman without a face.'

'The who?'

But the old woman turned away, picked up the bucket and walked on.

Ingi swung the rucksack up on to her shoulders. She was suddenly weary. Had she heard correctly? What lengths must she go to for these works of art?

Shanty towns where water lay in stinking pools and children relieved themselves squatting against tin walls with their clothing hitched high above their buttocks ... *Nouveau-riche* suburbs, where pretentious artists waited for her in caftans, with champagne on ice and CNN on TV ... Roadside stalls where curio-sellers sat dumbly behind their wares ... Shebeens, where she couldn't distinguish the artist from the rapist and car hijacker who all sat drinking together, hard-eyed. And now, behind the stone cottage, up the gorge, where the dark trees sighed ... Ingi wiped a hand over her eyes. 'I've only come to buy a wood carving,' she wanted to call out, but there was no one to listen – just workers far out of earshot, watching her from the fields, and a single car, twenty or more years old, coming slowly past with a driver in a hat, a woman beside him, her hair plaited into thick grey braids.

Ingi pretended she hadn't seen them. It was getting chilly, she realised. The sun had sunk below the mountain, the evening approached. My understanding of Yearsonend, thought Ingi, has changed radically in a few short hours. On the way here, I expected a drab and dusty Karoo town. But there was much more to it. A shift had taken place. What was it? A sense that the place was burdened with its own past?

As she walked back, the town was going through its evening rituals. People sitting on their verandas stared at her shamelessly. The workers had gone and the streets were quiet. The general store's veranda was deserted but for a few papers lying around and an old-fashioned poster advertising coffee.

Now she saw her Peugeot – the shocking yellow of it a statement against the surly gaze of the families on the verandas. And the trailer, which had already carried off so many sculptures to the gallery in the old government gardens in Cape Town, waiting.

She decided to light a fire in the stove, even though it was summer. The flames will keep me company, thought Ingi, and she stoked the Dover until it roared and she had to seek refuge in the fresh air on the wooden bench near the front door. She sat there sipping rooibos tea. In the distance she could hear cattle lowing and the shouts of herdsmen. Then even the dogs stopped barking and the evening breeze wafted over the town. Ingi fell asleep with the empty mug in her hand. Her head dropped and she dozed off as a gusty wind stirred the trees in Cave Gorge, setting the concertina gate a-tremble. Her chin rested on her chest while shadows stretched then swallowed everything.

It was just before ten when she awoke with a fright.

The wall was cold at her back; it was unexpectedly dark and she thought she saw a movement. She jumped up but one leg had gone to sleep and she limped round the cottage. It was so dark she could hardly make out the Peugeot. What was moving there? The rapid angle of a man's shoulder, a ponytail and the white underside of an arm? Could she smell a man's sweat?

Jonty Jack! Ingi wanted to call out. But it was only the wind: she was, alas, alone.

In the small hours, between dream and wakefulness, as she tossed in the humidity, she was awakened by a beautiful female voice singing an aria. It can't be, thought Ingi. I must be dreaming. Then she dropped off again, only to wake once more, cold now, with a late-night wind that pushed through the windows, filling the curtains. She sat up in bed, startled by the billowing curtains and the white splash of sheet that had fallen off her on to the floor. Yes, there it was again, soft, almost inaudible: '*Vissi d'arte, vissi d'amore* – I lived for art, I lived for love.'

Then Ingi knew: this was the voice of Edit, the singer of Italian arias; the wife of Mario Salviati, dimly visible behind glass.

6

In the late afternoon, Jonty Jack was in the habit of walking to town to get a bucket of cow piss. By that time he needed an outing and his forearms and hands were numb from working with mallet and chisel and wood.

This afternoon he made certain his best set of chisels lay concealed behind a pile of wood – he'd seen the foreign Cape

Town car with the sunglassed city girl at the wheel. He couldn't lock his house, as there wasn't a key, nor could he move the Staggering Merman, who was securely rooted in the ground.

Jonty was convinced the woman was a journalist: there was one in the city who'd written repeatedly for months, nagging him for an interview. This was probably the woman who'd arrived, he thought, here to interrogate him. He rubbed his eyes. I want to get away, he thought. Perhaps I should take the camper-van and disappear into the Murderers' Karoo until the strange car leaves. What do they want from me? Can't they understand that the sculpture is not my doing?

Before setting out, he peered through the telescope, which was set up so he could scan Yearsonend through it. Front verandas, gates, windmills and a couple of playing children slid slowly past the lens. The yellow Peugeot was nowhere to be seen.

Perhaps she'd already moved on, he hoped, as he set off with the bucket. High above him the two eagles circled the cliff-faces. They wavered only when they spied prey far below them. At this time of the afternoon, fragrances sank down from the mountain in the warm air that dammed up under shrubs all day and was now stirred free by the afternoon breeze and wafted out on to the plains. At times like this, Jonty always felt the body of the mountain was stirring: flexing its limbs and shaking off the oppressive heat of the day. The mountain had a body just like a person, he knew that, and you could read its moods in the fragrances.

When he came down Cave Gorge and approached the concertina gate, he stiffened: the yellow Peugeot station-wagon stood beside Salviati's stone cottage. He ducked behind a bush. Earlier this afternoon, he thought, the car came upon me so suddenly I didn't even have time to be startled.

And she'd gone past before he could get a proper look. Once she was out of sight, he'd swerved off towards the mountain, reaching his house in Cave Gorge by way of the old goatherds' path; a difficult rocky route he normally avoided. He'd sat the whole afternoon in front of his house brooding, picking up his chisels then dropping them on to the sawdust at his feet, picking them up, dropping them again.

But when the sun sank behind Mount Improbable, he started hacking furiously at a new piece of wood until his arms were stiff, and then he decided that there was nothing else for it but to go down and fetch the cow piss.

Perhaps, thought Jonty, from where he stood behind a tree-trunk watching the stone cottage, it's curiosity that's driving me back to town. He knew himself: one side of him wanted to escape, as he'd done earlier, up the goat path; the other side was inquisitive and wanted to know more about other artists and the art world in the big city. But when there was a tug-of-war between the two halves, the goat path always won: Jonty had no illusions about that.

There was no sign of life at the stone cottage. But just before he set off again, Ingi came round the corner. Her hair hung loose about her face and she was some distance away so he couldn't see her too well; just that she seemed preoccupied, hugging her arms to her chest. She looked up at the mountain, touched the stone wall and stooped to pick a flower. Then she walked round the station wagon, giving each wheel an investigative kick. Without her sunglasses, she looked less intimidating to him – and younger – than she'd seemed before.

He waited until she disappeared inside before he made a detour through the undergrowth. He couldn't go through the concertina gate: she might see him. So he had to force a path through the bushes.

As he passed the storekeeper's house, the man was sitting on his veranda drinking milk. Jonty just raised a hand in greeting but the man called him over: 'Jonty! Hang on a bit, man.' It looked as though he couldn't wait another minute to pass on some news. 'Have you spoken to her yet?'

'Who?' asked Jonty, the sweat running down his back under his vest. Here it comes, he thought, as he leaned on the garden gate and watched the man wipe the smear of white cream off his top lip with the back of his hand. They were distantly related, but Jonty didn't have much time for the fellow, one of the town's great scandalmongers. Moreover, the man was one of the few Yearsonenders who had, over the years, tried to quiz Jonty directly about his father's involvement with the lost gold.

'That child from Cape Town,' said the storekeeper.

'What child?'

'The girl, man. She's not bad, hey?' Jonty ignored the wink.

'No, I haven't seen any girl. Who is she?'

'She's staying for the week in the old Italian's house.'

'Oh.' Jonty shrugged. 'Right,' he said. 'Well, I'd better be on my way.'

'But what do you think she's after?'

Jonty shrugged once more and turned away. But as he walked on he knew: she's after me. He knew it with a certainty mixed with fear and anticipation.

The storekeeper called after him again. Jonty turned and had to strain to hear. 'She's got a Venter trailer behind her station wagon. She's come to get the Staggering Merman – you can bet your life on it!'

Jonty's head swam. He reached out for something to steady himself against, but his hands grasped hot air, stirred up by the wind and the storekeeper's mocking laugh. It felt as though time had gone backwards and Jonty was a teenager again, wandering through the streets of Yearsonend with a sculpture he'd just made, and everyone was eyeing him askance or laughing at his peculiar habit of playing with clay all day long. The other children were dancing round him, squealing, some pinning his arms behind him, while others snatched the sculpture and ran off with it.

He hid the bucket behind a tree and started running; slowly at first, and no one looked up because they were accustomed to the sight of Jonty Jack jogging round the block to keep fit for the heavy carving work he did up there in the gorge. But as the sweat dripped into his eyes and his anxiety increased, he ran faster, faster and faster, with pumping elbows and heaving chest, haring round the corners and scattering dogs and children in his path.

7

The next day, when he saw Ingi Friedländer's Peugeot creeping up the track into the gorge, Jonty Jack ground out his joint under the sole of his sandal. He watched how the grass growing on the centre of the track brushed the car's bonnet clean. Then he dug a hole in the wood shavings with his heel and buried the remains of the joint. Although everyone in Yearsonend knew about his dope smoking and the police turned a blind eye, he remained cautious.

He got up, went into the house and emerged again with a blanket, which he threw over the Staggering Merman, who stood ten paces from his front door, anchored in the ground like a totem. Then he turned and waited for the vehicle.

Ingi had no idea what to expect. All sorts of stories about Jonty Jack had come her way at the museum. She'd heard he was no longer young, that he was of mixed blood, that he was a descendant of the famous artist-explorer William Gird. His grandfather was the fashion designer and ostrich breeder Meerlust Bergh, and his father the water engineer Big Karel Bergh, for whom the earth was a canvas: he'd used his remarkable skills as a draughtsman to engrave ducts and roads on the landscape but initially failed with his boldest work of art, the Lightning Water Channel.

There was a great-grandmother from Indonesia, she heard, and a mother who loved to travel between South Africa and the British Isles by mail boat.

Mr Jack is on drugs, she'd been told. No, only dagga, someone else averred. According to another source, he runs round naked in the ravines at night; he lives in a cave and wears animal skins; and, in addition to eating locusts and honey like John the Baptist, he feeds on the flesh of the children he lures into the ravine with huge kites – he can be seen racing over the veld with a kite when the west wind blows.

And now here he stood in all innocence – apart from those

indisputably dilated pupils. Yes, he was the fellow she'd seen walking down the road. A big man. His shoulders were broad, though slightly stooped, and his arms sinewy, with prominent veins. Her glance took in the large-boned hands and the chisels lying in a neat row on the piece of tarpaulin beside his seat. He wore old jeans and sandals and his hair was tied back in a ponytail.

For his part, Jonty saw a winged woman; an angel with wings. No, with one golden wing on her back, a wing as graceful as the wings of the butterflies that wafted down the kloofs to flutter around his sculptures. Or was she a kite that would rise into the air, riding the thermals up into the gorge?

He saw more than that: a woman with an open, clear face, strong eyebrows, full lips and breasts that a chisel would yearn to replicate. Her nose, he decided, gave her character. She came walking up to him through the grass, put out a hand and shook his firmly, introduced herself: 'I'm from the gallery in Cape Town.'

He picked up the smell of the city on her. Her sunglasses were pushed back on to her head and, as soon as she'd shaken hands with him, she took off her shoes.

The clouds had drifted one by one through the blue all morning and now Jonty watched them sail into Ingi Friedländer's eyes. There were shiny bracelets round her wrist and she pulled up a blade of grass to chew.

'And . . .' Jonty hesitated.

Ingi was completely taken aback. She'd been prepared for eccentricity, but this fellow was completely out of it. Or was it booze? She leaned closer but there was no whiff of alcohol. Dagga, she decided, and asked, 'Where can I sit?'

Jonty waved to the chair beside his in the yard full of wood shavings. It was a handsome chair with a back carved from a rare wood. They sat down formally, as though they were taking part in a ceremony. In front of them, as though he'd been specially placed there, the Staggering Merman hid under his blanket. You could see the first metre of the sculpture, the lower portion, but Ingi Friedländer had to use her imagination for the rest.

They sat quietly for a moment and Ingi studied the landscape – the verdant, shrubby valley running up from below the house into the ravine; the huge oaks round the house; chunks of wood lying about everywhere; the rugged mountain slopes with a troop of baboons clearly visible on the cliff top.

Everything here has a strikingly earthy texture, she thought, a quality that makes you taste and feel the country anew. She shifted her bare feet – soft from always wearing shoes – in the wood shavings, stirring up the aroma of wood and leaf-mould.

The roofs and trees of Yearsonend lay nearly a kilometre below them. From this vantage point it looked like a toy town with neat fields and houses only just visible among the trees.

Jonty got up and she heard him clattering about inside. Ingi shook her hair loose and felt her body relax. He reappeared with two mugs of tea. Her tin mug was lukewarm to the touch. She sniffed the tea but couldn't place the fragrance. She took a sip and a light sensation floated through her upper body, as though a feather had been lifted by the breeze, had fluttered lightly then sunk down again.

Jonty sighed as he sat down. 'My father, Big Karel Bergh, is still sitting in his carriage up there in the cave.' He pointed to the ravine. 'He finally came to fetch my mother and me. He'd taken a momentous decision. He wanted to move us to Cape Town once he'd brought the water over the mountain. But he's still sitting up there.'

'Why?'

'The water refused.'

'What do you mean?' asked Ingi Friedländer. She took a second sip of tea and felt the fragrance of wet wood shavings rise like an epiphany to her nostrils, inside her head.

8

He was tall and dark, the man who woke in his bedroom at Yearsonend one summer morning in 1940 – nearly six decades before Ingi's visit. Jonty Jack's father's feet reached right down to the bottom of the double bed, and if he propped himself up against the pillows, you could see it would be difficult to make space for a second body.

The sheets on his wife Lettie's side of the bed were already cold anyway and Big Karel Bergh sighed. She'd risen early again, driven out by her worries. But then, like a rainstorm over the plains, the memory of the dream he'd just had sank over him. He could feel his heartbeat quicken, his broad chest move up and down more rapidly. He threw off the sheet and planted his feet firmly on the floor with the decisiveness of one who knows that getting up today marks the beginning of something momentous.

He dressed quickly in his riding clothes and hurried to the bathroom – smiling because he knew what they said in Yearsonend: 'Big Karel Bergh doesn't even stand still to pee.' He brushed his teeth vigorously, splashed his face with water, rubbing the coolness deep into his cheeks with his palms. He combed his wet fingers through his hair and pulled on his riding boots.

In the kitchen, Lettie stood with her back to him. He could tell from her shoulders that it was one of those times again. Neither of them said anything; both knew that everything had been said. His porridge was already cooling in the bowl and he ate it standing out on the veranda. From here he could watch Yearsonend waking up as their house was built on a slight rise on the edge of town between the more affluent houses and Edenville, where the poorer black and coloured families lived.

From behind the house, he could hear the sounds of Edenville waking: dogs barking, children yelling, adults calling to one another. Down there in front of him on Yearsonend's small-holdings it was more peaceful: smoke already curled out of most of the chimneys, somewhere he heard an axe strike wood, and the storekeeper's truck pulled up in front of his store. It was a black Ford with red guard rails and when he stopped there it was always a sign that, in Yearsonend, business could commence. Business was, admittedly, negligible because there was only one lawyer – Lettie's brother – one doctor, a pub that would open any time now, a butchery, and little more.

Karel's dream came over him again. He closed his eyes as he felt the blood dam up in his chest. Then, leaving the porridge bowl right there on the veranda table, he swung round and with a single glance at the house where he'd grown up – the Feather Palace – he sprang down the steps.

Without saying goodbye to Lettie, he mounted his horse and rode off. Whenever she got like this – so lost in the past, in things that still weren't right – he just let her be. This time had taught him. Then, to survive, he had to set his hand to something. He galloped through the gate, driving the horse unnecessarily hard. Why, he couldn't say, but today he needed to ride through the town before heading for the open veld.

People standing on their verandas, coffee in hand, contemplating the day that lay ahead, watched Big Karel Bergh galloping down William Gird Street. Where on earth was he off to now? they asked each other, curious but also slightly mocking. Because they knew Big Karel Bergh's helter-skelter flights – he got his ideas when his wife's spirits waned; that's when he made such grand gestures just like his father Meerlust Bergh had done. And it was especially when Lettie, Attorney Pistorius's sister, bemoaned the impossible relationship between the Bergh and Pistorius families that Big Karel saddled up his stallion with some great project or another in his head.

But Karel didn't feel the eyes on him. He urged his horse to the town dam where he paused on the banks, studying the dry, cracked mud crust. And then he estimated, with a practised eye, the gradient between the dam and the first foothills of Mount Improbable. He bent low on his horse's back to get a more accurate sightline. His gaze ran from the dry dam up the slopes over the first foothill of Mount Improbable. In his mind's eye, he was marking the landscape with a dotted line, and then he was on top, on the summit, envisaging the fall on the other side.

Karel jerked the horse's head round, digging his heels into its flanks. Such a dream, so clear and convincing, could not lie. It was a dream of prognostication rather than speculation. The wind was in his hair as the horse tackled the incline with flexing haunches.

On the summit, horse and rider turned. As clear as crystal, all was revealed to Karel: there among the pepper trees lay the house he shared with Lettie. It had become a sombre house these past years: Lettie could no longer endure the in-between life, on the border of Yearsonend's streets on one side and Edenville on the other. Lettie told Karel she had also had enough of spending the weekends at her brother's then walking back alone to her own house and husband, with the great silence that yawned between the two families lying increasingly heavily on her heart.

A mountain lay between the Berghs and the Pistoriuses, gossiped the town – higher than Mount Improbable, a mountain that would only permit them to traverse it after several generations had come and gone. When Lettie had fallen in love with the flashy young Karel, that handsome dark boy from the Feather Palace, the whole town had known it would never work.

But how could you know that in advance? wondered Big Karel, as he sat on his horse looking down at his house. How could you tell that a relationship would become as parched and dreary as the Plains of Melancholy behind me, as that stretch of landscape beyond the town, the emptiness known as the Murderers' Karoo?

He spurred his horse down the far side of Mount Improbable. They thundered into the empty basin, the rocky plain where the cicadas shrilled and the sun blazed a path up into the sky.

The dream was sent to me, thought Big Karel, as deliverance.

9

And it is seldom that a dream grips someone as fiercely as was the case with Big Karel Bergh, the father of Jonty Jack, in the time before the Italian prisoners from the Great Desert War arrived in Yearsonend.

After his dream, Big Karel remained out in the veld for three days. The town wanted to send out a search party on to the Plains of Melancholy, but after consulting her brother the attorney, Lettie Pistorius shook her head. 'He left here with a divine calling that morning,' she said. 'He has another plan. Karel isn't dead – he's busy with a scheme somewhere. Leave him be, he's coming back.'

And he did – on the third day, in the late afternoon. Townsfolk saw the horse stumbling down the slope to the dam, a bedraggled rider slouched in the saddle. They hung about on their verandas to watch the animal make its way slowly through town. Karel's body was exhausted but his eyes glowed with a fever they'd last seen in the eyes of his father Meerlust.

The townsfolk whispered among themselves, but asked no questions. One or two lifted their hats to Karel as he passed by. Salt caked the stallion's hide and Karel's face was burnt raw. The people watched the horse turn in slowly at the Berghs' gate and there, now, Lettie's white dress was appearing on the veranda.

They watched the way she waited for her husband, how the two of them stood there together on the veranda without greeting one another. And they kept a look-out, because that evening they expected Karel to come down the steps again on his way to town, washed, wearing clean clothes and fired with enthusiasm.

But it didn't happen. For two more days, neither hide nor hair was seen of Karel. From the Berghs' servants the Yearsonenders heard that Karel was sitting in his study, still wearing the same grimy, sweat-soaked clothes. Food and drink had to be taken to him there. He and Lettie hadn't exchanged a single word. He sat there writing and fiddling with the abacus his father had used in the old days to keep count of his ostrich flocks.

Servants had to scurry off to the post office with bundles of letters addressed in Karel's looping handwriting. The postmaster waited avidly for every handful, studying the addresses inquisitively, in the certain knowledge that he'd be cross-questioned in the vestry after prayers that evening.

Rotterdam, he read. London. Cape Town. Professor, Doctor. Engineers. Schools of Algebra.

Karel reappeared at the end of the two days. As though possessed by the devil, he cancelled all his projects – the pass over the Ouberg, the dam at Gariep, the suspension bridge at Keiskamma. He sat with the postmaster all day, firing off one telegram after another to his taskmasters, his suppliers, his foremen and his surveyors.

Then he went down the street to the general store where he stood drinking tea in the shop that smelt of flour and chewing tobacco. From now on, he told the storekeeper in the white apron, he was going to concentrate on one single project. A man had to have a dream and then you had to follow that dream's spoor. Otherwise you weren't worth your salt. What were you living for, otherwise?

He'd dreamed of the project again the night before he sent all the telegrams. The storekeeper couldn't believe his luck: he realised that the great mystery was about to be revealed to him. He leaned forward over his counter, wrapping his hands in his apron. Under the fabric, the knuckles bulged white.

It was a grand vision, explained Big Karel Bergh, which would restore the prosperous years of ostriches and feathers to Yearsonend. 'I dreamt of a map, as clear as though I'd drawn it myself, of the land east of Yearsonend.'

To the east – beyond the outstretched stone plains – the land was lusher. There were springs in the mountains and heavy winter snowfalls thawed on sunny days and set the streams rejoicing and dams overflowing. Big Karel had dreamt of a collecting dam in that area and an aqueduct – as he called it – bringing the water to the Yearsonend dam.

It wouldn't be easy and the dealer shook his head in disbelief, as did the other people Karel spoke to afterwards. Because between the meadows of the east and the dry plains of Yearsonend lay a hundred miles – or more – of forbidding stretches, stone ridges, gullies and dry riverbeds. In rainy seasons it was a paradise with fields of wildflowers beguiling the eye and white-tailed springbok bounding across the landscape. But in times of drought it was a hellish stretch of land dotted with animal skeletons, a time of celebration for the ant colonies who lived in the hundreds of anthills among the aloes and stripped the dead cattle's skeletons clean.

But the presence of Mount Improbable, against which Yearsonend lay, was the ultimate reason for their cynicism. There were also the foothills, lying like a clutch of dinosaur chickens with knobbly granite tails in the shadow of their mother. The water would have to go through all that, or round it, most people reckoned. But to everyone's amazement, Big Karel Bergh announced that the water would come *over* the mountain. People sighed: that was the style of Big Karel's father, Meerlust – the grand gesture of the ostrich age, when the feathers fetched top prices in the great cities of the world and every lady wanted to be seen with a plume in her hat or a boa draped from her shoulders.

To go round the mountain – so the calculations indicated, according to Karel Bergh – would take at least ten years of digging and millions of pounds' worth of masonry. But the distance as the crow flies, in spite of the steep gradients, would be affordable if the whole town and the farming industry chipped in.

Have you been possessed by the devil? the dominee wanted to know. Civic irresponsibility, sighed the mayor of Yearsonend. It was the same with women and Karel Bergh, said the rich Pistoriuses – always some drama, some embarrassment or other . . .

And when have you ever heard of water running uphill? Is this man trying to challenge Nature herself? Has he never heard of gravity? But Big Karel gave as good as he got in his response to the objections. The mathematics of water, he said, reflect the law and order of God's creation: the immutable order of the galaxies of stars and planets, the balances and counterbalances of orbiting solar systems. Once you understand water – especially its predictability – you'll be able to grasp the secrets of the universe. And on top of that, you will become reconciled to the irrevocable turn of the seasons, the inevitability of day and night and the knowledge of your own mortality – because is there not a mathematical precision in the way in which gravity draws your strength out from the soles of your feet throughout your life until you finally succumb and end up stretched out under the cypresses? These are the things he had realised during those three days under the harsh sun on the Plains of Melancholy.

And what could the townsfolk or, more particularly, the farm folk possibly answer to that? They remembered that Big Karel had studied algebra and geometry overseas on the ostrich-feather pounds earned by his father Meerlust. And now, in the weeks following his dream, Big Karel buried his nose deep in the books he'd ordered from abroad. He journeyed down to Cape Town. 'Chasing women again,' gossiped the town, but they knew that he was going to consult clever professors at the university, debating deep into the night with them about the fallibility and infallibility of mathematics.

The figures had driven him barmy, that's why he bought that big shiny carriage with six horses, the people would gossip in times to come. But Big Karel maintained he'd bought the carriage and horses for recreation, and he got into the habit of competing in agricultural shows at Yearsonend and the surrounding towns in his equipage. He usually carried off the prizes because everyone was impressed by the fancy horses and the posh carriage, which had apparently belonged to Lord Charles Somerset, a former British governor. In this neck of the woods, people had a weakness for horses and swagger.

And it was after these victories that Big Karel would draw a crowd of the district's richest farmers, right there in the arena, and canvass their support for his project.

'You invested so much money in that Boer movie-maker,' he said, 'and his dream of making the first film set in the Murderers'

Karoo . . . Now what about me, a true son of Yearsonend? Young Afrikaner businessmen come out here from the city like deacons, with their hats in their hands, going round the district, because they need funds for some venture or other, but for me, one of your own, you have nothing but cynicism? Even though numbers can't lie? Or don't you trust God's own creation?'

Urgent telegrams arrived each day from Amsterdam and Leiden in response to Big Karel's queries. They carried messages of advice and support from Dutch engineers and dyke-builders – people from a country where the battle against water was even bigger than the battle against drought in the Yearsonend district.

Chapter and verse, the proofs and formulae streamed in – this is how you measure the power of water flow, its depth and velocity. 'The deception of water,' said Big Karel enthusiastically, after reading the telegrams, 'can be predicted in advance. God didn't tell man to have dominion over creation for nothing.'

And his certainty acquired a name: the Law of Bernoulli, the basic Law of Flux. If you took this law and applied the formulae precisely, you could predict whether or not the water would come over the mountain. The formulae proved that his dream was true, said Big Karel, because in its eighty-mile journey from the east, the water would gather enough momentum to spurt the last twenty miles over Mount Improbable and into the Yearsonend town dam.

'Here is the density of water,' he explained to farmers at agricultural shows, while prize-winning boars with pink rosettes were paraded and the ladies' milk tarts and syrupy plaited pastries were applauded, 'and here is the depth of the liquid. That figure indicates the acceleration of gravity, that's the gradient and altitude of Mount Improbable, as established by the government surveyors.'

Feverishly he sketched his dream on paper, showing how, thanks to the slope down from east to west, the water would gather momentum for the climb ahead. Like a spring hare before hunting dogs, like a cheetah after an antelope, or like a homing pigeon in full flight – that's how the water would flash down to strike the waiting town dam.

'Cock and bull stories, just stories,' some Yearsonenders responded.

'The lightning water,' murmured others, captivated, chewing on their pipes.

'Exactly,' answered Big Karel Bergh, 'Bernoulli's lightning water.'

10

Ingi Friedländer liked to while away the time sitting on the stone sluice gate in the road that ran past her cottage. These constructions seemed to her an extension of the building itself. The network of furrows with their smooth-washed bases and weed-grown walls stretched outwards from the house with its smell of cool water. In between lay the stone sluice gates that watered the fields of trees or crops beyond them. She tried to imagine how the Italian had felt – he'd planned and laid all this out, according to what she'd heard down at the shop. How did the pieces fit together? she wondered. What was the connection the storekeeper had mentioned between Mario Salviati and Jonty Jack's father, Big Karel Bergh?

She tried to probe the storekeeper, but the man who'd been so welcoming and inquisitive when she arrived had suddenly become reticent. She'd also noticed that people who'd first stared at her openly from their verandas now turned away.

'All this marvellous stonework,' she said to the storekeeper as his pasty white hands carefully placed her purchases in a brown paper bag, 'was it all the Italian's handiwork, the one who was married to the opera singer?'

'There's so much stone lying around all over the place,' he muttered, snatching her money almost angrily before clanging open the antique cash register. 'It's just a matter of lifting and laying it.'

Well, Ingi thought, as she went out with her groceries, something must have happened since I arrived. Some rumour is doing the rounds. But the next afternoon, when she went down to the store for a loaf of bread, the storekeeper was all smiles again.

'Yep, after Missy spoke of the stonework yesterday, I cast fresh eyes on the sluices when I walked home. Very fine craftsmanship. That stonecutter knew how grain runs in stone.'

But Ingi was fed up with his unexpected shifts from surliness to friendliness, so she just nodded courteously, took her loaf and went to sit near Blood Tree in the shade of a young weeping willow, whose branches trailed in the pasture behind the fence and draped themselves over the sluice gate in front.

Smelling the dampness in the furrow, Ingi picked up an ant from the line passing her foot. She put it on her palm and sniffed at it: there was a musty smell of depth and secrecy. Just a whiff of a bigger stink, she thought, as the ant slipped off her hand, fell to the ground almost weightlessly and scrambled around blindly, until she edged him back into the stream of his co-workers with a gentle fingertip.

Something kept her away from the stone cottage; this part of Yearsonend was deserted at night. The wind blew black down the ravine, accompanied by all sorts of wild sounds and smells. And you couldn't really light the stove to keep you company, not in this summer weather: she'd already discovered that on her first night.

There was something of that first night, when she'd lain between dream and wakefulness, that still stayed with her. Even now in the small hours she'd wake and, there was no denying it. softly, lingeringly, lower than the breeze, Verdi's 'Addio del passato'. Surely she wasn't imagining it? She had a Maria Callas recording of the song in her own collection. But here in the nights of Yearsonend, it came from a world where song was no different from wind; it came from the ravine, the undergrowth and the darkness that dammed up there, from the great body of the mountain; from a place where sound could not be distinguished from time, or hearing from imagining and seeing.

Then Ingi would lie awake, and bite her arm lightly, to make sure that she was here, that she was indeed living in this dark house with its low ceiling and billowing curtains. She would smell the comforting living scent of her skin and her spit, and in time she would sink back to sleep.

The idleness of these first few days gave many things a chance to surface in Ingi's heart: quiet pent-up feelings that had accumulated all year; anxieties she had numbed for many weeks with hard work and activity; feelings she didn't know she still had. In Mario Salviati's house they all came back to haunt her, stirred up and drifting like the dark clouds across the moon when she pushed open the front door to dry her perspiration.

The moonlight shining on the familiar form of the station wagon comforted her. She stood out there in the cool breeze and raised her arms so it could get into her armpits and lift her, so she could billow like the curtains. She surmised, though couldn't be certain – Was it a kind of wish? she thought reproachfully – but, yes, she suspected that Jonty Jack spied on her from somewhere and that he was watching her even now: watching the air rinse her hair with silver, watching her pale arms and legs gleam as wisps of silver cloud swirled above her and the black trees in the ravine bowed their heads to her.

Then Ingi had fled inside, bolted the door securely, fastened the bedroom window and lit a candle. She studied the portraits on the wall in the flickering light, and scratched on the glass above the dull patches. 'Mario and Edit,' she'd whispered, then turned back to the bedroom to try to sleep.

Now she sat under the weeping willow with the ants filing past her foot, reluctant to go back to the cottage where the silence awaited her. Although she hadn't actually conversed with the Yearsonenders, at least she was not alone – even now people were busy at the nearby stables, just beyond the orchard, and she heard shouts and a tractor engine turning over; it travelled a little way then stuttered to a halt again. Dogs sounded an alarm across town from the poor neighbourhood; their barks blowing like dry leaves over Yearsonend.

Then she started, and snatched up the loaf that lay beside her.

Jonty Jack came round the corner. Tree branches hung over the fence and at first she saw only his legs; strong suntanned legs as long as an athlete's. Difficult to associate those fit, youthful legs with the first signs of a paunch and a face already marked by its quota of life experience.

He saw her, too, and hesitated a moment, but then walked on. He carried a bucket and even before he greeted her she picked up the stench of the cowshed.

'Jonty!' she cried, then immediately checked herself: Don't use that gallery voice of yours, Ingi; don't use the voice of authority and money. 'Jonty . . .' she tried again in another voice, and she preferred this one, soft amid the smells of willow and damp earth and cow piss.

'Don't you want to join me for a while?' asked Ingi.

But Jonty Jack shook his head. He looked like an animal about to take to its heels.

'Are you in a hurry?' she asked.

He tilted his head slightly, and she noticed the weariness under his eyes; the dagga-dreaminess of their first meeting was absent. 'No, I must get on,' he said abruptly, tightening his hold on the bucket and striding away.

'Come and have coffee in the stone cottage sometime,' Ingi called after him, but he gave no sign that he'd heard her: he strode on leaving a fresh whiff as a splash of yellow slopped from the bucket on to the soil beside one of his footprints.

She sighed and renewed her resolution to work on Jonty carefully. No direct offers; just win his trust first so that he pulls that blanket from the sculpture of his own free will. Then she would be able to talk to him. Until then, Ingi thought with a sigh, it's just me, alone in nights of wind and voices.

Actually, just one voice, and a silence: the voice of Edit and the silence of Mario, the stonecutter.

By then she knew that Yearsonend held many silences.

45

II

The Yearsonenders were Karoo people who knew about hardship and responded to overly good news with cynicism. Good news made them suspicious. At first they'd chewed over Big Karel's plans with some difficulty. But in time the name Bernoulli slipped more readily over the tongue – like the trusted and smooth-worn river pebble that the San, who roamed these parts in bygone days, would hold in their mouths when the water dried up on a hunt.

'Bernoulli, Bernoulli.' The Yearsonenders savoured the word while the train full of prisoners of war stood ready to leave Cape Town station for the long journey inland. The government troops yelled at the nervous Italian prisoners who bundled into the carriages and gazed from the compartment windows at the seagulls hovering over the shiny tracks. They had no idea what awaited them inland, though the prospect was at least better than it might be in a camp – they understood that they were to be billeted in towns and on farms that were devoid of men because so many South Africans had gone north to fight.

A stocky Italian caught the attention of the government troops. He had an angular profile with a strong nose and determined mouth. If you'd asked any one of the South African soldiers, they'd have described him as Roman legionary, with a forearm muscular enough to wield the short sword, and a chest broad enough to flex a bow. But what made him particularly remarkable was the strap round his waist by which he was attached to another Italian, the one with a red birthmark that all but covered the side of his face.

During the hurly-burly of banging and jostling and shouted commands, the short man with the strong nose was pulled hither and thither, and the government troops called to him derisively, 'What's your name? Hey, you! What do they call you?'

But he didn't answer and then the man with the red cheek indicated, He's deaf. And touched his lips, Yes, dumb as well.

And the strap, at which Red Cheek pointed, was to help the deaf and dumb man, because he didn't hear commands. They'd done the same up north during the war – they'd tied themselves together whenever they saw action. For the deaf and dumb man the war had been a silent affair, said Red Cheek. He couldn't hear commands, gunfire, bombs.

The government troops laughed and used the butts of their rifles to shove the two Italians towards a carriage. The deaf and dumb man looked back for a moment to the people in civilian clothing – mainly women and children – who climbed off other trains and gaped at the goings-on around the prison train; he looked at the huge flat-topped mountain behind them, which seemed to have been hewn from a single rock, with the clouds creeping over its crown, then spilling and dissolving into thin air.

Mario Salviati turned because the strap was cutting into his waist. He put his foot on one of the steel footplates, grasped the handrails with his powerful arms and pulled himself up into the carriage. Inside, everyone was looking for the best spot; there was a commotion as they dived for the window seats. Now that there were no soldiers yelling at them, the Italians could relax. Some swapped cigarettes with the South Africans on the platform. Salviati watched the mouths move and the hands gesticulate. As a concession to his deafness, his comrades allowed him to take a place beside a window. He thrust an index finger between his stomach and the thong. Then he drew a deep breath, and the train began to move.

At first they steamed through suburbs but then the houses grew sparse. Thinking of home, the Italians gazed at the vineyards they were now travelling through. The sky was radiant blue. A mountain range baked on the horizon like a line of breakers rising up from the sea. The closer they drew to the mountains the more open and beautiful the landscape became. White gables marked the more prosperous farmhouses among huge oaks.

There was a government soldier in each carriage. He sat at the front, facing the Italians, and the handful who understood a few words of English asked him about the countryside. They translated the information for their countrymen, and so the word went round that they'd leave wine country once they crossed the mountains and that the world out there would get drier as they travelled to the far-flung farms on the high plains known as the Karoo.

'Karoo. Karoo.' The young prisoners laughed as they savoured the exotic word.

'Make sure you get work as soon as possible, here in the Boland,' warned the guard. 'Life is tough on the other side of the mountains.'

So every Italian decided to do his best to get posted to a prosperous family as quickly as possible. But as time went by and the train pulled up at one station after another and the crowds of people on the platform scrutinised the young Italians critically, they noticed that the most important people from each district got first pick. 'Make sure you land up with a rich farmer's wife with a pretty daughter,' mocked the government soldier.

But all this passed Mario Salviati by. He sat at the window, captivated by the extraordinary light, the clarity with which mountain and vineyard, the blue sky and the green of trees spoke to one another. He looked out at the earth too: the shifts of brown and red and black; the stone and lichen and signs of earlier disturbances of the earth's crust.

At the first stop outside Cape Town men from the front carriages were shared out among wine farmers, brandy distillers and obviously prosperous businessmen. The stories about a shortage of South African men were not entirely true, the Italians realised, because everywhere the selection process was conducted by men, and men made the choices.

At the second stop the waiting farmers seemed more robust and abrupt. The allocation process continued until the Italians in the last carriage insisted on being given a fair chance – why should the train be emptied from the front? Pushing and shoving ensued, insults flew and a whistle blasted, then two young men who'd grown up as goatherds on Sicily broke loose and raced off over the tracks.

They were into the vineyards before the soldiers really knew what was happening, but by then two local mounted constables had set off in hot pursuit. Shots rang out; Mario Salviati saw heads jerk round on the platform, and then the two escapees were brought back. Both were wounded and one died there among the bystanders, blood dripping from his mouth, over his cheek and on to the platform.

The remaining Italians' mood grew ugly but they calmed down *en route* to the next stop. They stopped talking to the government soldier, who sat with his weapon at the ready on his knee. The trees were thinning out and the greenness fading. The station buildings looked smaller and word went round the carriage that it was high time to be posted out. Mario Salviati and his friend were passed over once more.

Night drew on and at the first stop next morning, again, they were not chosen. There were fewer prospective employers waiting on the platform, and only two of their number were selected. They left the train falteringly, and turned round once to wave to their comrades. The landscape was empty now, drab and desolate. Whirlwinds danced on the horizon, mocking the foreigners. The government soldiers poured water sparingly from the large cans. Meagre rations were issued.

It was then, as the train steamed into yet another station a day later with only one occupied carriage in a long string of empty ones, that the red-cheeked Lorenzo took out his knife, nodded to Mario and cut the strap that bound them together.

12

Afterwards the people of Yearsonend would say of that morning: And then Dumb Eyetie came, as if he'd been sent, to help out Big Karel Bergh with cutting and laying the stone.

These were the war years, the years of deprivation and partings, and Mario Salviati certainly had much to thank Big Karel for, because the day the Italian prisoners of war arrived and gathered on Yearsonend's small railway-station platform, without a moment's hesitation, Big Karel employed the short, stocky Italian with the rough stonecutter's hands, bandy legs and – strangely enough – a certain gracefulness.

It was early morning, and in the misty air the young Italian men looked drained and weary. They arrived in Yearsonend with their cheeks hollow from the long, southbound sea voyage and their sojourn in Zonderwater prison; their clothes were tattered and their eyes mournful with longing for loved ones and familiar landscapes. They arrived to find the district's businessmen and farming families gathered with picnic hampers on a hastily rigged grandstand.

This scene looked considerably better to the Italians than what they'd seen at previous stations. At least here a decent reception had been organised.

It was like the days of the slave trade, people often said afterwards, because the women and girls also waited for the train, chattering away in ostrich-plumed hats unearthed from hat-boxes for the occasion, twirling their open parasols in anticipation of the morning sun, working their crochet-hooks as industriously as their tongues.

The farmers paced up and down the platform in front of the pavilion, whacking their riding crops against their boots or jingling their motor-car keys impatiently. Inspired by American ranchers and the cowboy films that were shown once a month in the town hall, it was fashionable for farmers to sport big Stetson hats, trimmed with ostrich plumes. Every now and again they tilted their heads to check whether they could hear the train coming or not; then they returned to discussing the labour potential of the Italians.

One man needed an Italian with knowledge of sheep, of foot-and-mouth disease and herd management; another was looking for a young man skilled in servicing windmills and tractors; a third sought a carpenter. Each had his particular needs. The rich

Pistoriuses wanted a cook because they'd developed a passion for pasta during a holiday tour of Italy.

Mrs Pistorius, immaculately dressed as usual, graced the pavilion with her two giggling daughters, who blushed and twirled their parasols on the step below her. She was looking for an Italian who could cook with passion but who could also drive the Ford and prudently ferry her daughters to school. In addition, he must be able to supervise the housekeeping with the tact and dedication of a butler.

'And what will you do if he cooks with prudence and transports your daughters with passion?' asked some wag, quite ruining Mrs Pistorius' morning.

Her daughters evidently enjoyed the joke, and an alarm bell rang in her head. She wanted to call her husband – the attorney waiting there on the platform among the other men – and tell him they must go home, but she hesitated then let it pass.

Years later she would often think back to this moment. If only she'd stood up, taken her daughters and left . . .

Big Karel Bergh stood slightly apart from the other men – already isolated by the magnitude of his dream. One by one, despite their wariness, the farmers had begun to support him. They were herd animals, he had discovered: once one prominent personality took the step, they all followed suit. Or maybe they were just too caught up in their battle against the elements to think things through clearly. In any case, the bank account was growing daily – he'd opened it under the name Bernoulli Irrigation Properties Limited. The bank manager carefully recorded each new investor's contribution, and Pistorius, Yearsonend's only attorney and notary, issued small share certificates.

The lightning water pounds were streaming in, declared Big Karel Bergh, as he swung his new carriage and horses towards the main road in the south, with the wind in his hair and the smell of the steaming horses in his nostrils.

In his mind's eye he could already see the water snaking down the channel towards the Yearsonend dam; he could smell the wet fields after the sluice gates opened. The building contractor,

Goodwill Moloi, had undertaken to recruit sufficient Xhosas at Peddie for a shilling a head commission and to teach them how to work as a team with spade and stone.

Big Karel hoped there'd be an Italian on the train who knew how to cut the hard ironstone of the hills through which the water had to run – at the correct gradient too, because the water must gather momentum for the final push over the mountain. The man would have to be able to shape stone to size for building the channel wall. He would have to understand the effect of temperature on materials and respect water's power to erode over time.

'The channel will last for a hundred years,' Big Karel promised his investors, 'bringing prosperity to our children and our children's children.'

For this he needed a man with the spirit of stone.

When the train was heard in the far distance – as a soft drumming carried on the wind but fading again as the sun's gathering heat melted the morning mist and the cicadas began to pierce the air – the farmers gathered around the magistrate. He had put a table on the platform for the register. While the two mounted constables edged closer on their skittish horses, the farmers insisted that their names be ranked.

Attorney Pistorius had previously slipped the magistrate a pound and found himself at the top of the list – he would choose first. Big Karel put in a plea that his project benefited the whole community, not just himself, and his name was recorded second on the register. An unexpected greed overcame everyone on the platform. Some young farmers were spoiling for a fight: fists flew and the constables cracked their whips. The nervous women held back; suddenly guilty, they realised that this was about people and not about slaughter-stock.

The magistrate harangued the crowd, warning that he would wave the train past, sending it inland, deeper into the Karoo, if those present could not behave in a manner befitting the noble Boers that they were. Then all necks were craned . . . Yes: there was the first puff of smoke, just visible from behind the mountain.

'Order! Order!' shrieked the magistrate, unnecessarily, because dead silence had descended on the platform.

On the train, in contrast, there was a good deal of jostling in the close confines of the carriage. Everyone wanted to sit, or find standing room, next to a window on the side of the train that would face the Yearsonend platform.

Over the past few days, as the train lumbered through the countryside, the same impressions had been etched on each of their minds: fewer trees, less green, and a landscape that increasingly revealed its hard features; stations that were now no more than shacks under the pepper trees, set against a small hill or on the open plains with only one motor-car in which a farmer sat waiting, sometimes with no one at all.

Then there were the delays while the carriages baked in the sun, until the prisoners began to protest that they were being cooked alive and the commander of the guards, a young lieutenant, gave the order for the train to move on, and the locomotive stirred again, hissing and heaving.

By this time alcohol was flowing among the accompanying troops; their vigilance slackened – in any case, there was nowhere here to which an Italian could escape. The interpreter, who had to translate in and out of English, Afrikaans and Italian in the interests of maintaining order, now sat tipsily beside the engine driver with a half-empty bottle of whisky in his hand.

He liked the roaring furnace, the wind in his hair and the juddering instruments. And there was such a noise in here that he didn't need to translate anything for anybody: he felt free, free enough to unbutton his shirt and watch the drops of sweat trickle down his chest and paunch.

As the carriage grew quieter, excitement mounted in Mario Salviati's breast. He studied the landscape with keen interest. There was more stone than vegetation here. He gazed at the strata created when magma melted millions of years before; at the hills, which thrust up as heaped rock formations, and at the rock ledges, arranged in neat layers, as if a stonecutter had laid them.

He'd begun to feel more at home this past day: the world had been too green before, the houses too white and pretty, the people too garrulous, the farmers too arrogant and well-to-do. He had skulked behind Lorenzo while his fellow prisoners vied for the attention of the employers waiting at the various stations. With the sharp instinct developed over time by those who lack one of their senses, he knew something was waiting for him; someone who needed his love of stone.

The Yearsonend women stood up on the pavilion when they heard the train coming, but then thought better of it and sat down again. They folded their hands in their laps and waited. The mounted police horses were the first to pick up the smell of all those unwashed bodies in the carriage and they whinnied anxiously. They paced restlessly as the train appeared around the corner and steamed into the station.

The Italians leaned from the windows to scan the eager faces on the platform, trying to catch an eye here or there, appraising the women and nudging one another in the ribs when they caught sight of the two Pistorius girls sitting on the stand like two ripe, blushing apricots.

The farmers on the platform made a living from manual labour, and they scrutinised the forearm muscles, the hands and fingers resting on the windowsills. They tried to assess honesty and courage from the shape of the foreheads, the set of the chins and the look in the eyes. They all wanted a young blue-eyed blond because the dark Italians' reputation with women and their general exuberance had preceded their arrival by train.

There was complete silence on the platform as it was decided that disembarkation would proceed in an orderly fashion. To spare the Italians embarrassment, they were to be allowed to stand about in informal groups. The magistrate, the lieutenant in charge and the train conductor deliberated while everyone stood waiting nervously.

First the little Catholic choir, conducted by Big Karel's sister, Edit, was, as a special concession to the Italians, given the opportunity to sing. It didn't escape the notice of those present that a number of people – among both the new arrivals and the local residents – wiped a tear from an eye.

Then the interpreter appeared, his shirt buttoned askew and his legs slightly wobbly as he jumped from the locomotive on to the gravel. But he pulled himself together and greeted everyone in three languages. Shortly before the train left Cape Town, he had been lured away from the restaurant where he worked as a wine steward. This was after the government interpreter, afraid of the weeks-long journey into the interior, absconded on the eve of departure.

Everyone on the Yearsonend platform tried to ignore the unsteadiness in the interpreter's step, because due process was in everyone's interest and everything had to go according to the book. But afterwards there'd be enough reasons for everyone to remember how drunk the man had been that day; how, each time an allocation was made, he would shout out congratulations, shaking hands and bidding the family who led away the bashful young Italian a rousing '*Fantastico!*'

Nobody knew how much longer this second Great War would last; nobody could predict how many of these young men would ever find their way back to their families in Europe. There was an air of finality that day on the Yearsonend platform, of unpredictability; a premonition of great times to come.

This feeling was shared by the magistrate, who opened the allocations register and sat behind the table that had been placed on the platform. He indicated that the interpreter and the lieutenant in charge should draw closer. The ritual should do credit to the honour of Yearsonend, he decided. This was no cattle auction.

The prisoners of war bowed their heads, surprised when the magistrate opened the proceedings with a prayer. The intercessions and promises he directed to the Almighty were translated every which way by the sweating interpreter, who flourished a large handkerchief as he delivered an improvised version of the prayer to the young men. This was their first garbled intimation of what awaited them.

Attorney Pistorius, his thumbs in his braces, stepped up to the magistrate's table. He introduced himself to the Italians as a man of law and a civil leader. The interpreter translated in fits and starts. It was obvious that he struggled to find Italian equivalents for some of the words – perhaps he'd been in Africa too long.

They needed a young man, Pistorius explained . . . Everyone waited on tenterhooks while he searched for words. The interpreter mopped his face with his handkerchief. They needed . . . Pistorius found the words at last: Because they had an extensive household, they needed a young man who was slightly standoffish towards the ladies, because – and he nodded towards the pavilion where his two daughters sat beneath their parasols – our Heavenly Father had entrusted him with the devout education of two young maidens.

He rolled one shoulder, as was his habit, and expounded further. He and his wife had another ambition for their daughters: marriage in white to sturdy Afrikaner boys. And, of course, people could not help recalling these words as the years went by.

Attorney Pistorius explained that he was looking for a fellow who could cook pasta with passion, but who could also prudently and dispassionately transport his daughters in the Ford to wherever they wanted to go – piano lessons, confirmation classes, and so on, because in raising children parents must provide everything they can.

Expectant heads swung towards the young Italians while the interpreter translated, stumbling but bawdy – waving his hands, jerking his hips and pulling faces as he pointed to his genitalia. Immediately a forest of hands shot into the air. The young farmers hooted with laughter. Mrs Pistorius sprang up, grabbed her daughters' hands and flounced off in a huff. She waited in the brand new black Ford parked under the pepper tree in front of the station building.

Eventually her husband came to the car with a young man who hung his head, for he knew why he had been chosen: a large birthmark stained half of his face with a bright red blush. He limped slightly too, but, after all, Attorney Pistorius explained later to his wife, you don't need an athlete to keep an eye on the servants and the catering.

The tragic tale of this young fellow had been recounted at the station. The young man had explained, via the interpreter, how he was fathered by a priest who'd sinned with a widow of Florence – his mother. His father was defrocked, and had opened a small trattoria near the Ponte Vecchio, where he'd taught his son to make pasta.

The young man's name was Lorenzo, but the servants soon started to call him Devil Slap, because they believed that the devil, as punishment, had marked this child of a sinful priest with a hot slap across the face.

Mrs Pistorius decided that the young man added little grace to her kitchen and dining room; she wanted a fair young man, someone who could stand proud and strong behind her chair at the dining-table, in a white jacket and black bow-tie with a tea towel draped over his forearm.

She agreed with Attorney Pistorius that danger was danger, to be avoided at all costs, but ugly was also ugly. 'A club foot!' she complained at tea parties. 'He comes like bad news, limping across the wooden floors, from pantry to kitchen to dining room.' And in the summer that devil's mark glowed like a coal fire. The servants talked of the possibility, she once twittered to the dominee, that the red mark might set fire to the young Italian's pillow, and the whole house burn down. Was such a thing possible? she asked the dominee.

In the meantime, snippets of information from the other Italian men revealed that the interpreter had got it all wrong: on top of everything else, young Lorenzo Devil Slap was no cook, but a carpenter. His father was in fact an indigent pedlar. The story about the priest, the widow and the picturesque restaurant above the Ponte Vecchio was just the interpreter's way of keeping everyone happy.

Or maybe it was the interpreter's revenge on a country and a people who had never completely accepted him in his years as a foreigner in Cape Town and who in the years that stretched ahead, here in Yearsonend, would never make him feel like one of them. Because he, too, stayed on in the village. When all the young men had been allocated to families and the empty train was on the point of departure, the interpreter decided he didn't want to return to Cape Town with that rowdy bunch of government soldiers, now relieved of their charges.

He looked about him, at the trees and the mountain and the plains. Is there a place to stay here? he asked. He was told he could sleep over at the old Drostdy. And this was how he came to work for General Taljaard, the treasure-hunter who owned the Drostdy; and, in the years to come, take part in the gold expeditions that were orchestrated from there.

And when he was fed up with hunting for gold and treasure, he opened a pub, which he named Look Deep and which would be run by his sons and grandsons after him. This was the watering hole where Jonty Jack was wont to recount the story of the Staggering Merman.

As fate would have it, the only Yearsonender who made a good choice when the young Italians arrived was Karel Bergh. Because Dumb Eyetie could not hear or say anything, he had to find another way to explain his trade to the Yearsonenders. As they climbed down on to the platform to group themselves in front of the magistrate and the people on the pavilion, he picked up a stone. It was an oval ironstone that must have lain there for years, trampled by many feet.

He held it up above his head. Pistorius and Lorenzo Devil Slap had just left and it was Karel's turn to choose a young man. His eye fell immediately on the fellow with the stone. God, he thought, it can't be happening. Can this be mere coincidence? Nevertheless, he explained through the interpreter that he wanted someone who could work with stone and other raw materials; perhaps there was someone who had cut marble, or helped to build a cathedral somewhere? 'Someone,' explained Big Karel poetically, 'with a heart for water but a will of stone.'

Notwithstanding the number of hands that shot into the air, Big Karel called to Mario Salviati: 'You there.'

The interpreter called out in Italian, but Dumb Eyetie still didn't react, and at first Big Karel feared the man was an idiot. But when the other young men pointed to their mouths and ears and shook their heads, he understood. He noticed that Dumb Eyetie was shorter than he was, with a deep chest, and just as powerfully built as himself – maybe more so.

He saw the hands, too big for the arms; the way the feet were slightly splayed, as if the man was ready to pick up a heavy weight.

For his part, Mario Salviati saw a big man, a brown man, he thought at first, but then, maybe an Indian? Finally he decided that the man with the hat and the flamboyant gestures just spent a lot of time in the sun. He's white, yes, Mario thought, and he's important. There's also money: look at the gold watch and the expensive jacket, the handmade shoes and leather belt. And he stands slightly apart from the other farmers. Is he above them, Dumb Eyetie wondered, or have they pushed him out?

Big Karel walked up to Dumb Eyetie, took the stone from him, drew the side of his hand across it in a cutting movement and looked questioningly at the man before him. Dumb Eyetie felt the stillness surround them – even there on the pavilion and among the young farmers. He took the stone ceremoniously from Big Karel, and with an archetypically Italian gesture, he raised the stone dramatically to his lips and kissed it.

That evening the tipsy interpreter's mistakes came to light in various households. While housewives pointed to spice racks and shouted eagerly, 'Pasta! Pasta!' young men shrugged their shoulders helplessly. A tailor bent over the engine of a motor-car and scratched his head.

Only Big Karel Bergh and Dumb Eyetie sat together peacefully and contemplated one another with the knowledge that their understanding was a contract chiselled in stone; an understanding of certainty and durability. The building of the lightning water channel, in accordance with the immutable Law of Bernoulli, could begin.

13

Yes, thought Granny Siela Pedi, where she stood to one side of the platform observing the goings-on, yes, thank God we don't always know which part of our sorrowful history has gone before us and which is still to come.

It was at times like this – times when you could sense that things unfolding now would have huge implications in the future – that Granny Siela's heartbreak became too much for her to bear; when the memories washed over her, memories of the long journey riding on the ox tied to the black wagon bearing the gold, and she lamented the passing of the years, the cruelty of fate; the callous hand of war.

'I thought it would be the last war,' she murmured, 'the day the Boers were forced to bend their knees before the English; I thought it was all over and that only peace awaited us. And then it came again, and now it's here once more, with people who've been sent like cattle to a place where they don't want to be. Just as I was abducted from my home by that Attorney Pistorius's father, the field cornet with the red beard and the lightning blue eyes.

'Look how bravely these young men act: the proud stance and handshakes, and making eyes at the young women on the grandstand. But I, Siela Pedi, the woman who rode into Yearsonend on the back of an ox, can see in their eyes how they really feel inside.'

She looked out over the sombre cliffs of Mount Improbable without realising that Captain Gird – the man she'd heard about in 1902 when she'd arrived here in the wake of the gold-wagon – sat painting on the other side of the platform: Captain Gird, hunter and painter, traveller, smuggler and lover of Khoi women, artist whose drawings were bought by noblemen and kings, sat on the far side of the steam engine alongside the row of red fire buckets. Paint had stained his fingertips with the colours of the rainbow. He sat on his three-legged stool. The camp table was set up before him. Behind him, hands folded over his chest, stood his guide, Slingshot X!am, a man with a feather in his hat and a look on his face that said he'd had enough, his nerves were on edge, he wouldn't be able to put up with the captain's shenanigans for much longer.

An array of small bottles and brushes stood on the table in front of the captain. He studied the steam engine and the young Italians, the women with their twirling parasols and the men in their boots. He bent over his drawing, then looked up again so that his eye could follow the pipes and wheels of the steam engine and measure them carefully, intent on capturing the scene.

He had carried with him the restlessness and nomadic habits of his life into death; he was still in a hurry to capture everything. Even his horse stamped restlessly. And there on the red-hot boiler of the black steam engine, next to the funnel still spewing out wisps of smoke, the angel lounged at ease, his large wings relaxed and slightly spread as he surveyed the scene. He poked about catching fleas under his feathers and a thin white trickle ran from under his buttocks round the curve of the engine's boiler.

Granny Siela watched Big Karel Bergh closely because she was a contemporary of his father, Meerlust Bergh, and his mother, Irene Lampak, the beautiful Indonesian model and milliner. Yes, it was just as if Meerlust Bergh's big frame was back there under his son's wide-brimmed hat. Big Karel still had both his legs, while his father had lost one and stumped about on an artificial leg, but the broad shoulders were the same, the luxuriant hair, that set of the head; the gestures were as grandiose and his voice was as loud.

But the refinement of his mother, Irene Lampak, had also settled in Big Karel. One could see it in the way he inclined his head slightly when he talked to someone; in how he greeted everyone with a handshake and stopped to talk, giving them his full attention. One could see it in the profile: the finely chiselled lip and mouth, and the Oriental eyelid.

Granny Siela also recognised Meerlust's restlessness in Big Karel and she knew that those expansive gestures hid pain. Like his dead father before him, he would spend his life in search of water to fill those dry places inside him.

Unseen, Captain Gird bent over his work. He breathed in the sharp smell of paint as he captured the image of the stocky Mario Salviati holding up the stone. It was glistening yellow-gold – the same hue that infused the angel that he'd painted on top of the black steam engine.

Gold, thought Granny Siela Pedi. Gold – always gold.

Water, yes: ostrich feathers too; but in the end it always came back to the elusive gold.

The taste in her mouth was bitter as she turned round and saw them all leaving. The magistrate's table was removed, the clerks filed the list of allocations in a briefcase, cars revved up in front of the station, and the constables allowed their horses to drink out of the red fire buckets.

The angel's black shadow swept across the platform and over the shiny tracks and vanished as the engine gradually picked up speed. The driver had to take it round a special circular siding and, with a great roar and hissing steam, the engine hooked on to the end of the train. Its nose was now pointing towards Cape Town, and the rowdy government soldiers hoisted themselves up into it, made themselves comfortable in empty carriages and waved effusively to the stationmaster.

The train started to move and soon disappeared behind the trees. When Granny Siela turned round she imagined she caught a whiff of paint in the air. But Captain Gird and Slingshot X!am had already packed up and slipped away. The smell of the paint hung lightly on the breeze and then it, too, dissipated.

She sighed. Ah, the constant attempts to paint over things, to make them seem new: attempts to silence and conceal! There's nothing you can tell me about that, she thought. That's the story of my life, and of Yearsonend.

14

Jonty Jack focused his telescope on the stone cottage. Now and then a greenish haze passed over the lens: one of the pine trees that swayed in the wind between him and the stone house. Since the day after Ingi arrived in Yearsonend a chair had been stationed permanently near the telescope. He followed Ingi's movements through the moonlit nights, when she'd emerge to shake out her silver hair in the fresh air, standing outside for a while before going back in.

Then he went to bed and dreamt that Ingi was coming through the trees in her night clothes, walking through the darkness towards the Staggering Merman who glowed where he stood, anchored in the ground. He saw how something of her suppleness and fluidity was taken up by the wind and blown against the merman's wing and thigh, his fin and muscular arched back; and Jonty heard the merman's cry – whether of joy or of pain he couldn't tell – triumphant, like an eagle, and woke to it. It was his own voice: 'Like an eagle!'

Such were his nights, and his days were not much better. Ingi possessed him like a fever. When he picked up a piece of wood it was her body he saw calling for release from its depths. The cool chisels also held something of her in their smoothness, and the first drag on a dagga joint drew him in like an embrace.

Jonty sat there at the telescope watching the quiet road. And then, as if summoned, she was there, walking along with her hair pulled back in a cheeky ponytail, white sun cream smeared over her cheeks and bottom lip, the inevitable sunglasses. She wore lace-up boots, and the small backpack clung like a little monkey between her shoulders. Her beautiful legs startled him, as though he was seeing them for the first time.

He moved back from the lens, shook his head and looked again. She was gone, and he had to scan the streets hurriedly with the telescope to find her under the weeping willow at the sluice gate.

She was pouring coffee from a flask and breaking pieces from a loaf, which she ate with chunks of cheese. The simple meal was spread out beside her on a white cloth.

Jonty watched her until she turned and looked directly into his lens. For a moment her face was right there, close to him. The glasses were off and he saw worried eyes above the sun cream smudges, a hand that distractedly brushed aside stray strands of hair. Would she see him? See me! whispered a little voice in his head, but he knew that all she saw was the mountain, and a dark wood running up into the groin of the gorge, and there, above, the cliffs and ravines, the broad chest of Mount Improbable.

Jonty cursed himself and went to sit on the stump he'd braced on two supports a short way from the Staggering Merman. He examined the existing chisel marks in the wood. The image changed, became something else. It was Ingi who lay there, her hair loose against her upper arm and, because she was turned slightly on to her side, one breast hanging lower than the other. There was the curve of the stomach and the hip disappearing into rough wood, to be left just like that: a beautiful sleek form melting into raw nature.

Jonty took up his chisel and mallet and began to hack away at the wood furiously. He dripped with perspiration and his back ached by the time he paused to brew dagga tea. The warm liquid dizzied its way through his head and he laughed and laboured on and forgot about time. He was at her neck, her shoulders, and he worked away at the flesh and found breath and flow and warmth beneath it. 'Ingi,' he said, and when he looked up, suddenly, there she stood, tired from the walk, wet with sweat, her smile slightly askew.

'Am I interrupting?'

'But . . . I . . .' He looked down at the white flesh before him, the log he'd cleaved open, the chips of wood removed to expose the naked inside of the tree, vulnerable and shy beneath his hands. He fumbled around behind him, but there was nothing there. He stumbled over his mallet as he fled to the house, then re-emerged with a blanket, which he threw over the log. And realised, the moment he turned back to Ingi, that for her there was nothing to see in that stump on its trestles; he was still busy, working away the superfluous, clearing away the excess, shedding. There was no recognisable form or pattern yet.

'I . . .'

'Jonty,' she said, looking perplexed, 'I'm so, so sorry. I shouldn't have come here, not now . . .'

'No, please, sit down. Sit here.' He swept the chisels off the chair next to him, realising at the same time that she must have noticed the other chair so conspicuously positioned in front of the telescope. He whisked it away and they both sat, uncomfortable, once again almost absurdly formal.

'You're working,' Ingi said unnecessarily, pointing to the log under the blanket, as if it was only of passing importance.

'Yes, yes, always whittling away . . .'

Jonty rubbed his forearms. He saw how she looked at him, enquiringly, how her nostrils flared slightly and her eyes fell on the kettle with its last dregs of dagga tea.

'Hmmm . . .' she said, and burst out laughing.

'A sip?'

'Hmmm,' giggled Ingi.

He fetched her a mug. 'Listen,' she resumed, after Jonty had poured tea for her, 'I have to move out of the stone cottage one of these days. Apparently some Americans are coming.'

'Kudu hunters.'

'So I hear.' Ingi waited for Jonty to ask about her plans, but he just sat staring at the trees. 'I must find lodgings,' she said, and added hastily, in case he thought she was angling for an invitation, 'Somewhere in town.'

He sat thinking for a while. 'Everyone who passes through has always, all these years, stayed over at the Drostdy.'

'The Drostdy?'

'Yes, come and have a look.' He took her to the telescope. 'There, next to the palm trees. Do you see the turrets and the gables?'

'Who lives there?'

'Oh . . .' Jonty waved a hand, as if swatting at a fly in front of his face. Ingi recognised the gesture: the storekeeper had done the same when he hadn't wanted to talk to her that day. It's Yearsonend's gesture of avoidance, she thought, and asked, slightly sharply, 'Is that it? No one?'

'There are lodgings for travellers,' he said brusquely, and turned away. She could see he didn't want to discuss it further, and his use of the words 'everyone who passes through' and 'travellers' hadn't escaped her notice. Was he trying to indicate that he thought she was on her way somewhere else? Or was it a gentle reprimand: you must travel further, there is nothing here for you?

She wished she could say to him directly: 'I want to buy the sculpture, and then I want to go back to Cape Town.' But she was afraid of precipitating a final rebuff. And she wasn't ready to return to the art gallery. She had become more and more relaxed here with the passing of the days. There was something in the simple rhythms of the place that allowed her to forget about the infighting and conspiracies in the art world of the mother city.

She turned back to where they'd sat, and held the mug so that Jonty could pour her more tea. 'I'll try the Drostdy,' she said, in a tone that concluded the discussion. His silence made her uncomfortable until she realised that he was completely relaxed.

She untied her laces, took off her boots and socks and wiggled her sensitive soft-skinned feet in the earth, then sat back too.

Jonty watched her. 'City feet,' he teased. She laughed.

They sat with their elbows on their knees and Ingi buried her nose in the empty, warm mug. 'Ah, bliss.' She sighed.

'Hmmm . . .' murmured Jonty.

Ingi pointed at the log on the supports. 'What are you making?' she asked, casually, her earlier apology already forgotten.

Jonty looked sharply at her. What does she know? he wondered, something like irritation rising in him. Could he trust her? Pitching up here uninvited, making herself at home. 'Nothing,' he growled, and got up to go back into the house where he fiddled about, shifting pots and pans on the wood stove, then repairing a broken mallet. By the time he went outside again, she was gone. Her empty mug stood on the ground where she'd sat. And, like an accusation, the scuffmarks on the ground, and the chair back in its position behind the telescope. So soon, he thought. The same thing that has always happened to me has happened again, so soon.

15

When Ingi Friedländer pulled up under the big oak trees in front of the old Drostdy in her yellow Peugeot station-wagon, she had no idea of what awaited her.

Inside the Drostdy, the old general sat on the edge of his bed, staring moodily at the ham radio, which was mounted on the wall close by so that whenever he woke from a dream all he had to do was sit up, swing his feet on to the leopardskin and switch it on.

An old mosquito net suspended from the ceiling was draped around his shoulders. The radio was surrounded by leatherbound books full of maps and charts, so ancient that when he grabbed a volume too hastily pages often fluttered to the floor.

The yellowed maps on the wall were speckled with insect and gecko droppings. Rolled-up maps lay scattered on the floor, and two Great Danes rested their heads on piles of books as they listened to the crackling static of the general's radio and to his muttering as his fingers groped over a large globe of the world.

Whenever the gold lust seized him, the general spun the globe more urgently. The two dogs, Alexander and Stella, were accustomed to the scratching and shuffling of those long fingers on the surface of the globe as they slid over the degrees of latitude, up against the mountains, and down along the coastline, particularly at places where the major currents wash up against continents.

The general's uniform could be seen hanging in the open wardrobe, and swords and guns were mounted against the wall. There were photographs of old warriors from forgotten wars, flags tattered by bullet-holes or shrapnel, and at night, if you listened attentively, while the old man slept, pistol in hand, beneath the mosquito net, you could hear the sobbing of young wounded soldiers, dying on the floor, there where the Great Danes lay and twitched in their dreams.

Gossip in Yearsonend had it that the old general kept a woman locked up in a back room – an unfortunate girl without a face.

Next to the woman's room was the bedroom of the stonecutter Mario Salviati, the old man who sat next to the fountain in the Drostdy's inner courtyard with a stone in his hand all day: the very stone he'd held up to Big Karel on the day he'd first arrived at the railway station; that day when tailors became goatherds and bricklayers became butlers.

As time went by, Ingi would try to sift out how much truth lay hidden in these stories, but now she sat for a few moments in the Peugeot recalling Jonty Jack and the sculpture under the blanket. She wouldn't be able to buy that sculpture in a hurry, she realised. First she'd have to win the man's trust and, some day when he was more lucid than he'd been during their latest meeting, she'd have to convince him that the sculpture belonged in the lobby of the National Gallery.

Ingi thought about the Minister and the Speaker's avid faces and sighed. Then a big dog thrust his face in through the open window and stared at her enigmatically. His head was at the same level as the car window.

Ingi swallowed hard. 'And what is your name?' she asked, but still the dog showed no sign of goodwill. His tired, wise eyes focused on her. She was afraid to get out of the car: she felt as if the dog was holding her prisoner. Behind him, a clutch of bantam hens with feathered legs pecked about. She watched them scratch for a few minutes and then decided to make a move. The dog growled without taking his head off the window frame.

So Ingi sat there, in her car, in the shade. It was very quiet. At the quarter-hour she heard a clock chime in the house; doves crooned in the trees. The dog's eyelids drooped and eventually closed. He snored gently.

This is absurd, thought Ingi, preparing to make a move, but

the dog growled again, without opening his eyes. She sank submissively back into her seat. Perhaps it was better to wait. It was a legitimate time of rest, she decided – another city perception that had little relevance here. Because the old house, with its gable, its wide encircling veranda and the neglected formal garden, which had retained a certain decadent elegance, was pervaded by an air of timelessness.

While he sat on the edge of his bed, unaware of the young woman in the Peugeot, the general rattled off exotic names into the ham radio's microphone – the names of long-forgotten galleons and frigates; ghost ships that sailed on in the hearts of treasure hunters like him.

He knew it all by heart: the dates of sinking, the detail of the wreckage, drownings and losses, wave size and sea currents, tonnage and rescue boats, sails and steam engines straining against the swell, wrecks half buried in the sand like the gaping mouths of skulls exposed to decomposition and the coastal winds, half-drowned survivors on rafts who drifted further and further out to sea, slowly dying of dehydration and turning black as dried herrings, shrivelled and tough in death, to be picked up by ships, then stitched into sails and thrown back into the sea . . .

Images like these raced through the general's head while he sat before his maps, pulling the mosquito net over him when his memories of death and blizzards and the salt of the sea became too much to bear.

He was one of that dying breed of treasure hunters – the last of those who dived for treasure in sunken galleons, driven by dreams of gold coins and jewels waiting beneath the sand. Avarice kept alive men of his ilk as their birth dates sank, like sunken schooners, deeper into the sand, with the waves of time washing over them until they were lost for ever: men ageless in their gold lust and eternal faith in the great find; men watched over by generation after generation of Great Danes. Because if your desire is great enough, men like him knew, you can defeat even death itself.

Early on the same day that Ingi arrived at the Drostdy, the general had received a ham radio message from his agents about a search close to his own heart. A crackling report about the Fourth Ship came from the west of the country. The Dutch official, Jan van Riebeeck, sent in 1652 by the Dutch East India Company to establish a refreshment station at the Cape of Storms, arrived in three tiny ships – that was common knowledge. But only the chosen few, who searched the globe for sunken treasure, knew as a matter of fact that there had been another ship, a ship forgotten by the historians. The Fourth Ship had carried the gold that Van Riebeeck was to have used to bargain his way across the open seas, if necessary, and also his way through Africa. This ship had been blown off-course by cross-winds.

While the well-known three – the *Reijger*, the *Good Hope* and the brave *Drommedaris* – watched clouds boiling over Table Mountain from what came to be known as Table Bay harbour, the Fourth Ship had sunk in the cold Benguela current off the west coast of Africa, near to the mouth of the Great Gariep river.

The plot now thickened, according to crackles emanating from the general's radio, as he unrolled maps and drew circles with a pair of compasses and shooed the dog away while he paged through books and spun the globe: evidence had come to light suggesting that the Fourth Ship had been trying to evade a rapacious privateer, crewed by buccaneers from who-knows-where.

It was likely that the Fourth Ship had been plundered before it sank; perhaps the pirate ship also sank in the exchange of fire and the tangle of rigging when the two boats clashed on the rough sea and men fell upon one another with swords and blunderbusses.

Who knows? Gold glistened beneath the surface of the tale; the shining tides of the imagination washed over the treasure and now and then, if the light fell correctly, the gold would glisten on the bottom of the ocean, enticing, carnal, irresistibly desirable. The general knew all about that, as he sat alone in his bedroom, magnifying glass quivering over maps and old writings.

The Kruger Millions was the second trove that made him break out in a cold sweat, that brought on the old malaria attacks whenever he was hot on its trail: the knapsacks full of gold pounds, the ingots and other treasures that Paul Kruger had wanted to take out of the country when the British invaded the two Boer republics at the beginning of the twentieth century.

Some treasure hunters even maintained that the gold from the Fourth Ship had been found by Paul Kruger's cavalry, melted down and reminted as pounds to buy cannons from Germany, guns from France and provisions from the Cape Colony during the war.

That day there was a new report about the Kruger gold, just as Ingi stretched out a tentative hand to the Great Dane's imposing head. She stroked Alexander lightly, his eyes opened and he gazed adoringly at the pretty girl with the gentle touch. At the same time a fax stuttered through the general's machine: an old sangoma, reported the fax, a starving old witch from the far north, had summoned up memories and visions through the spirit of her mother – also a medicine woman: old tales of a valley with trees, one of them a great hollow baobab bowing sadly to the setting sun. A hundred paces further on lay a small hill with piles of rocks, one of which was clearly shaped like the profile of a bearded man. On the stroke of twelve noon on New Year's Day, and at no other time, the tip of the man's nose cast a shadow near an ant-heap. If you marked the place with your heel and dug there, you'd find the coins that slide shining through your hands, as slippery as water, heavenly, as if you were holding the sun between your fingers.

One day's ride south of the town without a railway line, dreamt the old sangoma, and the general's agents wrote it down, while the old woman wheezed over her divining bones and the light in the men's eyes turned yellow like leopard's eyes as they listened and wrote.

When she was done they killed her. She died with their faces petrified on her retina, and under Ingi Friedländer's hand the Drostdy's big brass lion's head door knocker felt unexpectedly cold. As if it were a winter's day, she thought, or a day of fever and sickness.

When the door opened, she recoiled at the smell of salves, old fountain water, grapes rotting on the courtyard floor, parrot feathers and, over the crackling radio transmitter, the sudden scream of a peacock. She stared at the middle-aged woman in front of her. 'Lodgings?' she squeaked nervously.

16

How do you lead a deaf and dumb man into a new town, a new life?

You watch him carefully, decided Big Karel Bergh, and you take note of what catches his eye. Then you bring him those things, or you take him to them. So you find a way into his heart and make of him a loyal partner.

On the first morning after the Italians arrived in Yearsonend, he went to wake Mario Salviati in his outside room, behind the Berghs' house. He saw with surprise that the sleeping man still held the stone he'd found next to the railway line and held up the day before.

Big Karel put down the mug of coffee next to the man, shook his shoulder lightly, then returned to the front veranda where Lettie Pistorius sat waiting for him. That morning she had a faraway, sullen look in her eyes again – the previous evening she'd reminded herself of something Big Karel had once said to her: he couldn't remember what it was, but she'd sat there brooding over it. As he came up the stairs, she looked up and said, 'And are you going to drag that dumb man out on to the Plains of Melancholy with you? Does he know what he's in for?'

'If you'd given me a son,' Karel snapped, as he picked up his coffee mug, 'who could help me with my projects, I wouldn't need to call on the help of foreigners.'

'You can have your son the day you listen to me.'

Forgetting his coffee, Karel threw up his hands, and the hot liquid splashed all over him. 'Do you know, Lettie Pistorius—'

Then, all of sudden, Mario Salviati was there, standing on the bottom step. He was wearing a clean white shirt, and his hair was wet and combed flat. Karel could see the stone between his thumb and his index finger. He exhaled slowly. When he turned to Lettie she was already gone. He turned back to Mario Salviati, but he'd also made himself scarce. Karel shook the drops of coffee off his hand.

Taking his hat, he walked slowly through the garden to where Mario Salviati was hunkered down next to the fishpond. For a while they watched the goldfish, then Big Karel beckoned to the Italian to follow him. The two men walked behind the house to the workshop. It was a big room, north-facing, with large windows. When Big Karel pushed open the door, Mario Salviati was surprised by the light streaming into the room, and by the large workbenches laden with measuring instruments and tools of various kinds.

Karel watched the Italian as he moved slowly between the tables. He picked up a compass, then a brass spirit level. He stopped for a long time next to a theodolite and held a telescope in his hand. But it was at the mallets and chisels that he lingered longest. He picked up the chisels one by one, weighing each in his hand. He looked at Karel and smiled.

Karel gave him a chance to explore further, but he was soon drawn back to the stonecutting tools. After a while Karel led him to a corner of the studio and a desk with land-survey maps and a few small-scale models of bridges and dams. Karel lifted the cloth covering a carefully built scale model that stood on its own table.

They studied it: there was Mount Improbable – even for the newcomer it was unmistakable – and the town dam, there was the railway line snaking along; the town roofs were visible; also the wide rocky plain that stretched out behind the mountain. And then Salviati bent forward, because Karel's forefinger was slowly tracing a line over the landscape. The finger began at the town dam and followed the fine silver line, which had been painted there so carefully. The line ran from the dam, up against the ridges, over the mountain, then shot out across the plain.

Karel stood in front of the Italian. He took the same forefinger and pressed it against Salviati's chest. The men stood there like that for a while, then suddenly realised that Lettie was outside, watching them through one of the windows. As Karel lifted a hand to her in greeting, she turned away.

Big Karel took a leather bag from a drawer. He went over to the chisels and thoughtfully selected six of the sturdiest in different sizes. While Mario Salviati watched him, Karel weighed the tools in his right hand one by one. Then he rolled up the chisel bag and tied it with a thong. He stepped towards Mario Salviati and gave him the bag.

'It's yours,' said Karel. Salviati couldn't hear him, but he understood, and an hour later, as they rode past the town dam, he kept his horse a short head behind the left flank of Big Karel's stallion. This was how Mario Salviati would always ride in the days that lay ahead and this was how Karel wanted it to be.

Just as Lettie Pistorius, who knew her husband too well, feared it would be.

17

In time it became known as the lightning water channel, the conduit that Karel created with the help of Dumb Eyetie and the Law of Bernoulli; the channel that shone like a snail's trail and led the abundant waters from the newly constructed dam on the other side of the rocky plains to Yearsonend.

Dumb Eyetie, the man who could not speak, made himself heard with thundering blasts of dynamite. Early morning was firing time – or the time to duck, as the inhabitants of Edenville called it – and the town was often roused by massive rumblings from the faraway plains.

They were a considerable presence, those explosions. And those were the days when Karel Bergh's name began to change to Big Karel Bergh, the time when the people began to look up to him; the days when the earth often trembled; the days before he was to be known as Karel Thin Air.

As time passed and the work toughened him and the sun tanned his skin, the stocky Italian began to look like a lizard. With his natural eye for levels and the theodolite that Big Karel had ordered from Amsterdam, he measured and dressed stone, working out a system of hand gestures so that he could make himself understood.

This was how Mario Salviati carved away his best years, the people said later – every stone he laid was a silent word of loneliness and longing for the world he'd left. The Italian laid stone after stone, handling each one as though it was the body of a woman, while Big Karel filled the world with words and – according to the rumours – love-making, and on Sunday afternoons proudly took invited guests in his carriage to see the excavation and building works.

Often the money ran out, and then Big Karel would ride from farm to farm. Or make speeches at agricultural shows, once the winner's rosette had been pinned to his lapel (section: Carriage and Horses). He usually chose the beer tent to get down to the serious business of persuading farmers to fork out more money.

'Just another four hundred pounds' worth of dynamite, seventy fresh Xhosas must be recruited and brought in, a second theodolite, a few milk cows to graze in the camp, free camping access for the work teams, and – again: please! no awkwardness about rights of way and servitudes. And the missionary must stay away from my blacks. They're here to work; not to prepare for entry into heaven.'

This was his tune and the farmers danced to it. Slowly but surely the lightning water conduit was chiselled through the landscape – in some places a dead straight line, in others as sinuous as a snake slithering across the landscape in lazy curves.

And they always raised their eyes to Mount Improbable, all of them: the workers, Dumb Eyetie, Big Karel Bergh, and everyone who'd scraped together an investment or laboured with them. Would the water really be able to get over the surly blue peak?

Prayer meetings were arranged at Yearsonend to bring vigour and momentum to the water, to call on the help of God's own powerful hand. Cynics from far and wide bet money on what they saw as inevitable disaster; optimists closed wagers in hope and expectation.

Only Mario Salviati and Big Karel Bergh did not pray and wager or doubt. They spurred on the work teams, Big Karel with expansiveness, threats, hundreds of bottles of cheap brandy and – on the sly – women brought in from the poor areas of Port Elizabeth; Dumb Eyetie with the quiet, intense labour of his hands, which came to resemble a crab's pincers as they grew larger and stronger – a man who could scarcely still hold a knife and a fork. His legs became more bowed from lifting stone, his eyes narrower and his eyebrows rougher as he weathered in the sun.

He was accustomed to the rituals required of him by Karel. At certain times he, Mario, had to strike an iron rod against the piece of train track that hung from a tree near his tent. Mario heard nothing but felt the vibration in the soles of his feet, and in the camp the workers stirred. All the teams had to get their equipment, and then Big Karel had to be called from where he sat at work in front of his tent, on a camping chair next to a folding table with open plans, a compass and a pair of dividers.

Karel allocated the daily tasks. The pickaxe team had to break the ground between two ropes, which had been restrung the previous day after careful measuring. The team with spades had to follow them, with the shovel team bringing up the rear. The ox-carts must be on standby here, Big Karel indicated with his hand, to move stone, and the mule-carts must carry the soil that way.

The best stone had to be stacked to one side under Dumb Eyetie's watchful eye where his hand could quickly test the grain and stability; the small team of stonecutting assistants had to get to work after the first rest break.

Dumb Eyetie was always busy among them, and the pile of cut stone grew, and was laid and mortared every second day to make a clean, finished length of duct – neat, watertight, as if it had always just been there.

The evening before any blasting was scheduled Big Karel would summon Mario to his tent. They'd sit drinking grappa by lantern light. Big Karel explained with sign language what they could expect, and Mario responded after he'd inspected the grain of the outcrop of stone that was obstructing the works.

They'd decide on the number of dynamite sticks, laying out the charges to one side on an oilcloth. Then they'd turn in, both now slightly unsteady on their feet from the grappa.

The following morning the workforce was under strict instructions to remain in the camp. Big Karel and Mario would plant the dynamite sticks and unroll the fuses themselves. Big Karel stood far back while Mario lit the fuses, but Mario was instructed to fall back behind Big Karel during the explosion. Before the dust had settled Big Karel was back out there in the cloud of dust. Sometimes he stumbled over rocks and uprooted Karoo bushes, but he made sure he got to the hole as quickly as he could. There he stumbled about, rubbing his eyes until the worst of the dust had settled and he could relax and look around properly; eventually he'd beckon to Mario, You can come closer now.

After Mario had carefully inspected the scene, he'd strike the piece of railtrack and the workers would emerge with picks and shovels, the ox- and mule-carts would be hitched amid whistling and shouting, while Big Karel walked back to his tent, head bowed, deep in thought.

And then Mario wished that he could offer his employer a few words of comfort. He didn't know what this was all about, but he had begun to suspect. And he stored the word in the back of his mind, as if it was something you should keep locked away because it was too dangerous to use.

18

Jonty heard on the town grapevine that Ingi Friedländer had been asking around for a horse to hire. According to the talk in the Look Deep pub, she wanted to ride out to the Plains of Melancholy. It was a little after eleven o'clock and Jonty was already propping up the bar with a few of the town's more hardened drinkers. That stump was giving him trouble, becoming ever more lifeless in his hands.

The barman rubbed his eyes and flicked a shot of brandy with a practised thumb and forefinger down the smooth wood to Jonty's waiting hand. 'I heard she said she wanted to go out after the secret,' said Look Deep, the barman.

'The secret?' asked Jonty, leaning on one elbow and undoing the thong that fastened his ponytail. As he shook out his long red hair he was aware that Look Deep and the little group of regulars were all watching him closely. So before they could respond, he added hastily, 'And where is she going to hire a horse?'

'She's already got one,' said Look Deep. 'I fixed her up with a tame old mare from the Pistoriuses. She said she knows how to stay in the saddle, she didn't want an old nag.'

'So she really wanted to go riding in this hot sun?' Jonty took a swig of brandy.

'She passed the pub a good hour ago. And she does know how to stay in the saddle, we could see.' Look Deep laughed when Jonty, clearly alarmed, gathered his hair, retied the thong and emptied his glass in two gulps. 'Are you going to follow her?' he called, but Jonty was already outside.

What on earth was Ingi up to? What fantasies had the town gossips painted for her? What was she looking for? 'Secret' could only mean one thing – and it was madness to think you could solve the riddle on horseback in one day. Jonty was afraid Ingi would get lost on the Plains of Melancholy. But then he remembered: wherever you are out there in the open, you can always see the sullen bulk of Mount Improbable. So there was really no cause for concern.

But suppose her horse broke its leg in a meerkat's burrow and she couldn't get back before dark? Or a snake bit her. With that fair skin, she might have underestimated the sun; and maybe she hadn't taken enough water with her.

He hurried up the pathway to Cave Gorge; like a lovestruck

schoolboy, he mocked himself, whose girlfriend has gone missing. At his house, he grabbed the binoculars, two bottles of water and an extra hat, in case she didn't have one.

What else could he take to her? he wondered, dithering. What about a piece of biltong? No, too salty in this heat. He buckled another bottle of water on to his belt instead.

He trotted down to the smallholding where he always visited the cowsheds in the late afternoon, and borrowed the horse he sometimes used when he went out looking for driftwood in the gullies under the cliffs.

'She went that way,' the workers told him, laughing knowingly as he galloped off. Why don't you get on with your bloody work and dig up the weeds? Jonty snarled silently.

He followed the route they'd indicated, out of the town, in the opposite direction to the stone cottage. He checked the town dam. There was no sign of her. But beside the lightning water channel, where it came down the mountain slope, he picked up the marks of skidding hoofs and her bootprints. She'd led her horse there, and it was obvious that she wanted to follow the channel.

Jonty also led his mare up the slope; it was steep, but she was used to clambering around with him through the gullies and across the rocky slopes of Mount Improbable. Once they'd climbed the steep parts and crested the first foothill he rested the horse. The animal's hide rippled as Jonty swung himself back into the saddle.

There was the channel again, neatly built, its base black with dried frog slime. It ran at a slight gradient then climbed steeper slopes to reach the back of this part of the mountain, angled, then ran steeply down to the Plains of Melancholy.

The lightning water channel was baked dry because, these days, it was only necessary to open the sluice gates at the source, far to the north, twice a month. Then the water would travel across the plains and flash up over the back of the mountain to stream down and fill the town dam with enough water to keep the townsfolk and the owners of the smallholdings going for fourteen days.

Jonty dropped down behind the mountain, and soon he could

no longer see any trees or fields when he looked back. Like a grey ocean, the Plains of Melancholy surged out before him, and he and his horse were no more than a dark speck creeping down the length of the mountain, weaving between bushes and rocks.

He never caught a glimpse of Ingi, but her trail was easy to follow. There were indications that she had dismounted here and there to stand around for a bit. There was even a damp patch, with her bootprints on either side, which made him smile in spite of himself.

You'll get thirsty today, Ingi, he thought. What does a girl from Cape Town know about the Murderers' Karoo?

While he rode, Jonty hoped that Ingi hadn't heard too many scandalous tales about the Berghs and the Pistoriuses. He knew how it was in Yearsonend, and he shuddered to think of some of the stories in circulation. Like stray dogs criss-crossing the streets in search of the carrion of falsehood and rumour, sniffing at every doorstep, and sometimes a story became rabid, berserk, biting poison into everybody in the town.

What would she know of the ox-wagon carrying the gold and his grandfather Meerlust Bergh's role in it? What would she have heard of his father, Big Karel Bergh, there in the pub or at the bony-handed storekeeper's?

Jonty dug his heels into his horse's flanks and pressed on, because the sun was already at two o'clock. Her water would be finished by now, he knew, and if she had any sense she'd be starting to think about turning back.

The circling crows led him to where she sat in a dry sand ditch, next to her hobbled horse, in the shade of a thorn tree. So she hadn't come across any mysterious carriages or discovered treasure chests, he thought compassionately: just stone and plains and Karoo bush. He was surprised that she'd not heard him approaching, and he sat for a while in his saddle looking at her. She had scraped her hair back under a cap and her cheeks were white with sunblock.

Her horse lifted its head and the jingle of the bridle made her look up in alarm. But she wasn't entirely surprised to see him. It's as if she was thinking about me, thought Jonty, as he dismounted and led his horse closer. The cicadas shrilled and he pointed up towards the crows.

'They're reporting for supper.' He laughed. 'Looks as if you're on the menu.'

She laughed with him. 'I was just about to turn back. It's a big stretch of the earth.' She looked around her, eyes narrowed against the light. 'Makes words seem redundant.' He laughed again and sat down beside her. They could smell the horse sweat and she drew patterns in the dust with a twig. He didn't know what to say. Then she looked up. 'I see you have water?'

'Indeed I do.' He passed her one of the bottles. He watched her drink, her cheeks glowing red even through the smears of sunblock, drops trickling from the corners of her thirsty mouth and slipping down over her chin to fall into her lap.

She was breathless by the time she stopped and screwed the cap back on to the bottle. 'And what brings you out here on to the plains?'

He pointed into the ditch. 'The most wonderful pieces of wood are washed down here when it rains. And stones. Tortoiseshells. Porcupine quills. All sorts of things. I scavenge about for whatever I can find.'

She nodded and picked up the water bottle to drink again. Then she turned to him. He'd known the question would come, but he hadn't been able to think of an appropriate answer on his way here. At times he'd contemplated turning back simply because he dreaded the question.

But now the time had come, and she asked it simply; offered it almost as a proposition. He wished he could answer her with matching simplicity. 'I wonder about the gold?'

He laughed, slightly relieved, and wiped a hand over his face as he stared over the plains. Then he sniffed and scratched in the sand. 'Stories,' he said eventually. 'Gossip.'

She was silent for a moment. Then she said quietly, 'Just gossip?'

He stood up and dusted the earth off his backside. Then he

looked into the face turned up towards his. He shook his head and went off to get the horses.

'Look at how low the sun is. The leopards come out of the mountain at night and prowl around these plains. We'd better move on.'

He could see that she was irritated by the way he'd avoided her question, but she only said lightly, 'And they eat city girls.'

'Their favourite meal.'

They rode back slowly. And, as always when he followed this pathway beside the lightning water channel, Jonty thought of his father's carriage, which, according to legend, had raced along here on the day of his disappearance.

Here, he always felt something of the urgency and horror of Karel Thin Air's helter-skelter flight.

It's ironic, he thought: it's when there's no wind and everything is quiet and still that you hear the rumbling and the hoofbeats, the desperate swaying of a carriage travelling too fast, crazy out here on the open plain; absurd, just as his father's dreams and plans always were.

These are things I would have liked to tell you about, Ingi Friedländer, he thought, but I cannot afford to. Because I know what I would do as soon as I'd entrusted these things to you. I'd try to take them back. Furiously, with all my strength.

As if you had stolen them from me.

19

On the day when the water was to run at last, everyone gathered at Turncoat, in the mountainous area to the east, beyond the rocky plains.

There was a lord from England, bored and preoccupied – he'd been retracing the footsteps of the famous explorer and artist, Captain William Gird, and just happened to be around at the right time. There was a bishop in purple robes with a shining cross on his crozier. The angel sat on the dam wall, a little way away, cooling his feet in the shallow muddy water. He kept an eye on Mario Salviati, who couldn't really join in the celebrations. He watched the heron on the other side of the dam, wading in the shallows and fishing, as if unaware of the crowd of people and the excitement at the deep end of the dam. The angel dipped the ends of his wings into the water. He waited.

There were also three sangomas sitting on blankets. The black workers had summoned them from the Transkei by bush telegraph and since early that morning they'd been possessed by the spirits of the ancestors, trembling so violently that their teeth chattered. Captain Gird made rapid sketches of them. He'd arrived late, looking slightly the worse for wear and escorted by his guide Slingshot X!am leading their pack mule. When he felt more rested, he'd complete formal studies in ink and oils. Today he had to hurry to capture the fast movements, the big gestures, the immeasurable landscape and these larger-than-life people . . .

Big Karel Bergh's carriage and horses stood next to the dam wall among the cars and pick-up trucks. There were other horse-carts, because the region was in transition between horse-drawn transport and the car. The missionary was there, with his weathered Bible and his flabby backside; the dominee with his solemnity and glib tongue; the Minister of Agriculture had sent an assistant secretary – a young man with a *pince-nez*, who had to keep slipping behind a bush to relieve himself during the endless prayers, the shuddering wails of the sangomas, the signs of the blessing from the priests and the flag-waving of the schoolchildren.

And amid it all stood Big Karel Bergh. In those days, during the build-up to Grand Apartheid, which would become law in 1948, he was something of an enigma: a man of mixed blood, son of Meerlust Bergh, the fashion king, and Irene Lampak, the model and milliner from Indonesia.

His father was descended from the Huguenots on one side, and on the other side, he was related to Captain William Gird. There were also other, more indigenous forebears, but they were not much spoken about, because Meerlust was an influential man and the Yearsonenders knew when it was in their best interests to keep silent.

Big Karel's mother had appeared from 'nowhere', it was said. One morning the flamboyant Meerlust drove into town in a Cape cart and stopped in front of the general store. He put out a hand to help the lady in the hooded cart. She peeled off her white gloves and alighted elegantly. She was beautiful, that Indonesian girl, with the grace of a leopard, recalled the Yearsonenders, and skin the colour of the springbok that the San rock artists had painted on cave walls.

These were Big Karel's parents and he was proud of them. The father was fabulously rich and fascinating. In bad times his blend of creativity and lust for gold might have led Meerlust Bergh into the life of a swindler and spendthrift, but he struck it lucky in the ostrich-feather boom.

And the mother: such a fine-boned girl, obviously of royal descent, a princess; a fashion designer, an artist from the exotic East.

And there stood Big Karel on the dam wall on this, the first day of the lightning water channel. Unexpectedly, you saw smouldering in him the erotic elegance of his mother. Today he wore a suit and his shiny black hair was combed back; he was lean with tension and expectation. Handsome and important, he stood there, tall like his flamboyant father, a man who rose above other men, a man of vision as he looked out over the gathering, over the banks of schoolchildren, over the cars and the carts and the restless horses, over the black workers, crouching under the thorn trees, with their spades and picks ceremoniously laid out (as if it were a contest of arms), and over Dumb Eyetie, behind the carriage, to one side, somewhat lost now that everything was over.

That was how Big Karel looked that day, the people would say later. The look of a dreamer, the gaze of an idealist – a man who tried, with grand gestures, to escape the limitations imposed on him by his mixed ancestry at a time when there was increasing talk of the natural division of races.

Maybe Karel had known what was coming: the strict laws, the

removal of brown families from the street in Yearsonend that would later become known as Eviction Road; the other idiocies. Maybe he wanted to buy his whiteness once and for all with one huge project; buy citizenship on the privileged side of the dividing fence that was to be erected within a year or ten.

'Trying for white,' whispered people behind their hands. 'Look at him standing there, all puffed up with his own importance.'

And yet they were all there, because they all had an interest. The whole of Yearsonend was there to watch. Big Karel scanned them all then settled his eyes on the distant, hazy summit of Mount Improbable. While an actress recited stanzas by a folk poet – about water bringing relief to a parched land, about swarms of locusts devouring greenness down to the stalk, about thunderclouds blooming over the earth like cauliflowers – Big Karel ceremoniously loaded his gun.

When the poem was finished and the last trembling rhyme had descended on the goose-pimpled crowd, he fired a shot into the air. Immediately a group of uncouth farmers also whipped out their firearms and fired several celebratory rounds. The nervous assistant secretary from the Department of Agriculture raised the sluice gate: he struggled with the winding mechanism and had to be helped because too much deskwork had weakened his arm muscles.

With a gurgling roar, the water spurted out of the dam, into the furrow and began to flow down the stone duct with such amazing speed that people caught their breath.

'See? The gradient is exactly right for maximum flow,' murmured Big Karel, and his eye, shining with gratitude and relief, caught Dumb Eyetie's – the very last time their eyes were to meet.

Or was it? What was yet to come, in the next hour? It would never be possible to investigate or unravel it properly. But this meeting of eyes was a kind of closure, even though the two men did not know it; even though the angel, sniggering, was the only one who understood what was going on; even though the angel was the only one to splash his wings in the water in excitement.

Dust had collected in the base of the canal, and as the water pushed through, a hellish dustcloud rose into the air. People gasped for breath when they witnessed dry earth visibly yielding to water. The priest lifted his staff and smote the water, the missionary praised the Lord, the schoolchildren waved their flags, the workers chanted a seditious political freedom song, which the whites didn't understand and took to be some devotional psalm or other. The sangomas frothed at the mouth and one cast herself on to the dam wall; the spirits of the ancestors are angry, she was informed, in a fresh visitation, because the channel runs over old, forgotten graves ten miles further on.

But it was too late because there went the water, shining and sly as a snake.

Signallers with heliographs were installed on every ridge from First Sluice, also known as Turncoat, to the highest point on Mount Improbable. They had to report back on the water's progress. As the water progressed the message was flashed on from one heliograph to the next, back to the crowds at First Sluice.

Big Karel's calculations, based on the miraculous Law of Bernoulli, showed that the water would run as fleetly as a scrub hare over certain predetermined sections; over others, which he had measured precisely, like a horse at the trot; and then, eventually, as laborious as a mountain tortoise, it would creep up Mount Improbable to the vertiginous summit, reaching a state approaching inertia, only to tumble down the cliff with renewed vigour, to reach Yearsonend's dry town dam within a mere six and a quarter minutes.

The journey of that first shining arrow of water would, according to calculations, last four hours, twenty minutes and thirty seconds, and therefore the assembly now turned its attention to picnic tables and the lighting of cooking fires. The workers had been given an ox, which they ceremonially slaughtered by slitting an artery with a spear, and by the time the ceremonial champagne corks popped, the first heliograph was already flashing.

The water had passed Struggling Stream, and glasses were raised by jubilant revellers round the improvised picnic tables. Games had been organised for the schoolchildren of Yearsonend and the surrounding districts: sack races, egg-and-spoon races, and a tug-of-war. General Taljaard had set aside his treasure-hunting for the day, and he and the bishop got roaring drunk.

It didn't take long for the general's eye to focus on the bishop's golden crozier. This was not lost on the bishop, who'd honed his nose for lust and other sins of the flesh. During their discussions he got the general's drift. As he grew the worse for wear, and the general's rantings about sunken frigates and forbidden treasure grew more enthusiastic, the bishop pushed his crozier deeper and deeper under the table.

'And as one old man to another, may I ask how old you are now?' asked the bishop, with British punctiliousness.

'Hell, man, I don't know,' answered the general. 'I can still recall a visit from Napoleon at the old Drostdy: he complained of stomach-ache and we discussed maps and war tactics; and obviously I fought at Colenso and at Dellville Wood. I only saw action in this war for six months before collecting a salvo of shrapnel in my arse, as you no doubt heard, so now I just sit at home and look for gold. But the German submarines are up and down our coast in these days. Cruising over the gold that lies buried below the sea currents. Silent as sharks.'

The bishop looked away. Perhaps he thought the old general was talking codswallop; perhaps he didn't have much time for living legends with a passion for war and gold; perhaps he was no longer all that sober himself. Who knows?

As the minutes ticked by and the guests grew rowdier, Big Karel's tension mounted. He looked for Dumb Eyetie among the people, but he was nowhere to be seen. He went to look among the noisy township workers, who were cooking chunks of the recently slaughtered beast over an open fire; he went and peered inside the carriage; he looked between the cars and carts and among the horses, but he couldn't find the Italian anywhere.

Everyone was celebrating and no one saw Dumb Eyetie standing near the heron in the shallows. Slowly he undressed as the water gurgled out of the dam. Where it had been exposed to the sun, his skin was almost black. But the rest of his body was snow white as he slid and dived and spluttered about in the mud dam in his underpants.

He could see people moving and gesticulating excitedly in the distance, but he couldn't hear his own snorting and blowing noises, or the splash of water or the hiss of the lightning water channel as it shot through the landscape. He imagined what noise was, and from the way flocks of birds had taken flight above him, he deduced that they'd been startled by something. But he had no way of knowing what noise is, and how was he to know that the air was filled with a rushing, an urgent, almost ominous droning, as the water sang over Rocky Plains?

The walls of the lightning water channel were built, by chance, in such a way that the water moving between them created an acoustic miracle. At times it sounded as if the channel was singing. This was why people would always talk of the singing water – the lightning water's first swish over the dry channel floor. And, thus, First Sluice would be named Singing Water by some people, in memory of that first day.

Others would refer to Many Names, because First Sluice was given so many names on that one day that the Yearsonenders would joke about this in the weeks that followed. Are you talking about Washout or Singing Water? they would ask. Or First Sluice or Many Names?

Mario Salviati, there in the dam, felt tremors in the water and a change in temperature as he moved in deeper; he felt the sun's changing warmth and his hands grasped at the water and relaxed, as if he wanted to find a handhold there, but couldn't.

The war was over, and Dumb Eyetie was treading water: which way should he go? There was Edit Bergh, Big Karel's sister: they'd become friendly. But he had so little money and this was a country, he'd discovered early on, where one needed money. And work was hard to come by.

It was said in the district, and in Yearsonend, that Dumb Eyetie would become an important man when the flashwater ran, because he'd have to lay out channels in the fields below the town dam, install irrigation sluices and aqueducts; he was the man with an eye for levels and for stone.

But they didn't make this known to him: he'd been living in a tent, sleeping like a lizard among stones. Only Edit Bergh had come to visit him with her picnic basket, and now and again Lorenzo Devil Slap, and Big Karel. But with Big Karel it was always to do with business; could only be about business, because he was such a driven man.

From there, in the deep water, Mario Salviati could feel the current pull over his body, lightly, teasingly, as it gurgled out at the sluice gate. He saw Big Karel walking up and down, but he didn't hear him call his name. Nor did he hear the celebrations when the lightning water reached the next heliograph, ten miles further on, and the light signals flashed through.

Afterwards people would ponder over Big Karel Bergh's nervousness that day at First Sluice. He paced up and down like a caged lion, and with each heliograph flash he went and stood impatiently next to Old Sheriff, a retired man with heliograph experience from the previous war. He'd trained the team of young men as heliograph operators and placed them in a chain on the highest points from First Sluice all the way to Yearsonend – all especially for the first opening of the lightning water channel sluice gates.

Old Sheriff had always stammered, and this was possibly why he was drawn to the light stutterings of the heliograph – so the story went. While he gave Big Karel Bergh a stammering translation of the sun signals, the channel-builder grew more and more fidgety. The sheriff complained later that he became sun-blind from all the heliograph messages, every quarter of an hour as the water flashed onwards, but Big Karel said, 'We can't do without you. We have to push through. Have another glass of wine, Old Sheriff.'

He promised the sheriff fifty ewes if he persevered, and the old man duly received them from the estate once Big Karel Bergh had disappeared and was renamed Karel Thin Air and Attorney Pistorius had had to sort out the estate for his sister, Lettie, and for the child who was born on the *Windsor Castle en route* back to

South Africa – Big Karel's only acknowledged son, Jonty Jack, the future sculptor who'd live in Mount Improbable's Cave Gorge.

But the heliograph flashes took their toll: Old Sheriff's eyes were burnt blind in their sockets that day. For the rest of his life he could see only the outlines of things. The core of things, people would say, was lost on Old Sheriff for ever from that day on: 'He sees only the frame, never the picture.'

The hours passed, then Big Karel stripped off the gold watch he had inherited from his father and walked around with it in his hand. In the dam Dumb Eyetie floated on his back in a circling, drifting stillness and thought about stone and form, about texture and wind, about the sun and longing – about the things that a man who works in lonely landscapes and has almost no contact with other people ponders upon; a man of the chisel and the trowel, of the spirit level and of deliberation.

And then the flash came from Mount Improbable, as everyone sat waiting on picnic blankets and tarpaulins, bloated and hung over, and even the children rested under the trees, worn out with play. The flash came from the heliograph on Mount Improbable through to Dreamstone. Then it was read and signalled over to Nowhere, in the centre of the rocky plain, where chunks of black volcanic rock lay strewn over the face of the earth, and from there to Gorra, where the Khoi had dug for water, and finally on to Old Sheriff, who looked at the signal and rubbed his eyes, while Big Karel stood beside him and, his chest heaving, asked, 'What do you see, old man?'

Maybe I am blind now, thought Old Sheriff, rubbing his eyes again. 'I think, no, I think . . . the water . . .'

'What?'

The anguish in Big Karel's eyes was too much to behold, people said afterwards. 'Failure. Failure like you've never seen it before.'

When Old Sheriff, dizzy with shock, cried, 'The water refuses!' Big Karel shook him and slapped him a couple of times.

'You old blind fool! Jingo! Turncoat!'

But then the flash came again. 'The water is surging back!'

whispered the people to one another, and cried, 'The water refuses!'

Then Big Karel bellowed, 'Get away from here! Get the children and the cars away from here!' He was the only one who realised that the water, which had crawled a good way up Mount Improbable, would fall back with the same energy that had brought it to that point. And so it happened – and that was why that day became known as the day of the stubborn water, the day the lightning water ran backwards.

Luckily everyone got out of the way in time: the work teams, the trancing sangomas and the schoolchildren. They also rescued the cars, the Cape carts and the picnic blankets. The water turned back with a fury that swept everything away before it: the ash from the cooking fires, the urine patches left by the men behind the trees, the horse dung and the heelmarks left in the ground after the tug-of-war.

From then on that piece of ground beneath the dam wall was known as Washout, and it is still a popular picnicking place for people who go there to rake up the story of the stubborn water, and who want to speculate about all the names – yes, even Stubborn Water – or who want to make up stories about Karel Thin Air's last days as a visible presence.

What no one saw was how that returning flood swept up poor Dumb Eyetie and deposited him like a half-drowned fieldmouse on the plains some distance away; poor Dumb Eyetie who'd been minding his own business as he floated dreamily in blissful ignorance on the water. Perplexed, Mario Salviati shook his head then realised what had happened.

He looked around for Big Karel Bergh. But by that time Big Karel had already disappeared into thin air, because when the stubborn water swished back and washed everything away, Big Karel jumped into his carriage, whipped up his horses and fled as if from the scene of a crime. The last people saw of him was the black carriage, which bumped across the plain in the direction of Mount Improbable and Yearsonend.

Then they also spotted the half-drowned Mario Salviati, as he jumped onto a horse and gave chase. And hard on his heels, as if he'd got wind of something big in the offing, was Lorenzo Devil Slap who, having arrived at the event as chauffeur of Attorney Pistorius' Ford, also commandeered a horse.

No one at Washout knew that the events of the coming years had been set in motion by this triple chase across the plains. Perhaps the sangoma who'd passed out had sensed something of this. Hold on: what about the angel? The angel knew, for the angel followed the two riders with great, leisurely – even bored – sweeps of his wings. He kept a sympathetic eye on them as he wheeled in wide circles over the plains, and he, of course, could also see Big Karel Bergh's black carriage swaying along far ahead of them. They were headed for the angel's own territory: Mount Improbable.

The guests hung about at First Sluice. They stood gawping at the aftermath of the water's violence, at the indiscriminate power of nature, at the uprooted trees and shrubs. They went home eventually and that evening there was no end to the talk of the dismal failure of Big Karel Bergh's lightning water channel.

'He set himself up too high,' preached the dominee that evening during a service that had been arranged in advance to serve as an act of thanks for the water. Now everyone sat slightly dazed, but enjoying the sanctimonious condemnation of Big Karel's project. They forgot that they were all, to a greater or lesser extent, shareholders in the project, and that Big Karel's loss was also theirs.

'We give you thanks, O Lord, for keeping us humble, and reminding us of Your power and might; of the greatness of Your creation and of the feebleness of man,' prayed the dominee while Mario Salviati wandered through the streets of Yearsonend with his stone in his hand.

What he'd seen after following Big Karel would remain with him for ever. For the first time in his life there was something in him so big that he felt it was going to burst out past his dumb tongue. It was like a dam of water in his breast, and his disability was a stubborn wall with no floodgate: the silence of Mario Salviati.

20

At times it seemed the wood flamed under Jonty's chisel; at others the log lay there morosely, dull and lifeless, and he felt that he was extinguishing it with every blow of the mallet. Every day, before he got to work on it, he'd throw a blanket over the Staggering Merman's head; and in the late afternoon, when he returned from the byre with a bucket of cow urine, he'd remove the blanket and whisper to the merman's gleaming form, 'There she comes, Staggers, old chap. Look, she's taking shape . . .'

Then he sat in his yard and wondered: How can I explain to her that she isn't the first one I've desired with a burning in my hands? But I snarl until they leave, I talk them away, I turn aside as if I have no choice but to do so – and then eventually it's just me again and these bits of scattered wood, driftwood from the mouth of the Great River, white, sunbleached whale-ribs from the Wild Coast, old stumps from the cliffs of Mount Improbable.

'Ingi,' Jonty repeated, when the shadows began to stalk him, and he rolled a joint because something else was creeping up on him too: the feeling that yet another sculpture was going to end up with all those others, rotting on the pile behind his house – out there in the gully that had started as a scar left by a rockfall long ago, and was then gouged deeper by wind and rain, out there where he threw all his aborted sculptures, his crippled lambs.

The cemetery: that's what he called the place. When a piece of wood went dead under his hands it had to be disposed of, consigned to the place where wind and weather would take its course; where termites and small scurrying creatures would do what needed to be done with the old wood: working it over, devouring and digesting it and ultimately converting it into something else – dung and mould and compost and, in dry years, dust.

'Ingi . . .' Jonty looked at the sculpture, and all at once he couldn't recall her face. It seemed a portent that the piece was already eluding him. 'Ingi . . .' He hurried to the telescope and focused it on the stone cottage. It shimmered in the midday sun and the Peugeot was parked so that she could drive straight out when the time came.

Tonight was her last in the stone cottage: arrangements had been concluded for her indefinite stay at the Drostdy – so he had heard in the pub.

How can I tell her the reasons for all I do, thought Jonty, and why I stay in this isolated house, tell her why I choose to breathe life into hard, unformed material, while other people breathe the breath of passion into their lovers?

I cannot love, he wanted to tell Ingi, and as he sat there he spread his arms in explanation, as though she were with him. I know that love is the giving of life, of space and energy. But the fear never leaves me: the thing you love will disappear and you'll be left alone. And thus the sculptures: the chopping and chiselling and whittling – to fix the loved one in permanence.

Towards evening, Jonty went off to his open-air shower. He'd erected the reed shelter and the metal drum, and once a week he took the camper-van down to Lampak's Dam to fill the drums. Then, back at home, he'd pump the water into the drums above his shower and in the ceiling above the kitchen. He undressed and soaped himself, shivering under the cold water. He rubbed his body, over the hair and the rough patches, his hands working as a lover's would, and he lifted his face into the water and spurted and spat against the stream. Always with the work of my own hands, he thought, every bit of woodwork in the house, every nail and roof sheet, this scaffolding and the levelling of the yard, all with my own hands . . . The hands that can never desert me, betray me or let me down.

He pulled on a clean white shirt and sat outside to rub his hair dry and comb it through. It fell in a loose fleece that reached down to his shoulder-blades. He pulled on new black jeans and socks under his black boots. Finally he put on the bracelet he'd inherited from his mother – a silver snake coiled round his sinewy brown wrist, a reptile swallowing its tail.

He went to pick arum lilies in the meadow that lay in the damp ravine behind the cemetery. The long stems pulled loose from the plants with a popping noise and he didn't stop until he held a large bunch of the deep-throated flowers. Angel flowers he'd called them since childhood. Flowers so exquisite in their simplicity, so different from the succulents and marigolds and anemones they grew down there in the gardens of Yearsonend.

He set off down the Cave Gorge path, light-headed, with a Bob Dylan tune on his lips. He remembered the advice a lovely young woman had given him a long time ago: perhaps one shouldn't explain; perhaps one should simply give the body and the self, flowers and aromas, but few words. Least of all words. Meaning lay elsewhere.

He hesitated at the concertina gate. Shouldn't he turn back? The impulse was strong. But he flexed his shoulders. 'Buck up, Jonty,' he said quietly. He went through the gate, then closed it behind him, fastening it with the hook.

'Florentine Cottage', he read on the small signboard as he walked past the Peugeot. He didn't have to knock at the door for it was open. Ingi sat reading at the table. She looked up and started when she saw him. 'Hello,' said Jonty, and thrust the bunch of lilies against her. 'From Cave Gorge.'

'Th-thank you!' Ingi turned, searching for something to arrange the lilies in, then turned back to him. 'Please sit down.' She gestured vaguely at the empty space opposite her. He drew up a chair from against the wall. 'Where have you come from?' she asked.

'I always come from Cave Gorge,' Jonty said simply, and once again – as so often before – she had the feeling that he wanted to say more than his words told.

'From Cave Gorge?' She made a joke of her own confusion. 'And pray tell me, kind sir, where that great city lies.'

'Against a mountain.' He took up the game. 'Far, far away from the castle, far from the wicked king, and far from the sea and all the tumult.'

'A mountain? And what are the houses like in the city?'

95

'Humble dwellings. Made of wood. Tarred poles that stink. They make the elves sneeze. And the wind frightens fairies who like to flit about at night.'

She looked up sharply. He read it in her eyes: the telescope.

'No, no,' he continued. 'No, there're no fairies, only a water snake with a diamond glittering in his forehead.'

'And where does he live?'

'Between the floodgates. In the reeds. In the duct. The flashwater channel.'

'Oh, indeed! And what does this snake seek?'

Without warning, he lost interest. She noticed, and said, 'Thanks for the flowers. And you look very smart tonight.'

Jonty shrugged. He regarded her with his head on one side: it was that nose he'd been unable to liberate from the wood; the way she tossed her hair back. Self-confidence, confidence in my own inspiration – that's what I lack, he thought. Here she is before me, but she was up there too, in my hands, ready for me to liberate her. Then my courage failed . . .

'Hey!' Ingi called him back to the present. 'Would you like a glass of white wine from the Cape?'

She poured for both of them and they clinked glasses.

'You've got a lot to tell,' she said, after a while, teasing.

'About what?'

'I've watched you and the storekeeper. You only want to talk about certain things.'

Jonty recoiled. Not about my sculpture, not now, he thought. But he relaxed as she continued.

'Since my visit to the Drostdy I have lots of questions.'

'But you're moving in tomorrow. Then you can see for yourself.'

She continued to tease him, her face half concealed by the wineglass. 'And what is there to be seen? A water snake with a diamond in his forehead?'

He laughed. 'Well, there's the general. And his Great Danes.'

'And . . . ?'

'Well, that's just about it.' Again he waved an imaginary fly away from his face. She got up and went over to the portraits on the wall. She pointed to the picture of the prison train. 'Were you there?'

He laughed again. 'It was before I was born. Just.'

'Forgive me.'

'Do you think I'm that ancient?'

She smiled. 'Was Mario Salviati on this train?'

Jonty cleared his throat and stood up. 'Yes, he was,' he said, running his fingers through his hair. Ingi saw he was clamming up: the hand in the now-familiar gesture in front of his face, the body half turned away. His fingertips started to drum on the table.

She's watching me, Jonty knew. He got the feeling she was testing him, and he felt his anger rising. But he controlled it. Look at her, he told himself, so beautiful standing there, her elbow on her hip, the head tilted, the wine-glass high next to her face, the teasing eyes.

He got up and came round the table. Still holding his wine-glass, he came to stand before her. He was much larger than her: her face was on a level with the grey hairs thrusting out from under his shirt. Up close, she was so completely different from a piece of wood. He wanted to turn and run away. He could smell her: the smell of buchu leaves and a light perfume; traces of a world far from here. Tiny drops of perspiration beaded her upper lip.

They stood like that. She looked over his shoulder; he stared at the portrait of Mario Salviati and Edit Bergh behind her. The wine-glasses were between them: glasses held up as an excuse; as though they were proposing a toast to something that would never happen.

21

From the day he arrived in Yearsonend, Mario Salviati watched Big Karel and Lettie Bergh closely. In them he sensed something of his own longing for Italy. It was as though they were cast adrift, circling each other in a strange no-man's land.

Lettie didn't pay Salviati much attention: she was too busy with her own thoughts. Sometimes he wondered if she wasn't afraid of him, but in time he came to realise that, to her, he was simply part of one of Big Karel's projects. Once he'd realised that, Salviati took pains to avoid her. Whenever he saw her approaching, he made himself scarce.

Gradually he came to know the lie of the land between the Berghs. As he was deaf, it took him weeks to figure out things that others might discern in a flash. But the advantage of the slow osmosis of his observations was that he weighed up every drop of information. Mario Salviati never jumped to conclusions, he thought wryly. It was slow going but in the end it was all as clear as a mountain stream.

He kept an eye on the Berghs from where he sat reflecting in the sunshine at the door of his outside room, and from the pond in the garden where on Saturdays and Sundays he sat thinking while the fish played about in the water.

He considered the connection between the studio and the living room. In the living room Karel and Lettie sat stiff and silent, but by and by spirited words were exchanged and then the predictable happened: Lettie hurried down the steps, out through the gate, down into town to her brother, who sat in his office behind stacks of files; the brother with whom Karel had almost no contact even though his firm administered the finances for the lightning water channel – with the aid of bicycle messengers who went to and fro between Karel's house and the attorney's.

When Lettie tripped down into town so indignantly, it was the cue for Big Karel to hurry to the studio, hesitate a moment in indecision, then get down to work. He worked with abnormal haste, stooped over the drawing tables or the columns of scientific formulae through which he applied the Law of Bernoulli to the landscape. It was complicated work, and Karel burnt the midnight oil over the notes he and Mario had made with the aid of a measuring tape and theodolite on the Plains of Melancholy: the gradient of the mountain slopes, the distance from the lowest to the highest point, the ideal breadth and depth of the channel.

And then all of a sudden, Big Karel would emerge, leap on to his horse and race down to the big house with the towers and dormer windows – the Feather Palace where he'd grown up. After galloping round the house once, as if he was chasing something away, he'd come pounding up the road again, sending frightened animals fleeing across the smallholdings as the labourers leaned on their spades to watch.

After one of these spurts of energy, Karel always seemed calmer. And then Lettie would be walking home again, slowly but also visibly calmer, even though her shoulders were hunched, resigned like a lamb to the slaughter.

Salviati had no idea what it was the two of them berated each other for, but he had known since childhood that the faculties he lacked – tongue and ear – could cause greater damage than anything else.

He grew attached to Karel Bergh, the big man with those big dreams: the man who strode over the veld gesturing impatiently at the theodolite, who cleaned his equipment and buffed it to a shine punctiliously every night; who did everything meticulously and professionally – the project's bank account, the list of shareholders, the recruitment of labourers, the placating of impatient townsfolk, the figures delineating gradient and distance and resistances.

It gave Mario Salviati great pleasure to see Big Karel standing in his doorway with a cup of coffee to wake him up every morning. For the remainder of the working day, Mario was the subordinate. But from the first, their days always began with this gesture by Big Karel, and Mario, who noted his employer's other relationships, realised just what a privileged position he enjoyed.

He could feel Karel watching him too, and responding to his wishes. Whenever they had to select equipment for the project, Karel would pretend he was looking at something else, but Mario could feel Karel's eye on him, and he knew that if he stood holding a specific piece of equipment for a while before he put it down again, it would be included on the final shopping list.

So Big Karel made him part of the project; and Lettie turned her back on him more than ever. In the early days she had still greeted him; later on she pretended not to see him. And it was no surprise to Mario when she appeared on the veranda one morning with a large trunk beside her.

It was at that time that Mario came to realise how much on the fringes of the white community Karel Bergh lived, with ultimately only Lettie Pistorius and his big projects binding him to it. And he realised that Big Karel identified with him, Mario Salviati; also – maybe especially – with his deafness, his dumbness. He realised that Big Karel always wore wide-brimmed hats, and always moved into the shade of a wagon or a tree when they worked on the Plains of Melancholy.

In this world, a swarthy complexion counted against you, Mario quickly discovered. And if you were in Big Karel's position you were involved in a perpetual war on that account: against the prejudices of the narrow-minded congregation who stood in front of their church each Sunday morning talking in subdued voices with narrowed eyes.

After Lettie's departure, Karel stepped up the pace. The first teams of labourers arrived. Men from the rural Transkei who soon worked out that Mario was a foreigner and mocked him behind his back – but in a way that ensured he knew it. Big Karel had a word with them. After that they were more friendly and respectful. Mario had no idea what Big Karel had said to them, but the first time some rock had to be blasted away and he appeared carrying sticks of dynamite, the men reeled back and kept out of his way for the duration of the project.

That suited him well enough and he was pleased with this demonstration that Big Karel knew how to manage his project. And it was for that reason that the day after he was possessed by his great mystery, like a malady that would never leave him, the day Karel Thin Air disappeared, he decided to do everything in his power to disprove the town's conviction and show that Big Karel's faith in Bernoulli was justified.

And so, the day after the water had refused to flow and everyone had accepted that the dream of the channel had gone to the devil, he went on his own to open the sluice. The channel floor was damp now so the water slid over it more easily, progressing three-quarters of the way up Mount Improbable. On the third day when he rode alone to First Sluice, he knew this time it would work.

The water slipped with practised ease into the damp channel and then, with an exuberant glittering dash, it flashed up over Mount Improbable – just as Lettie Pistorius unfolded the telegram as she sat, with the sickly baby Jonty Jack at her breast on the *Windsor Castle* moored in Table Bay Harbour, and learned of Big Karel's disappearance.

In Yearsonend people were startled out of their afternoon snoozes by the singing of the lightning water channel, and all of a sudden their back gardens and the fields of their smallholdings and the wetland and the town conduit were filled with water – sheets and sheets of sweetly capricious water from out there in First Sluice country. Someone had forgotten to shut the sluice gate on the dam and the first flashwater spread like a generous hand through the town.

Amazed, everyone rushed up to the dam. A couple of young men managed to shut off the sluice gate, then everyone stood staring at the water, churning, foaming, glistening and swirling with the energy it had gathered while racing down the mountain. The water had the strange smell of a faraway mountain world of deep chambers from which springs flowed, strange roots and plants unknown in this part of the world.

And when Dumb Eyetie came riding into town late that afternoon, he was welcomed as a hero and a citizen. Everyone had already realised that Big Karel had forgotten the power of the smallest unit of creation: the speck of dust.

That first day the tongue of water had to consume and chase the dust for miles and miles. Everyone remembered the gigantic cloud of dust that had risen into the air the first time the sluice gate was opened. The furrow had first to be broken in. 'It's the same with love,' said those who knew. 'You must plough the earth to reap a bountiful crop.'

22

The old Drostdy had its own rhythms, Ingi soon discovered. Even though soap was no longer cooked up in the old soap vat in the outside kitchen, the smell of lye and fat hung heavy in the air every Friday afternoon, at the time when soap would have been made in the old days in preparation for washday the following Monday.

And at about eleven on Monday mornings, Ingi could hear sounds like the cracking of whiplashes as the laundry flapped on the line. But when she went to investigate, she found little hanging up to dry, only one line with the general's white long johns, the matron's substantial bras, a couple of dishcloths and a few items of clothing she didn't recognise. But she made out the shadows of shirts and trousers flapping against the ground when the wind came up – the clothing of gallant young men and lovely women from another age. When a huge tablecloth from a forgotten banquet spread like the sail of a frigate in an unexpected gust of wind, the two Great Danes slunk off with their tails between their legs.

What is going on here? wondered Ingi Friedländer. Why can't the past leave this house be? On Saturday nights she heard the notes of a mournful accordion under the vine trellis. The instrument must have been left behind by the lover of the young woman without a face, the one who lived in one of the back veranda rooms, behind the door that was never opened.

It was the woman, the poker-faced kitchen helpers told Ingi, with the beautiful plait of hair, the body of a goddess, the voice of a nightingale, but an invisible face.

How did this woman end up here? Ingi wanted to know. Oh, whispered the servants, once they'd glanced over their shoulders to make certain neither the general nor the matron was in earshot, she came on the black ox-wagon, the ox-wagon with the gold, and she was looking for her little boy. That's why she can never rest in peace. Her little boy was lost in the war against the British, and the thing in her that was broken then can never heal.

What happened to the boy?

Oh, he . . . But then they lost the thread of the story. She didn't press them any further because she realised it was about old beliefs and legend, and she thought: I am going to find out. This place is riddled with secrets, but I will not allow myself to be put off.

On Sundays the murmur of old prayers haunted Ingi. They woke her on the first Sunday. She belted her dressing-gown securely and went out, surprised that the general and the matron were religious. But Alexander lay sleeping peacefully outside her room – the Great Dane had fallen in love with Ingi upon her arrival. Peacocks, with sleepy heads still tucked under their wings, roosted on the various angles of the great pergola in the courtyard, their long feathers drooping like wilted flowers.

A good many grapes had fallen in the night and had begun to ferment on the paving. Ingi was annoyed when she trod on some as she tried to slip discreetly over the courtyard, holding up the hem of her dressing-gown. With the smell of old raisins in her nostrils, she hunted for the source of the murmuring.

She found nothing and ended up standing at the door of the woman without a face. The sighs she heard inside made her shudder and she fled past the two-hundred-year-old vine with its base as thick as the trunk of an oak, past the kitchen, where the previous night's embers still smouldered in the old stove, and past the general's bedroom, where she saw him still lying under his mosquito net with half-open eyes. Stella, the other Great Dane, was stretched out on the bed beside the general while morning light streamed in through the window on to the globe of the world.

The murmur was louder in the dining room. Ingi couldn't make out the words but she picked up something like a supplication. She imagined she felt a hand grab at her calf as she walked past the corner of the table; something brushed against her; she smelt ointment and flesh. She rushed into the kitchen where a drowsy servant was trying to coax the coffee pot to boil.

'What's making that noise? What's that I hear?'

The servant looked round at her. 'Wounded people lay in the dining room during the Boer War. It's them you hear moaning. They're in a lot of pain.'

'Oh,' sighed Ingi, and hurried to her room where she sat trembling at the dressing-table. She heard the parrot cage being opened and the flock of parrots, the general's pets, flying into the foliage on the pergola, disturbing the peacocks, who woke with loud screams. The Great Danes made their way towards the kitchen, in search of their morning porridge; the courtyard fountain that had been imported from Italy started spewing water through its lion heads, and the koi fish flitted here and there, knowing it was feeding time.

In his room the general stretched and passed wind before turning on his ham radio, tearing off the night's faxes and calling for coffee. Dumb Eyetie's bedroom door also creaked open, and the old man appeared, aged but still as strong as an ox. He stood immobile in the morning sun, very grey, a man of over eighty, who'd suffered a stroke twenty years earlier that had left him blind. Or had it been a stroke?

No one knew for certain, Ingi discovered, but ever since then Dumb Eyetie had lived in a back room at the old Drostdy, emerging only when Alexander the Great Dane came to fetch him. Then he would rest the fingertips of one hand lightly on the dog's back and Alexander would lead the blind-deaf-mute wherever he thought he should be: to the bathroom, into a patch of sun if it was chilly, into the shade if it was hot, under cover if it began to rain.

Ingi watched the old man as he shuffled along beside the dog, in a world of his own; his eyes empty, his ears empty, his mouth empty of words, the stone clasped in his hand, his head tilted as though other instincts guided him. And then she realised – his senses of smell and taste were virtually all that was left to him, apart from touch. Already, on the day of her arrival, when she stepped into the courtyard with the matron, she'd noticed how he tilted his head slightly, keeping quite still for a moment as he registered the presence of another lodger.

In time she learned to stay downwind if she wanted to observe him as the dog led him slowly round the perimeter of the courtyard. She watched the dog take him to the fountain, where he sat for hours on the edge of the pond with his hand in the water while the fish nibbled at his fingers.

One particularly large fish, gold with a black patch on its back, would often come to rest under the old man's hand. Gently, the fish would move its fins against Mario Salviati's hand, and the old man would stroke the fish in return. Sometimes he took the fish gently in his hand and rocked it to and fro in the water, like a father lulling a child to sleep.

They spoke to one another, Ingi realised, this man and the fish. The big koi was the father of the school in the fountain pond; so she had heard in the kitchen. The three original fish had been presented to the general by King George during his visit many years ago.

Apart from the huge dog, who stood patiently with his head against Dumb Eyetie's shoulder when the old man sat playing with the fish, that ancient koi was the only living creature with whom the old man had any contact, Ingi realised, for she soon noticed that everyone in the house gave him a wide berth.

She wondered how it felt to live in a world without sight or sound, without human contact or the ability to speak. It's a dark cave, she thought, sealed off by a rockfall, and you're in there – in numbing silence, full of memories and forebodings, fearful anxiety and nightmares; a cave with bats whirling through your heart. Old stalactites drip ever longer, fingers grow up from the earth to grip you ever tighter. Nothing new or fresh comes in – you must rely on what is already stored in your heart and imagination, and it all swims round and round in a sealed dam.

For Dumb Eyetie there was only Alexander's rippling back and the cool caress of the fish. Utter silence, thought Ingi, with only scent and touch giving access to the world. The old man's head responded to every breeze, moving almost imperceptibly, but she saw how he reacted when a kitchen window was thrown open, when the general passed wind, when rainclouds banked up against the peaks of Mount Improbable. The night became a fragrance: you smelt the sunrise when the peacocks and parrots shook their wings and you caught a whiff of musty feathers; when the Karoo rain banked up in white cumulus clouds four days away you could already smell it.

So Ingi decided that she'd get up one night, slip over the paving and the old zebra skins that served as rugs in the passages, past the lion and sable antelope heads and African masks on the walls, tiptoe past the sleeping parrots, and under the pergola where the peacocks dozed in the moonlight, past the fresh coolness that lingered round the courtyard fountain, to Dumb Eyetie's room.

She would push open the door and give to the old man what she could not offer Jonty Jack: the warm, fragrant, freshly bathed, silky body of a young woman in her prime.

23

It was a long story, the story of Big Karel Bergh and Lettie Pistorius, daughter of Field Cornet Pistorius, the man who'd brought the ox-wagon laden with gold to Yearsonend. Just one of the many love stories to play out in Yearsonend over the years, and Ingi, with her youthful interest in the things that took place between men and women, couldn't wait to hear it all.

She wanted to know all about Lettie and Big Karel and, yes, also about Karel's parents, Meerlust Bergh and the Indonesian princess. Was she really a princess? And, of course, about Mario Salviati and Edit Bergh, Karel's sister. And who else? Ingi looked about and asked questions; she walked along the dusty roads among the smallholdings, greeting people, introducing herself. And often, without her needing to ask, they started telling her things, as though they needed to unburden themselves to a stranger.

And the stories always came back to water, to gold and to feathers – and to the love affairs that were interwoven with these three things. All these stories were painted on to the great canvas and what Ingi didn't realise was that Captain William Gird regarded her with growing fascination.

He followed her about with his bemused attendant trailing behind, and whenever she kicked off her shoes on the banks of the town dam and rested a while in the shade of a willow, the table had to be set up and the ink bottles laid out.

He loved drawing this young woman: her beautiful strong back, her nose, and the mass of thick hair, the narrow waist and strong calf muscles. And Ingi was drawing too – but only in her imagination. Something here is awakening my need to paint – all these stories, she thought, and she kept on asking questions with the instinct of someone who knew there was a special message for her in the story of Yearsonend. So she began with Lettie Pistorius, the woman who'd arrived on the *Windsor Castle* the day Big Karel Bergh disappeared.

Perhaps it was because Ingi's ancestors had also come out to South Africa on the *Windsor Castle* – Jews who had had to flee from Europe. Or perhaps it was because she recognised something of her own loneliness in the story of the small town in the middle of nowhere. Or possibly it was the angel subtly directing things, keeping an amused eye on it all while he wafted about, high above everything, free of earthly desires and longings.

Lettie Pistorius fell in love with Big Karel; and, such are the ways of love, there was no reversing it. As with many romances, theirs was born in blossom time with sunshine, and it deepened with fiery kisses on moonlit nights, and it rushed on towards tragedy as surely as water flows in a well-built channel.

Their love was to spew them out into a churning dam full of turbulent foam, flotsam and jetsam eddying against the wall; a dam in which uprooted plants and drowned insects swirled and sank, then came up to the surface only to sink again. They had the choice of braving the dam or giving up and allowing the banks to give way while watching where the floodwaters dragged the debris and the dead creatures.

In 1943, Lettie Pistorius sat in her small cabin in the *Windsor Castle* thinking about these things, while the ship's great hulk shuddered as it scraped against the wall of Cape Town harbour, the orchestra up on deck played a jolly march, and balloons and paper streamers were tossed by officers and passengers down to family and friends waiting on the quay.

The baby Jonty Jack lay at her breast sucking fitfully. He'd been born on the equator. God knows, it hadn't been easy: a sweaty birth, bloody, with mosquitoes and the ship's doctor who had to be called from the salon where he was fooling about with girls and sailors. The boat ploughed slowly forward through the black water. With every contraction, Lettie felt as though she, too, were a boat plying through deep waters. The burden in her body was too cumbersome, too much was being asked of her and she was rocking with an ocean waiting to suck her under.

It had all been so well planned – Karel's tender love letters sent from Yearsonend to London, promising her he'd mend his ways in future, her replies saying she'd think it over, and then, shortly after her arrival in London, the news that she was pregnant, and the telegrams that had flown to and fro between her and Karel amid increasingly ominous rumours of war.

The baby was restless: he swung his head back and forth against her nipple; he sucked and spat it out, writhing with colic. This was the story of her voyage: confined to her cabin with a red-faced infant, her breasts swollen and tender, with the perpetual fear of a German submarine possibly lurking like a shark under the belly of the ship, biding its time.

She was completely removed from the frenetic wartime flirtations of the other passengers. Fear and uncertainty were the undercurrents as conventional caution was thrown to the winds: the wild socialising began shortly after they sailed from Southampton, and continued with a feverish intensity that became legendary on the Southampton–Cape Town passenger line.

More babies were conceived and more marriages wrecked on that one voyage than ever before, it was said. Whenever she looked through her porthole, she saw champagne bottles diving off the upper decks to drift on the sea then disappear into the foaming wake. At night she heard giggles and drunken stumbling in the passages, more champagne corks popping, and on one occasion, because of a party raging on the bridge, the ship sailed dangerously close to a friendly naval frigate, missing it by a hair's breadth.

After dark, the ship resembled a nightclub adrift on the high seas, filled with desperate people seeking oblivion in quick sex, alcohol and grand meals served up in the saloon with its sparkling chandeliers and a seven-man band with a black jazz singer from New Orleans. The steward who brought breakfast to Lettie's cabin told her that late one night the singer had stripped down to her navel, singing gospel blues with jiggling breasts.

Lettie hugged her baby close, longing for the open Karoo, the evening breezes fragrant with Karoo scrub and moonlight and dust, the noonday smells of sunbaked rocks, and the murmuring of doves in the orchards of Yearsonend. She travelled in the certain knowledge that something irrevocable was taking place, that this Second Great War was taking the world in its hand and overturning it, just as the general lying in his room in the old Drostdy put a hand on to his globe and spun it as if he were God and the earth his toy.

The war was the general, she dreamt one night, an old man of cruel and mysterious origin, a professional soldier, a power more carnal than the lusts of people confined on this ship, almost hysterical in their fear of a dark German submarine.

Lettie had left Big Karel and headed for London to get away from the suffocating space of Yearsonend. She came from a respected family – one of the most prominent in the area. Her father, the red-bearded field cornet, had led the team of rangers who brought the black ox-wagon as far as Yearsonend, where he had set himself up as an attorney. Her brother, who had followed their father into practice, was recognised as one of the best mayors Yearsonend had ever known – particularly in the difficult years of the depression, when money was scarce and Afrikaners suffered greatly. It was he who had arranged for the Italian prisoners of war to be sent to them.

Coming from such a family, it hadn't been easy to marry a man with an Oriental mother and a father who, according to the gossips, was a half-breed – the more so because Big Karel always strained and fought against the boundaries around him. One great scheme followed another – all attempts to prove himself and win the full acceptance of Yearsonend's white community.

Lettie could no longer bear it. The town had closed around her like a stranglehold. So, using money given to her by her father, she had left for London and what was to be an indefinite stay. But on the eve of her departure, both in tears, she and Big Karel had created a child in their desperate passion – this snotty-nosed, crumple-faced child that she now pressed to her breast as she opened the telegram, unaware of the steward's lustful gaze on the nipple that the baby suckled, spat out, nuzzled and spat out again.

'Can I help you?' asked the steward. 'Telegrams always bring bad news in wartime.' She shook her head and he withdrew. She read the telegram, suddenly dizzy.

This is what I sensed, thought Lettie, the premonition that has haunted me for the whole voyage. She looked at the telegram again. Her brother had sent it two days after the water had refused: 'Water project fails. Karel disappeared. Believed dead. Love from your brother.'

She jumped up, almost dropping the baby, and stumbled out of her cabin, bumping into the Friedländer couple: the pair who had been such a support to her during the voyage, even though it was a difficult time for them too, fleeing from their homeland, seeking a new life at the southern tip of Africa, far away from Hitler's rousing slogans, and from alienation in the English-speaking world.

Their eight-year-old son, Ingemar, ran up to Lettie. He was blond with his father's features and none of the dark beauty of his Jewish mother. The baby fascinated him. His pale, nervous parents were dressed in their best clothes. They each held a balloon and carried a suitcase, and stood staring in surprise at the weeping woman.

The balloons had been thrust into their hands as they left the dining room after their last breakfast on board; they hadn't really been hungry, too anxious about what might await them, their son and their descendants, in this country that seemed to promise so much.

'Bad news,' stammered Lettie and fainted, overcome with weakness from the demands of the voyage, and the noise of the band and the cheering people. Ingemar fielded the baby as though he had been practising the catch for a long time. For decades to come in his new country he would tell the story of how he'd saved that baby from injury, and he often wondered what had become of the redheaded mite and his unhappy mother.

24

Ingi brushed her hair with a hundred strokes just as her mother had taught her. She fastened it up in a ponytail, pulled on a T-shirt advertising Cape Town as a tourist destination, added a pair of Bermuda shorts, red woolly socks and her lace-up boots.

She gulped down her breakfast in the Drostdy kitchen while the servants fussed about her, always wanting to offer her more information. Then she packed sandwiches, the water bottle and a flask of sweet tea in her small backpack and swung it over her shoulders.

With her sunglasses on her nose and her camera slung round her neck, she strode out into the beautiful morning, through the radiant orchards, along the quiet gravel roads of Yearsonend, the little town that was really not much more than a collection of smallholdings with cultivated fields and orchards and houses sometimes as much as four hundred yards from one another. The old Drostdy stood apart, sunk amid trees and history, timelessly, on the outskirts of town, with its back to the open plains to the north. Its gables and towers and the large radio aerial, which rose high above the roof like the feeler of a huge grasshopper, were visible from the other side of town.

She walked out along the Drostdy road and under the huge old pines, which arched towards one another forming a tunnel. When she reached the first fields the workers looked up from their hoeing, curious, and waved to her. She waved back, imagining their tongues wagging: that young girl in the creepy old Drostdy, the place where so many had checked in because it was one of the few places that opened its doors to visitors – who would never be the same again afterwards.

But she'd always been drawn to the unknown and challenges, like trips to Turkey, Morocco and Chile, by danger, the feeling of flirting with risk. And she travelled light, carrying one bag with the bare essentials: two pairs of jeans, a light dress, a T-shirt and two tops, a sweater, a laptop computer and printer, a camera with lenses.

She felt very light this morning. The balmy early-morning air made her skin tingle as she paused at the place called Giraffe Corner. This was where, she'd been told, Jonty Jack's ancestor, the English captain, had shot a giraffe in the old days – the man from whom Jonty had inherited his artistic talent.

She'd seen the photograph of Prince Charles with Captain Gird's painting on the wall behind him – it had been clipped from a glossy magazine and was on display in the small library between the police station and Attorney Pistorius's offices.

Ingi paused a moment on the corner then decided to steer clear of the general store and the café, keeping to the quieter streets. She was aiming for Mount Improbable. She wanted to head up Cave Gorge and track down Jonty Jack. And, after the stories she'd had to listen to in the Drostdy over the weekend, she wanted to see the cave sealed off by a rockfall high in the mountain.

As she walked past the station she remembered the stories of how Dumb Eyetie had arrived there as a young man; of how Mrs Pistorius had fled to the new Ford with her daughters, and of how Lorenzo Devil Slap had become involved with the daughter of Attorney Pistorius.

Outside the town, she had to pass a poplar grove, cross a sandy stream bed, climb through the concertina gate that marked the boundary between the town and Mount Improbable. The route ahead was no more than a two-lane track, already familiar to her: it was here she'd driven in her station wagon the first time she visited Jonty Jack. The hump between the tracks was wild and overgrown. The route veered between trees and grew steeper, passing a quarry, which had provided the stone for the last stretch of the lightning water channel. Then it wound between trees again and Yearsonend sank slowly into the background.

It was steep here, and when she looked up the sky was blue. She came upon a small antelope, which darted away, and the sound of the cicadas was shrill. Then, high above the treetops, against the brown cliffs, she saw a giant kite tugging at its line. It was blood red and fluttered in the crosswinds that gusted round the steepest ravines on Mount Improbable.

She hurried up higher, out of breath now, because she knew Jonty Jack must have something to do with the kite. Then suddenly something leaped up in front of her. Someone running as though startled. Ingi thrust her way through the bushes and saw it was a woman. She caught sight of a handsome thick plait of hair, a slim neck, a model's figure, a young girl's calves with long muscles like a fish. For a moment the head turned and where the face should have been there was nothing – or had she imagined it? Yet she tried to follow, crying, 'Wait! Wait! I won't harm you.'

But the woman had gone and Ingi bent to pick up a black silk scarf. It was feather-light in her fingers; it floated up as though it wanted to become a kite or a butterfly or a spirit. Pressing it to her nose and cheeks, she smelt tears and a longing for death and Ingi knew that she had already discovered too much about Yearsonend for her own peace of mind.

'Jonty Jack!' she shouted, anxiously now, because the wind had risen and was surging through the pines and she was afraid to go on alone. But suddenly the wind dropped and the kite sank down. As she stumbled into the open ground on this side of the first cliffs where Jonty Jack's small house lay, she was just in time to watch him reel in the kite and catch it as it dipped down to the ground.

He turned and she ran up into his arms and wept against his broad sculptor's chest. She wanted to tell him she had seen the woman without a face, the one who was supposed never to leave her room at the Drostdy, but she knew which words her mouth would utter: an admission that she'd seen something of herself; something of her own feeling that there was nowhere she belonged.

Jonty didn't ask her the reason for her distress, but held her close and let her cry herself out. Then he held her at arms' length and said, 'Come, I want to show you something.'

Ingi was surprised at Jonty; he was more lucid than he'd been during their previous meetings; in fact, he seemed almost a different person. His dilapidated camper van was parked behind the house. They climbed in and when he turned the key in the ignition, blue oil smoke belched from the exhaust. She thought back to those stories from the Drostdy kitchen: the huge estate Jonty had inherited when Lettie Pistorius died. It was old money, as they used to say those days – Meerlust Bergh's money, made from selling ostrich feathers in the fashion capitals of Europe. Jonty had invested it in the bank, the servants had told her. He lived up here with his sculptures as though he was dirt poor.

As they pulled haltingly away, she saw that the Staggering Merman was still covered with a tarpaulin. Leather thongs were bound around it and the sculpture stood there, restrained. Bird droppings suggested that an owl perched on top of it at night, waiting for mice to come out from the stacks of wood. Or perhaps a stork sat there during the day waiting for something to stir in the wood shavings.

What Ingi didn't know was that the angel loved to perform a balancing act up there at night. He would alight on the Staggering Merman's head, his widespread wings balancing him precariously, and he'd perch there listening to the jackals howling in the distant gorges of Mount Improbable, looking up at the stars that shone so brightly in the Karoo night and sometimes dozing off and often losing his balance.

The camper van crawled up the slope. The road evened out and Ingi realised that they were moving around the shoulder of the mountain, away from Yearsonend. Then the road got steeper again, becoming almost impassable. They got out to walk.

'Where are we going?' she asked.

'To a place where you can forget Yearsonend,' answered Jonty.

They had to scramble over black volcanic rocks. There was hardly any vegetation here because rockfalls decades or even centuries earlier had scattered a thick layer of stone. Snakes and lizards were the only living things on this dark stone under the harsh blue sky. I may as well be on the moon, thought Ingi; I'm in another reality here with this man with a suntanned chest and a strange glint in his eye.

As they came round a huge outcrop, she cried out in surprise. Below them stretched a small valley dotted with boulders. The sharp dragon's teeth of encircling cliff walls enclosed this plain. In the gaps between the black boulders stood huge sculptures: some made of concrete, others painted bright blue or orange. There were totems hung with spangles, twirling wings and mirrors; there were polished wood-carvings that reflected the sun.

It was a lifetime's work, this sculpture garden. She recognised the significance of what Jonty Jack was showing her – something no one in the arts community outside Yearsonend knew about.

For the second time that day she felt like bursting into tears, but Jonty unfurled the huge red kite he'd brought along and showed her a track he'd levelled through the boulders. It stretched a couple of hundred paces, and he and Ingi Friedländer ran along it, squealing and laughing among the sculptures as the red kite rose triumphantly up against the stark cliffs to hang emblazoned against the sky.

25

It seemed to Lettie Pistorius that the last few years had been one long, unplanned journey. Against the advice of her husband, Big Karel Bergh, and her brother, Attorney Pistorius, she withdrew her nest-egg. Then she announced she'd be leaving Yearsonend to live in London for a while.

This came as no surprise to Big Karel. He'd married a woman

who was always on the point of fleeing from some deficiency in her life and he'd anticipated it for years – that she'd go on a long journey, that she'd 'leave', as she'd so often threatened to do. But he knew that in this world you could never escape from yourself. You could travel to distant continents, find adventures in unknown places, begin a new life in a foreign country, but you could never get away from yourself. Thus, early in his life, he'd decided to carry out every task that came his way, with haste and energy.

Lettie Pistorius, on the other hand, was married to a man who was admired for his energy and enterprise yet was the butt of gossip, to be given a wide berth because he was a so-called half-breed.

What she admitted to herself with more difficulty was that she was fleeing from herself, trying to escape from the superficial space in which she lived: an emptiness that could not be filled. She was dissatisfied, frustrated and could find nothing to turn her hand to that would fulfil or excite her – the opposite to Big Karel. Where this sense of anxiety and uselessness came from, Lettie had no idea.

Ultimately she felt as though her entire life was just a kind of departure, a journey without a discernible goal, an existence full of farewells but no arrivals, with thoughts packed away in suitcases and trunks, because her strict upbringing had smothered her, forbidding her to free her thoughts and feelings and dreams.

How could she explain to Big Karel that she never felt at home, to this man who always found his home in the future, in some exciting undertaking that smoothed a path before his hasty feet, a foothold in the storms against which he pitted his strength?

She left for London intending never to return to Yearsonend. Big Karel stood on the platform as the train left for Cape Town and the harbour. She had never seen him look so tired and downcast. He stood there with his hand raised as she leaned out of the window, and then he was gone, and she wiped the mixture of tears and soot from her cheeks.

She knew he couldn't understand why she chose to raise problems at precisely those times when his projects hovered at the delicate point between success and failure. The lightning water project had reached a critical stage. He'd brought it this far in spite of the cynicism and scorn of others; he'd toiled through many a night and he was almost there now – or completely off the mark.

And she chose a delicate time like this to announce that she didn't see any point in any of it; that there were no prospects for her here; that she should go and find herself. In London.

She'd hardly reached London, after the long sea voyage, when her suspicions were confirmed: she had fallen pregnant, on that night of desperately urgent leave-taking. The long letters from Yearsonend started to arrive, creased from being bundled in postbags from continent to continent. From where she sat in her London flat, even the postage stamps looked exotic and homesickness suffused her.

In the letters Karel proclaimed his love for her. She sniffed at the pages – perhaps there was a whiff of his clothes, or of the evening breezes that came down from Mount Improbable, or of dust and stone and Karoo herbs. She kissed his handwriting and his tentative words. He had no idea of what she was struggling with. He wanted to perform and accomplish; she was swimming slowly and painfully against the current, which threatened to drag her down into a deep black dam where she knew she'd ultimately sink.

I had no choice, she wrote back. Of course I love you as you love me. But, alas, at our age we have to discover that love is not enough; it is only the beginning. I have to work through this, Karel, and you must reconcile yourself to that. What are you running away from? she added, much to her later regret. But by then the letter had already been posted.

He answered placatingly. 'Come back,' he begged. She vacillated for months. The child grew in her womb. Finally she packed her bags and sent another telegram to Big Karel: I'll try again. But you must make an effort too.

On the ship from Southampton with German submarines lurking, invisible in the dark water, she thought long and deeply. Why did she love this man, this rash man from a controversial family – after her upbringing in the conservative home of Gwen Viljee and Attorney Pistorius?

From the beginning, Lettie Pistorius realised, my love for him was a rebellion against my parents. And a rebellion against myself, for do we not often fall in love with someone who personifies that which we are not. It is precisely the one who heals the absences in ourselves that we seek out as a life partner.

To make matters worse, the Berghs and the Pistoriuses had never got on – not since the black ox-wagon arrived in Yearsonend. Over time, the relationship had ranged from open hostility to cautious reconciliation. It wasn't easy for the two families to try to develop a relationship within the Yearsonend circle of gossip because the Yearsonenders never missed an opportunity to point out that the great secret of the gold lay in the respective hands of the two families, like the two half-shells of an oyster, the one half here and the other half there.

For was it not Lettie's father, Field Cornet Redbeard Pistorius, later the first Attorney Pistorius, who'd gone out into the darkness that night to bury the gold with Meerlust Bergh, Big Karel's father?

To fall in love in such a climate was madness, Lettie decided on the ship. But since childhood she'd been drawn to the boy who had galloped through the streets of Yearsonend on a thoroughbred in the wake of his flamboyant father.

After the drab offices of her father's practice, the Berghs' Feather Palace was a great novelty with its fashion studio and displays of hats, its visiting dressmakers, models and fashion leaders from the world's greatest cities.

She would never forget the day her friendship with Big Karel Bergh blossomed into love. Irene Lampak always remained aloof and busied herself with her work up at the Feather Palace. Nevertheless, she once agreed to give the young ladies of the town a few lessons in dressmaking and the art of choosing outfits and dressing with style. Lettie couldn't imagine who had persuaded Irene to do this.

It was a daring undertaking and there was much debate in prosperous homes as to whether it was advisable or not. Doing business with Meerlust Bergh was all very well, but he was still a half-breed. And his wife, beautiful though she might be, is not one of us, it was said. On top of that, all sorts of strange foreigners visited the Feather Palace – people who did and saw things differently from the Yearsonenders.

But it did seem a pity, when the town boasted such a talented woman, that the young should not benefit from her skills.

The course was advertised at school and church meetings, the general store and the convent. But the day it was launched, Lettie Pistorius was the only young woman who walked up the long avenue to the Feather Palace. Karel Bergh, a well-built young man, was grooming his chestnut stallion on the lawn in front of the big, gabled house. It wasn't until years later that she realised he had been lying in wait for the town girls, that he'd installed himself there in his gaiters and riding breeches, brushing his horse over and over again – all in anticipation of the girls' arrival.

When she walked up alone, he regarded her with compassion, which she came to know later as a form of defence, then he hobbled the horse and led her up the steps to the front door. Irene Lampak took her completely by surprise. Lettie had only seen the fashion designer ride through the streets of Yearsonend a couple of times, and now here she was, standing in front of the woman for the first time. Lettie was overwhelmed by her exotic beauty as she took the cool hand in her hot and sweaty clasp.

She was led into the Feather Palace, and was amazed by the furniture from faraway lands, the huge library, and the studio with its high windows, drawing tables and plaster models. While Irene Lampak was still showing her around and explaining how it all worked in a sort of sing-song voice with a strange accent, Lettie glanced across the room.

The boy stood in the doorway watching her: the boy who was to become the husband she'd fight with for nights on end in a relationship whose intensity would always startle her, the husband from whom she could never tear herself away.

Sometimes in life there comes a decisive moment; a moment that, with hindsight, you would have preferred to live without. It was just such a moment when Lettie's and Karel's eyes met. They would always be bound together in this moment; committed to one another in dependence and doubt.

And that was how their relationship began. In the weeks that followed, Lettie came to the Feather Palace at four every Monday afternoon. She was trained patiently by Irene Lampak and learned to respect colour, texture and the beauty of line and form. She discovered the anxiety of a blank sheet of paper – the moments before your pencil began to move, the moment when possibilities spun away and you had to catch one as though it were a butterfly, and hold it, because it was the one meant for you.

Lettie thought about all these things on the ship and after she'd received the telegram about Big Karel in Table Bay harbour. She climbed wearily on to the train at the Cape Town station. At first she and little Jonty had the good fortune to have a compartment to themselves and, with the child's wet mouth at her breast, she watched the landscape shifting past.

She felt exposed and defenceless; she had no idea of what awaited her. Once the train had gone through the mountain pass, and slid snakelike along the bottom of the Hex River Valley, they left the vineyards behind and the landscape lay open and empty.

What if Karel is dead? wondered Lettie. All those years of conflict and neglect, rage and passion – how will I ever forgive myself for my part in it? So he has finally come up against something too big for him: the most ambitious of all his projects took on such mythical dimensions that it was beyond human power. He has tackled something greater than his own energy and determination.

And where would she take refuge now? She who had always held him back because of her background, her inability to find meaning herself, her feeling of unease in the world.

In a strange way she felt that the baby at her breast was not hers.

He belongs to Yearsonend, she thought; she'd carried him in her womb quite by coincidence. She struggled to connect with him as she did with everything and everyone around her. She comforted and caressed him, she gave him what he needed and more, but deep down inside her she was afraid he'd turn his back on her and go off into the world, leaving her behind.

Jonty, she named him, Jonty Jack Bergh, and when people asked her later, 'Where on earth did you get that name?' she'd answer that she'd looked for one that had nothing, absolutely nothing to do with Yearsonend and its people. A name that had no connection to her people, either.

When she'd arrived in London a poster for a singer and cabaret artist had caught her eye: 'Jonty Jack performs', it announced. When it was confirmed that she was pregnant, the phrase came to mind again: 'Jonty Jack performs'. Lettie decided obstinately that that would be the child's name – a rebellion against her mother Gwen Viljee's obsession with her Huguenot blood; against the Pistoriuses, with their men who could only be attorneys and nothing else, each one too nervous to break away; and, naturally, a refusal to let the Berghs get a hold on the child by giving him a name from their side.

'You were born at sea,' she whispered to Jonty Jack's wizened little face, red and screwed up with the pain of colic, 'in the middle of nowhere. You don't owe anyone anything. Keep yourself free, keep yourself detached, look down on Yearsonend from afar.'

She would never know how closely Jonty Jack followed her admonition. How he withdrew into his house in Cave Gorge, and lived as though the Bergh fortune had nothing to do with him. How he tried, not always successfully, to become a sculptor who honoured the more enduring things.

26

As he sat beside the fishpond, caressing the fish and scenting Ingi Friedländer's approach, Mario Salviati the *scalpellino* strolled through the streets of Florence, his home town, as he'd often done as he sat with Edit Bergh beside the excavations for the lightning water channel, with the picnic she'd brought spread out before them.

The remains of a great boulder lay steaming beside him and Edit, just broken into fragments. He would get the labourers to build a fire under the largest boulders lying in the path of the channel. Once a boulder had been heated all day, a chain of singing Xhosas would pass brimming buckets from hand to hand and douse it with cold water. The rock would crack, making it easier for picks and crowbars to break it into pieces small enough to be carted away.

It was beside such a rock that Mario and Edit sat as the aromas of steam and of the stone's core, previously untouched by air, wafted around them. They broke the bread Edit had baked and sipped coffee and lemon syrup, while Mario strolled through the narrow *vicoli* of his home town inhaling the fragrance of fresh-baked Tuscan semolina bread. His mind was on chopped chicken livers with raw onion marinated in wine, as he reached out for a peach from Big Karel Bergh's orchard.

He ambled onwards now, as he sat beside the Drostdy fountain: across the Ponte Vecchio, towards the Duomo that reared up out of the city like a great curved boulder. He strolled past pavement stalls and people sitting outside trattorias, past the gypsies who patrolled street corners looking for mischief, and children laughing as they played on the paving. Eventually he reached the Piazza San Marco and made his way to a regular rendezvous with a certain painting.

It was an image he visited every Sunday afternoon, before the week's work began in the quarry Le Cave di Maiano, where

Salviatis had plied their trade as stonecutters for centuries. In the old days, building stones were carried to the city along the steep and difficult route through Fiesole then past the monastery of San Domenico and after that slowly, cautiously, because many a *scalpellino* had lost a foot on this route when a stone was shaken loose from the wagon, onwards, past the cypresses, dark green-blue in the shadows of the great stone buildings. And from there on into what was now the inner city, where the stone would be worked into the *facciate*, the façades, of building after astounding building . . .

Every Sunday, Mario followed this route to visit the painting of the monk Fra Angelico, which he had begun to think of as his own. The work was called *The Naming of John the Baptist*. A father who could not speak naming his son. Mario stood before the painting thinking about dumbness and the naming of things; the question of whether he'd ever have a son of his own; and naturally, Sunday after Sunday, the realisation that he would never be able to pass on to his son the stonecutters' stories that his father and grandfather had so wanted to tell him, but weren't able to. I am like an absence between the generations, Mario often thought; the gap where a note has fallen out of a composition; a silence.

Then he saw seven of the Xhosa workers, armed with sticks, chasing a lizard. They laughed as they scrambled over the picks and spades that lay scattered there. They kicked up dust as they tried to kill the small reptile, and Mario reached deep into the pond, frightening the koi who darted away, to return cautiously to his hand a little later. Edit leaned closer to him, talking to him with her eyes as she'd learned to do, and he picked up the fragrance of the young woman, the new lodger who hung about him day after day.

Years have passed, he warned himself, and your hands itch to cut and dress stone. You sit here without any idea of day or night; you smell your memories, and times and imaginings wash through your head, and you are no longer certain whether it's the smell of Edit or of this woman who, these days, circles you and the parrot cage endlessly.

He no longer knew whether he was helping his father restore the façade of the Palazzo Vecchio before the Great War, where they worked close to the beautiful courtyard with its fountain, and where, from the top of his scaffolding, he could eye the tourists who posed with Panama hats and sunshades for street artists.

Or was he lying on his stomach beside Big Karel out on the endless plains with his cheek where the water level should be, taking a sightline through thorn trees and anthills at the dark back of Mount Improbable, blue in the distance, but a shadow that guarded your dreams like a dragon?

Was that smell the fountain water of Florence or Yearsonend, or was it the first bucket he and Edit had poured one weekend afternoon into the duct that scaled the mountain? An impulsive experiment, very much against Big Karel's instructions, just to see water running there, even if it was only a bucketful, and watch startled grasshoppers and ants fleeing from the stream's shining tongue.

He had to remind himself frequently that years were separate from other years, that times do not flow in one stream of insepa-rable droplets, that memories and the here and now were not one single present.

He had to fight off the madness of utter silence and darkness; he broke out in a nervous sweat whenever he caught a cold and his nose was blocked or when the wind blew so strongly that no recognisable smells wafted round him. Then he would shuffle off to his small room and pick up his few trusted possessions, sniffing at them eagerly: his chisels arranged on his chest of drawers; his clothes; the books he could never read, but which contained the works of Cicero and Dante; his trowel and binoculars; the spirit-level.

He sat in the shade of a thorn tree in front of his tent, beside the excavations. It was Sunday afternoon and Big Karel was dressed in his formal suit, at home with Lettie. Every Friday afternoon, Big Karel would roll up his bedding, mount his horse, wave goodbye to Mario, and only come riding back over the plains at daybreak on Monday. The labourers went off to live it up in Edenville over the weekend, so Mario was left behind alone at the excavations to keep an eye on the sticks of dynamite, the picks and spades, the theodolite and other equipment.

He sat beside the tent and he felt the fish's cool fins on his hand, and the general's smell came past briefly, in a hurry, making Mario stiffen and remember where he was. Then he was back with Michelozzo's relief, *Madonna and Child,* and Mario's fingers were sliding over Edit's face, soft stone carved by Michelozzo, worked lovingly, bit by bit with the tender chisel-edge, cheek, nose, forehead, eye and eyebrow.

Mario sat lost in memories – his mind a lake without a bank, flowing out into the past – with over his head the motto he held fast to in the days when the wind tore at the vine leaves in the pergola.

Above the hearth in their house in Borgo di San Frediano was an inscription chiselled by his grandfather. The grandfather who, shortly before Mario had had to go off to war, had died of the disease that had killed generations of Florentine stonecutters. Silicosis, the lung sickness, caused by a lifetime of working with stone, stone gravel, stone dust.

The motto he had carved hung over the shimmering Plains of Melancholy as the channel crept slowly onwards, while boulders smouldered and dynamite clouds mushroomed into the air, while Mario grew harder and more muscular in the endless days of soul-destroying chopping and dressing stone.

The motto danced in his dreams when he lay on his bed in the back room, thinking about what had been given and what taken away; what was granted and what was withheld.

Omnia in mensura et numero et pondere disposuisti. That was the family motto: By measure, number, and weight you have ranged all things.

Even for me, thought Mario Salviati, the stonecutter.

27

Let me be the one who keeps an eye on the womenfolk, thought Granny Siela Pedi, since it's me, Captain Gird, his guide Slingshot X!am who are the most restless souls around here. They can watch over the men. Just as I never sat comfortably on that ox during the gold-wagon's journey, so now I find no peace in the Hereafter either. And just as I had to turn away my eyes from the man I loved throughout my life, so I must also look the other way now.

And so she kept a tender eye on Lettie Pistorius, the child who in another country at a different time would have been hers. It might have been her, Siela Pedi, who had carried Redbeard Pistorius' children. If things had only been different.

In fact, her heart should go out to Karel Bergh as well: it was always uphill for him in Yearsonend, a life always on the margins, because of his skin. But it was for Lettie, the daughter of Redbeard Pistorius, that she had a soft spot because she, Siela Pedi, knew every freckle on the attorney's white body.

Yes, she knew where Lettie came from; she knew how Redbeard, the bloody-minded field cornet from the north, could tighten his mouth, and how his blue eyes could get even bluer. Nothing was ever good enough for him; you had to try harder, aim higher. From Edenville, Granny Siela had watched how Field Cornet Pistorius had slowly changed from soldier to eminent attorney.

It was common knowledge that the field cornet had once been a respected man of law in the Transvaal, and the Yearsonenders were only too pleased when he decided to stay on in their town after the war ended in 1902.

'For the sake of law and order,' he said, in announcing his decision, 'to balance the scales of justice even hereabouts.'

With the emphasis on 'hereabouts', the field cornet stated his relationship with the Yearsonenders. They were never allowed to forget that he came from elsewhere, from a place where things were done better. And they were expected to be eternally grateful that he'd been prepared to give up a better life in the great city in the north to serve them here, on the edge of the Murderers' Karoo.

Redbeard, as he'd been known during the war, used the same method to control his men during the long journey that was to bring Granny Siela Pedi to Yearsonend. Granny Siela remembered it only too well: that 'I'm doing you a favour' attitude of his. With 'you owe me one' following close on its heels; the stern, tight mouth, the flashing blue eyes, the freckles like rusty nails' heads.

How could Lettie help being affected by a father like that – obsessed with quality and striving and order, so punctilious and correct – any more than she could help falling hopelessly in love with Karel Bergh when she breathed in the aura of the Feather Palace, that exotic world of hats and plumes and travels abroad?

Only to learn later – this was how Granny Siela Pedi came to see things – that as you grow older, you become more like yourself. A self with a good dose of what your parents were – especially in those things you once rebelled against. But by then the Berghs' grand gestures had become too much for Lettie. Under the pressure of adult life, she'd begun to long, without realising it, for the order and rules she'd grown up with. She might have started to recognise, thought Granny Siela, why people like Redbeard needed such unbending rules; the fixed framework of what was permissible. The great unknown, to which you must never abandon yourself, must be left lying out there, waiting.

Scarcely nine months after Lettie had run off to London just as Big Karel's water project reached the critical stage, she returned to a phrase she could never have predicted she would hear used around her so often: 'disappeared into thin air'. On her first day back, Lettie was sitting on the steps of the house she'd shared with Karel and at first she didn't see the old woman coming down the street. When Granny Siela saw Lettie sitting there, she'd hesitated a moment, then came on through the gate.

Granny Siela sighed. Perhaps I shouldn't have done it, but that was my first and last chance to talk to the child of Redbeard's loins. I watched her growing up during the years I had to live in

Edenville; when I walked past on the way to the shop, I saw her playing in the schoolyard; and later, when Karel was courting her, I saw her walk with him over the ridge behind Edenville towards the mountain; I've watched her her whole life without her ever speaking a single word to me.

And now, on this day when the whole town is in uproar about the flashwater that came through on the third day, with all the excitement and hullabaloo down there, so that no one is in the mood to start searching afresh for Big Karel and his carriage, here she sits on the step, with her father's glint in her eye, at a distance, just as he looked on that long journey from Pedi to here. That look, just as though the eyes have swallowed the sky, that slightly stubborn bitterness, the handsome lines of the face framing disillusionment.

Granny Siela didn't know whether Lettie knew about her. Pistorius had thought her, Siela, away, out of his life, once they reached Yearsonend at the end of that long journey with the ox-wagon and the gold. And it was certain he'd never say a word to his family about the woman down there in Edenville; the one he and his men had brought with them from Pedi. But perhaps Lettie had heard about her from some other source.

Granny Siela pushed open the gate and walked slowly up to the woman who sat on the veranda step cradling her baby in her arms. In the town below she could hear the sounds of excited Yearsonenders busy with all sorts of plans and arrangements.

She was about ten paces away when Lettie first became aware of her. Lettie looked up with eyes reddened by tears, those eyes Granny Siela knew so well, and said, 'No, sorry, I don't have work for you. If you want work, go and ask down in town.'

Then Lettie put her head in her arms, but in the few moments of eye contact, Granny Siela Pedi saw a desolation she recognised as her own. But with Lettie it was different: she had been born with it. Granny Siela knew it was true that some people were born that way, even before life got a chance to give them things and then take them away again; even before that happened, yes, already there was a sense of loss.

The loss of things that had no name.

28

As he raced away from Washout in his carriage, leaving behind him the chaos of hastily shifted cars and picnic baskets, under his formal suit Big Karel Bergh's skin was turning the colour of his mother's.

He watched his hands turn brown as they held the reins. By the time he'd passed the first rise and seen one of the heliograph operators on his way down, he was dark all over.

He swung the carriage aside in an attempt to avoid the man, looking away as he thundered past, so that the fellow would later report: 'A coloured man was driving Big Karel's carriage. Dressed in Big Karel's church clothes, even the hat, and I'm sure I saw Meerlust Bergh's gold watch on his wrist.'

And thus the first red herring was drawn over the trail. Shortly afterwards, it started to rain and people said, 'There you are: God's sending water in His own way.' Yearsonend's four constables, reinforced by a search party, set out in the pouring rain to find Big Karel or apprehend the rogue who'd stolen his carriage.

They called first at Edenville, that row of train houses, so-called because the dwellings were packed so close to one another they looked like the carriages of a train.

Here, the four constables and their posse of farmers kicked open doors and dragged out suspects. Crime had shot up since construction of the lightning water channel had begun. Often Big Karel got the blame – after all, he was the one who'd brought in all these strangers to help dig and build.

The people of Edenville denied that any of them had been involved in Big Karel's disappearance or the theft of his carriage, but now that the prayer-hour had passed and frustration over the stubborn water was mounting, the townsfolk had to take out their feelings on someone. Things got ugly. Late that afternoon, in pouring rain, they dragged a half-drunk Fielies Jollies, christened Fielies Moloi, out of his house. Afterwards it was said it only happened because he was cocky with the constables. He was strapped to a pepper tree right near the gate to Cave Gorge and dealt seventy lashes with a hippo-hide sjambok.

No one would later acknowledge who had beaten him, but in fact everyone had a hand in it, because above the pouring rain Fielies Jollies' screams had rung out over the whole town and people had just drawn their curtains. No one lifted a hand to stop the beating.

Fielies passed away late that afternoon. Blood Tree – that's what they named the corner where Ingi had felt a slight chill on her back just as she took the road up Cave Gorge that first time. Blood Tree, where the relationship between white and brown reached an all-time low in the days after Big Karel Thin Air's disappearance.

That became evident when Lettie Pistorius came back to town a few days later with her sickly baby and heard to her horror that Fielies Jollies, who'd often helped out in her garden, had been beaten to death by the police and a posse of young farmers.

And it was the brown community, the people of the Mission church, who organised a welcome tea in the old church hall and sang to her and the baby, who screamed as though hellfire threatened him. And they offered to christen him.

But Big Karel Bergh knew nothing of all this. As he fled from Washout and realised he was taking on the colour of Irene Lampak, he stopped beside the lightning water channel and bent over a puddle. He gazed at his reflection for a long moment as the first drops of rain spattered into the puddle, breaking up his face. He was the spitting image of his mother.

The new colour actually suited him better, but he didn't notice that. It was as though the darker skin gave his features new dimensions. They seemed even stronger and more refined. But knowing the world he lived in, Big Karel's heart was filled with panic. He washed and washed his face with the muddy water, trying to scrub his skin with wet sand, bent, sobbing, over the puddle.

It was then that Big Karel looked up and saw the gash in the earth torn open by the lightning water channel as it rushed backwards down from the heights of Mount Improbable and on to the Plains of Melancholy. He knew the spot. As a child he'd often watched the family of lynxes who lived here in a crack in the rocks. The wild red cats had lived there for generations; only moving on when building began on the channel.

Big Karel saw something white protruding from the gully. He drew closer, looked and reeled back. He had to look again, in fear and trembling, for the dead lay there, hidden from sight for many years. The skeletons lay sprawled over one another with black cloths tied round their skulls – evidently to cover the eyes, which had long since rotted away.

Big Karel had to wipe the water from his face for it was raining harder now. He looked once more at the gruesome scene, then swung round because suddenly Mario Salviati was there on horseback and Lorenzo Devil Slap, and it was Lorenzo who clambered down into the gully, slipping and sliding in the mud, and tried to open one of the bone hands to get at the gold coin it clutched. Why were they blindfolded, wondered Big Karel, these forgotten dead people who'd been washed out by the stubborn water?

Big Karel realised Mario Salviati was gaping in astonishment at the brown man who looked just like his employer. He scrambled back into the carriage and took off at a cracking pace. It was only when he'd put some distance between them that he decided how he'd get up the mountain. Big Karel picked his way up in that carriage at an angle from the back, on the Plains of Melancholy side, so that no one would see him from Yearsonend. Bouncing and unwieldy, the big carriage was hauled up Mount Improbable as though it were a mountain tortoise with a big clumsy shell.

Fed up with the drizzle, the angel sat on the carriage roof, behind Big Karel, who sat on the driver's bench holding the reins. The angel sat and swayed as they struggled over rocks and bushes, and he listened to Big Karel cursing and cajoling the horses. His huge wings drooped from the carriage roof, dripping.

While the carriage climbed up the mountain, tongues were

already wagging in Yearsonend about Big Karel's failure. He'd rushed off like that because his unshakeable belief in the predictability of water had been toppled when the flashwater refused to do what his formulae had predicted it would do, said the gossips. For Big Karel, it was whispered, this was the end of his predictable world.

And there on his carriage he realised it too: he would exist from now on in a realm of uncertainty and unpredictability. Once the predictable becomes unpredictable, all certainty is gone. And, moreover, what he had seen in the gully was a sign of the apocalypse, thought Big Karel.

The horses found the route to the cave of their own accord. He drove them in. They were show-horses, perfectly trained, and even though they were afraid of the dark cave and in spite of the stench of old fires, the lairs of predators and earth that had never known the sun, they ducked their ostrich-plumed heads and stepped bravely into the gloom.

Big Karel steered his horses around between the stalactites, some of which had been blackened by the cooking fires of the San, who had lived here centuries ago. Herdsmen, youths playing truant, escaped slaves and deserters had also all lit fugitive fires in here down the ages.

The carriage now stood so that the horses looked outwards, to the mouth of the cave, which usually glowed like an oven as the flaming sun streamed in, but today was shadowed by rain and clouds. Big Karel sat with the reins slack in his hands. The rain is starting to wash away my tracks, he thought; before long no one will know where I am.

Still gleaming, but with the sweat turning to saltpetre on their coats, the horses stood in harness. Now and then a bridle clinked as one moved its head in the otherwise silent cave. As the rain seeped through, the stalactites began to drip around Big Karel. The droplets sounded like a muted orchestra, and Big Karel imagined he could hear the primitive guitars of old hunters, San voices and the plucking of strings. He saw shadows against the walls, slow-shuffling feet starting to dance a sad reel. They're my ancestors – the ones I denied – come to seek me out, he thought. Sara Bruin and Titty X!am's people.

29

It was then that the angel appeared to Matron Taljaard and told her, 'The gold lies hidden in Gold Pit.' Matron Taljaard, who suffered from the falling sickness, could never distinguish between an attack and a visitation from the angel. She would just get the taste of cinnamon in her mouth, something would begin to flutter in her like a butterfly against a windowpane, and then her consciousness would slip away; or the angel would appear before her, with his muscular, feathered body, his four wings – two large and two small – and beautiful legs.

He held a short sword . . . no, she was imagining things: it was a bushy horsetail, with a gnarled stinkwood handle, or an oxtail perhaps. A symbol of power? Like those carried by tribal chieftains? 'An African angel,' murmured Matron Taljaard. And his name was . . . but it eluded her again, even though he'd whispered it to her in a strange creaky voice, which reminded her of a blue crane's call.

But she knew that the taste of cinnamon often heralded the appearance of the beautiful, glistening man: he of the lovely skin, which lay in silvery shades all over his body. The shoulder muscles extended into the powerful cartilage of the wings with their branching blue veins and thickly packed feathers – ranging from fine down, against which she wanted to press her cheek, to great quill feathers like those on an eagle's wing.

Whenever he stood before her like that, she smelt his sweat, the musty aroma of feathers, the smell of man and god and beast all at once, and when he left, with a mighty flexing and gasping as he gathered his energies for flight, Matron Taljaard had to go and lie down as pleasure contracted in ripples through her loins – she couldn't help herself. Was he from the kingdom of the dead, from the heavenly choirs, or had God Himself sent the young man? Why did he single her out?

She rushed into the dining room where Ingi and the general already sat at the breakfast table. Grapefruit lay sliced open before them, hard-boiled eggs ready in silver eggcups, and the porridge pot steamed away under its lid. A peacock, his plumage in full display, stood in the doorway that led into the courtyard. The matron stared at the general who sat holding his compass with a map rolled open before him, and at Ingi who was staring at the general over her grapefruit, thunderstruck.

'Kruger millions? Here?' asked Ingi – just as the matron rushed in and the peacock looked her impertinently in the eye and fanned out his splendid tail feathers. Why do these animals have such an eye for me? wondered the matron, as she blurted out: 'Gold Pit, General.'

She still called the old man 'General' like everyone else did; even though they were married, he was still 'General' to her. Perhaps it was the difference in their ages; perhaps because he'd never been anything else but a general – even when he sat on the lavatory, or brushed his teeth, he did so as a general. Could he ever be anything else? Had he ever been anything else? Had he ever even been young?

'There you have it!' cried the general triumphantly, stabbing his knife-point into the map. 'Gold Pit!' He looked at Matron Taljaard. She trembled, her hair stood on end and one shoulder twitched.

'The angel?' he asked.

She nodded. 'The angel.'

Then she fainted and the general rang for the servants, thrust his spoon into the sour flesh of the grapefruit and, with one stern glance, sent the peacock scurrying out. When Ingi tried to get up, he stopped her: 'The servants will attend to her, Miss Friedländer. The most important thing is that you enjoy your breakfast.'

Ingi tried to appear nonchalant while three servants carried out the matron. She ate her grapefruit carefully, then asked, 'And where is Gold Pit?'

'We don't know,' answered the general. 'It is still no more than a name, a legend. But if the angels start to enlighten us, we must take heed. It might not even be on this earth.'

Ingi looked at him nonplussed. 'But then where are you going to look? How will you find it?'

He pushed away his grapefruit and drew the eggcup closer. His big fingers broke the shell deftly and peeled away a piece so that he could poke the thin silver teaspoon into the quivering white of the egg.

'My searches,' he said, 'have taught me patience. Gold does not lie silent in the earth. It calls out. And if you search long enough and you get close to it, you can hear the call.'

'A . . . sound . . . ?'

'No, you feel it in your body. If you are an experienced hunter, you know when the antelope is on the other side of the rise, or when the lion crouches behind the bush. When two commanders have met in battle a number of times, they come to know in advance what the movements of the other's army will be; where his divisions lurk; what he seeks to conceal. It's the same with gold. It stirs in your blood, even though it might lie buried deep beneath stone and sand.

'It's only when gold is buried in a lead chest that you can't hear it. Lead is thick; lead is dead. But if the gold coins lie under seawater, or buried in the sand, or waiting in the belly of a sunken galleon, they cry out to you. They call for attention. Because gold is nothing when it's hidden, and gold knows that. Gold is meaningless when it lies in seams in the belly of the earth. Gold only gains value when a human hand takes hold of it or when greedy eyes fall upon it. Gold needs to be desired.

'There is a special understanding between humankind and gold. Just think of a fine gold chain round the neck of a beautiful woman, a gold bracelet on a woman's wrist. Gold was meant for people, just as water was meant for fish.'

Ingi wanted to ask more but a servant entered and, without saying a word, laid a large feather on the white tablecloth in front of the general. The general nodded and the servant left the room.

Ingi studied the feather. She picked up a strange smell: cinnamon, she thought, and something singed.

The general looked at her and nodded. 'The angels are guiding us.' Then he pushed back his plate, wiped his mouth with the large white table napkin and asked to be excused.

Ingi heard the heavy footsteps making their way to his room. She heard the hiss of the radio and the buzz of the fax machine. She was so bemused by it all, she had to pull herself together forcibly: You must remember, Ingi Friedländer, why you're here; you must remember who you are and where you come from. You're here on a mission and that mission is to get the sculpture that sprang up from the ground away from here and into the lobby at the Houses of Parliament. You're not here to immerse yourself in the heartbreaks of the past, in the lust for gold, or in chasing kites through lunar landscapes.

She pushed back her chair decisively and stood up. She took her plate and cup to the kitchen. There she found the two Great Danes pressed up nervously against one another in front of the wood stove. The parrots had fled from the pergola to their cage, she noticed through the open kitchen windows.

'And now?' asked Ingi, as she put down her cup and plate.

'The angel's been here again and the peacock fanned his tail feathers at the matron.'

She looked in surprise at the frightened women and at the dogs who watched her with anxious guilty eyes, and she could smell cinnamon and scorched feathers hovering over the normal kitchen smells.

'And what does that mean?' she asked Princess Moloi, the daughter of Goodwill and Mama, who'd taken a job here after making it plain that she had no time for her father's plans for her in the big city.

'You'll see for yourself,' said Princess, and fled to the pantry. Ingi went out into the courtyard and saw the peacocks sitting far off on the highest vine trellis. And Dumb Eyetie, on the edge of the Roman fountain, with the water spurting over his shoulder from the statue's mouths. He sat with one hand in the water, but when Ingi came out, his head jerked round.

He wore a hat against the sun. It was a shabby old hat – one he'd probably worn to build the lightning water channel, she thought. He didn't wear a watch, just a fine gold bracelet with an array of delicate figures worked on it. His forearms were brown, burned almost black, as were his neck and throat. He held his smooth stone as though it were his only grip on the world, apart from the fish stroking his other hand with its fins.

Ingi knew that the old man was aware of her. She approached slowly, until she stood five paces from him. He tilted his head slightly. His eyelids fluttered as he concentrated. She caught herself moving quietly, on tiptoe and holding her breath. But he's deaf! she reminded herself.

But here in his presence she found that his silence sharpened her ears, and that his blindness focused her vision; here in the proximity of this poor man, surrounded by so many legends, the progenitor of all that was damp and fertile in the fields and gardens of Yearsonend.

She looked up to the sun glowing through the fresh green vine leaves on the pergola; she saw the way the water struck the surface, shining and joyful, how the colours merged and flashed on the parrots' wings. She heard the breath sigh from the Great Danes' throats, the splash of water on water, the kitchen clatter, a dove calling in the trees.

Then she walked round the fountain. The old man's nostrils flared. She saw how his head turned, almost imperceptibly. She walked slowly, warily, and she noticed his body turning with her; slowly, as if he didn't want her to notice.

After she'd come round the fountain and stood between him and the kitchen door, she moved slightly closer; but then Alexander was suddenly there. The old man had smelt the dog when he got up from beside the stove and had already put out his wet hand. The dog slid in under the hand with surprising agility. Dumb Eyetie stood up, remarkably quickly for his age, and with the old man's hand resting on his spine, Alexander led him away to his room.

Just once the dog looked over his shoulder at Ingi: reproachfully? Accusingly?

'Mario Salviati!' Ingi called out the old man's name after them, because she felt sorry, guilty. What had got into her? Teasing the old man with her smells! Was she trying to vex him? Test him? 'Mario Salviati!' she called again, but then the general suddenly appeared beside her.

'He can't hear you,' he said sternly. 'Perhaps you'd better take a little walk, Miss Friedländer. To clear your head after the morning's excitement.'

Ingi swung round to him. 'And who do you keep locked up in that little room?' she cried.

The general looked towards the door of the woman without a face.

'People create their own prisons,' he said tersely, and turned back into the house to walk with his heavy tread to his room.

Ingi stood there for a few moments, and when the sounds of sighs and groans that she couldn't place started to push slowly through the rooms of the house and echo over the paving, she hurried outside.

The past, she thought, that's your prison, all of you.

30

Not long after the arrival of the Italian men in Protestant Yearsonend, Dumb Eyetie felt the need to strengthen the presence of Catholicism.

When the Italians, wearing borrowed suits that were either too baggy or too tight, attended the church service from that first Sunday morning with their various adoptive, firmly Calvinist families, they made the sign of the holy cross on their chests as the dominee came in, which drew censorious glances from the congregation.

Here in the Karoo worship was as elemental as the plains. No likenesses of God or His Son were permitted in the churches; there was no question of charismatic gestures or ecstatic worship. Just as the endless plains taught devotion, and brought home the virtues of control and sobriety, so, too, must you approach God, Creator of this sparseness. This was the people's belief and so, on Sunday, they wore dark clothes and walked stiffly into church with sober faces. Their professions of faith were restrained, their supplications were restrained, they were christened and married with restraint, and died with restraint, with controlled, courageous stubbornness.

Then along came this bunch of Catholic Italians who fidgeted during the service with the crucifixes that hung round their necks on fine chains; they made the sign of the cross on their chests and, if you moved your ear closer to their lips, you'd sometimes hear the name of the Mother of Christ slip out.

The congregation, especially the children, watched all this with patent amazement. 'Idolatry,' growled the dominee, and the young Italians soon learned to keep their eyes closed during prayers, to restrain their warm Italian hearts, to utter the Blessed Mary's holy name only in their thoughts, and never in the hearing of this suspicious congregation to refer ever again to His Holiness the Pope, successor of St Peter, who established God's Church on earth. Calvinism, the young Italian men quickly learned, was as hard as a Karoo rock and as straightlaced as a Jesuit.

The situation was not improved by events over at the Pistorius house. No sooner was their young Italian installed than their house servants and the labourers on their smallholding decided he had a pact with the devil. They called him Devil Slap because of the mark on his cheek. And one night Lorenzo Devil Slap was visited by a feverish dream featuring one of the Pistorius girls and the mark glowed so fiery red that his pillow caught fire and the ostentatious house nearly burnt down. The proverbial fat was in the fire.

The dominee was called in, the servants insisted that, in addition to idolatry, the Catholic had given his heart to the devil so he must be thrown out of town, and Attorney Pistorius had to explain that he couldn't send the young man away; that the young man, red mark and all, had been placed under his legal jurisdiction and guardianship, and that he would get into trouble with the government if he drove him out of Yearsonend. 'Next thing I'd be branded an enemy collaborator,' he explained, 'and where do you find a greater curse than that in these times?'

'Then we must excommunicate the young man until his face stops glowing,' declared the dominee, somewhat at a loss as a result of this unusual course of events. He'd heard of exorcism, of course, and he knew it had taken place in Biblical times, but he had no taste for it.

'The young man is barred from the church for a month, during which time he must repent of all his sins. He must give his heart to Almighty God, our Father and His chosen Son, our Lord Jesus Christ, with the aid of the Holy Ghost. And that is my final word.'

The front door slammed behind the dominee, and Attorney Pistorius was left to pass sentence on the young man who hung his head in shame as he held a wet cloth against his cheek on the instructions of Mrs Pistorius, to douse the fire.

It was a terrible blow for it was only on Sunday that he got the chance to see his countrymen outside of work. On Sundays the young men came to church with their families, and after that, the town had decided under the leadership of the magistrate, the young Italians were permitted to go for a walk together or cool off in the shallow waters of the stream, or (with special permission from the owner) swim in Lampak's dam – named after the beautiful Indonesian model and fashion designer, who had been in the habit of bathing in the dam every Sunday afternoon.

Devil Slap had to stay at home on Sundays now and he missed his comrades: the quiet, controlled yet powerful deaf-and-dumb stonecutter; the mercurial one, a cook; and the refined one who loved working with clothes but now had to play mechanic. He thought about each of them as he lay in his room pressing the wet cloth to his cheek.

And it was around that time, whenever Dumb Eyetie was alone and had nothing else to do, that he'd climb Mount Improbable and sit up there chiselling away at a tall slab of rock, twice as high as a man. At first he kept it a secret, but once Devil Slap had served his sentence and was allowed to attend the church service again, with the wet cloth pressed to his cheek, and go for a walk with his comrades afterwards, Dumb Eyetie led the men up the mountain. He walked ahead with many encouraging hand gestures, looking round often to make sure that they were following him.

He couldn't explain what he was up to, and they had no idea what to expect. Their amazement was great when they saw the head and torso of the Virgin Mary's figure, with her soft features, her gracious hand gesture calling you closer, and the lower half of her body still trapped in a rough block of stone.

Tears streamed down their cheeks and right there and then, in the winds that gusted over Mount Improbable's spine, in the warmth of the sun, with an unsuspecting Yearsonend sleeping off a heavy Sunday lunch down below, the young men conducted a Catholic mass using a loaf they'd brought with them for a picnic and a bottle of sweet wine someone had pinched from a farm pantry. For holy water they had the contents of a water bottle that one had brought along for the stiff climb; they sprinkled the water over each other and the statue, and they thanked God and the Virgin Mary that they'd survived the war, that they had one another and that their loved ones in Italy still thought about and loved them.

Then they sat in the shade of the rocks and thorn trees, watching Dumb Eyetie as he continued to chip away with his mallet and chisel, and the Virgin Mary as she rose like an angel from the stone: a lovely, gentle woman, Mother of God, mother of all tenderness and humility.

Within three months the statue was ready to be hauled upright. Two days went by before someone in Yearsonend directed his binoculars at the mountain and sounded the alarm. The townspeople stared upwards in shock, narrowing their eyes and pointing their fingers at the strange apparition high on Mount Improbable. Two constables were dispatched to investigate.

'Idolatry,' they reported on their return. 'There's a statue up there, with dead flowers strewn at her feet: it's the Italians.' But thank God there were no weapons or ammunition or any other signs of an armed insurrection, the town was informed.

Within half an hour the church council had assembled in the vestry. The elders and deacons were sombre and sanctimonious. The dominee sighed and prayed for guidance, and Devil Slap was sent for – still in his apron, fresh from making pasta. And Dumb Eyetie was fetched from the Plains of Melancholy where he and Big Karel Bergh were busy with a theodolite.

By the time a perspiring and breathless Dumb Eyetie arrived, escorted by Big Karel, the chief elder was busy reading the riot act to the young Italians, who hung their heads. 'You may not make an image of God, or of any other thing in creation; you may not bow down before it; you may serve no other god but the Lord your God, the Father of Israel and Yearsonend.' Thus the old man thundered forth.

At first Dumb Eyetie could make no sense of what was going on. He only saw the seething anger of his comrades. But gradually he caught on and grew terribly angry. He saw the redness rising from Big Karel's collar and flooding his face too.

Big Karel glared at the deacons but realised he must restrain himself. To suffer because you are different was nothing new to him – not among these people with their inability to accept difference. But he couldn't afford to speak out – not at this stage. A number of the members of the church council had invested in the lightning water scheme; they sat on the town council and on the board of the bank. And he knew he was going to need lots more capital before the channel was completed. 'No!' he wanted to bellow: that was the one word pounding against his temples. But he just stood there and eventually followed the young men out into the harsh sunlight, shaking his head.

The next day the two constables and three deputies from the church council clambered laboriously up the mountain carrying crowbars. Their instructions were to chop the statue of the Virgin Mary into small pieces. But when they reached it, they were met by Mario Salviati, standing with legs braced in front of it. For the first time, they noticed his powerful forearms, the strong legs and the arched back of a fighting bull. He stood there with a .303 across his chest. It was Big Karel Bergh's rifle – earlier he'd thrust it into Dumb Eyetie's hands and gestured: 'Go up the mountain.'

The men took one look at Dumb Eyetie and realised: We can't reason with him; he won't hear a thing. So they sat down on the rocks and laid aside their equipment to light their pipes. Dumb Eyetie also sat down – in front of the statue, under the Virgin Mary's outstretched arms.

They contemplated the statue and started to feel a twinge of guilt. They saw the dry flowers at the Virgin Mary's feet and they looked up into the blue sky above them and at the rocky peak of Mount Improbable. And all at once the stuffy vestry with its indignant church council seemed very far away. The wind cooled their faces and they were filled with a feeling of humility and peace.

Eventually, they went one by one to shake Dumb Eyetie's hand, without a word, then stumbled down the mountain again with their heavy crowbars and picks. At the bottom, they had to face the raging of the dominee, Attorney Pistorius and the chief elder. But they insisted: The Catholic Mary is causing no harm. Have mercy on her. The Italians are only practising their faith, after all.

And to this day, the statue of the Virgin Mary, now slightly weathered by sun and rain, still stands on the place that came to be known as Madonna's Peak. If you stood there, Ingi discovered, you could see all of Yearsonend. You could look up to the summit of Mount Improbable and its forbidding cliffs. Or you could let your eyes drop to the Plain of Melancholy with the shiny lightning water channel tracing a line across it, like a snail's trail to the horizon. You could look left to the Cave Gorge, where smoke trailed lazily up from Jonty Jack's chimney. You might even see a bright orange kite fluttering up into the wind. Or you could follow the flight of the kestrels, leading your glance over Edenville, the gables and towers of the old Drostdy, the smallholdings and neatly cultivated fields, the streets of town with a single car puttering along and the windmills turning and the schoolchildren romping in the playground during break.

And all around stretched the immeasurable plains – first a

greeny brown and then a deeper brown and eventually dull grey and finally a hue that merged so perfectly with the sky you couldn't tell with certainty what was earth and what was the heavens.

I must paint again, Ingi thought, the first time she stood at Madonna's Peak, smiling at the statue of the Virgin. You can only deny colours and textures for so long; then your hands begin to tingle; then your arm begins to burn with excitement and canvases seem to rise up in front of your eyes.

I am an artist, Ingi realised, and I'd forgotten that: tangled up in administration at the museum, too close to the anxious sweat and urgent strategies of the cultural commissars. But here things are raw and pure, and light is light once more.

Here heavenly colours lie about you naturally, dappled, evasive, blended into the landscape and people's hearts. And if you want to capture the textures here, then there is one great metaphor: the lightning water channel.

Yes, thought Ingi: Mario Salviati's singing water.

31

Lettie Pistorius on the train: a seemingly endless journey in the long brown snake dragged by a lugubrious steam engine.

If Karel comes back, she thought, I'll try again. But separate bedrooms. Or maybe he could go and live for a time in the Feather Palace, which hasn't been touched since Meerlust left. She and the baby would stay in their house, or perhaps she should buy a house of her own closer to the general store and Attorney Pistorius' office.

Little Jonty was soothed by the landscape. He clung to her breast and she sat at an angle so his watery eyes could focus on the dun-coloured plains. It might have been the rhythm of the train; perhaps he had some sense of homecoming. Perhaps he remembers his first journey along this track, she thought, when we travelled towards Cape Town and he was smaller than a seahorse – just a tadpole in my womb.

She stepped down on to the platform at Yearsonend in the heat of the day. No one expected her. The stationmaster came out of the signal room and circled round her and her two suitcases, worried and inquisitive. He bent over the baby, studying his features, then examined her outfit.

Lettie knew that before she'd stepped out into the bright dusty street he would have rung the pub, the storekeeper, his friend the church elder, and goodness only knew how many other people.

He offered to get someone to come and fetch her, stammering something she didn't understand about the stubborn water. He asked her could she not smell the water in the air and, yes, as a child of the Karoo, she was able to smell water from afar; and, yes, in spite of the scorching sun the unmistakable smell of wet earth did hang in the air.

She refused his help, asking him to store her suitcases behind his signals. As she set off down the street, she was amazed at how many herons patrolled the smallholdings. Great flocks of white storks moved from field to field. Everything was green and fresh. What has happened? she wondered. Yearsonend is sparkling. According to the telegram, the channel had failed.

Gradually she pieced together the events: Big Karel Bergh fleeing; Mario Salviati determinedly raising and raising again the sluice gates at Washout; and finally, the bubbling, swishing water proving the Law of Bernoulli as it rushed into the town dam only to gurgle out again through the open sluice gate, pouring and spilling out all over the place, mocking the people's amazement and their lack of vision.

She discovered that not only was Big Karel still missing, but that the name Karel Thin Air was even used in conversation to her face, though with some hesitation, and people tended to swallow the new name, but it seemed to her that they had a need to try it out on her. She was not certain why, but she settled back into their house, made contact with family and friends and, on the third day after her return, she decided to look for Mario Salviati.

'What do you hope to achieve by that?' grumbled her brother, the attorney. 'Your husband obviously pocketed a lot of the money himself and that's why he's hit the high road. Half-breeds have no conscience – I always warned you.'

But something drew Lettie to Mario Salviati: an instinct told her that he knew more than the others. She settled Jonty Jack – the baby whose name had so outraged the Pistoriuses – into his pram and set out through the moist plots of Yearsonend.

She found Mario Salviati on the plot nearest to the dam. He was bent over his theodolite, surrounded by impatient, anxious men with maps. She recognised the town clerk, the water superintendent – he usually sat idly at home drinking beer and breeding pigeons – and a couple of the younger landowners.

They'd already seen her coming from a long way off. She dragged the pram over the clods of earth and mud splashed up to her knees. She wore a modish London hat over her curly hair. They greeted her and tapped Mario Salviati on the shoulder, so he straightened, his eyes blinking as they refocused. Then his eyes met hers and she saw his mouth open and close, just once. Then it was gone.

32

Heavy with the burden of all the things she'd been told and the sorrow of unfinished business, Ingi plodded wearily up Cave Gorge. The trees offered blessed shade as she sweated onwards.

She turned round once to look down at the stone cottage, and marvelled at how long ago her first night there seemed. What I knew of Yearsonend then, and what I know now! It was just a town to me when I arrived, with dusty streets, water furrows and sluice gates, quiet verandas and curtains drawn against the heat. And now it's like a tree with branches stretching everywhere and tendrils reaching into every house. Every branch grows from another and sends out its own shoots in turn, and when a story is startled from the branches, flying up into the air like a bird, it takes a flock of other stories with it.

Jonty lay sleeping on the shady side of his house. She glanced at the chisels and mallets strewn among the wood shavings. An empty wine bottle lay near his hand. She bent over him and the smell of old sweat and alcohol rose off his large body. He was unkempt; his clothes were stained with perspiration and his fingers were rubbed raw in places.

She turned to the Staggering Merman. Now is my chance to take a peep under the tarpaulin, she thought. I want to greet this sculpture. Then she thought better of it, noticing that the trestles, which had supported the log he'd been working on, were empty now: two steel prongs almost like mouths with gap-teeth. Dragmarks and Jonty's footprints, stalling here and there, led round to the back of the house.

While he lay snoring behind her, Ingi followed the trail. It led past the old camper-van, behind a disused fowl-run, around a stack of whalebones and a heap of scrap iron and then through the trees. She followed the marks carefully until she came to the ravine with the grey scar left by that mountain rockfall so long ago. She gazed down at Jonty's disintegrating failures. The latest lay on top, its exposed flesh still white.

There was a noise behind her. She turned and there he stood, hattered, with lines of bitterness round his mouth. The shrilling of the cicadas in the trees was almost deafening. Without a word, he turned and walked away.

When she got back to his house there was no sign of him. It was only now that she noticed the telescope had also been covered with a heavy oilcloth. She knew he was somewhere there, that he was watching her.

She set off down the gorge and the further down she got, the lighter her step became. A breeze came up, fluttering in the small of her back, playing with her hair. She felt as though she had been relieved of an obligation; as though she'd escaped from something that threatened to smother her, an oppressiveness she'd been fleeing all these years.

As she walked past the stone cottage, she felt the telescope in her back, like a hand pushing her forward.

Ahead, there is always more to see, she thought.

Part Two

Gold Pit

I

The black ox-wagon carrying part of the Kruger Millions and
five children's hands reached Yearsonend on a quiet Saturday
afternoon in 1901. It was the time of the South African war,
fought from 1899 to 1902 when Great Britain challenged the two
Boer republics in the southernmost region of Africa. The war was,
of course, about gold.

The black ox-wagon moved through the country like the Ark
of the Covenant: from Pretoria, over the endless plains of the
Orange Free State, past Winburg, down towards the Cape Colony,
skirting Ficksburg one cold winter when snow lay on the Maluti
mountains, and further, over the green hills to East London, to
Grahamstown, Port Elizabeth, Graaff-Reinet, Oudtshoorn, Prince
Albert . . .

The wagon loaded with gold groaned forward, mostly at night,
but on the open plains where there was no sign of life they'd push
on in daylight, through the thirsty land. The small commando
consisted of hand picked scouts, appointed by President Paul
Kruger himself the day before he left by train for Lourenço Marques
en route to Switzerland, where he died on the shores of a lake.
Their job until the war was over was to keep on the move and
to preserve part of the treasury of the embattled republic as it
staggered under the British invasion. Their instructions were never
to rest; and to keep moving ahead of rumour, speculation and the
enemy.

The ox-wagon was specially reinforced. Trunks were fastened
to its base. An old State Bible, signed before his departure by the
president himself, lay in the wagon-chest. The salted hands were
packed in a sealed lead casket.

The oxen were tough and hardy, selected from the best northern
herds, descendants of the stalwart beasts who'd trekked from
the Cape Colony, through bloody skirmishes with the Zulus,

braving spears, foot-and-mouth disease and marauding lions as they pushed on to the Transvaal, to the gold fields, and to the Highveld's beckoning grasslands where the Boers, hardened and craving independence in Africa, declared their own republic.

The Kruger gold was of the purest, cast into bars and coins stamped with President Paul Kruger's bearded head. The gold reserves were to be kept moving until the president returned from exile; they had to keep trekking from town to town, from friendly farm to loyal community. It didn't matter how far they detoured as long as they kept ahead of the enemy. And if they found a sympathetic ship, they were to use some of the gold to negotiate for the shipping of the children's hands.

They left a trail of rumour and myth behind them, and fabulous tales of the small commando of horsemen with their valuable cargo preceded them, even though everyone along the road who helped them had to swear, on pain of death, to keep silent about the black ox-wagon, which was guarded at night, hidden under bales of lucerne in isolated barns or under thorn-tree branches in lonely dry riverbeds.

Sometimes they had to buy secrecy, because the Cape Colony, in particular, was crawling with turncoats, and loyalists to the Queen. It was a journey of huge risks, along rough tracks, over mountain passes and across swollen rivers. When they arrived in Yearsonend that day in 1901, they were ragged and emaciated, nothing like the heroes they'd become in the legends.

They should have waited until nightfall in the ravines of Mount Improbable, but they'd come to the end of their tether, exhausted from keeping ahead of the British spies. They were sick of the outmanoeuvring, of hiding their tracks, of lies and threats and bribery; they were feverish with loneliness, hunger and longing; sickened by their own misdeeds. They were ready to murder one another; it was a journey marked by strife and dissent.

And they had to find women, desperately. The sole woman with them, astride an ox, had only brought trouble. And that was the one injunction the old president had given them before he heaved his heavy body on to the train: 'Stay away from women, my boys.'

For the first eight months of the journey, they had managed, until that night near Pedi in the Transkei. God have mercy on them, sons of the Republic: that night when the devil seized them.

That was a day that Field Cornet Pistorius, father of Lettie Pistorius, would remember for the rest of his life. The day before, when they had come across the small settlement, had been a disaster. The wagon stuck in a ditch. At dusk, as they battled to get out, one of the oxen broke its leg.

From then on the wagon would have to manage with fewer oxen. The extra ox, which had now lost its yoke fellow, was tied to the back of the wagon with a thong.

Pistorius and Fourie had to kill the crippled ox. They had to slit the beast's throat because a shot in the night would have attracted attention. First they tied him securely to a tree so that he couldn't jerk and then they tried to slash his artery while he bellowed and wrestled against the thongs. Eventually, sickened by the struggle, they hit the artery. As the beast's blood drained away, it sank, bellowing, to its knees, and then keeled over.

As it fell, the thong fastening it to the tree snapped and swiped Pistorius across his shoulders leaving a mark like a whiplash. That was the first task for the woman they called Siela Pedi, after they brought her to the wagon: to rub salve and herbs into that wound, as he lay groaning under her hands.

But before she joined them, while they were butchering the ox – the meat still steaming – one of the other men came up with the idea that before deciding which route they should now follow, they should go and see whether there was life down in the settlement they'd spied out that afternoon.

Perhaps they all knew exactly what lay behind this – for who had not seen the women hoeing in the maize field next to the small houses? The place was somewhere between a Xhosa kraal and a small settlement. The people were clearly not Xhosa – through the binoculars most looked coloured

Pistorius gave the order that choice pieces of meat be wrapped in tarpaulin. He posted guards round the wagon and, with two gold pounds and two men, he set out for the settlement. They stumbled along, cursing, in the dark and in the distance they could hear a dog barking and people chattering – Afrikaans with snatches of Xhosa.

A heated debate was in progress, and as they approached, they realised that their arrival in the district had been noted and that the argument was about them, about the 'funeral wagon that had come past with Paul Kruger's body', and 'black riders' who were taking the president's body to the Queen of England to show her what the war was doing to the elderly and to beg for her mercy.

As the people chattered on round their fire Pistorius and his two men suddenly appeared. As long as he lived, Pistorius would never forget that scene. One moment it was all lively argument, with dogs lazing by the fire and children playing around the houses, and a group of youngsters romping and giggling a little way from the adults and their beer pots. The next moment there was no one: just fires, ash, empty seats, and a puff of dust in the air.

Only then did Pistorius realise how he and his men must have looked in their tattered black clothes. Their faces were drawn from hardship, from clinging to one grim command, and their clothes were caked with the blood that had spurted from the ox's artery, and with dust that clung to it from the walk.

Only later did he realise that the unsheathed slaughtering knife was still stuck in his belt, and that he'd smeared blood on his face when he'd wiped it after killing the ox. What was more, behind him stood two men carrying bloody chunks of meat on meat hooks. Who wouldn't be scared out of their wits at such a sight?

It took some time to entice the people outside again. Sweet talk and cajoling were necessary; the meat was laid down near the fire; explanations and yet more explanations. And eventually the two gold pounds were tossed with a flourish into the open space between the fire and the thatched huts.

Heads bobbed over windowsills and all eyes were on the coins that lay glittering in the firelight. A dog must have picked up the scent of ox blood, which had smeared from Pistorius' hands on to the coins, and came out of one of the doors to sniff at one. A stone flew from behind a house hitting it in the ribs, so that it ran off yelping.

'The blood on our bodies is from the ox we slaughtered for you,' called Pistorius. 'We aren't murderers, we are soldiers of the Zuid Afrikaansche Republic. And the president is not dead. He's on a ship *en route* to Europe. We come in peace. We are tired. God, can't you see what we look like?'

Siela peeped out first. Yes, it was the future Granny Siela Pedi who, at a tender age, first ventured out. She wasn't particularly beautiful, but radiated curiosity and a spirit of adventure – you could see it the moment she stuck her head round the door. And then she darted outside and scrambled on all fours in the dust to snatch up the coins as quickly as possible. The firelight played over her beautiful legs and strong body and around the mischievous smile she threw the haggard men, and then she was back indoors.

Silence fell. An old man appeared from the door through which Siela disappeared. He doesn't look in much better shape than us, thought Pistorius; a man cured by the sun and this rugged goat country, here on the border where the Xhosa, the Khoi, the San and the white pioneers had come to a stand-off.

'Why do you throw your money at us?' He held the two pounds in his hand.

'We are alone. We need salt. We're tired of eating unseasoned meat. We have travelled far. We're looking for news of the war.'

Pistorius kept quiet for a moment and thought: Is this my voice begging? His men drew up closer behind him. 'We haven't come to hurt you. We could have shot you all long ago if we wanted to. We are seven men with guns.'

There was murmuring in the houses. 'We could have crept up and murdered you tonight.'

Then, one after another, the people emerged. They picked up the meat and hung it on the hooks from a tree branch – before the dogs got at it. Someone began to cut slices and a grid was put over the coals. The old man came up to Pistorius: 'How long have you been on the road, Field Cornet?'

'Eight hard months.'

'And what is on the wagon?'

'This I cannot tell you.'

'We have heard it's the president's body, embalmed.'

'Rubbish.'

'The people also say you're carrying the severed right hands of children who died in the British concentration camps. You're taking the hands to the Queen as proof.'

'That is true,' answered Field Cornet Pistorius, his eyes resting on Siela's breasts as she straightened the grill. 'They are the salted hands of small children who died in the Winburg camp. The world won't believe us when we tell them women and children are dying like flies in Kitchener's concentration camps. We asked five of the mothers each to give up the right hand of her dead child before it was buried. We're taking them to England. The ship is waiting.'

'It's a wagon of doom,' mused the old man, studying Pistorius through narrowed eyes. 'And, with respect, you have the red beard of the devil.'

'We are exhausted,' answered Pistorius. Something in him had died during the trek over the endless plains to the mountain world in which they were now trapped; and still, the knowledge that these eight long months were just the beginning and much hardship lay ahead. At the same time he had no idea of the state of the war, where his men's women and children were, or whether their farms had been razed by the British troops.

The old man looked at him for a while, then offered him beer, and later on a piece of the ox, tenderly grilled. 'We have no salt, sorry,' he said. And then it happened, the thing that started it all. While Pistorius was eating, he saw one of his men reach for his gun. It was an innocent gesture, a soldier pulling his trusty weapon closer. But a woman saw it, read it as the beginning of a massacre, and began to scream. The fellow meant no harm, but as the woman screamed, one of the young men from the settlement produced a battered Mauser from behind a barrel. He was just getting to his feet when one of Pistorius' men shot him in the forehead – a neat red hole. His eyes rolled back and, with a look of surprise and a resigned sigh, he fell face down into the dust.

Pistorius had instinctively drawn and cocked his gun; he and his men had been handpicked because of their lightning-fast reflexes in a tight corner. He summed up the situation instantly: saw that no one was pointing a gun at him and fired a shot into the air.

'Murderers!' screeched the old man. Pistorius grabbed Siela by the arm and jerked her to one side. Carefully he and his men started to retreat, with the woman in front of them. The people, who'd fallen flat when Pistorius fired his shot, lay with their faces in the dust. This wasn't the first time something like this had happened to them, Pistorius realised. Blood dripped slowly into the dust from the meat on the hook.

God knows, we were desperate, hungry and thirsty, and reports had reached us that one Boer commando after another was surrendering – so Field Cornet Pistorius would console himself in years to come, long after he and Siela Pedi had stopped talking to one another.

Back at the wagon, they found the oxen already yoked and the men lying fanned out around the vehicle, at the ready. They'd heard the shots. Pistorius had Siela's hands tied behind her back and they lifted her on to the unpaired ox. They needed her as a hostage, they told themselves.

Another eight month journey lay ahead of them before they were to arrive at Yearsonend. They made their way cautiously through outlying districts. At night sometimes they came upon animals that watched them with calm eyes. Seldom people – just once in the moonlight: two young boys who took one look and fled. Wanting to see if the boys would sound the alarm, they holed up in a gully for three days, the wagon concealed under thorn branches, the oxen and horses tethered under an overhang some way off.

Then they trekked on, more forlorn than glad that the boys hadn't betrayed them. Perhaps we're ghosts, they joked in the evenings. But Pistorius watched his men: how emaciated they became, how they sat like hyenas, watching one another for a sign that one would betray the blood oath.

Eight hard months, and the woman's body swaying on the ox. The wagon held together miraculously, but every now and again they had to steal supplies and bridles from a quiet farmhouse during the night. Here sympathetic families were few and far between. Sometimes they travelled for four days before they came to a trustworthy homestead to which they'd been directed. But even that happened less frequently. Eventually they stopped thinking about allies. All that remained to them was the wind, the plains, and the long, lonely nights. And then, eventually, the small town in the shadow of the mountain.

The black ox-wagon groaned into Yearsonend. The oxen strained forward with their tired heads swaying from side to side with every step and the weary men slouched in their saddles, tired eyes under their hats surveying the sleepy village, the barking dogs and the children who ran along beside the wagon.

The Plains of Melancholy had finally broken Pistorius' men: the desolation, the lack of water, the burnt-out farmsteads left behind by British troops, the skeletons of farm animals, which had either been shot or had their tendons cut, or had died of thirst because wells and waterholes had been filled in.

It was Meerlust Bergh – ostrich farmer and Cape rebel when he wasn't visiting fashion houses overseas – and Lost Cause Moloi, black rebel field cornet and grandfather of Goodwill Moloi, Yearsonend's mayor in Ingi's time, who rode out to welcome them.

Meerlust Bergh, in the flamboyant clothes he favoured, climbed down from his carriage, swinging his plumed hat in a sweeping arc – 'Just like Jan van Riebeeck,' Field Cornet Pistorius was to remark bitterly in later years – and noticed that the scouts were staring at his artificial leg. An old tracker had carved the ivory peg during the long months after a young male lion had bitten off Meerlust's right leg, just below the knee. Lying on the banks of the thundering Zambezi, just above the Victoria Falls, Meerlust had had to sweat out fever and sepsis and wait for the stump of his leg to heal.

Meerlust began to dress like a dandy after he lost his leg, people said. That was when he began to resemble the models who worked in his ostrich-feather business.

Meerlust bowed low before Field Cornet Pistorius, Jonty Jack's other grandfather. His eye took in the wild red beard and the eyes that had lost all lust for life.

'Welcome to a community of sympathisers,' he said. 'We are friends. This is Moloi, the famous black field cornet. We can offer you hospitality. You look as if you've been through hell.' Meerlust couldn't help but notice the tears running down the cheeks of the young woman sitting on the ox.

What are you fellows doing with a woman like that? he wanted to ask. But he could see the answer in their guilty eyes, in the way their hats were pulled low on their brows, but more especially in her demeanour, which clearly said: I want to get away, I want to be free, but they've made me do things that have taken away my freedom for ever.

Moloi looked at the black ox-wagon and sniffed. 'What's that stink?' was his first question. 'Hides? Did you hunt much?'

'It's the right hands of five dead children,' answered Pistorius. 'We wanted to get them to the Queen of England so that the burning down of farms and the deaths in the concentration camps could be stopped. But we've decided that we won't be able to get them to a ship. We want to bury them here, decently.'

'Good God!' cried Meerlust.

And that's why Yearsonend's first street corner was named Little Hands, because it was there that Field Cornet Pistorius decided: this far and no further.

2

There was a map, Iugi heard, while sitting over a beer in the Look Deep pub, the very same watering-hole opened by the interpreter who decided to stay on in Yearsonend after he'd ridiculously misallocated the Italian prisoners of war. His son, also known as Look Deep, was in charge of the bar, the only public drinking hole in Yearsonend.

The map showed the location of Gold Pit. This she heard in the heat of late afternoons, but no one knew where the map was. Only three families could possibly have it.

The Molois were a possibility, because Lost Cause, the black rebel field cornet, married Granny Siela Pedi shortly after she arrived in Yearsonend on the ox. Ingi gathered that maybe, in the course of that miserable journey from Pedi to Yearsonend, Siela had learned what the men planned to do with the black ox-wagon.

Then, of course, there was Field Cornet Redbeard Pistorius, who married Gwen Viljee, scion of a Huguenot family, shortly after his arrival in Yearsonend.

The third family who might have the map was the Berghs, because Meerlust Bergh had met the black ox-wagon that Saturday afternoon when those shattered men limped into Yearsonend.

There were all kinds of stories about the map, she realised, as she raised a cold beer to her lips and a tractor droned away in one of Yearsonend's distant fields, someone on the storekeeper's veranda called a worker, and a train chugged slowly out of the station, hauling its heavy cargo into the Karoo.

The Look Deep regulars had been unaccustomed to female company in a pub. But once they got used to the idea, they spoke freely to Ingi. The most persistent rumour, the one she heard from one regular after another, all in varying degrees of inebriation, was that during the excavations for the lightning water channel, Big Karel Bergh had come upon Gold Pit – or, at least, a trunk containing the map. Hence his disappearance into thin air.

A second rumour was that Meerlust Bergh financed his business with the Kruger gold, his extensive farms and feather-plucking business, the export warehouses on the Cape Town docks, the hat factory and the fashion house in Europe, and the modelling school and all his fancy trips with the exquisite Irene Lampak at his side.

And the third most persistent rumour claimed that the gold map lay forgotten somewhere in Attorney Pistorius' strongroom and filing cabinets as part of an old pile of estate documents, and that the map wasn't drawn but explained in the form of a story. The story, however, contained so many scandalous details about the journey of that black ox-wagon to Yearsonend, and particularly about the way President Kruger's scouts had treated Granny Siela Pedi, that the Pistorius family could not afford to unearth the documents.

Or the Molois: perhaps they were sitting on the money. Then the drinkers would lean closer to Ingi and she got the bitter taste of isolation and inbreeding, of old hates and suspicions. The Molois and the revolution . . . who forked out the money for the political upheavals of recent years? It was obvious! The Kruger gold, Boer gold, had been scandalously misappropriated to run the Boers into the ground.

She stumbled out of the bar. It was broad daylight, but she'd had too much to drink. She shook her head as the sunlight hit her. The general's Plymouth crawled slowly up the street, from the direction of Little Hands. The old man was watching her movements, she realised; whenever I go for a walk, it's not long before I hear the purr of that Plymouth approaching from behind the trees, up and down the streets, between the smallholdings and houses, till he catches sight of me.

She shook her head again, and through the white light and quivering mirage in the street the general drove by. He looked ahead, as if he hadn't seen her. Alexander lay on the back seat. The Great Dane's head rested on the windowsill and he sniffed the wind. And the angel sprawled on the front passenger seat, next to the general, looking very pleased with the way things were going.

Ingi rubbed her eyes and looked back. The sun burned through the red dustcloud. A few men in front of the pub gazed after her. Ahead of her the dust mushroomed higher. She didn't know what was happening; she knew only that the stories were getting the better of her, and that she must make a call to the art museum, or perhaps send a fax.

She decided to take a detour back to the Drostdy, and walked to Camel, swung left into Eviction Road, then right to Blood Tree, after which she walked in the direction of the town dam. The big black Mercedes caught up with her as she passed Blood Tree and now it pulled up beside her in a cloud of dust.

Goodwill Moloi, in a black Sunday suit, rolled down his window. The glass was tinted, but Ingi had been warned by a finger-wagger in the Look Deep bar, 'That shiny car is Goodwill Moloi's. He rides up and down, lording it over us.' His face was so large it filled the car windowframe.

'Miss Friedländer, I presume?' smiled Goodwill, with the charm that had won him the position of first citizen in the Yearsonend council chamber. 'May I offer you a lift?'

Ingi couldn't suppress a 'No, thank you,' but then Goodwill's charm caught up with her: in spite of her refusal, he kept on smiling at her. 'It's hot,' he said. 'And there's no mercy.'

'All right. It's very kind of you.'

She went round to the passenger door which was already open, waiting for her. For Goodwill, this was not a chance meeting. He'd received a request from the legislative capital that he must extend his protection to the young assistant who worked for the new black artistic director of the National Gallery.

He'd asked a sympathetic supporter, Attorney Pistorius' messenger Pedal Quick-Quick, to keep an eye on Ingi. At the time of Mandela's release when the residents of Edenville had exercised their new municipal rights and voted him on to the council, he'd recruited Pedal to keep him informed of affairs in the mainly white business community of Yearsonend.

When Pedal Quick-Quick rang to say that Ingi Friedländer had just left the Look Deep and was acting strangely, hovering about in the dust of the general's Plymouth as if she'd seen a ghost, Goodwill leaped into the Merc and revved up, only to approach Ingi slowly, seemingly calmly, as she wandered through the streets of Yearsonend, sweaty and a little tipsy, and not quite certain whether she'd really seen an angel or not.

Goodwill knew that people in Edenville were saying that the

girl from the city was obviously completely clueless. Jonty Jack talked a hole in her head, the general had bamboozled her, and the drunken ravings of those white farmers propping up the bar had created all sorts of fantasies in her imagination about the history of Yearsonend.

'One shouldn't venture out in this heat,' Goodwill cautioned her in a fatherly tone. Before she could say she resented being made to feel like a helpless little girl, he continued, 'You're here on a very important mission, I believe.' Ingi took in the fine black suit and the enthusiasm. But she wasn't going to be caught offside by a man who wanted to patronise her.

She decided to ask the question foremost in her mind. 'Is it true that Granny Siela Pedi was your grandmother?'

He looked at her sharply. 'Is the young lady interested in the history of Yearsonend?' She nodded and he pulled over under a tree opposite the school. He kept the motor running; the air-conditioner hummed and Ingi realised that while they could see the children in the playground, she and the mayor were hidden behind the Mercedes' tinted windows.

'How could I not be?' she asked. 'I've never been in a place where the past lingers on like this. You can smell it and feel it and taste it.'

'Too long under the African sun,' Goodwill chided. 'The young lady should wear a hat. This sun can addle the brain.'

'And your grandmother, Mayor?'

Goodwill looked away 'Did you hear me remark on what an important project it is you're busy with?'

'I heard you,' said Ingi. She looked at the school in silence.

'Yes, it's true.' Goodwill slipped the Merc into gear. He could tell she wasn't impressed by the praise. Out there in the big city, he thought, they're so blasé. He decided not to mention that he'd also built the school. 'Can I take you on a tour of my town?'

Ingi smiled. 'I'd love that!'

While they drove, she thought back to the morning she'd been busy at her desk with statistics and transport costs, when she had received a call from the Speaker of Parliament. The Speaker, an

Indian lady with the motherly seriousness of a maths teacher, needed her help with removing the old paintings.

Ingi hurried to the parliament buildings, where workers were already busy in the foyer removing huge oil paintings of the previous rulers. An old cellar had been cleared and the portraits were to go there. Ingi had stood with the Speaker watching memorabilia carried out of the cellar: huge mahogany desks with built-in microphones and hidden tape recorders, old ceremonial swords and ensigns, machine-guns carved from ivory, medals and piles of leatherbound visitors' books in which generals from South America and lords from Britain had left their flamboyant signatures.

'Three-quarters of the stuff has already been stolen,' the Speaker explained, 'because it seems that our new politicians only feel they've really triumphed once they can flaunt one of these distasteful items on their desks.'

The air was filled with a musty, dreary smell, and the cleaners' cheers echoed through the corridors: they'd stood behind the rope railings waiting until the last of the enormous oil paintings – a massive work depicting the last apartheid cabinet – was taken down and lugged off to the cellar. Ingi pointed out that the cellar was no place to store paintings: the air was too damp. Everything is being done too hastily, was her objection. These things may refer to a distasteful period of history, but they are still artefacts from the past. But the Speaker explained that other arrangements would be made – a museum of neglect and transgressions, perhaps.

While they were busy, the Speaker mentioned that the president had decreed that a new parliamentary mace must be carved, inlaid with gold leaf and diamonds; a mace without the colonial connotations of the existing one.

It gives the president dyspepsia, explained the Speaker, rearranging her sari, to have that imperial mace lying there right under his nose every day. 'Can the art museum organise something for us? Perhaps an outstanding artist from a rural area? A black woman, ideally, who has a way with a knife and an instinct for national symbols?'

Ingi sighed and looked out of the window.

'And the sigh?' asked Goodwill.

'Everyone is suddenly interested in the arts,' said Ingi.

'But we value our artists! They're our pride!'

'Oh, absolutely, Mayor. Please tell me about Granny Siela Pedi.'

Goodwill smiled and pointed. 'Look, there's Blood Tree. Do you know about that?'

Ingi nodded. 'I heard.'

'My grandmother Siela was on her deathbed when she first spoke about the black ox-wagon.' Goodwill stopped again, this time under a tree near the Drostdy. He told Ingi how Granny Siela, broken by fever, sweated out her hardship on her deathbed. She babbled feverishly but always came back to the black ox-wagon and that time in the veld. After the young cavaliers, as she called them, took her prisoner that day near Pedi, they sat her on an ox and trekked on.

In Goodwill's calm voice – he could well have made a career in radio – the story of Granny Siela unfolded for Ingi. Granny Siela had said she could hear the wailing from her home, when the ox-wagon crested a rise, and for a few days men from her settlement followed the black ox-wagon to see if the black cavaliers would set her free. They kept their distance, stood as quiet as the aloes on the hills, and disappeared if one of the cavaliers fired a shot at them. An hour later they were there again, this time on another hill. But a few days into the hinterland one morning she had to face it: they'd gone; they'd turned back. 'I'm alone,' lamented Granny Siela on her deathbed. 'Alone.'

It wasn't Redbeard Pistorius who began the lewd jokes about how she had to ride astride the ox day after day, she said; it was one of the others. But it was Redbeard who watched her by the fire in the evenings, more than the others. And night after night she had to rub salve into the thong wound on his shoulder.

It was he who called her aside the first time, one hot afternoon in the middle of nowhere, with the oxen lying panting in the shade and the wagon hidden under thorn branches. Cicadas shrilled in the thorn trees and the bored men sat around speculating quietly about the progress of the war.

She thought about the wagon, she said, as her head tossed feverishly on the sweat-soaked pillow; she thought how the gold on the wagon shimmered in the murderous sun while Redbeard took her, behind the agave; she thought how the gold would reflect the sun if the tarpaulin was to be removed; that dark wagon; that black wagon; the funeral wagon as it would always be to her; and the dust was like water offering her no handhold; and then the stone she grabbed, with which she tried to hit him, but he was too strong, too angry, too crazed with loneliness; and he'd wept afterwards and brought her water.

But the following day it was one of the others. And after three days Redbeard again. ' "And so they treated me rudely for nearly a year," ' Goodwill repeated his granny Siela's own words. ' "In time we were on first-name terms, we knew each other so well. They shared me out like their rations – so many days with each man.

' "But when we arrived at Yearsonend, they threw me away like a slut, and in the years to come you'd never think that Redbeard ever knew me. I met him often, often in the street, or there at the general store, but he'd always look away. He was busy becoming a big man, a leader of the town. I was his scandalous reminder – me, Granny Siela of Pedi, who came into this town riding on an ox, many years ago." '

Goodwill sighed and looked at Ingi. 'Now you understand why we need our beautiful statues and paintings,' he said quietly.

'I'd like to go home now,' said Ingi. 'Will you excuse me?'

'No,' said Goodwill. 'Wait, there's something else.'

Ingi shook her head. 'I feel dizzy.'

'Redbeard's greatest burden of guilt . . .' he carried on, regardless, and, it seemed to Ingi, in an unnecessarily loud voice; his deep voice filled the car. Perhaps he normally spoke that way, or maybe it was just the three quick beers in the bar and the unnatural air from the Mercedes' air-conditioner that overwhelmed her. And then, to make matters worse, there was the general's sullen

Plymouth creeping like an admonition down the street, idling, grumbling.

Goodwill Moloi spoke as a man driven to do so. 'Redbeard's biggest guilt is that only four children's hands were buried under that memorial on the corner.'

Ingi looked at him, stupefied. 'Not five?

She'd read the inscription chiselled on the tall granite obelisk, the inscription that said the right hands of five children who'd died in the concentration camps were laid to rest here when it was no longer deemed possible to take them to the Queen of England. 'Five Small Hands,' she'd read the inscription out loud, 'who play no more, but point accusing fingers at the Empire and the transgressions of England.'

Goodwill told her that one night Redbeard Pistorius had unlocked the lead chest and stolen one hand. During the long journey, a few months before they reached Yearsonend, he'd sought out a sangoma at one of their stops, a woman under a lion skin, with rattling divining bones and deep sighs and foam around her mouth. She must help free him from his enslavement to that woman who'd trekked with them on the back of the ox for over half a year.

The sangoma had promised that she'd do it, and questioned him about the black ox-wagon's journey. Redbeard told her of the gold and the hands in the lead chest. Eagerly, the woman insisted, 'You must go back, Field Cornet, and bring me one of those little hands. It's powerful medicine. Then I'll heal you, as compensation, and take the lynx from your loins. I will take away your lust for black women.'

Redbeard Pistorius lifted the little hand out of the lead chest, thinking no one had seen him. But Granny Siela was watching him. She wondered for whom the sangoma would brew muti from those little fingers – it had to be rich people, who were in great trouble. Child-muti is expensive. Which powders would the nails be ground into? Granny Siela wondered. To spice someone's love again? To bring forgetfulness to someone plagued by the past? To lure back a lover, lying with another woman? To help heal a cancer?

Only the one little finger was brewed up for Redbeard – with other powerful herbs. 'Human flesh: eat,' the sangoma hissed. 'Great muti . . .'

To the end of his days Redbeard carried the guilt of that theft, that cannibalism. He knew that now the child could never be at peace in his grave in the concentration camp in the north. The little boy would roam restlessly for ever, because he had lost his hand to witchcraft, because a man who was growing rich and prominent walked around with that little finger in his stomach, feigning innocence.

Because if you consume human flesh, you never digest it. You carry it inside you for ever – that is what makes it such strong muti. Right up to the time of his death, the people of Edenville called him 'Pinky', and every morning of his life, on the way to his attorney's office, he took a detour and stood for a moment before the monument. The white people thought it was out of respect, but the coloured people knew: this was a man with a great burden of guilt.

'Thanks,' called Ingi, as she opened the Mercedes' door. She ran through the hot sunlight to the Drostdy, pushed open the heavy front door, and found herself breathless in the cavernous living room with its stuffed animal heads, swords, heavy furniture and leatherbound books.

She could smell cinnamon; she could hear the servants' muffled voices in the kitchen. The parrot screeched and the general's transmitter crackled. She fled to her room.

'May the angels guide us!' she heard the general shout from his office.

Then she pulled a pillow over her head and waited for her heartbeat to settle. 'Remember why you're here,' she whispered to herself. 'For the sculpture; for the Staggering Merman.'

3

Jonty Jack stood before the Staggering Merman. Like standing in front of my vanished father, he thought; as if opposite my own mother. Ah! How much this sculpture signifies to me! Father, yes, and mother, too. And now the Staggering Merman is a perch for that angel-man, who comes to sit on his head and crap so that I have to wipe it carefully, amazed by the little mouse skulls, seeds, birds' claws in the feathered man's droppings, all of which has to be worked loose bit by bit, and cleaned and painted over with cow's piss so that the fish-man just gets more deeply bronzed than ever in the harsh sun.

But the merman is definitely Father; see how he runs; see how he's taking flight and turning himself away, aiming that way, turning his back on Yearsonend. Father Thin Air. Jonty sat on his folding stool in front of the sculpture. 'Yes, Father Fuckoff,' he sometimes muttered to the sculpture, and, 'Mama Mournful,' when he saw something of Lettie Pistorius in the soft lines of a body seeking sanctuary, of gestures too tentative for this world. 'Yes, look, there, the one hip and shoulder, that soft, painful line: the little Mother of Despair.'

It was when he was maudlin, deep in his cups – especially when he drank brandy and dagga tea too soon after each other, to take away his anxiety about the unformed wood under his hands – that Jonty sat and stared like this at the Staggering Merman. Then he'd get down to work on the wood again. A few days after he'd thrown away the failed sculpture of Ingi he'd put his new piece of wood on the trestles. An image had to emerge. He rolled it over, raised one end and weighed it in his hands. What was lurking inside? Today it was just a piece of wood. It smelt of forest and wind and sun – nothing more. He stripped off pieces of bark, and relished feeding them into the mouth of the wood stove. 'Burn, you bastards,' he said, as though the impulse to carve something from the stump would go up in smoke as the bark curled in the flames.

For Jonty, Ingi's arrival broke open so many things: all her questioning and nagging and observing. He still watched her constantly through the telescope. Every morning, at the same time, she emerged from the Drostdy avenue with her backpack, swinging her arms with gusto.

She'd brought with her so much of what Yearsonend had forgotten: lively curiosity – not the surly meddlesomeness of the Yearsonenders. No, it was a naïve questioning and probing, as if she found herself caught in a maze and had to question her way out, fiercely.

He watched her wave to the workers who leaned on their spades to gaze after her, gossiping among themselves about who and what she was; and how far she was going to get with 'that crazy Jonty Jack up there in Cave Gorge'.

Jonty watched her walk down Captain William Gird Road, stopping to pass the time of day with the stationmaster, as was her custom now. She would usually slip her bag off her shoulders and stand astride it, accepting a mug of coffee from him. Jonty watched the man in the black jacket gesticulate to Ingi and how she listened, nodding. Yes, thought Jonty, the story of Ingi Friedländer and the men of Yearsonend is another story. She has the knack, with that vulnerable air, those innocent questions . . .

Sometimes she made Jonty furious. But then again he knew those were genuine tears that filled her eyes whenever she heard a sad story about some Yearsonender; she laughed when a happy story was told. And, most importantly of all, her insistence on buying the sculpture was gentle and courteous. Almost like a butterfly wing against your palm, thought Jonty – gently, gently she persuades.

But then he'd berate himself for thinking of her in such romantic terms. Of course, she was still an artist herself, he knew, but one of those who'd gone astray in the city, getting snarled up in the responsibilities of arts administration. He knew what it was like with museums and art collections in this time of change and adjustment under the new government: endless meetings and piles of documents, ceaseless arguments about policy, budget cuts and affirmative action; a new bureaucracy, touting all kinds of new initiatives, but quickly becoming just as cumbersome and confusing as the previous phalanx of pen-pushers.

It was a deadly time for artists who often became involved in it all in spite of themselves. And Ingi was one of them – one of a new generation, fresh from university, determined to help with the transformation of society. Yes, thought Jonty ruefully, these days you don't join the liberation movement, you throw in your lot with the pen-pushers – that's all that's left of the struggle.

He took another sip of brandy. Fuck you too, he thought mournfully. He focused the telescope and saw Ingi walking away from the station, towards the Look Deep pub. It made him feel suddenly vulnerable and he took another swig. She was finding out more all over the place, he knew. About him. About his father Karel Thin Air. About his mother, Lettie Pistorius. About all the things that should be left unspoken and worked into sculptures instead. Because art can capture the past so much better than the writings of historians.

How can you ever comprehend a community like Yearsonend if you only look at dates and forced removals and statutes and facts? No, thought Jonty, raising his mug to the wind and the trees, to the mountain's rocky cliffs. No, come to my sculpture garden and there you'll find the true story. Look at how those clowns and gnarled half-breeds eye each other, those tree stumps one-eyed among stones, those pieces of tin and metal and ostrich feather, and plastic junk and scrap iron, and wood and paint, and kitsch and earnestness, and sadness and imperfection. Just come and walk through my garden of images and feel the wind on your shoulders and smell the sun on stone and know you are far from art journals and fashionable theories.

Come to my sculpture garden, and you will find the grief, the tears, the blood, yes: all those old-fashioned things – oh, I can't spell it out for you, God forgive me, I try to emulate the perfection of a Staggering Merman, I try night and day, look how I isolate myself here; I have nothing to show but dedication and honesty. He smiled sardonically: And my, how the brandy inspires me to pontificate about my art!

And isn't the story of Yearsonend also the artist's story? Didn't Mario Salviati revolt against myopia with his statue of the Blessed Virgin Mary? And before him: Titty X!am's people who drew on cave walls; and that Captain William Gird whose drawings hang in the palace; and Meerlust Bergh and his designer wife, Irene Lampak – in the fashion world of their time didn't they outstrip the old boundaries of line and interpretation, of grace and texture?

Yearsonend had its artists, yes. They'd always kicked over the traces of convention, so the story of Yearsonend was in a sense a tribute to its artists – those chroniclers of sorrow and mythology. Yes, the artists had left their mark on the landscape . . . and perhaps Ingi Friedländer will too. Who knows what she'll create?

Jonty rolled the piece of wood over and over on his lap and felt it pressing against his body. It fought against him, hard and mute, heavy as lead. He shoved it away, cursed, and went into the house. After fumbling around inside, he re-emerged. The stump of wood had rolled up against the Staggering Merman and Jonty studied the two pieces – the brilliant, charismatic merman, which kept drawing the eye, inexorably. And, at his feet, the raw log.

He drew his stool up to the telescope so that he could sit more comfortably, and focused the lens. Forget about Father Fuckoff and Mama Mournful, he told himself, watch that girl instead. Look at her beautiful breasts, so you can chisel them with your bare hands. And look at her face, carried high, with that Florentine nose, look at her hair streaming in the wind: Ingi!

He was still in love with her, Jonty Jack realised, and that was why he sat up here watching her. But he'd decided a long time ago, long before he came to live here, that love wasn't compatible with a life free of compromise. Love demands so much compromise that you lose yourself in it. Love demands the kind of sacrifice that thwarts the essentials for creativity – impulsiveness and selfishness. You must choose, Jonty had decided many years ago: love or art.

So consciously he built up his resistance to the smell of Ingi's sweat when she came up Cave Gorge and appeared with rosy cheeks in front of his house. Perhaps she'd come again today. He knew he could charm her. He'd captivate her with conversation and seduce her during mountain walks. He'd invoke her suppressed creativity and encourage her to blossom. He'd take her hand in his, drawing imaginary lines, or ask her to look through his eyes at the colours and textures she had long forgotten.

From the way she spoke and looked, he knew she was ready to fall in love: with a man, or a group of people, or a town and a past. Ingi Friedländer, he realised, yearned for belonging and sanctuary. She was looking for a homeland, and in her nosy probing was an anxious questioning of the right of abode. Could she be at home here? What did the town and its history have to tell her? What lessons could she learn here, infatuated with life as she was?

Jonty smiled as he saw her slip into the shade of the roof in front of the pub. She was going in to talk to Look Deep, that incorrigible gossipmonger. He knew it. And he, Jonty, felt bereft. Jealous! he thought, turning back to the Staggering Merman and the piece of wood at his feet.

Stick to your stumps, Jonty, he admonished himself.

4

'Water, gold and feathers,' said Meerlust Bergh, that afternoon in 1901 to the redbearded field cornet opposite him. They sat in the study of the Feather Palace, drinking brandy from showy Boland goblets, twirling the liquid round and round as they sparred. 'These will always be the three main motifs in Yearsonend.'

Field Cornet Pistorius watched in surprise as Meerlust unbuckled his artificial ivory leg and had a servant bring a wooden peg closer. 'This one,' Meerlust indicated, with a smile, as he fastened the wooden leg and the servant stored the ivory leg in a special case, 'is more comfortable than that elephant's tusk. I wear the ivory when I go out. It just makes a better show.' Then he raised his brandy glass high and cried, 'Cheers!'

The field cornet nodded and looked around him. The house was exceptional for this part of the world. It resembled the pretentious homesteads of the wine farms of the south-west Cape. And the furnishings and décor were unusual. That chest, for instance, certainly didn't originate in this country, Pistorius thought. He reflected bitterly: While we were fighting the British in the northern republics and our children and wives were dying in concentration camps, these bastards were swilling brandy in the Colony.

But before the old bitterness could get the better of him, he was overcome with weariness and the dull, gnawing feeling that it was all in vain: the unending trek over the landscape, the stock they sometimes had to steal when they were ravenously hungry, the struggle to build rafts on which to float the wagon over rivers during the rainy season, the perpetual watchfulness for turncoats and Empire loyalists – and, of course, Siela on the back of the ox; Siela Everyman's Wife, as the others began to call her.

And, all the time, the feeling in his stomach that reminded him the little finger was still there, undigested, lying in his gut like a blob of bitter gall, and that it would always be there as a punishment for the day he turned his back on the Christian God and sought the aid of a black witch-doctor.

Oh, how many nights had he lain beside the ox-wagon wondering about the little boy whose hand it was. An exquisitely delicate hand, looking almost alive there amid the grains of salt before he wrapped it in a rock rabbit's skin and took it to the sangoma.

'You must be very tired, Field Cornet,' said Meerlust Bergh to him then.

'No, no. I'm just thinking about my men outside.'

'They're being taken care of.' Meerlust poured another shot of brandy for each of them. As the grandfather clock struck the hour he continued, 'We'll always covet water.' He looked at the quiet, obviously moody man in front of him and decided to tease him. 'Now you've kindly brought us gold, and the ostrich industry will undoubtedly develop after the war.' But the field cornet didn't smile, just sat staring into his glass.

'What was your trade before the war, Field Cornet?'

'Jurisprudence. I had to give up my practice when the British invaded.'

'Oh!'

'My men . . .'

'Yes, I can offer you all hospitality, and as for the ox-wagon . . .'

'The ox-wagon cannot stay here at Yearsonend or remain in your yard. It must be hidden.'

The field cornet saw Meerlust's eyelids flicker. His experience as a man of law warned him: beware. He stood up. 'The gold must be guarded; the children's hands must be buried.'

Pistorius downed his brandy. He looked out through the window. The black ox-wagon stood under the large oak trees in front of the buildings and the men lounged on the lawn under the trees. The servants had brought them food and drink and it looked like a communion picnic. Where was Siela Pedi? he wondered. Then he turned back to Meerlust. 'The gold must be kept safe.'

'There's a cave in the mountain. No one ever goes there. It's big enough for the wagon and a span of oxen. Or the oxen can stay in my kraal once we've got the wagon up there. When we've eaten, we can yoke the oxen and saddle up and then . . .'

'Now. It must happen now.'

'But first, let's calmly . . .'

'There's no time for calm while women and children are dying . . .'

The field cornet heard indignation in the sound of the peg leg on the wooden floor as Meerlust grabbed his plumed hat, swept it flamboyantly on to his head and went outside. He's full of swagger, thought Pistorius. How did he make his money? Just look at the furniture! An establishment like this, with a garden too, in this part of the world?

The settlements they encountered had become progressively poorer, he'd noticed, as the black ox-wagon moved deeper into the Karoo. There were few farms with a homestead to match this. He watched how Meerlust stood on the veranda, called to his workers and gave them instructions to bring back the oxen and yoke them to the wagon. 'You take a horse,' he said to one worker, 'and fetch the black wagon's maid. She's at Field Cornet Moloi's place.'

Then Pistorius understood where Siela Pedi was, and he realised that they were making one mistake after another. Not once during the past year – or was it longer? – had they ridden so trustingly into a town and accepted hospitality without questioning it. They had been always on their guard.

He looked at his men, who got slowly to their feet and knocked the dust off their hats. We've come to the end of the line, he realised. We've transgressed in ways we'd never have contemplated in our former lives. God forgive us, look what they've come to, look at their eyes: here, among normal people, we're unable to look anyone in the eye. We've come too far. This was a mad undertaking, conceived in the insanity and desperation of war. We must bury the gold in a secret place, rather than risk dragging it through the country any further; we cannot keep running like this.

But, at the same time, there is no one we can trust, he thought. Who is this man with the wooden leg and the black field cornet at his side? Since when was it possible for a black man to become a field cornet?

But they'd been told along the way: When you get to Yearsonend, ask for Meerlust Bergh, the man with the wooden leg, and for Moloi the black field cornet.

And when they'd arrived exhausted at a farm on the Plains of Melancholy a week earlier, the farmer had sent his son ahead on horseback to warn Meerlust that the black ox-wagon was on its way and to tell him that the men looked like death. They won't be able to carry on much longer, said the message, find them shelter. Redbeard only heard about this later.

But whom can you trust?

'Taljaard is the man who could have helped,' said Meerlust, when Pistorius came out to join him on the veranda.

'Taljaard?'

'The general.'

'General Taljaard! But he was shipped off to the prisoner of war camp on St Helena!'

Meerlust laughed and shook his head. 'The old geezer and two men jumped overboard as the ship sailed past Robben Island. The lepers there helped them to build a raft. While the British reported in Cape Town's newspapers that General Taljaard had drowned during a foolhardy escape attempt, he was riding on the waves towards the beach at Blouberg. The two men – both from Bloemfontein – fell foul of sharks, but the general survived and made his way over here. He shaved off his beard, dyed his hair, began to wear glasses and bought the old Drostdy under a false name.'

'And where is he now?'

'He's leading the Cape rebels in this region. They went west a week ago to stop the building of the blockhouses. The British want to set up a series of blockhouses right across the Cape Colony. The general left here with sixteen dynamite sticks and a few young hotheads. Watch the newspapers.'

I could stay here, thought Pistorius, and join the Taljaard rebels. There's no longer any sense in trekking with the gold reserves. From Meerlust's veranda, he looked out over the fields and further on to the rooftops and trees of Yearsonend, and then to the high mountain beyond the town.

Meerlust followed his gaze. 'Mount Improbable,' he said. 'The cave is there. Are your men ready?'

'No,' said Pistorius suddenly. 'We must wait until dark.' He didn't wait for Meerlust's answer, but walked down the veranda steps and summoned his men.

As he stood talking to them, they formed a tight, subdued circle around him, with Meerlust watching from the veranda. His peg leg tap-tapped impatiently on the veranda floor. A fanatic, he thought, as he watched Pistorius. And a band of strays.

5

Ingi Friedländer could no longer bear to think of the silent black cave Dumb Eyetie inhabited. She sat at the Drostdy breakfast table with a fax she'd typed on her laptop. Opposite her, the general was engrossed in his naval maps. He'd received a report that a gale-force wind on the west coast near Paternoster had shifted a sand gully and that divers had noticed distinct signs of a long-buried galleon sunk in the sand.

The matron, with the help of the servants, had already brought in steaming dishes of scrambled eggs, kidneys, cooked tomatoes, pork sausages and bacon. Alexander slavered on the arm the general was using to eat and page through documents at the same time.

The matron sat down and looked up at Ingi. Her eyes are quite transparent, thought Ingi, and she hardly ever shows any emotion. Except after visitations from the angel – then she was animated, even transported, and for days afterwards she'd supervise the baking of cakes for the poor people of Edenville. After a while the fancy left her, and she became calm and serene, occupying herself with the care and organisation needed for the smooth running of the big household.

'I'm going to take Mr Salviati out for a stroll today,' Ingi announced, after holding her breath as she plucked up her courage.

The general's head snapped round. He looked at her over his half-moon spectacles. 'Who?'

'I'm going to take Mr Salviati for a walk. Alexander and myself. And Stella.' Ingi looked at the dog for support, but the animal kept his eyes fixed on the general's plate as if his only loyalty was to food.

'But that's a crazy undertaking!' The general pushed away his documents angrily. 'The man cannot hear or see. It's all the same to him wherever he sits daydreaming. He'll gain nothing from an outing.'

'I'm sure it'll do him good.'

'The strange smells in town might upset him,' the matron ventured, softly. 'He's so used to things here.' Dreamily she chanted, 'At the fountain, dripping; at the parrots, smelling; at the vine leaves, feeling.' She rocked back and forth, only stopping when the general put his hand on her shoulder.

'You're keeping him prisoner. He sits here day after day and he can never leave the Drostdy.'

'It's his choice,' growled the general. 'He's been living like this for years.'

'Why do you keep him here?' Ingi looked directly at the matron. Maybe the woman would give her a straight answer.

The matron shook her head, brushed back the hair that had escaped from her bun, and sighed heavily, as if she had shored up the information inside herself for too long, through too many tiresome years. She looked at the ceiling as she talked, as if the information didn't come from her, as if she wished to deny that she was passing it on, even as she said it: 'He knows where the gold is.'

The general thumped the table with the flat of his hand. Alexander jerked his head away so quickly that he left a strand of saliva quivering in the air. The matron fled from the room. They heard her bedroom door slam.

Ingi stared at the general. 'The gold?' The old man's jaw muscles were working and she knew that he was restraining his mighty temper. Then the throbbing of the artery at his right temple subsided. He breathed deeply, obviously fighting to control himself. Then he looked at Ingi and placed his hand over hers. Briefly, she had a vision: my hand is a rabbit and a Great Dane has lain on it and smothered it to death. She wanted to pull it out from beneath his warm palm, but couldn't. 'Miss Friedländer,' he began quietly, 'what you don't realise is that Mr Salviati is my father-in-law. He's her . . .' and he indicated with his head '. . . father.'

The general waited for Ingi to absorb this news. Why has no one told me this before? she wondered. But before she could ask, he continued, 'Mr Salviati has lived a hard life. Our people aren't sympathetic to foreigners. In addition, he was a prisoner of war. And a Catholic. As you know, people are wary of the Catholic Threat. He was beset by a series of unforeseen circumstances. He's earned the rest that we can offer him here at the old Drostdy during his last years.'

Ingi tried to pull away her hand again, but the pressure of his had cut off the circulation to her fingers. She stared straight into the general's eyes. She had never been able to tolerate injustice. You can mislead and upset me with your stories, she thought, but what's right is right. If I'm the only person who can help that poor imprisoned soul, then I'll do it.

'You keep him here like a convict,' she hissed through her teeth. He didn't answer, but the pressure on her hand increased. 'I'm going to help him.' Ingi moved her face closer to the general's: she could smell his breath. It smelt the same as the odour of his bedroom: the four-poster bed with the mosquito net draped across it, the huge dog baskets he'd had woven for the Great Danes, the musty maps and the smell of gun oil and Brasso.

She looked over the general's shoulder and shouted, 'But, Matron!' When the old man started and looked around, releasing the pressure of his hand, she snatched her hand out from under his and grimaced at him. The she grabbed the fax, which she'd hoped to be able to send on his fax machine, crumpled it up and marched out of the room. At the door she turned. The old man sat with his back to her, his large head slightly tilted. She looked at the profile: the heavy, crooked nose, the grey hair curling behind the ear, the red ear-lobe and the crinkled artery against his temple.

'Wars,' she hissed, 'do that to people like you.'

Then she went to the kitchen in her town shoes, which she'd put on that morning to feel different, to walk in the passages and reception rooms of the Drostdy, to pace over the terracotta paving of the courtyard. When she'd woken, something had made her feel like a townie on a journey; she wanted to dress inappropriately for this remote town; she wanted to look out of place. It would confirm her independence and show that she was not prepared to fall into their ways.

But now she went to her bedroom and changed into more comfortable clothes. She threw down the fax and thought: It can wait. Back into the walking boots, which she carefully laced, the chirpy T-shirt advertising Cape Town's mountain and sea, the small rucksack and the sun-protection cream.

For the first time since her arrival, she picked up her mobile phone and switched it on, but to her disappointment the little screen showed that she was still outside the network's reception area. Maybe I should climb to the top of Mount Improbable, she thought, and try to contact normal people from up there. It's those high cliffs that block the signals.

Once she was dressed, she stood for a moment listening to the general's booming voice. She heard the matron's distressed answer, and suddenly imagined she heard something Italian in the cadence of the woman's voice. She had no idea what they were shouting at one another. They were behind closed doors, and the high ceilings and thick stone walls only carried the sounds of their arguing to her.

She hurried outside, through the kitchen. There was Princess Moloi, the pertly pretty girl who, she'd heard, was the mayor's daughter, chattering to the parrots in the sunshine. She was teaching them to speak Xhosa, the other servants always teased, laughing at her. Now Ingi walked quickly towards her.

'Is the old man the matron's father?' she asked abruptly. For a moment, Princess was startled by the directness of the question. She, too, seemed to feel it was something that shouldn't be spoken of. She turned and fled indoors, to where Ingi could hear the matron's long, shuddering, wrenching sobs.

She looked around and saw Dumb Eyetie standing at the parrot cage. He had pushed his arm through the wire mesh and his cupped hand was full of wheat. The breeding birds, which stayed in their nesting boxes rather than clambering around on the vine-laden trellis with the others, came one by one to peck the grain out of his hand. Now and then he bent down to the full bucket beside him, pushed his hand deep into the wheat as if it were water, then withdrew it again.

He became aware of her while she was still walking towards him, and turned his head a little. She waited until the parrots had all finished eating and he'd turned round. Alexander was also there, and the Great Dane watched both Ingi and the old man. Ingi stretched out her hand to Dumb Eyetie, carefully and softly, and touched his cheek with her fingers. She brushed his face very softly, but his head jerked back as if she'd slapped him. The parrots on the vines screeched and clambered to the furthest corners of the pergola, the peacocks flapped over the roof to land under the trees behind the house, and Alexander and Stella fled into the kitchen.

I've broken some taboo, Ingi realised, something that set everything in motion – even the animals perceive it as a transgression. It had probably been years, she realised, since anyone had touched the old man. As an untouchable he'd existed in the small living space of his bedroom and the courtyard, sometimes taking a short stroll under the trees with his nervous hand on Alexander's back, and always keeping to within smelling distance of the house.

His nostrils were dilated; he stood huddled. Then she reached down and took the hand that always held the stone. She carefully opened the fingers to take the stone out of his hand. But then she saw that his skin had grown over the stone. It sat in the palm of his hand as if he had been born with it. Ingi took the other hand and moved closer. She brought his hand lightly to her face, brushed it over her cheeks and forehead and her hair. Slowly, without expression, the old man began to move his own hand. Carefully he felt her nose and mouth and eyelids. He fiddled with her ear and brushed his fingers through her hair. Ingi closed her eyes and heard the fountain murmur and the peacocks complain under the trees. She smelt the old man's musty body while his fingers eagerly explored her face and throat.

Then a great sigh coursed through him and he let his hand fall. She took the hand in hers and began to walk. Alexander slipped in under Dumb Eyetie's other hand. They walked towards the gateway that led outside. Suddenly Dumb Eyetie stopped. Ingi looked around. The general appeared at an open window. Dumb Eyetie's face was turned towards the general. He sensed the general's presence before I saw him, Ingi realised.

The general looked at them. He took a matchbox from his pocket and lit a match. The old Italian started when he caught the smell of the match. He wanted to pull back to his bedroom, but Ingi held his hand tightly. 'You can control him with a match,' thundered the general. 'Remember that if he tries to run away.' Then he pulled the shutters closed.

Ingi began to walk with the old Italian, through the gateway, out from beneath the trees, past the sprinklers, which sprayed long arcs of water over the lawns, under the oak trees with the crooning doves and down into the fir tree avenue. After a while he fell into step with her. And so they walked, linked, with the dog slinking along guiltily beside them.

6

Jonty Jack was busy oiling the Staggering Merman. He rubbed the smooth-whittled wooden fins and arched muscles, the curves, furrows and crannies with a flannel cloth and the oil mixture made from a recipe given to him by that lunatic woodworker-genius from Zimbabwe, the black man with the lynx hat.

The sculpture glowed in the early-morning sun. It was as if it grew with each polishing, as if it possessed an inner life and energy that shone more distinctly in the morning light. When you touched the wood, you felt energy pulsing under the palm of your hand.

The sharp smell of the oil – which also contained a good dose of cow urine because the wood absorbed the salts which made it hard and shiny – mixed with the scent of wood shavings wet with dew. When Jonty worked with the Staggering Merman like this, the smell made him lightheaded and gave him courage to tackle the new sculptures that were yet to be created. It was the smell of possibilities, he thought, taking another sip of dagga tea.

He turned to the old telescope. It always came in handy. From up above, he was often the first Yearsonender to see a new visitor standing on the platform, suitcase in hand, as the train wove its way through the brown hills. He was the first to see a strange car approach from the south-west, with its dusty paintwork, carrying passengers who might climb out under a tree in one of the roads, looking around in vain for a McDonald's or some other restaurant.

He had inherited the telescope from his grandfather, Field Cornet Redbeard Pistorius, who'd used the instrument to scan the hills in search of empire loyalists and turncoats while the black ox-wagon trundled slowly across the landscape. Now, through the same telescope, Jonty Jack spotted the odd threesome emerging from under the trees near the Drostdy, then walking down William Gird Road towards the station.

At first he thought his eyes were playing tricks on him, but it was Ingi, and she was with Mario Salviati! And one of General Taljaard's Great Danes; yes, it was the male, Alexander. There they were, walking along down the road, somewhat stiffly and close together as if they were afraid of the big open landscape around them.

The long brass telescope was reputed to have been sent to President Kruger by the Tsar of Russia as part of his aid to the Boer forces and it carried the ZAR stamp of the old Zuid Afrikaansche Republic. When Jonty drew it out and let it rest on the forked stick, he often thought back to his grandfather.

Redbeard had been a bad-tempered man, Jonty remembered, a man who got stuck in Yearsonend although he really didn't belong there. When he, Jonty, was a baby, when the shiny lightning water ran through the town's furrows while Big Karel was on the run somewhere or lay dead, it was Field Cornet Pistorius who had looked after his daughter Lettie and her young son.

He bought them a small house, one of those little Karoo houses that front right on to the pavement, with a veranda and backyard and cement floors, in what was later called Eviction Road, between the practice and the 'eviction houses' themselves. These were the houses occupied by thirteen brown families who would subsequently have to move to Edenville, fifty years after the Boer War, after D. F. Malan and the apartheid government came into power.

Attorney Pistorius, old and decrepit but officially still practising with his son, Lettie's brother, nailed shut the doors and windows of Big Karel Bergh's posh house after he'd ensured that Lettie had taken only necessities and brought them to her new small house.

The field cornet had definite plans for his daughter. Lettie had to get away from Big Karel's influence, which still haunted their old house, said Grandpa Pistorius; she had to forget about her marriage to the Runaway, the Big Talker and Showman, the half-breed, Karel Bergh, son of the Indonesian model and that rich bastard Meerlust Bergh with his collection of artificial legs: one for each occasion, even a special one, according to rumour, for love-making – a limb inlaid with rubies and silver filigree work, Zulu beads, with lewd images worked on the calf and a diamond on the shin.

The idea made Jonty smile. A Meerlust totem will still come, he thought, a large sculpture of wood or stone, with a cheeky feather in the hat, and that leg, covered with small relief figures and mocking slogans.

It was really against her will that Lettie had come to live close to her brother's practice with her baby son. 'He's a brat of a child,' said Field Cornet Pistorius disapprovingly. 'Obviously not a farmer or a lawyer or a soldier.'

Indeed, little Jonty was always playing with the clay he found next to one of the many irrigation channels through which his father's water flowed – as if he found his father in the wet earth he fondled and modelled.

He often went for a walk with his grandfather on Sundays. The old man was already grey, but his beard was still red. Walking beside him holding his hand, the little boy's flaming red hair glowed during their wanderings through the streets of

Yearsonend – wanderings that always led them to Little Hands, the monument near Lampak's Dam.

His grandfather would pause there for a long time with his head bowed, Jonty remembered, as he watched Ingi's slow threesome swing off in the direction of the Look Deep pub. And after his grandfather had paid his respects, they would walk on to Lampak's Dam, named after Irene Lampak, who liked to bathe there in the old days.

Then Attorney Pistorius would sit and watch the naked boy jumping into the water, again and again, playing as happily as a fish.

One day remained vividly etched on Jonty's mind – it had inspired one of the works in his sculpture garden, though he was the only one who understood the reference. He'd been swimming in the dam while his grandfather sat on a stone near the windmill. Granny Siela Pedi arrived on foot. From the water Jonty noticed the woman before his grandfather saw her. He began to tread water and, with his hands on the cement dam wall, he floated and waited.

From his earliest childhood he'd heard stories from the children of Eviction Road; and he'd picked up snippets when the grown-ups talked in whispers. He knew that there was a bond between his grandfather and the woman, but he didn't know what it involved – only that it was a union of secrecy and shame.

That was why he kept as still as possible in the water, moving his legs very slowly, while his grandfather sat on his stone, absentmindedly sucking his pipe and staring out over the ridges, and Granny Siela Pedi came walking out of a mirage of shimmering heat. She limped slightly, old age had made her crooked, and she wore black, for she never, ever wore any other colour.

She was in perpetual mourning, the people of Edenville said, for her people in Pedi to whom she could never return in this life because of her shame, and her sorrowful time on the back of the ox, and everything she had lost and given up during the war.

To this day Jonty didn't know whether Granny Siela had planned the meeting. But he knew it was a Sunday, and that he and his grandfather went walking every Sunday. Granny Siela must have known of this routine.

Jonty saw Ingi and Dumb Eyetie and the Great Dane stop for a second in front of the Look Deep pub, hovering around one another indecisively, the old man shuffling on blind feet and the dog with its tail between its legs. Then a decision was obviously reached and Ingi led them up the steps.

They disappeared on to the veranda, swallowed up by shadow, and in his imagination Jonty heard the bar's door screech open then swing closed. The old general's Plymouth came gliding out from under the Drostdy's trees and crawled slowly through the streets. The general seemed to be driving aimlessly, up and down, in second gear.

Granny Siela had appeared out of the heat, her black shoes coloured white by the dust. She walked briskly for her age, and her ankles were also white with dust. Jonty trod water, his eyes peeping over the edge of the dam wall. He saw how Grandpa Pistorius looked up and how the pipe fell out of his mouth. As he bent to pick it up, Granny Siela Pedi stopped next to him.

As children do, Jonty forgot the most important part; he couldn't remember the words they exchanged, whether it was an angry discussion or a soothing reconciliation; he only knew that his body grew cold and his arms went stiff from staying under the water and his fingers turned blue as he hung on to the dam wall. Then his grandfather suddenly remembered him – 'Why is everything so quiet in the water? Oh, God, the child!' – and the two old people pulled him out of the water and made him sit in the sun, shivering, with blue lips and the water streaming out of his hair and into his eyes and the landscape spinning before him. Then there were a few last words, and something Jonty would never forget: in a time when physical contact between white and black was confined to that between nursemaid and child, or between a trusted house servant and housewife, Granny Siela Pedi rested her dark hand on Grandpa Pistorius's cheek, against his white beard, for just a moment. Then she swung round and walked away down the dusty path in her black clothes; he remembered the scuff-scuff of her feet on the ground.

Then Attorney Pistorius turned around, and there were tears running into his beard, and he bent over near the windmill, his body shuddering as he vomited.

When Jonty was older he heard the story that his grandfather had vomited out the sins of his past that Sunday morning. What he actually remembered was going nearer, worried about the old man whose body was jerking with spasms, and seeing that, with the final heave of his stomach, Field Cornet Pistorius brought up a child's little finger. The old man hastily dug a little hole with a stick and buried the finger, as though he were concealing a murder.

His grandchild watched him, shivering at first but gradually relaxing as the sun caressed his shoulders like a trusted hand, and the doves started crooning again and the windmill turned slowly and the afternoon sounds of Yearsonend came floating towards them on the breeze: children playing, dogs barking excitedly, cows lowing and also the sound of the stones singing, as the old people always said. That was the silence of the Karoo – you hear nothing, but even so, there *is* a sound. It's not the wind, nor the cicadas, for they're silent now: it's the stones, singing.

Jonty straightened up from the telescope stiffly. In his memory the old man took the boy's hand and started to walk slowly homeward. I never knew a father, thought Jonty. My father disappeared into thin air with the lightning water; my mother always felt abandoned and tearful. The person who came closest to giving me a sense of belonging was that obnoxious grandpa of mine, the Red Transvaler, the man with the secret, which never was a secret because Yearsonend's stories are carried forward by the wind, from yard to yard, from doorstep to doorstep, from year to year.

7

'Yes, Jonty Jack often comes past here,' the barman, Look Deep Pitrelli, told Ingi, 'on his way to the cow byres at the smallholdings, there below the Drostdy, to fetch cow piss. Every evening at milking time he scoops a bucketful from the drain in the milking-shed. It's to coat his wooden statues. It makes the wood shiny and as hard as glass. The Xhosa fighters used to do the same to their assegai shafts in the old days.'

The man leaned towards her, his elbows on the bar counter. He still spoke with the accent he'd picked up from his Italian father, the interpreter. 'But some people say he pees on the statues himself every day.' Look Deep tossed his white cloth over his shoulder. 'Artists, you know.' He shrugged meaningfully. 'We Yearsonenders know all about artists.'

Ingi nodded. She didn't like this man and his compulsive gossiping, but he was a valuable source of information. Although the sign 'Men's Bar' still hung above the door, he never seemed to mind her coming here. On the contrary, it was obvious that he enjoyed her visits and her receptive ear.

He'd already told her about his father, the drunken Italian waiter who'd been dragooned into accompanying the prisoners of war into the hinterland on the train. 'My poor father got it wrong,' he said, in his singing accent. 'He'd thought the train was going right up Africa to the north. He was homesick and he thought the train was taking the young men back to Italy.'

Look Deep Pitrelli rubbed over the damp circles on the bar counter and looked at Ingi and Dumb Eyetie and the dog lying in the corner. He opened early in the morning, more out of boredom than anything else, and usually had to wait until about ten before the first regular settled in under the sign with the arrow – it was usually ancient Old Sheriff from Eviction Road, a quiet man who sat drinking, day after day, and never referred to the time when the water refused to run and he was blinded by the heliograph flashes.

It was a pleasant surprise to have the odd trio arrive that morning. First the dog's huge suspicious head peering round the screen door, then the girl with those lovely breasts swelling under the T-shirt with Table Mountain on it, a sight which already had all the men in town in a lather; and then, holding her hand, his nose wrinkling as he sniffed and tried to work out where he was, one of the old prisoners of war, Salviati, the blind-and-deaf mute.

Look Deep realised: This is a special day. The old man never went out, and here he was allowing himself to be led around by the young woman. And the general's dog, who didn't like anyone but the old Italian and the general himself, he was here too. Look Deep poured long beers and watched Ingi settle the old man into a seat. She took the beer mug and folded Mario Salviati's hands around it, dipped her little finger into the froth and put it to his lips.

He watched the old man lick her little finger and half turn his face to her when Ingi took away her hand, how he leaned slightly towards her. Then he raised the beer mug to his mouth and drank deep and long, so that the froth trickled down over his chin on to the counter, and Ingi watched and smiled and the dog lifted his head and gave a little bark. Outside, the Plymouth drove slowly past, shortly followed by Mayor Moloi's Mercedes with its tinted windows. As if the two cars were patrolling the territory, wary of the intrusion of a girl from Cape Town, as if they were watching and weighing up; throbbing, vigilant engines, not just gliding casually round corners but making their presence known deliberately, slowly.

Ingi lifted her beer and her cheeks began to glow. Look Deep poured his first beer of the day – a long one out of the vat, with thick froth, just the way he liked it – and outside the sun beat down murderously. Ingi began to massage the Italian's neck muscles gently, and he groaned like an old dog. Alexander moved closer, jealous, and rested his head on her thigh, so she laughed and stroked him too.

Ingi and Look Deep grinned, and Look Deep proffered more about the people of Yearsonend. She was especially interested in Jonty Jack's family, in Lettie Pistorius and Big Karel Bergh, in the grandfather who'd ridden as field cornet with the black ox-wagon, and in the family connections between the Berghs and the Molois who, according to tradition, shared the same forebears: Ensign Moloi, the legendary free slave and officer of the Fourth Ship, and Titty X!am, the San girl who loved to perform her shuffling dances by the light of the full moon, her ostrich-egg beads around her ankles.

Look Deep didn't know much about the hazy past, but he could tell her about Jonty Jack, the man who'd withdrawn from the daily life of Yearsonend, the artist of the mountain, the one who first saw a sculpture – and here Look Deep Pitrelli pointed at Mario Salviati – the day his mother, Lettie Pistorius, took him to see the statue of the Blessed Virgin Mary on Mount Improbable.

The redheaded child broke out in goosepimples, Look Deep told Ingi, and from then on Jonty Jack was hopelessly addicted to mankind's greatest sin: the imitation of God, by the making of graven images. Many people around there, said Look Deep, believed that the Almighty would never forgive Jonty because he'd made likenesses of God and His creation, even though the Bible's commandment forbade it.

And the people said, he gossiped on to Ingi as he wiped imaginary dregs from the bar counter, polished and rearranged glasses, and simultaneously kept an eye on the window so that nothing happening outside would escape his notice, people said that Field Cornet Pistorius' punishment had been passed on to Jonty Jack in the form of craziness and artistic inspiration; an infatuation with images and shapes and all sorts of unfathomable things . . .

He leaned towards Ingi and said: 'Do you know, Miss? They say there's a place in the mountain where he's laid out a devil's garden, with all sorts of likenesses and lewd things; sculptures of devilish birds and sangoma dreams . . .'

Look Deep was so agitated that his eyes pulled into a squint. This is a man who lives his days, she thought, amid all sorts of drunken stories, seldom getting out to test things or to weigh them against reality.

'Devilish birds?' she asked.

'Yes,' nodded Look Deep. 'Take this new story about the Staggering Merman, the statue that sprung up out of the ground. With respect, Miss, I heard the art gallery had sent you here because of that sculpture. But the people of Yearsonend think it's a statue born of idolatry, that it came up like a toadstool. One morning it was suddenly there, a toadstool from the devil.'

It was the sangoma who bewitched Field Cornet Pistorius, Ingi heard from Look Deep and everywhere else she went; it was the old Xhosa woman who cursed the black ox-wagon. The curse rested on Pistorius' descendants, and Jonty was one of them, everyone knew that, and the people said the black ox-wagon could still be seen on moonlit nights, lumbering across the plains.

Only the week before, the wagon had been spotted on the far side of Rocky Plains, on the Washout side of the Plains of Melancholy. It trekked on with that load of gold and Little Hands and it could never stop or rest; it was like the Flying Dutchman or the Fourth Ship, which went down again every month at new moon with the same anguish and screams and drownings. It's the same gold always reburied, always soaked in blood, always sinking under the sea to be covered by driftsand. That's why the general never dies: it's the hunger and sorrow of years of unresolved misdeeds . . .

Ingi looked at the sweaty red face in front of her, the slightly squinting eyes and the stained white apron. Whenever he disappeared behind the partition, she thought, he takes a nip of brandy: I can smell it on his breath. She looked at the coarse hair on his hands and she thought: No wonder Jonty Jack stays up there in the mountain, no wonder he's turned his back on this bunch of inbred idiots following all their old habits as if nothing had ever changed.

'Give Mr Salviati another beer, please,' she said, if only to stem the flood of words from Look Deep's mouth, 'or, better still, bring a whole lot of different drinks for him to smell so he can show us what he'd like to drink.'

Look Deep lined up open bottles in front of the old man: Cognac, whisky, liqueurs, dessert wine, white wines and red wines, sherry and port. He enjoyed the game.

Ingi took the old man's hand and let him feel the bottles in front of him. Then, one by one, she held the bottles under his nose. As always, Salviati's face was immobile. He appeared to understand what was expected of him, and after a few moments of hesitation the stone in the palm of his hand clinked against a bottle of grappa.

Ingi and Mario Salviati were slightly tipsy when they finally left the pub with Alexander the Great Dane, while the barman stood in the shadows of the veranda and waved them goodbye, and their morning shadows stretched out before them over the dust road as they sauntered towards Giraffe Corner, then to Eviction Road and Blood Tree. Finally they took the contour path and started to climb slowly up into Cave Gorge.

At the concertina gate Ingi let the old man's hands glide over the droppers, the sneezewood straining-post and the rusty wire. She watched his fingers see and hear, and his head turned towards the wind that blew from Cave Gorge carrying the smell of Mount Improbable's plants and secret places. She saw him breathe in deeply and fill the broad barrel of his chest with air, and she noted how determinedly the old legs took on the challenge of the mountain.

8

He couldn't tell what she looked like, but her smell was the fragrance of young women round a fountain in a forgotten city. Yes, Florence. The city's red roofs had become redder in his dreams over the past years, and lovely stone streets had become labyrinths of anxiety there in the courtyard, with the water beneath his palm, with the parrots who pecked at his hand with small pricks of pain, so that sometimes there was a wetness between his fingers and the salty taste of what he thought might be blood when he brought his hand to his mouth.

But it might also be parrot piss, he often thought, it might be anything. How many people are there around me, staring at me, stalking me? When are they finally going to drag me up the mountain, tie me to the Holy Virgin and execute me with those guns smeared with the gun oil I can smell?

Why does no one take my hand any more? I sit and I dream of stone: first rough-hewn, serrated in places, ripped out of the earth. Damp, with bits of earth that broke out with it, maybe fine plant roots that still cling, or a spider that spun a web between the rock and a bush, still sitting there like a dot of soot you crush before rolling the stone over and feeling the ridges to see where it might split and whether it would withstand the chisel's crude point.

Soft, hard stone: I smell your burning as the fire in you complains because I want to tame you; I smell in you the lava and the eruptions of long ago, when God was still dreaming man and woman into being, when you, older than all of us, were born here of materials as soft and as fluid as water. You were there at the beginning of all things, with your rough cheeks like the face of an old father, maybe God himself, maybe God as stone, as the quietness among us, nothing and everything, omnipresent, the ground beneath our feet.

But she came and wrapped her scents around me, like a scarf, woven of colours I had forgotten existed. She'd smelt pale pink, the soft pink of a sunset, the blue where water and sun meet in a flash of light, and her touch was as soft as a tongue, her breath like the wind, which blows autumnal yellow across the plain. I smell her bleeding: I know when she is in the red time; I smell her, the shy young woman who circles around me not knowing how it frightens me when people circle me like vultures around carrion and think I don't know they are there. But I feel, I feel how the breeze is blocked off, the temperature changes, the warmth of a body near to me, north-east, because I still have my sense of direction, as clear as a compass, thank God for that. I've just forgotten exactly how things look.

Do I remember correctly? The peacock that sometimes walks into me, fanning his tail feathers in fright. So many eyes in his tail! Are they laughing at me?

She touched my cheek. It burnt like fire, the touch of another person when you only have your own hands and they no longer want to touch your body because you don't know who's watching. Are you ever alone? Is something fidgeting in the corner of your bedroom, at the foot of the bed, at the closed door?

That one night, Mario Salviati, that mad night, old man, when you imagined you smelt parrot or peacock in your room, or ostrich, and you were certain you weren't alone and you strained your sense of touch and smell and first pulled the blanket over yourself then kicked it off and sprang up at the thing there in the corner.

It was a man's body, but it was covered in tough quill feathers, curved like those on an eagle's wing, and a big sinew that was neither an arm nor a proper wing, and a hard muscular chest but with soft down and a terrible smell like newly split rock, and it smelt like gunpowder or cinnamon. You wrestled with the thing: it was a big man or bird, a something that struck you with a steel wing and whose heart you could feel hammering under his ribs, and his wet breath, afraid, just like yours, against your cheek as you wrestled, rolling on the floor, over the bedstead. Then he dealt you a giant blow and you made a last grab and thought. God, they've sent a demon for my final undoing, they've sent a birdman down on to me to drive me completely mad.

And when he left, with a smell of fright and fart, and you lay sweating and puffing and groaning, holding the great feather you'd pulled out of the wing as you broke free, then you smelt your daughter, the quiet one, the one who wanted to be a nun, should have been a nun, who should have started a small Catholic school here, but the general led her astray, the man with the melted flesh where his left buttock should have been. He was naked, one day, as the men with guns cooled off in the dam and mockingly speculated about the flashwater, and his buttock looked like melted candlewax where the shrapnel from a cannon shot took away his flesh. Do her hands stroke that piece of molten flesh?

But she was there and he couldn't hear his own voice, but he thought he'd lain groaning on the floor beside his bed, with the long feather in his hand. He could smell the humidity of night on his daughter's clothes. He had to swallow his own bile, shuddering as he remembered the body of that bird-thing writhing against him, and she'd wrenched the long feather from his fingers. He could feel her breath racing as she helped him back into his bed and pulled the blanket up to his chin, stroking his head as he'd always stroked hers when she was little. That was the last time she had touched him.

She was the last one: her touch was a farewell. The beginning of death, he always thought, where nobody can ever touch you again; or perhaps, no, perhaps God was waiting; or maybe Mary, mother of all mothers, especially for those who'd lost their mothers; mother of touch and caressing peace.

And then the woman of the fragrances. She'd smelt like – how could he put it? – another place, yes, from afar, a little sweaty on the day of her arrival, a whiff of car seat. As time went on he'd grown accustomed to her smell and sometimes, when he thought no one was watching, he would station himself in the courtyard so he could breathe in the aroma that came from her bedroom.

It wafted out of her window, through the rampant bougainvillaea – he didn't know if it had purple or orange flowers – and he could tell exactly what she was doing, if she was in her bedroom or not, if she was brushing her hair, if she was pulling a dress over her head, if she was lying there under the sheets in the dusk and longing for a lover.

Mario Salviati knew all these things about Ingi Friedländer; he also knew how frightened she was of the general, and how stubborn she could be. He could smell the prickles of sweat when her scent was close by and the general's smell mingled with it; he could sniff out her fragrance of fear; and then he could smell how it changed slowly into anger; how she pulled herself together and straightened up in front of the old general, who sometimes came and stood close to Salviati with matches and put a gold coin into his hand then lit a match close to him.

Gold Pit

While Salviati's fingertips traced Kruger's head on the heavy coin, he felt the heat of the match against his cheek and the smell of sulphur and flame would drug him. Then the general brought it closer and blew it out lightly, mockingly. Then another match, and he retreated slowly over the paving until he was against the parrot cage and Alexander was around his legs, frightened and restless, and the general's breath smelt like garlic and brandy. The next match was even nearer to his face, and then his back was against the wire netting and he shook his head violently from side to side, no, no, no, and then he smelt the arrival of someone else.

It was the matron or a servant, and the scent of the match was blown away and the general plucked the gold coin from his hand and his smell swished angrily away.

He knew that the new woman tried to resist the general's power, but he didn't know why she was there. He just knew that she was different; that she did things the people of Yearsonend didn't normally do, that she broke old rules.

He also smelt on her, and felt it, that she was consciously making a stand; that it didn't come as naturally to her as she would have wished. He smelt her hesitation and her vacillation, but at the same time a youthful certainty, an attitude he'd forgotten.

Maria, he named her in his thoughts, while they walked on, beginning to perspire as the gravel path sloped upwards and big, loose stones and grass tufts made the going difficult. He knew what he smelt. He smelt the quarry that was dug here for stone and gravel for the lightning water channel. He'd recognised the concertina gate's straining-post and droppers when she put his hands on them; he knew this gorge and the scents that funnelled down from the rockfaces and the mountain peak.

He lifted his face to the heights and felt the big stone cliffs leaning above him, the scowling rockfaces, the dark holes, the clefts and the merciless heights of Mount Improbable, and he took the young woman more firmly by the elbow. He smelt the Great Dane's breath and his own sweat, and he felt like a young man, a young man striding out into life, as if everything still lay ahead of him and little behind; as if there was only anticipation.

He remembered youth; he felt it move in him again. He could become young again on the arm of this woman. He turned his head to her and his heart sang like a stone with water spilling over it; but he did not laugh, because he'd long since forgotten that he had a face.

9

Jonty Jack was painting the Staggering Merman with a brush when Ingi, Dumb Eyetie and the Great Dane came up through the trees, against a backdrop that looked like a painting: the roofs and chimneys of Yearsonend and the railway line that snaked off towards the curve of the earth.

The sculpture gleamed yellow-brown, because the cow urine that Jonty Jack was painting on again had already penetrated deep into the wood and given it the quality of a semi-precious stone.

He'd put away the telescope hurriedly when he saw that the three of them were on their way; he'd swept the blanket off the sculpture and fetched the bucket of urine, which he kept behind the house. Don't let them suspect that I watch them, he thought; and something in him wanted the young woman from the gallery to see his sculpture today.

The old man . . . well, he couldn't see. Jonty regretted that because he remembered his first sight of Salviati's Virgin Mary on Madonna's Peak many years ago. But for Salviati, the Staggering Merman would only be a smell now – the smell of cow piss: ammonia and the sap of pastures where the cows grazed during the day.

Ingi brought the old man right up to Jonty who was standing on his short ladder. She was pretending she hadn't seen the sculpture, Jonty observed. At first he felt his temper rising; he felt like asking her if she'd kindly leave her pretentious city ways in the corrupt self-conscious galleries on which he, Jonty, had for ever turned his back. But then he hesitated. Perhaps she's waiting for a cue from me, he thought.

'Okay, you can have a look,' he said eventually, as the brush plopped back into the bucket and he came down the ladder. He moved the ladder aside, laying it on the ground. 'You can look!' he shouted, making the Great Dane's hackles rise. The dog growled at him, and the old Italian felt the hair bristle on the dog's neck, turned his face to Jonty and stiffened.

'With my own eyes or the museum's?' Ingi asked Jonty, as though the sculpture didn't exist.

'With your own eyes.'

But still she didn't look at the sculpture. She came closer and the old man shuffled along with her. 'Will you consider the museum's offer, Mr Jack?'

Jonty smiled. 'I know it doesn't matter to you either way, Ingi,' he said quietly. 'Your heart isn't in the deal. And never will be.'

She dropped her eyes then turned to the sculpture. The Staggering Merman glistened wetly in the sunshine as though he had just been born from the earth.

The base was as broad as a tree-trunk that she'd only just be able to get her arms round. The sculpture swelled out with lines that might have been those of a dolphin breaching the surface of the water. Or something with the speed of a shark. The smoothness ran into carved muscles plaited over the Staggering Merman's trunk, linking with a wing that lay pressed against the back, giving the figure a streamlined fluidity. The wood on that side of the sculpture was pale yellow and delicately finished, and it gleamed in the sun.

As she walked round it, the sculpture changed colour. The wood on one side was darker. The upward thrust had become a surly hesitation here. It seemed as though on this side there was a falling backward, thought Ingi; a defensive hunching in the back and wing as if to ward off a blow – as though the sculpture didn't trust the energy on its brighter side.

It seems to have been carved from two trees, she thought, twined together as they grew: a tree of shadows and a tree of light.

But then she looked up at the neck and head: something between a human face and a primeval fish snout and the narrow head of an antelope. Here the sculpture had overcome its gloomy side, she saw: it thrust up, reaching for liberation, as though the darker side had been vanquished and the Staggering Merman was breaking free into the blue sky above.

Her head swam. She thought of the stories and legends about the sculpture that were already flying around Cape Town. And the stories here in Yearsonend, especially in the pub, as the drunkards breathed over her with their gossip about evil toadstools and the angry earth pushing out warts – while the city was starry-eyed about the primal artist of a rocky world, the man who'd turned his back on city art circles, who'd worked with dedication for years and had finally produced an image that symbolised everything this new country was striving for.

The sculpture is already so much more than I see before me here, she thought. It has grown: not just miraculously out of the earth, but also in the imaginations of people in the remotest corners of the country. In her mind's eye she saw the sculpture, bought and standing in a small cordoned-off space with gilt-framed paintings hanging on the walls around it. She saw Madam Speaker posing beside the Minister with a glass of wine, the arts journalists, the critics and the art dealers circling each other, and she smelt the stink of money and sparkling wine and savoury snacks and envy. 'And are you absolutely certain that the gentleman is . . . not white?' the museum director had asked.

And Ingi's answer clinched the museum's decision to acquire the sculpture: 'I believe he's of mixed origin.'

'No, my heart isn't in the deal,' she answered, as she stood there amid the wood shavings at the sculpture's base, in the yard strewn with half-worked logs and dry tree-trunks and driftwood collected from old riverbeds, beside the shining chisels and mallets laid out on the tarpaulin, with white arum lilies in the damp corners of the yard, in the greenness and, behind it all, the cool gorge stretching up into the windy cliffs.

'No,' she said, and turned and began to walk away.

The old man and the dog followed her. Jonty called, 'And where are you off to now?'

'Up the mountain,' she called back. 'Are you coming? The old man never gets out. Let's go and show him the mountain.'

Jonty took off his apron and caught up with them. 'I hope I haven't said anything to upset you.'

She shook her head. 'No, I have my own things to be upset about. I've found a lot to think about here in Yearsonend. In the city we live as though there's no time to think. We argue about Afrocentrism and Eurocentrism and tangle ourselves up in gestures and symbols that in the long run don't . . .' she searched for words, gesticulating wildly '. . . that don't *smell* of anything. We have to go back to being . . .' and she pointed at Dumb Eyetie almost angrily. 'We need to go back to being like him; with just the faculty to taste, smell and touch . . .'

'Do you hear me, Jonty Jack?' She looked at him desperately.

'I hear you, Miss Friedländer!' he cried jubilantly into the wind, which was blowing towards them now. The mountain veld lay wide before them and they looked out over the landscape, the blue Karoo hills and the horizon. 'This is my gallery,' cried Jonty Jack, throwing his arms wide in the wind.

He fell silent, and so did Ingi, as the old Italian came to stand, out of breath and open-mouthed, before the statue of the Blessed Virgin Mary that he had carved from the rock and erected decades earlier. They watched him gently fingering the statue: his fingers explored the changes wrought by wind and weather; in the worn rock he fingered the years that had passed.

Eventually he turned and sat with his back to the statue. Like a rock, thought Ingi, he looked like a rock himself.

10

The general stood at the kitchen window watching Ingi work the soap into a lather on Mario Salviati's cheeks and chin with a shaving brush. She'd placed a kitchen chair under the pergola then led the old man to it. Then she had fetched the shaving soap, the razor and a towel from his room, let him sniff the soap, brushed her hand across his shoulders and wrapped the towel round his neck. Normally he shaved himself by feel, and Ingi couldn't help but notice how much stubble he missed.

The peacocks had taken themselves off to the furthest reaches of the vine and sat there, eyeing the general guiltily over their shoulders. Alexander and Stella lay with their heads on their paws in the shadows near the gateway that led outside, as though ready to flee when the explosion came.

I must keep an eye on the two of them, the general told himself, as the servants crept about their chores, whispering to one another, I must keep a close watch on those two. She is beautiful: look at those lovely arms, the nipples pressing against Table Mountain on her T-shirt, the strong pelvis and the way she stands with her legs astride in those lace-up boots. Her youth and naïvety make her all the more dangerous. There's no caution; just the impetuous rushing forward of youth.

He watched the old man sitting with his face tilted up as the razor scraped the foam away to leave an open path of skin. Am I jealous? wondered the general. I who have had so many women that I can't keep a tally, out on commando, in lonely farmhouses, war widows waiting desperately for tidings of their tattered menfolk fighting a British patrol somewhere out there, with only an old Mauser and twenty rounds of ammunition, mouldy biltong and stale biscuits in the saddlebag; trembling women, thin and famished, starved of both food and caresses, women who came to me while my men camped outside under the trees and I, as the senior officer, stayed in the house.

The guest room with the flickering oil lamp, the jug and washbasin, his own shadow sliding over the portraits of family ancestors, and the woman with the guttering candle whose light made her face leap about. 'Put the cloth over the Bible,' she'd always say, before he pulled her down beside him, surprised anew at the body's smell of privation, the limbs' angularity.

'Our womenfolk are getting thinner,' he'd remark to his smirking field cornet next morning as they rode out of the yard.

He watched Ingi wipe the old man's clean chin with the towel, then dab a nick on his cheek with cotton wool. The old man's blood is red, thought the general, when he saw the stains on the cotton wool, red with things we don't know about coursing in his veins, red with knowledge and stubborn silence.

I'll keep an eye on him; I'll use her to get it out of him, he thought, on a sudden inspiration, to make him talk, to make him tell us what happened that last day when the flashwater turned back and Karel Thin Air yelled at everyone at Washout to make way. What happened after Karel Thin Air made off in such distress?

Why had Dumb Eyetie and Big Karel Bergh become so introspective during the last weeks of excavation of the lightning water channel? Why had Karel disappeared off to Cape Town so often? Where had they found the money for Lettie to go to London for months on end? What had Lettie been up to in London?

The general felt his blood pressure rise, as it always did when he thought of gold flowing like water, of gold glistening on your hands like water, of gold washing things away just as water cleanses you.

'There's only one difference,' he murmured. 'Gold doesn't evaporate.'

'Perhaps gold is more like stone.' He swung round to find Ingi Friedländer standing behind with the damp towel over her arm and the tufts of bloody cotton wool in her fingers, and realised he'd spoken aloud. She was smiling at him, and he saw that she meant no harm. At first he felt his temper rising, but controlled himself. Anger helped – anger helped a good deal, but not right now.

'Have you appointed yourself his nurse?'

She tossed the cotton wool into the bin beside the woodstove. 'Me?' She was still smiling. Her mountain walks had put a bloom on her cheeks like the bloom on new fruit in the orchard, he noticed. Her arms were much browner than they'd been when she arrived at Yearsonend, and she'd given up on the lipstick she'd worn for the first few days. She didn't need it any more. She shook her head. 'No, I'm only trying to give him back something of a life.'

'Be careful you don't let yourself get drawn too far into a past you know nothing about, Miss Friedländer.' He rubbed his nose, aware that the servants were still around, working silently. They can overhear us, he thought. Tonight tongues will wag again in Edenville and the story will be all over town by the morning. 'Old men are all about the past. Your life lies ahead of you.'

She grinned, tossed back her hair and put her nose in the air; the nose that reminded him of a Roman soldier. A little Caesar, he thought in spite of himself, but she doesn't choose her battles well and she doesn't know much about weapons and tactics either.

Suddenly he loomed over her. 'Take him no further than the municipal boundaries,' he hissed, then turned on his heel and made for his room, leaving her amazed at his vehemence. He shut his door firmly and sat on the chair before his radio among the maps. He heard Alexander scratch an enquiring paw against the door. And the memory seized him like a cold hand on his spine: echoes of the same sentence, 'Take it no further than the municipal boundaries,' in another era, long ago.

God, thought the general, so much can happen in one life and one life can involve so many others: the night of the black ox-wagon, Meerlust Bergh screwing on a wooden leg painted black especially for night missions, the ravaged Redbeard Pistorius and the black field cornet, Moloi, who stood arguing while he, General Taljaard, and his fifteen men came riding in after attacking the British blockhouse builders down Washout way. It was in December of that year, shortly after the turn of the century.

'Take it no further than the municipal boundaries.' He heard

Pistorius' voice crack out like a whiplash once again; he saw the reluctant men who'd trekked all this way with Pistorius, he looked at the black ox-wagon, and immediately recognised it from the legends that had reached this district months earlier.

It couldn't be true: the general remembered that this had been his reaction. But here it stood: the wagon really existed. We dismissed it as a fable, yet here it stands: the wagon whose belly groans with gold coin, guarded by seven shabby, emaciated men with twitchy fingers on the triggers of Mausers and legs bowed from a year on horseback.

'What happened?' whispered the general, into the ham radio microphone, and people bent closer to radios all over the country as far afield as the deserts up north, the southerly vineyards, the windswept diamond coast, the Bushveld near the border and the massive dunes of the east coast. What happened? the general's whisper rumbled over the airwaves. It's a ghost voice, shuddered his listeners nervously; a voice from an unresolved past.

The general shook his head from side to side as if to find clarity. The radio receiver hissed like the wind over the plains. Like the wind that whistles past your ears as you gallop in the night, praying your horse won't put a hoof into an antbear's burrow. You dash along with the bullets stinging past your ears like hornets, you wait for the wetness somewhere on your body, for pain, for injury. The wind envelops you like a piece of cloth, a sheet as when you were feverish; you're shrouded in the wind.

The general's eyes ran over maps portraying battles on Bloubergstrand, neatly drawn-up columns firing on one another, and the Battle of Blood River, with the water stained red by Zulu blood. He looked at the guns hanging on the walls, the sabre and bandoliers; and suddenly he swept the compasses and maps off his desk, so that the maps rolled up like frightened centipedes on the floor, and he yanked open his door and stumped out.

'Matron!' he bellowed.

She'd been dreaming of the angel and when she emerged timidly from her room, he growled at her, 'From now on your father will sit at the table and eat with us like a civilised human being. And you're to fetch him out of his stinking lair yourself for meals. Be sure he can smell it's you: wear your Italian perfume. If he thinks it's me he'll soil his trousers.'

I I

Granny Siela Pedi stayed in the background when the people of Edenville organised a tea party for Lettie Pistorius and baby Jonty Jack, after they'd returned from England. She'd already stamped her feet in the police station about the constables' apathy over Karel Thin Air's disappearance, and under the strict supervision of her brother, Attorney Pistorius, and at the insistence of her father, she'd removed the necessities from the house she'd shared with Karel.

The windows and doors were nailed shut and Lettie, who initially stayed with her parents, eventually moved into a small house close to the Pistorius Attorneys' offices. She was to end her days there, as Yearsonend went its irrevocable way, as she watched the mail for a letter from the vanished Karel, as the yearning of all those years sank deeper into her eyes.

Granny Siela kept her distance because the blood of Fielies Jollies was still wet on Blood Tree. Yes, they came and grabbed her grandson in their haste to catch someone that day when the water refused and Karel disappeared. Those were tense times for the relationship between the white and brown communities of Yearsonend.

Granny Siela kept her distance but she heard that balloons were bought and cakes baked; that the women of Edenville wanted 'Miss Lettie' to feel welcome at home. Why this unexpected gesture? she wondered. Were they trying to prove something to the white community? Were they trying to claim Lettie Pistorius? Were they trying to say that Big Karel Bergh had always been theirs, even though he'd never acknowledged it? After Blood Tree, did they want to show that they respected people who'd been kind and considerate to them in the past?

Whatever the reasons, Granny Siela Pedi stayed at home that day and she heard afterwards about the pale silent woman at the top table, the baby doubled up with colic and the grief he'd sucked from his mother's breast. She heard how Attorney Pistorius tried to cancel the tea. He apparently considered it inappropriate – a celebration like that among the brown people for a white woman so soon after her husband's death. 'What purpose does it serve?' he'd asked in his office, and the cleaners heard him and took the news back to Edenville. And Redbeard, the old field cornet, now twisted and bent double by his own rigidity, was, it seemed, also opposed to the tea for Lettie.

But what could you do? Lettie had always gone against the Pistorius ways of doing things; she was always stubborn and awkward about the things the Pistoriuses regarded as good and right. This is what they whispered in the offices of Pistorius Attorneys.

Granny Siela Pedi walked the outside paths, as she called them. These were Yearsonend's furthest streets, the boundary road. She walked while balloons were hung up and the people of Edenville sang to Lettie 'Lord, lay Your blessing on her' just before everyone fell on the syrupy plaited pastries and milk tarts. The women wore their church hats; the men were dressed in their shabby black church suits, the holes darned. Lettie struggled with the baby; she expected Karel to appear in the door of the hall at any moment. She had to tear her eyes away from it and pay attention to the people around her.

And, of course, there was the scandal. A woman who leaves because of marriage trouble then returns with a baby, and the husband disappears at almost the same moment! In a way the story also reflected badly on the Pistoriuses. Even though they'd never approved of Karel, it was still an injustice that he had abandoned the love of a Pistorius woman. And that colicky baby with his peculiar name. It's been a long time, it was gossiped in Yearsonend, since a woman was so shamed.

But Lettie watched the door in vain. Karel never came. The closest she could get to him was the water that gleamed in a field far away, beyond the trees, when a sluice gate was raised. The shining water that glistened between the lucerne stubble, slowly spreading its glistening way over the dry ground: Lettie stared at it, hypnotised, until someone tugged her elbow.

Now that everyone had had their fill, they came up to shake her hand and the children pinched the balloons and ran outside with them into the hot sun where they were spiked on the thorn trees and burst, or drifted away into the blue sky. Empty plates were stacked and the remains of milk tarts were slipped into boxes to be taken home. Lettie saw off the last of them and turned back to the empty hall: the crumbs on the floor, the coloured ribbons on the back of her chair and the words 'Welcome back to Yearsonend, Miss Lettie' written on the blackboard, above 'May God grant you His richest blessings'.

What was that all about? she wondered, turning back to the clear white light outside. She didn't know whether the people of Edenville were using her to get at the Pistoriuses; she didn't know what role she played. Blood Tree was still wet, she heard people say – even during the party tears had flowed over what had happened that rainy day. Fielies Jollies had been dragged out of his house by the legs; he'd hung on to the doorjamb shouting his innocence. But the constables and their helpers – hot-blooded young farmers from the Murderers' Karoo – wouldn't listen to reason.

Perhaps, was Lettie's eventual conclusion, the welcome really had come straight from the hearts of people in Edenville. But Granny Siela Pedi knew better. Behind the great gesture of decorating the church hall, baking and speech-making lay the thing without which the people of Edenville could never have got this far: hope.

The hope that Lettie, as someone with a foot in both the Bergh and the Pistorius camps, could bring together the two pieces of the puzzle. The gold would mean a lot to the people of Edenville – it could change everything. Just think of it, they often said. Just think of it! A wagon full of gold! If we share it out surely everyone will get a bucketful? And just think what you could do with that. Clothes for the children, a new lintel for the front door, now that the ants have eaten the old one right through; a new stove, perhaps a bicycle, or – no harm in dreaming! – an old Ford or some other wreck as long as it has an engine and four wheels; a new hat to wear on Sundays, white gloves for the wedding!

This is how the people talked in Edenville and the old people had grown uneasier when the Xhosa labourers had arrived to work on the lightning water channel. What would these new people, so foreign in the Karoo, bring with them? Say the gold was found, what would they demand for themselves? And were they going to settle here in Yearsonend?

Yes, Big Karel had never bothered too much with the people of Edenville, but he was never far from their thoughts – he was their man, who'd been accepted there among the white farmers and businessmen. Now that he was gone they felt a sense of loss. But, yes, there was Lettie. 'Miss Lettie,' Granny Siela Pedi heard, 'Miss Lettie's heart isn't cold towards our kin.'

But people also kept Granny Siela at arm's length. For years, even after she'd married Lost Cause Moloi, the black field cornet, the people of Edenville eyed her with suspicion. After all, he'd ridden with the Boer soldiers from goodness knows where on the back of the ox and she knew them well, those men who'd guarded the wagon. Hadn't she, maybe . ? Granny Siela Pedi saw it in their eyes and turned away; she walked the boundary road, beyond the houses and fields; she walked and kept on walking. What would they know of what she had been through and what she'd left behind?

Let them just wonder if she knew where Gold Pit was; let them speculate. The years would go by and the gold, she sensed, was like water that had seeped into the ground. In time they'd forget she'd arrived with the gold; they'd accept her. And it did happen that way because she'd married into an important family – the Molois were well respected in Edenville – and she'd done her bit for the community.

But when Big Karel Bergh disappeared, that important link with Meerlust Bergh and the wagon with the gold, the eyes were fixed questioningly on her again. It was a few days before she heard about the tea party they'd planned for Lettie; it had all been arranged without anyone saying a word to her. And so she'd kept even more to herself. It would all blow over again, she thought, with the passing of the years.

And, after all, she had her family: the memories of Lost Cause, her beautiful son Goodwill Significant Moloi I and his children Goodwill Moloi II and Fielies Jollies, the man of the bloody tree trunk, Blood Tree, where Granny Siela stood as the first knife cut into a milk tart and a balloon in the corner of the hall burst in the heat.

12

In time Lorenzo Devil Slap came to be known as 'the dark Italian' – not only because of the glowing red strawberry on his right cheek but also because of the rumour that the cheek was so red because he steadfastly refused to obey the biblical injunction to turn the other cheek.

And then, of course, there was the night his glowing right cheek had set his pillow alight. No one knew that he hadn't been alone between the sheets that night. Flames licked at his pillow as he held Attorney Pistorius' daughter in his arms – one of the daughters dragged away from the grandstand at the station by Mrs Pistorius in a huff on the day the Italians came.

Italian passion, so the townspeople said, is a terrible passion. That was acknowledged during the first week after the young prisoners of war arrived, because with them, a certain Mediterranean vigour had flowed into the reserved little town. They were strong young fellows, confined for too long, first in a cargo ship, then in the Zonderwater prison and then in a train, far from home, with lynxes in their loins, as the saying goes in this part of the world.

On Saturday afternoons, they'd play around in the street, wrestling with one another, keeping an eye open for something to do. Fortunately they never got up to mischief, and they let off steam with wrestling matches, card games, expeditions up Mount Improbable and long conversations about Italy.

But curtains often twitched in the Yearsonend houses where young women lived, moved ever so slightly as the lively young men went past. Their high-pitched voices and their language fell like foreign rain on the roofs.

In their innocence, one or two tried to get involved with the girls of Edenville or girls from the other coloured families dotted about in Yearsonend, but they learned quickly that there were things you did and things you didn't do round here. There was a glass wall: you could watch people on the other side and they could see you, but if you stretched out a hand it hit an invisible but impenetrable barrier created by white Yearsonenders.

They were attractive young fellows – from the stocky Dumb Eyetie to the elegant blond who was to become a big game hunter. Only Lorenzo, the dark Italian, Devil Slap, was undeniably ugly, crossing the floors of the Pistorius' fancy house with that dragging gait, pausing before the family portraits of Field Cornet Pistorius, whose red beard had been coloured by hand once the photo had been developed.

Lorenzo was billeted in a back room as far from the girls' rooms as possible, but from the beginning, people told Ingi, he and Gwen Pistorius had an eye for each other. No one knew if her love had been born out of sympathy, but the Pistoriuses cloistered their daughters so strictly with hair ribbons, modest frocks and Sunday-school lessons that what else could you expect? Something had to give and it was Gwen, the older of the two girls, who let herself go, to use the Yearsonenders' expression.

And just to think she let herself go with the dark Italian, sighed the gossips, as in their mind's eye they saw the lovely Gwen's face glowing next to Lorenzo's, that dark head with the purple cheek. What was true was that as he lay in the arms of his lover during their secret trysts at Lampak's Dam, in the sandy gullies below the town dam – or wherever else they could steal a moment – Lorenzo heard stories that made his head spin.

He was particularly captivated by the stories about Field Cornet

Redbeard Pistorius, Gwen's grandfather. The old field cornet's hair and eyebrows were grey but the red beard still flamed with conviction and a passion that could only be caused by frustrated bloodlust, according to the townsfolk.

When Lorenzo took him out now and again in his wheelchair, they made an odd couple. The red twins, they were called – the flame and the devil's slap – and the spoor they left was two narrow wheel-tracks with the single club-foot dragmark after Lorenzo's healthy footprint. Look, people said, pointing at the spoor when the two of them came round the corner at Eviction Road: the marks of two snakes and a club-footed ghost.

The Pistoriuses didn't talk much and they would always remain outsiders in this part of the world – not only because Field Cornet Redbeard had only arrived with the black ox-wagon towards the end of the war, but also because of the distance their lifestyle created.

The field cornet had been accustomed to a different life up north; people were different there, he had felt. In Yearsonend he kept himself aloof, but also took care to secure positions of leadership in the community. He wasn't a man with whom you could just have a couple of drinks. They were as open as the safe in their offices, people were wont to say of the Pistoriuses, and maybe the reason for their behaviour lay in what was locked up in that safe; in their rumoured vast fortune; and in what had happened that night when the black ox-wagon arrived at Meerlust's house.

Shots had been fired. There were bloodstains on the veranda next morning and Meerlust's servants had to wash them off quickly. And the black peg leg was never seen again – reportedly burnt or buried hastily because it had been splintered by a bullet and had Transvaal blood splashed all over it.

These things were whispered in Lorenzo's ear by the sweet mouth of the breathtaking Gwen Pistorius, scarcely nineteen, with an exquisite body and a mischievousness that generously compensated for the restrained evenings spent in the sitting room with Attorney Pistorius behind his newspaper. His wife sat crocheting beside her lamp and the old field cornet nodded off in his wheelchair before the hearth, dribbling into his beard. In his good hand he held a half-glass of Cognac, which tipped dangerously so Lorenzo had to be on standby to rescue it. In their rooms the daughters played the harp or brushed their hair five hundred times.

Lorenzo had to keep nipping in from the kitchen with his white tea-towel over his arm to attend to the ashtray at Attorney Pistorius' elbow; he had to answer the telephone and top up the old field cornet's Cognac until Mrs Pistorius raised her eyebrows to indicate that he'd had enough, and finally Lorenzo had to draw Mrs Pistorius' bath, lay out the towels, wheel the old field cornet to his room and help him to bed.

It was during one of these evenings, when the red beard brushed against his cheek and the old man felt surprisingly light as Lorenzo lifted him from the wheelchair, that he had the inspiration: he should pay more attention to the field cornet's ramblings, maybe even prompt him with a question or two – or better still, help him regain his health. One side of the old man's mouth hung lower than the other, and his one hand curled in towards the wrist so it looked like the devil's claw.

Lorenzo sat down beside him on the bed, thinking: We're both red, you with the beard and me with my devil's cheek; and we're equally deformed, me with my clubfoot, you with your backhanded claw and sagging cheek. But you are old and I am young. Your life is almost over and no one is going to love me for my looks. Even Gwen doesn't: she loves my Italian tales, my stories of the war, my deformed foot, which she rubs against her breasts to comfort me; she loves the way I battle to understand what's expected of me, the way I suffer under Madam's sharp, imperious tongue. No, it's your cheek, Gwen Pistorius would say, your glowing Roman cheek – press it against me, kiss me, Lorenzo. Oh, Lorenzo! But sitting there on the old man's bed, he thought: Her love for me will blow over, like the wind.

A handsome young Afrikaner will turn up, some respectable clerk will be articled to her father, and everyone will see the advantage of having him to carry on the family tradition. The safe could be entrusted to him: all the title deeds and old wills and estates and current business, all the letters and documents, the history of the town in the form of charges, letters of demand, summonses, deathbed wishes, property bonds and stock sales – all these could be handed over to a young man who would discreetly assume responsibility for Yearsonend's secrets, caprices and passions.

All this he had already heard, there in the sitting room, as the notes of the harp came from the girls' rooms and the old field cornet sat before the hearth holding his glass at a dangerous angle so that Lorenzo had to right it again and Madam sat crocheting in furious frustration, and behind his newspaper Attorney Pistorius sighed over the falling price of merino wool and gold.

Then he would hear Mrs Pistorius crocheting her dreams for her daughters. The two men didn't pay much attention to her busying, and as soon as the grandfather clock struck nine, Attorney Pistorius folded his newspaper, knocked out his pipe, went over to the old man in the wheelchair and – a moment that never failed to surprise Lorenzo – kissed his cheek.

Then he went to stand outside on the veranda and listen to the jackals howling in the ravines of Mount Improbable. Or he tilted his head to listen to the laughter from Edenville, where people gathered round their fires with more exuberance than you found in the Pistorius household.

As Lorenzo lowered the old man gently on to his bed he felt the claw grip his shoulder awkwardly. The field cornet was regaining some strength in his hand but it was still pulling askew, and he could hardly use it. It's the gold claw, they whispered in town, the one he used to slam the lid over the coins and fasten the lock, just before they covered it with soil and trod it smooth, and the wind and rain and wild animals' spoor closed over it and removed all signs so that no one today has any idea where Gold Pit is.

It's the claw that swings the safe door shut, people said, with the whole town's scandals behind it; it's the claw that leafs through the file, points in court, and pulled the trigger during those wild years out in the veld on commando.

It was the claw that the old man brought up to his mouth every night, as his beard flamed on the pillow and his eyes glazed over and the lids drooped, and it was the little finger of this claw that he sucked as though it were a baby's dummy.

Oh, yes, the stories about the children's hands had also reached Lorenzo, and the first night he'd watched in amazement as the old man dozed off with a finger in his mouth. Once he was sound asleep, the hand fell away from his mouth so the finger, wet with saliva, lay on the pillow.

Now Lorenzo sat on the bed surveying the collection of things that might be regarded as the field cornet's personal possessions. Is this all that's left at the end of a lifetime? thought Lorenzo. That jabbering mother had already taken possession of the rest, and the daughters would bring strange young men here who would take over while the old man, who'd created it all through his own labour, lay here forgotten.

Hardly anyone tried to engage him in conversation, because the paralysed side of his face embarrassed them on his behalf, or they were revolted by the claw or, now that he was harmless, they could finally allow themselves to feel their anger at him – at the years of humiliation when they had appeared in the witness box before the flaming red beard and the black robe, the man whose voice cracked like a Mauser during a closing argument, at his inflexible summonses, at the failure of long-awaited legacies to materialise because he'd influenced his clients to favour someone else when they were drawing up their wills. Or perhaps it was jealousy over money and status, diligence and determination, or whatever else piles up over a lifetime in a community's attitude towards one of its members.

Lorenzo moved the hand away from the old man's face. He leaned over and stared for a long moment at the old field cornet. He heard the soft notes Gwen's hands plucked from the harp. He heard Madam plop into the bath and Attorney Pistorius urinating – a slow trickle. Then he looked at the old man again. Why don't I just ask you? he thought. Then he thought better of it. Not tonight. Later. When you have your strength back, old man. And Lorenzo decided to devote himself to the healing of the old field cornet. It took many months of devotion and exercise, the redbearded man struggling along, with his arm over the Italian's shoulder. But gradually they overcame Field Cornet Pretorius' first stroke and miraculously he walked again, albeit with a slight limp. It would be some time before a second stroke put him back in a wheelchair.

Now Lorenzo got to his feet, blew out the lamp and closed the door behind him, then walked round the house to his room. He unlatched the window and slid the frame up a little so that Gwen Roubaix Pistorius' pretty hand could easily slide it further open an hour later while he lay waiting for her in his bed – stark naked and glowing like an ember. On her body he exacted passionate revenge for his difference. And she accepted it as a tumultuous form of penance.

13

Whenever she could Ingi asked questions about all the tangled relationships, the married couples and families who shared so many branches it was difficult to separate one family from another, or the present from the past.

But she asked no more questions in the Drostdy because her first innocent query about the matron's mother and the connection between the Berghs and Pistoriuses was received with icy silence. In the kitchen the servants turned away, putting their noses into the pots or rubbing the silver fiercely. The Great Danes scuttled outside and the general barked out a few noncommittal sounds. The matron sat dreaming in the bay window that looked out over the garden and oak trees, murmuring something about her guardian angel and the Blessed Virgin Mary.

So Ingi looked for someone else to help her. But as she laced up her boots first thing in the morning, smeared suntan cream on her face and arms, and swung the small backpack over her shoulders, she had first to ask herself the question that had hovered on the borders of her consciousness since she'd held Mario Salviati's clean-shaven cheeks between her fingertips and studied the expressionless face, which might have been carved from rock then weathered by wind and rain.

That question, which she knew was half crazy yet valid: Are you, silly girl, falling in love with an old, old man? In the flower of your youth? A blind man? You who make a living out of what others conjure from colour and image? You're a painter yourself, Ingi Friedländer, and you're attracted to someone who lives without colour in darkness, in night. You, who can't go hiking in the mountains without your Walkman, who always feels surrounded by sounds and the sighing of the winds – why do you fall in love with the silence, your opposite?

Where do sympathy and pity end and where does love begin? Where does curiosity about this town, with its hidden secrets, end and attraction to one of its inhabitants begin? Isn't he merely the personification of the mysteries you're trying to unravel? She chided herself with every stroke of the hairbrush.

Today her hair crackled with electricity, tingled with the excitement of the day that lay ahead. The fax she'd wanted to send to Cape Town lay crumpled on her dressing-table.

It was all so far away: Table Mountain, the busy streets, the museum with its framed paintings, her desk with the computer and the bundles of mail and the budget books, the fax machine and the gossip about art and funding in the corridors. Here, thought Ingi, as she brushed her scalp to a pink glow, it's all cerise bougainvillaea and peacock tails draped from the pergola like a cascade of eyes, the fountain that smells of coolness and moss, and the fishes flitting about beneath the sunshine on the water.

There's the smell of grapes rotting on the paving in the afternoon and the sprinklers spraying water in huge, graceful arcs under the oak trees; the Great Danes who, when she took them for a walk, were beginning to trot along with her more freely and happily, sometimes breaking into a clumsy gallop as they sniffed out the route ahead.

Then there was the Drostdy driveway with its over-arching pines and the fragrance of pine needles and resin; hundreds of doves crooning as they sheltered from the sun; the scents from the fields, land turned by the plough, diesel tractors and the friendly labourers, who leaned on their spades to wave to her as she passed by the smallholdings.

She liked the white dust on the streets that looked cool in the morning but baked mercilessly in the sun by eleven and radiated heat waves by midday, so that Mount Improbable looked black, its rocky cliffs cruel and dark, while the sky turned a blue you found nowhere else.

She liked the idleness on the storekeeper's veranda, the couple of layabouts who ambled over from Edenville each morning to hang about there, sometimes moving into the shade at Attorney Pistorius' office when the sun moved, where their friends were waiting for a consultation in any case. She liked the smells and noises in front of the store: the moist smell of sugar, the smell of flour and paraffin and tobacco, the clang of the old-fashioned cash register and shoppers who tied their change safely in their headscarves and went out for a breather on the veranda before coming back inside to make another small purchase.

And the deserted station, where she sometimes sat on a bench on the platform, imagining the arrival of the young prisoners of war. She pictured the lively suntanned young Italians, the improvised grandstand with the townsfolk and farmers, and heard the train's whistle blow before the locomotive came into sight.

And all the events that had taken place down the years! she thought. But the memories were so tattered and threadbare, tossed by the wind. Desire and hope, jealousy and betrayal: these were the words in Ingi's head as she walked up William Gird Road with her headphones in her ears and her hair flying in the wind, up past Little Hands for the umpteenth time.

Round and round, all over town, the labourers and the old women leaning on the gates gossiped. The young miss walks, round and round. There she comes again, watching everything, but it doesn't look as though she's going to get anywhere with the Staggering Merman business – those Berghs are impervious to foreign money; they've got their own, they're their own people.

It's the way they treat the old man that bothers me, thought Ingi. He lives like a prisoner, and the general is after something he knows. And there's the woman without a face in the back room next to Dumb Eyetie's. Talk has it that when she goes out for a walk, she must go down the passage past the coal room and the laundry and the old pack-rooms and the maze of passages and rooms that were once the slave quarters. And then through the rickety old gate made from planks salvaged from the Fourth Ship, the wood that washed up on the beach and was brought here. A wagon was the first thing made out of it in the old days, then rough wardrobes in the first wattle-and-daub houses built by the farmers who had ventured furthest from Cape Town; then the wood had been sawn up to make doors.

And now all that remains of the ship is this little gate. Or so they say in the kitchen where, it seems, they'd rather talk about the gate than the poor woman who has a room out there at the back. They'd rather lose themselves in chattering about something in the distant past than let slip something about her, preferring to push a plate of food under the gate for her and run away again, as Princess Moloi does three times a day. Then she'd run back over the paving stones, with her apron pulled high up on her legs, escaping from the ghost woman, fear bringing up goosepimples on her arms, which she showed breathlessly to Ingi.

It was these thoughts that brought Ingi to the attorney's waiting room. It was eleven o'clock and all the walking had made her thirsty so she dropped in at the general store for a Coke, turning inquisitive heads and setting them a-whispering.

Now she walked past the brass sign that read *Pistorius Attorneys: Criminal, Conveyancing, Estates, Water Rights* and pushed open the door. The waiting room was crowded and the receptionist looked up. Once Ingi had explained that hers was a social visit, not about business, she was told that, yes, the attorney would see her now, fortunately it was time for his tea break.

She'd already observed Pistorius' red hair, his freckled face and clerkly manner as he walked through town, nodding to her and minding his own business. He hadn't inherited the fiery spirit of his great-grandfather, the field cornet, or the formal crustiness of his grandfather, the attorney who'd taken Devil Slap into service. These qualities had been watered down over the generations. He was an insipid little fellow, thought Ingi, a real country bumpkin who couldn't help but adhere slavishly to the formulae and conventions of this little town.

He was the son of the younger Pistorius girl, Jeanne, the one who was tucked up safely in bed while her sister Gwen slipped out as soon as they heard their father's snores and their mother sighing in her sleep. He'd inherited something of his mother's caution; he was the ideal person to inherit the practice, thought Ingi, to guard with small-town precision that safe with the secrets of the past. No more than a pen-pusher, someone who'd never be able to comprehend the historical value of his collection of documents.

He was slightly taken aback by her visit, especially once he learned it was purely social. He was uncomfortable in this role, particularly because he was wearing his professional clothes, a dark suit and somewhat old-fashioned tie. 'Just to talk?' he asked in surprise, as the receptionist showed Ingi in and offered to make tea.

'Chat, actually,' said Ingi, offering her hand with a smile. She was warm from the walk and still held the Coke. The headphones dangled from her neck. 'Just to say hello.'

'Oh. Please take a seat.'

He started rearranging and straightening the files in front of him, so she had to protest, 'Don't worry: I know all about messy offices. I work with artists, remember?'

'Oh . . .' He smoothed his hair.

'Have you worked here long?'

He laughed. 'As long as I can remember. As a child I used to come and sharpen my father's pencils and file documents. It made sense to study law and follow in his footsteps. My great-grandfather . . .'

'Yes, I see his sign is still hanging outside . . .'

He shrugged. 'There's no point in taking it down, even though I am a Terreblanche. Everyone knows us. We rarely get clients from out of town.'

'And I suppose it's a way of acknowledging what your great-grandfather Field Cornet Pistorius achieved.' She threw the Coke can in an arc, and it clanged into the wastepaper bin. He jumped, whether at her words or her action she didn't know.

'Yes . . .' he stammered uncomfortably, and then the tea appeared. They sat in silence while the middle-aged secretary poured it then withdrew with a knowing smile. He was unmarried, Ingi realised, and tonight the woman would fill her friends in on the details of Ingi's visit to the wealthy young heir.

'Typical small town,' she said, 'full of gossips.'

That startled him too. She could see that her remarks were totally unexpected. 'Yes,' he said, sipping the hot tea. 'I suppose it shows a kind of community spirit. People care about one another.'

'Are you certain of that?'

He looked at her questioningly and put down his cup. A sort of officiousness came over him. 'You're very critical for an outsider.'

She couldn't ignore the sharpness in his voice. She waved a hand and she saw his eyes flash to her bangles. 'Only joking. Don't worry.' She glanced at the files on the desk. 'I know you have a lot of clients waiting. You're very busy. But I hoped you could help me with something.'

He raised his eyebrows. 'I thought this was a social visit?'

'Must I pay a deposit first?' she joked.

He laughed. 'I'll do my best to help. What is it?'

She frowned and sighed, and looked down at her hands. She could feel his eyes on her T-shirt and tugged at her hair self-consciously.

'Well?' He was playing a familiar role now.

'The Drostdy.' She paused, hoping he'd say something, but when he didn't she continued carefully, 'It's a strange set-up. The old house is beautiful, but . . .'

When she looked up she saw that he was very tense. He fidgeted with his fountain pen and one eyelid twitched. 'Yes?'

She paused. 'Am I . . .' she hesitated '. . . am I saying things I shouldn't?'

'You haven't actually said anything yet, Miss Friedländer, except that it's a lovely house.'

'Yes, that it certainly is. And such interesting people living there . . .'

'Interesting is certainly the right word.' He laughed again, pleased to have the scales tipping in his favour.

'Well . . . I . . .'

He leaned forward suddenly, a decisiveness that belied the earlier clerkish ineffectuality. 'What is your question?'

Ingi gazed at the pale blue eyes and the freckles round the too-pink mouth. The hand on the pen was motionless. He waited. They heard voices from the waiting room. A telephone rang. Steam rose slowly from the teacups. A framed degree certificate hung on the wall.

'There's an old man . . .' she stammered, angry with herself for making such heavy weather of it.

'Mario Salviati. Mr Mario Salviati,' he repeated deliberately, in a way she couldn't immediately fathom.

She nodded. 'Yes . . . and . . .'

'And?'

She spoke quietly, as though she was making a personal confession; as though she was voicing something she'd kept hidden for a long time, deep inside her. 'And the woman without a face.'

He threw down his pen and sat back.

They heard the voices outside again. Then there was a knock at the door. He spoke quickly, sharply: 'Come in!'

The secretary came in behind Ingi. 'You have to go to court, the public prosecutor rang, he's calling your case in half an hour.'

'Get out the file for me, please.'

With the secretary fussing round them and the steel drawer of the filing cabinet sliding open noisily, Ingi couldn't ask any more. She felt herself trembling. And then, after a quick handshake, she had to go back out into the harsh sunlight, and past the inquisitive eyes.

14

The year out in the veld with the black ox-wagon had sharpened Field Cornet Pistorius' instincts. And when he stood with his men under the trees looking up at Meerlust on his veranda, he had a sixth sense that things were going wrong.

Siela had disappeared with the black field cornet Moloi who'd promised her a bath and clean clothes; Meerlust Bergh paced up and down, limping on his black wooden leg, his eyes glued to the black wagon.

Field Cornet Pistorius knew that a dull smell of salt and putrefaction hung over him, his men and the wagon. It was a smell similar to biltong, with thyme and coriander and salted meat, but it didn't make your mouth water, because something in you recognised the smell as that of human flesh. The smell of the children's hands had grown stronger with time.

It's in our clothes, thought Redbeard Pistorius, we breathe it in and out. He remembered the farm dogs that had been abandoned when British patrols were burning farmhouses and barns to the ground and moving women and children into concentration camps. During the black ox-wagon's trek, the dogs had picked up the scent out there on the plains and started trailing them, afraid to come close but drawn in their desolation to the smell of meat and salt. The pack of dogs grew until a dozen or so fanned out behind the wagon, their tongues lolling. When the riders tried to drive them off, they ran away, only to return later.

There was a risk, the commando knew, that the dogs would get out of control – as their numbers increased, so did their daring. From one razed farmstead to another, new animals joined the pack. At night they crouched beyond the circle of firelight and they'd disappear for a couple of days to prey on the sheep that had escaped the British scorched-earth patrols. The sheep were wild and took shelter in the rocky hills, and once Redbeard watched the dogs, as skilled as a pack of wild hunting dogs, ambush a sheep and tear it to pieces. They would return a day or so later, calmer, with distended bellies, almost lazy when the men tried to drive them off.

And there was the day when an argument broke out in the commando about which direction they should take; about the possibility of spies ahead; about the struggle to make camp at night after finding a dry riverbed to hide the wagon, which had to be camouflaged with thorn-tree branches.

As Meerlust's wooden leg tap-tapped on the veranda and a jackal howled in the mountain, Redbeard remembered how he'd taken up his Mauser and shot the closest dog in the shoulder – the one that had emerged as pack leader and ventured closest to the ox-wagon. The dog, a Ridgeback-Alsatian cross, had collapsed, yelping, rolled in the dust and lain there shuddering.

Then out of pent-up rage and frustration the other men started shooting and Siela screamed at them to stop. The dogs made off in all directions and the men pursued them on horseback. By the time they came to their senses, thirty-three dogs lay on the plains and on the slopes of a nearby ridge. Some were still alive and it was he, Field Cornet Pistorius of the ZAR Presidential Guard, who had to go from dog to dog, and make sure that they were dead.

As he walked out there on the plains he had thought of the hands that had stroked these dogs' heads, the verandas where the creatures once lay, the children with whom these dogs had once splashed in streams or played ball.

That night Siela comforted him as though she were long past anger, as though she had come to care for him, as though she loved him, he realised the next day when they looked back to see the crows circling over the dogs' carcasses.

Now Field Cornet Pistorius turned to his men. He was startled afresh at their faces: it was as though exhaustion had suddenly caught up with them now that there was a chance of ending the trek. Overcome with a weariness he hadn't noticed build up in him, he studied them. How intimately he had come to know them this past year! Their whims, their mutual betrayals, their affections, their aversions. First they had been comrades, then friends, and then friendship had crumbled under tension and hardship; then they had hated each other until now, finally, they were no more than a gang of victims.

'What do you want to do?' he asked, and he saw in their faces the eyes of a pack of starving stray dogs yearning for a stroking hand, the familiar smells of a home, the familiar rituals of a family. He saw fear of the open veld, the wildness of open space and privation; and he remembered that in civilian life they'd been ordinary respectable young men – lawyers, successful farmers, accountants, the pride of the Republic.

He realised they were on their knees, destroyed, and he could tell by the way they watched one another out of the corners of their eyes that they were no longer individuals but pack animals.

You hunt in formation, he thought, as he watched them. These strays I command, who travel with me and in whose dissipation I as their officer have played my part; this war trash with their whore riding on an ox, their terrible year-long rape of the woman, who endured it in silence behind bushes and rocks and who has now disappeared with the black field cornet, leaving us with no idea of what reckoning she will exact.

'Are we going on?' he asked. They looked at him without seeing him; they were watching one another, he knew, they breathed in unison with pack instinct, they . . . He raised his Mauser and aimed it at them. They reeled back. 'What do you want to do? Do we bury the gold or push on?'

He could smell their sweat, the anxiety at the decision they had to take. The tired shadow of the old president fell over them; they thought of the women in the concentration camp cutting off the hands of a child before the corpse was wrapped in a tarpaulin, rolled in slaked lime and consigned to the grave. They thought of the mothers who had given them those small hands for salting; he could feel the little finger scratching in his stomach.

Then he swung round to Meerlust. 'Mr Bergh!'

'Yes, Field Cornet.' The man with the extravagant plumed hat drew nearer. He'd almost lost his limp; he walked with a new confidence.

'Where will you lead us?'

'Do you mean . . . ?'

'I mean we must make for a hiding place.' Redbeard glanced at his men. He realised he was still aiming his Mauser at them and dropped the barrel. 'We must bury the gold first.'

'There's a Bushman cave high in Mount Improbable.'

But Redbeard shook his head. 'No, a cave is the first place people will look.'

'There's an overhang further south.'

'That's the second place they'll look.'

Meerlust rubbed his eyes. He stood a good head taller than the tired men around him. I could wipe them off the map with one blow, he thought – words or a gesture. They look like reeds shaken by the wind, this tatty crew who cart round a republic's gold reserves – can you believe it? Then he looked into the field cornet's intense bright blue eyes and thought: I'd better watch my step.

'There's an old pit . . .'

'No, an old pit is the third place.'

'So where?'

One of the other men stepped forward. 'You can't hide a wagon this size.'

Meerlust gestured into the sky. 'There's no moon tonight. We can move silently.'

Another man grunted a warning: 'Treachery.'

'God,' murmured Redbeard, 'it's the state reserves . . .'

'We must divide it into four parts and hide each in a different place.'

Redbeard turned on the man with flashing eyes. 'Are you mad? That's the last thing we should do. How do you guard four treasures?'

Suddenly a man asked, 'And how do we know we can trust him?' Now all eyes were on Meerlust, teetering on his wooden leg. He swept off his hat – too much for the occasion, thought Pistorius, too grand a gesture. The man is too extravagant; his whole house radiates appetite, a love of money. Too demonstrative – just like those suddenly rich Transvaal families who'd found gold on their land.

Careful, he thought. Careful.

'I—' began Meerlust.

'We were referred to this man by trusted people,' Redbeard reminded his men. 'We were assured he was trustworthy.' He glanced at Meerlust. 'We must bury the gold in the most ordinary place, where no one would ever look for it. Where there's no landmark in sight. On God's naked earth.'

'On God's naked . . . ?' asked Meerlust.

'Yes,' answered Redbeard, 'and we are going to devise a plan to ensure that no one possesses all the information about where the gold is.'

'And how are you going to do that?' asked one of the men. They fidgeted in the darkness. The evening star had appeared and the smell of mud and plants wafted over to them from the irrigated vegetable garden nearby.

'God knows,' Redbeard told them quietly. 'We must conduct this business correctly. The war will end one day. Then all eyes will be on us. Do you realise that?'

'Yes,' they answered in unison.

'Only two men will share the knowledge of where the gold is,' Redbeard continued. 'You and I.' He pointed at Meerlust. 'But neither you nor I will have complete knowledge.'

'How—'

'Have you any black cloth?' Redbeard asked Meerlust. 'We need blindfolds. Enough for everyone, including the two of us.'

'And the kaffir field cornet,' said Meerlust.

'Why?'

'He's on his way back. He took your . . .' Meerlust hesitated. 'He took your . . . the woman to where she'd be cared for.'

Redbeard swung round. 'Bring the blindfolds.' He stood staring into the night as he listened to Meerlust's wooden leg dragging through the grass then limping over the veranda and the wooden floor inside the house. Frogs croaked in the moist vegetable garden. And there was that jackal he'd heard earlier, howling in the mountain. He rubbed his face, and his hand was cold on his burning cheeks.

Too long, too long and too far. Too much was placed on our shoulders. The old president was no longer thinking clearly when he gave us our orders. War does that to people: without your realising it, it erodes your judgement, like floodwaters eat at the sides of a furrow, and it all caves in before you know it. O Lord, help us tonight. Help us to honour our republic, help us to make the right decision. Wash away our sins. God, redeem us.

'God, redeem us.' He heard a quiet echo, and when he looked up at the dark faces around him, he realised he'd whispered his thoughts. He felt his beard grow wet with tears.

'God, redeem us,' he said again quietly, and walked to the veranda, up the steps and into the brightly lit farmhouse with the books, the gracious furnishings, the hunting trophies, and all the trappings of old Cape money and sophistication.

Ignoring the glasses, he took up the crystal sherry decanter that stood on a silver tray beside the oil lamp. He didn't know that Meerlust was watching him from the front entrance as he drank deeply from the decanter and the sherry overflowed and trickled into his beard where it mingled with the tears. The black blindfolds Meerlust had cut hastily from a length of mourning cloth hung from his hands like dead starlings.

Each man had already decided that the other members of the commando must die.

15

Gulping at the gusts, hovering on wings as strong as men's backs, his buttocks straining together against a wind that chased black stormclouds over the naked plains, the angel kept an eye on developments: the lumbering ox-wagon, the man with the wooden leg limping on ahead, the ostrich plume in his hat bobbing white in the darkness.

The rest of the men kept one eye on the feather and the other on the threatening weather, because water erases, obscures; water would change route to rumour. The oxen swayed and strained, and the creaking wagon was like a black ship in a heavy swell. The angel lurched with fright when a man rode up suddenly out of the night and Mausers spat fire. The rider fell to the ground and the plume bounced over to him, while his horse galloped away over the plains with tossing stirrups.

Then the angel somersaulted in the air. He thrust with his powerful shoulder muscles, filled his lungs and winged away as if he, too, had a share in the shame down there on the plains where the stooping men discovered that they'd made a terrible mistake. They stooped to hear the words murmured by the wounded man, while blood bubbled out over his cheeks.

The angel was gone and there was only an empty channel in the night wind, a shred of mist against the mountain slope, a smell of fright and regret and cinnamon hanging faintly over the northerly cliffs.

After Meerlust shouted, 'He's my man, don't shoot,' and Field Cornet Pistorius dropped his Mauser, he realised he wasn't the only one who'd fired. Our position has been given away, he thought, and, simultaneously: there's a disturbance in the air, a stronger wind than we expected, and it blows over us away from the town. The sound of these shots, God willing, will have ducked into the burrows of the night like meerkats.

He bent over the man. Then he called Meerlust over. 'You know him. Tell us what he's trying to say.'

As the plume hovered in the air, Pistorius looked at Meerlust's back. Eventually Meerlust turned to him and said, 'The black woman has asked to be taken before the magistrate and a coloured dominee: she wants to lay charges of abduction and rape over the past year. You must put a stop to it.'

Pistorius' head swam and he smelt the blood on the man's

breath. As he knelt there beside Meerlust, his knees grew warm from the urine that left the man's body as he died, and his hands were wet too: he had to wipe them on his trousers. 'Piss,' he said, under his breath.

'Blindfold him,' he ordered, grabbing Meerlust's wooden leg. Meerlust staggered down beside him and Pistorius stuck his pistol into Meerlust's face. 'Listen carefully, Mr Bergh. I apologise for what we're going to do to you now. My men are going to take the wagon on for two hours. You will accompany them blindfolded. Wait for me there.' He looked at his men. 'Make sure he can't see where you're going. Make a couple of full circles and double back on your own tracks to confuse him.' Then he whispered to one of his men, 'Keep a close watch on him. He's full of tricks. And shoot him like a dog if he tries to peek or escape.'

'Like a dog!' he shouted over his shoulder as he galloped off, back, to stop what could be stopped.

Meanwhile the angel had returned, hovering indecisively, now over the men who, having loaded the corpse into the wagon and covered over the blood and urine stains, were moving away with the blind-folded Meerlust and the oxen, now over the redheaded rider who was digging his heels into his horse's flanks and racing back over the plains with steel in his eyes and his beard glowing like hot coals.

Caught in disbelief, the angel strained against the wind and then, making a decision with a sound between a whinny and a coo, between that of a horse, a dove and a man, he dived away and disappeared, leaving them all behind, because there was nothing to be done; there was only the unfolding story, the horror that was taking its course as though it had been predestined.

The evil seemed so finely spun, so intricate yet deliberate that you could imagine a guiding hand behind it, an intelligence. This was something to flee from, the angel realised, to escape.

The angel fled and because fear brought him out in goose-pimples, a few soft feathers came loose and fluttered downward, but the wind snatched them up and swept them off to the east, bobbing over the black plains, into the emptiness where, for six full days' journey, there was nothing.

16

The dead could never leave Yearsonend: the wind out there was too cold, or the sun too fierce, or the plains too sullen – or perhaps it was the angel who waylaid them and persuaded them to turn back. Maybe it was an experience common to them all – to try to escape, to go, after death, on the journeys that had been forbidden them in life, only to find with the first attempt that the angel was waiting for them on the plains. With wings spread, feathers ruffled and chest puffed out like an angry vulture or a turkey cock, a proud peacock of death, dancing, step stepping like a blue crane marking out his territory, that wide-winged angel with the blue veins that branched over the muscles and could even be seen through the down on his belly and chest – and the two breathtaking larger wings, beautifully matched, as though carved from marble, one and a half times the height of a man. The angel breathing heavily, warning, threatening: Go back, go back.

The woman without a face had to give in, turn back, when she caught the smell of buchu sweat and birdshit and cinnamon and the huge creature up ahead began to make a racket, dragging and sweeping his wings in the dust, making her sneeze and flee, back, back to Yearsonend.

Perhaps it was also the angel who made Captain William Gird bring down the giraffe over and over again, as though it was the only deed that had distinguished him in life – not the brave expeditions in India, not the medal parades or the discussions of strategy when his sharp mind showed him to be superior to his fellow officers. No, the only deed he had to repeat over and over again after death was to appear with his scout and see the giraffe's long neck rising above the trees right there at the spot they now called Giraffe Corner, twenty paces from the first houses in Eviction Road.

And then the careful licking of a finger, which he held up to determine the direction of the wind before he slipped from the saddle and the table was unfolded, the sharp odour of ink as the guide unscrewed the caps on the bottles while the giraffe nibbled a leaf from the top of a tree growing in what was now the middle of a road – Eviction Road, with everything that was to take place there centuries after Captain Gird's painting session. And once the ink had been blown dry and the bottles carefully and neatly stowed again, once more the scraping sound as the firearm was drawn from its case, and afresh, through the rifle sights, another chance to marvel at this beautiful animal.

When the shot rang out, children playing in Eviction Road would turn their heads, thinking it was some so-and-so hunting in the mountain again, or a tin falling from the shelf in the general store, and a flock of doves coming to land near Lampak's Dam to drink would fly up again, spreading into the air like the fingers of an opening hand.

The general, who always had an ear pricked for gunfire, would jump as he dozed in the coolness under the vine, then realise he'd imagined the sound, and Dumb Eyetie's head would toss restlessly on his pillow, as though he had heard something, deaf as he was. He would hug himself, imagining he was getting a fever; he could smell dynamite and dust settling, or cool water flowing over stone.

Only Matron Taljaard was not surprised. She sat in the bay window watching the doves flutter about and the Great Danes with their sensitive ears, yelping and galloping through the trees in fright, and she smelt something but she wasn't sure what. She looked round the room half expecting a visit, but there was nothing: just the stiff furniture, the rugs, the paintings, and the grandfather clock.

Then Gird had to remount and turn away from the beautiful animal stretched out there in the veld, promising himself he'd return as he had done so many times before.

That was just the way it went round here, and there was nothing that could be done about it. Only the dismal hand of the inevitable held sway.

As you had lived, so would you be in death, Ingi heard in

Yearsonend, and as the days went by she began to understand. Choose your days and your deeds carefully, because you might have to repeat them for ever.

And so she battled to fall asleep that night, tossing her hot head on the pillow, and crying out and drumming her heels on the mattress. No dreams drifted through her sleeping mind, there was nothing, just unease, nameless, imageless. Once she sat bolt upright in her sleep, reached for a glass of water and, when she brought it to her mouth, poured it all over herself.

Later she lay awake, bathed in sweat, listening to the peacocks sneezing in the vineyard, the tap of Alexander's paw as he lay jerking in his sleep. She'd heard so many stories recently. The voices buzzed like bees in her head, or rather, she thought, bright and colourful, a swarm of butterflies that fluttered silently around her, brushing their wings against her.

She sat up and swung her bare feet to the floor. The task she'd been charged with was a simple one: buy the sculpture from that artist in the gorge on Mount Improbable. And if he hesitates to sell, hang around, make friends with him, make him understand the full implications and what a great honour it is to have the National Gallery request your work.

Yet the longer she stayed, the vaguer reality on the other side of the plains seemed, the world from which the train came every day and to where it disappeared back, like a snake emerging from its hole then gliding in again.

She heard an aircraft only once or twice and looked up: a scheduled passenger flight that had evidently had to change course owing to poor weather conditions somewhere in the interior, flying through the vast empty space above Yearsonend. We are just a slight smear on the brown earth, she thought, a greenish brushstroke on the brown canvas of these widespread plains.

Maybe they saw roofs shining and wondered what went on down there, but we wouldn't have any name or meaning for them – and yet down here we are so tightly packed, so dense, so interwoven and excessive; we are so *here* and they . . .

Ingi shook her head and got up. She went through the quiet

house to the kitchen. The general's light was still on, but he was stretched out on his bed, under the mosquito net, snoring so loudly that the rolled-up maps on his desk trembled. The radio receiver hissed, and a long message had curled on to the floor from the fax machine. Ingi looked at the yellowed sole of his foot, the black voids of the nostrils and the hawkish nose, the long underpants and the vest he slept in. She shuddered and rushed past his open bedroom door into the kitchen.

Then she unlatched the door carefully and stepped out on to the patio. It was deliciously cool in the moonlight and a peacock stirred on the pergola. The fountain had been switched off and a fish plopped in the water. She looked over her shoulder then tiptoed to Dumb Eyetie's room. She heard a noise coming from it, a thump and a hiss, and hurried when it grew louder. She stood listening at the door. Wrestling? A body fell to the floor.

It was dark and she was breathing fast as she pulled open the door. Two bodies were thrashing about in a wild wrestling match. She couldn't make out any detail but she was visible, standing there in a shaft of moonlight, and one of the figures fled past her with rustling, snorting sounds, sending her flying with the passage of its huge body.

It swished past her with a strange smell and a shimmer and then they were alone in the quiet room – she and the old man, who gasped for breath and groaned as he knelt beside his bed.

She waited until his breathing settled. He sniffed at the smell that hung so heavily in the air. Then gradually, her smell – perfume and soap – wafted towards him and he turned his head. Crouching on all fours, he turned his body in her direction, his head bowed, as though he were expecting another assault.

17

Ingi was up next morning even before the servants began trying with crumpled newspaper and kindling to coax a flame from yesterday's coals in the wood stove. She'd hardly slept and at daybreak, when the roosters on the smallholdings started crowing one after another, she decided to walk up to Jonty's and ask him if they could go out for the day in his camper-van or her car. She had to get away; she needed breathing space, away from everything that was happening around her and threatening to overwhelm her.

Next thing, she shuddered at the thought, I'll lose my face too and I'll have to spend the rest of my life – and my death – in a back room here. God spare me that. She brushed her hair quickly – no time for rituals today – packed her rucksack, with a sweater just in case.

She bumped into the general in the passage outside her room. 'Good morning, Miss Friedländer,' he drawled, his voice still thick with sleep and dreams, as he pulled his dressing-gown across his chest. 'You're up early. Don't city girls ever lie in?'

'I am going up the mountain,' she said, trying to get past him. He slopped some of the coffee from the large mug he was carrying. 'After breakfast, surely,' he purred, closing in on her. He was staring at her hair as he spoke. 'We're having a whole ostrich egg this morning. Hard-boiled and served in slices. Have you ever tried it done that way?'

She shook her head, wanting to retreat, feeling claustrophobic in the dark passage, but the backpack she'd swung over her shoulders now wedged her against the wall.

'Not hungry, eh?' he said, right up close to her now, reaching out a hand. 'What's that shining in your hair?'

She pulled back. 'It's just the colour.'

'Here, in this dark passage?' She could smell garlic on his breath and old wounds; she heard a lame leg dragging down the passage behind him and the groans of a wounded man. During the night, after she'd given Dumb Eyetie a chance to pick up her scent and to realise she was there and that they were alone, she'd gently helped him to bed. She'd crept in under the sheet beside him and allowed him to breathe in her smells deeply. At first he had lain trembling, and then the wind had blown up and rattled the roof tiles, loose there over the rear of the house. She thought: he hears nothing; he knows nothing of that wind; it isn't even night to him for night is the same as day.

Slowly she shifted her body so that her softness was pressed against him. She stroked his head, his face, his back and his chest. As his body relaxed it began to steam with new smells: smells that simultaneously absorbed and repelled her. She took the hand that didn't hold the stone and stroked it over her back, over her hips. He moved his head slowly into her armpit, and lay sniffing like a dog; then his head moved down against her nipple, which pressed against her nightdress, and he put out his tongue to lick it through the fabric and fell asleep like that, with his open wet mouth at her breast, his breath gurgling and snoring.

The general ran his fingers over Ingi's hair. Then, without warning, he grabbed her by the arm, bellowing, 'Matron!' He marched Ingi into the breakfast room and pushed her into a chair at the table. The matron appeared with her hands folded in front of her and he ordered, 'Sit down.'

'I want to go,' said Ingi. 'What's the problem now?'

'Look,' said the general, holding his fingers out to Ingi. The tips glistened. 'From your hair.'

'But what is it?' Nervously, she put up a hand to it.

'Gold dust.' His voice brushed over her.

'But . . .'

He leaned over her. 'You've been with the angel,' he hissed.

Stella and Alexander slewed their clumsy bodies round and scrambled through the door, all but knocking over a chair, their paws skidding on the highly polished passage floor.

'The angel. Angel Gold Dust, angel.' The matron rocked, hugging herself, as steam rose from the gigantic ostrich egg, which lay sliced on a silver salver.

'Angel . . . ?'

Ingi jumped up and ran from the room.

'Breakfast?' asked a startled servant on her way to the dining room with a tray.

'No!' screamed Ingi, running past her. 'No!'

Then she was in the courtyard with the peacocks fleeing before her. Dumb Eyetie stiffened where he stood at the parrot cage with his arm through the wire and his hand full of seed with the parrots flapping round it. The dogs, grateful to escape, surged through the gate with Ingi, making her stumble, but then she was running under the sprinklers that the matron had switched on earlier; running down the dusty road, with her hair streaming out behind, gleaming in the sunshine.

18

Ingi carried on running even after she'd put a safe distance between her and the Drostdy. She felt like a little girl on roller skates. She flashed past the trees, a honeybee in the morning sun. She flew through the smells of earth and pine logs and composting leaves and sun on skin, and she put a hand in her hair and knew that she shone because she had been touched by a miracle and a mystery.

Even the dogs sprouted wings: they galloped ahead of her, their noses to the ground, frightening the doves, sending guinea-fowl scuttling for cover, leaping into the air to snap at butterflies.

Their frequent walks with Ingi had made them fitter: they were leaner, more joyous. Every day she took them through the streets of the town or up Cave Gorge, or even further, over the shoulder of the mountain to the statue of the Blessed Virgin Mary, even further than that, down the back slopes, with the wide panorama of nothingness that was the plains, and there might be five eagles soaring over the silence of the plains, or a single dust worm crawling along in the distance as a railway lorry drove supplies to town or, incongruously, Jonty Jack's red kite flaunting itself against the black cliffs.

At first the people on the veranda of the general store were nervous when she came by with the two Great Danes – two dogs the size of overgrown calves, the girl with the rucksack and Walkman striding along behind them. She walked quite differently from the locals: people here ambled along, chatting, carried forward by gossip and the breeze, gently edged along by the sun between their shoulder-blades. But she walked like a city dweller, with speed and determination.

Only she knew the insecurities that lurked behind her confident stride. How could they know, these Yearsonenders who had almost no contact with outsiders, here so far from the tourist routes and commercial centres? The few strangers who visited were usually palaeontologists who wanted to explore the cave, or archaeologists who wanted to fossick about for dinosaur bones that were still trapped in the petrified mud, from the time when everything here had been one great swamp.

Or they were kudu hunters with their Land Rovers and their tents and their searchlights and the preoccupied air of predators focused on their prey. They passed through here, stocking up their provisions at the general store and quizzing the locals for information about farms where hunting concessions were available, and a week later you saw them coming through again, stopping for cold beer or petrol, the load of fresh kudu horns making the vehicle look like a porcupine – just a mass of quills.

And the town dogs clustered round the Land Rovers because the smell of fresh-cut and salted biltong lured them from their front verandas and backyards and they followed them out of town in a pack, past Giraffe Corner and Little Hands. Baying with meat-lust, they followed them to the outskirts of town, where their breath ran out and they turned to slake their thirst in the spillway of Lampak's Dam then flop down for a rest in the cool shade of the dam wall.

These dogs, people were fond of saying, were the descendants of the pack that had followed the ox-wagon all the way to Yearsonend in the old days. They were Boer War dogs, who had slunk into town behind Field Cornet Pistorius' black ox-wagon, the disappointed, tortured animals from far-flung districts who could not understand why their world had perished in fire and tragedy; dogs that hunted in the ravines and plagued bitches on heat in surging lust-crazed packs, sowing their seed among the house and yard dogs of the town.

They'd passed on to future generations their memory of an ox-wagon that stank of salt meat, and it was that memory, Ingi heard in the kitchen, that rose up in their minds as the hunters drove their Land Rovers southwards, loaded with freshly slaughtered kudu meat.

Ingi made her way slowly up Cave Gorge. She called the Great Danes to walk closer to her: she was apprehensive about encountering the woman without a face again. She remembered the day the woman had fled before her through the undergrowth; the beautiful body of a young woman who'd never aged, the slim neck and the long braid. It's the beautiful Gwen Pistorius, folk whispered, the elder daughter of Attorney Pistorius, the one who let herself go with the black Italian; the man who, Ingi realised, was perhaps the true bearer of the secret; the man sent summarily back to Italy when the official paperwork had been completed, in record time, at military HQ in the castle in Cape Town. In two days flat, she'd heard tell, that young man had been packed off back to Italy. Against wartime regulations, he had been dispatched as though he had the plague.

He'd seen something, people said, and that had made Attorney Pistorius decide to get rid of him. 'Get out, Devil Slap' had become a popular expression in town when you didn't want something near you; when you felt the goosepimples of the evil tokoloshe come over you. Get out, Devil Slap, said the Drostdy kitchen-maids, when Ingi went past, and they argued among themselves about who was to undertake which tasks. And when the matron talked about her angel in that dreamy voice, they'd wait until she'd left the kitchen then whisper, Get out, Devil Slap.

What had Lorenzo Devil Slap discovered that made it necessary to get rid of him so fast? Ingi wondered, as she went through the trees with Stella beside her and Alexander a little way ahead. And why did the woman without a face have to stay in the back room under the rattling roof tiles? Why did the angel confine her there? Or was it the general? Or perhaps the whole town was involved in the secret, gossiping about her, Ingi Friedländer, the naïve city girl.

Were they laughing at her from behind their drawn curtains as she walked down Eviction Road, those people who'd endured so much, from the time before she was even born, those labourers who leaned on their spades as she passed by, the people on Attorney Pistorius' veranda, or the naked children splashing in Lampak's Dam and climbing on to its wall to watch her go by.

Ingi's step would not betray any of her thoughts. She waved to the children frolicking in the dam, she waved to the people on the veranda of the general store, those who gathered aimlessly and lazily beneath the flies and the dustclouds from the odd vehicle that occasionally passed by, she nodded to Attorney Pistorius' clients waiting on his veranda, she smiled to the children behind the school fence, who might be greeting her or making fun of her – which she couldn't tell.

What she was certain of was that she had to get away for a day or so; that it was all becoming too much for her; that she couldn't bear the silences; that she alone was unearthing all the grief of the past – grief that these people tried to ignore for the sake of their survival.

And she was the onlooker, she was the one who asked too many questions, and she was beginning to feel they were pushing her out, and mocking her.

Perhaps it was only that she was too tired and too concerned about everything she'd come across here; perhaps she just needed to take a break and get things back into perspective. But she knew that her soul wanted to soar unhindered past the cliffs like one of

Jonty's kites, defiant in the wind, laughing in the late afternoon, because an angel had touched her, even if he had been somewhat flustered and hasty at the time.

When Jonty's house came into view and the track narrowed in the tall green grass that grew in the moisture there, she quickened her pace. She knew already what she was going to say to him. I am that woman without a face, she'd say. It isn't Gwen Pistorius, it's me, Ingi Friedländer; I anticipated myself, it is I who cannot escape from this place because I am trapped here, just like the rest of you.

And do all of you know that already? Is that why you laugh at me and gossip about me? But when she saw him polishing the Staggering Merman, busy and preoccupied on his stepladder, she swallowed her words and greeted him as though she didn't have a care in the world. 'Hello, Jonty! Isn't it a lovely day?' And the dogs rushed up to the sculpture, attracted by the smell of cow piss. Alexander lifted his leg and peed against the Staggering Merman while Ingi and Jonty looked on, laughing, and Stella hurried to the arums, tensing her hindquarters, and the lilies nodded round her as she dropped a turd as proof that she was enjoying the day's outing.

19

'Yes, but what about Granny Siela Pedi?' Ingi asked Mayor Goodwill Moloi. The questions haunted her: it was impossible to leave. The mayor sat across from her, at a modern desk, and the new national flag was displayed in the corner of the office. The door to the council chamber was open and Ingi peered in at the modest chairs and tables. It was, however, obvious that the mayor's office had been recently refurbished: deep-pile plum-coloured carpeting, a desk chair in the latest design, newly framed portraits on the walls.

'You're really on my grandmother's trail, aren't you?' The

mayor laughed. He added milk to her tea and waved at her to take the cup. 'And I've heard, Miss, that the purchase of the Staggering Merman is not going too well.'

'No.' Ingi shook her head. 'But I'm learning all sorts of things about Yearsonend in the process.'

He took a sip of coffee and regarded her through narrowed eyes. 'You shouldn't believe all the stories – you do realise that, don't you, Miss Friedländer?'

'You've already told me that.'

'Yes, I keep forgetting you're a city girl. You'll be on guard against your fellow humans.'

'And against politicians like you!' she teased.

He laughed and put his cup down in the saucer. 'Do you know,' he said, leaning forward confidentially, 'that Jonty Jack's first sculpture – the first thing he ever made – was for Granny Siela Pedi?'

Ingi straightened up, surprised. 'Really?'

Goodwill Moloi nodded solemnly. 'The sculpture still adorns my house. My wife Mama and I treasure it. We know it might be worth a lot one day. Probably already is.'

'What does it look like?' It struck Ingi that the art museum could benefit from this. She put her cup down and leaned forward too.

Moloi laughed. 'Hold on! Next thing you'll want to buy it as well.'

'Well, the first piece made by an important artist is always valuable. For historical reasons, even if it isn't so good intrinsically.'

'I can assure you, Miss Friedländer, that this work has none of the wings and gold paint and peculiar totem poles that Jonty Jack busies himself with these days – it's a beautiful, simple sculpture.'

'What does it portray?'

The politician in Goodwill Moloi enjoyed playing with Ingi's curiosity. 'Oh, you'd never guess.'

'I'd really like to mention it in my report.'

He got up to close the door into the council chamber. Then he came back to his chair. 'It's a bust of Field Cornet Redbeard Pistorius.'

Ingi leaned even further forward. 'Jonty's grandfather?'

'That's him. Old Redbeard himself.' Goodwill Moloi rocked in a belly laugh.

She sat back to think this over. 'And he gave it to . . .'

'Yes. He presented it to Granny Siela Pedi. Without anyone knowing about it.'

'Ah!' sighed Ingi, quite carried away.

Goodwill laughed triumphantly. 'Children have more honest eyes than adults. As a little boy Jonty Jack must have sensed the bond between his grandfather and that old woman in Edenville.' Moloi emphasised the name with an ironic smile. 'A number of white Yearsonenders also sensed it, but there are things one simply doesn't talk about. Only a child had the guts to see things in their nakedness.'

'So you think Jonty knew that his grandfather and Granny Siela had a relationship?'

'No, Miss Friedländer, I'm saying that everyone knew there was a relationship. But Jonty Jack was the only one who had the guts to tell Granny Siela Pedi that he knew. And after Pistorius' funeral, he took the statue to her in Edenville. He was only a little boy, but he used clay from the grave to make the statue on the afternoon after the funeral, baking it secretly in his mother's oven while Lettie was at her welfare office, and took the statue to Granny Siela. After a bad night she was still sitting in the arms of her husband, my grandfather, crying over the red-bearded white man who'd used her then never even greeted her again.'

Ingi sighed and combed her fingers through her hair. They sat in silence. Behind the door, cleaners were busy dusting and sweeping the council chamber. Their brooms bumped against chair-legs and their dusters slapped on tabletops.

'I don't really know . . .' whispered Ingi.

'What don't you really know?' asked Moloi quietly.

'I don't know whether I'm strong enough for all the stories of this town,' Ingi Friedländer said, over her shoulder, as she made for the door. She ran down the street and the mayor stood at his office window.

They're only stories to you, he thought, not entirely without bitterness. But for us it's all we know. For us it's our Yearsonend.

20

How do you draw love? wondered Captain William Gird, one-time hero of the Indian Raj and now in love with the African veld, as he sat grilling ribs over an open fire with Slingshot X!am. The exact year had momentarily slipped his mind because they were puffing on a cigarette containing a herb Slingshot X!am had introduced him to: a weed that flourished in these damp gorges and helped you to forgive and forget.

But how do you give expression to what ultimately decides territorial fate: the attraction between men and women, passion? The mating instinct, thought Captain Gird, that's what you're really talking about when you study the great movements of troops, the fall of kings and the rise of empires. In the long run it all hinges on what happens between lovers.

Once you understand that, you can give up being concerned with the great gestures of history, the greed, the craving for power and the subjugation. If you wish to say something meaningful about the history of a given place, you should concentrate on the beguilements of lovers. And just look at how artists have given expression to this! Because isn't the creation of art that takes as its subject matter a specific place or time an act of love in itself?

Captain Gird didn't know which of these thoughts were sucked out of the small cigarette and which of them made sense, but he had already lost himself on the pathways of love. Once, while he and Slingshot X!am were journeying, Slingshot had told him about a verdant gorge grazed by wild antelope who were so tame you could catch them by hand for your cooking fire; a paradise where crystal water bubbled from an eternal spring.

It was a region far to the east of what was now Yearsonend; yes, it was the region that would be called Washout in times to come. It was damp and temperate, the earth always moist from good rains. Slingshot X!am led the exhausted Captain William Gird there, to a small house against a cliff under a waterfall. This was the house that Ensign Moloi, the pirate, the escaped slave and bandit, had built and to which he brought his lover Titty X!am in his old age, when leprosy crippled him.

Slingshot X!am told Captain Gird that his father Ensign Moloi had brought his mother, Titty, here after annihilating her family with his blunderbuss and sword and abducting her. But it was also true that Titty was treated well by the buccaneer and, in turn, she cared for him when he started dropping fingers and toes on the byways of life – and at this point Captain Gird could not suppress a smile.

When she was finally caught and taken with her husband to Robben Island to die there in the leper colony, within sight of Table Mountain and surrounded by the restless waves of Table Bay, the house stayed behind for Slingshot X!am, guide to big-game hunters, prodigal, smuggler, former pandoer. And confidant of the artist who trod this landscape, William Gird; the man who crept under overhangs and through caves to see how Slingshot X!am's forefathers gave expression to their love of man and beast, to melancholy and to landscape.

It was after one of these long expeditions when the captain made endless tracings of the rock paintings that Slingshot X!am took him to the small house against the cliff. And it was in the late afternoon, when they unsaddled the horses wearily, that Captain Gird met Little Titty X!am, Slingshot's sister.

Little Titty had stayed with a white family in Cape Town for a short time and she and the captain got on well – so well that on the first night they excused themselves from the fire where Slingshot crouched in a trance over his pot of honey beer. They strolled a short distance to observe the effect of the moonlight on the San rock paintings. Captain Gird was stirred by the surging energy of the herds of animals painted in ochre and orange on the rock walls, and he looked at Little Titty and in her he saw the refinement and the myths of ages, the moon and the stars and the calling of centuries; he saw the small breasts pressing against her little bodice and in her he could smell the veld and the wind.

And that was where Sara Bruin came from – from that night under the overhang; from the allure of landscape and line and colour. And Sara Bruin, who grew up under the cliff with the waterfall long after Captain Gird had been forgotten in the area, roamed down south to settle in the Boland on a wine farm owned by Huguenot Viljee. And there, in those unsettled times of new settlers and old wars, she bore a baby – a baby who, right from the very beginning, was always restless and noisy: Meerlust Bergh.

But of course Captain Gird had no idea of what lay ahead. What worried him was the sardonic – no, mocking – smile on the face of his scout, Slingshot X!am. Gird knew that Slingshot wasn't terribly impressed with his habit of drawing or painting everything, human or animal, they came upon. Nothing more came of their lives than the eternal drawing, the endless recording of everything they encountered.

They often argued about it. Slingshot was diplomatic because, after all, he was only the scout, and he knew his place. But whenever those rolled cigarettes worked their magic, or the honey beer took its natural course, they became equals – two men of more or less the same age, both adventurers; 'orphan rock rabbits', in X!am's words, 'without kith or kin'.

Then Slingshot would pester the captain about why he found it necessary to record everything. Why couldn't he just enjoy the exploring, the womenfolk they came across, and the fruits of their barter, the wildlife and the landscape? You should smell and feel and taste everything, Slingshot X!am berated the captain; instead you lie on your back and copy what the old people left there; you sit behind your folding table obsessed with getting everything right, exactly right in colour and form.

How could the captain defend himself against this accusation? 'I am an artist,' he would say. 'Circumstances tried to make me into a soldier, and succeeded. I was awarded a medal for bravery. It's there in the saddlebag. But I'm more than a professional soldier. Really, I am a man of paint and oil, of colour and line.'

'Not much help when the river comes down in flood.' And the cynical Slingshot X!am drew deeply on his dagga cigarette.

'The traces of earlier travellers – those drawings on the rock walls – amaze me. I touch them with my fingers and it seems as though the people and animals spring to life under my hands.'

'Not much help when the lion charges.'

'Someone has to record the things we encounter; someone must sit between past and future and assume responsibility for the passing of things. Someone must say: "Wait, it's like this now, this is the way I see it, here it is . . ."'

'Not much help when lightning strikes to the right and left of you.'

'. . . and I find that there's nothing else for me. I've watched other explorers grow rich on ivory and lion skins and tell tall stories about gold in the interior, but I find peace when I can breathe in the smell of my paint mingled with the fragrance of dry grass and a wild animal stands under the trees before me and I can document something about his existence. I . . .'

'. . . when the water runs out and the sun grills the back of your scalp.'

Then Captain William Gird drew himself up to his full height. 'I am an artist. But that doesn't mean I'm frightened of a gun.'

He called Slingshot X!am into action, they saddled the horses, and rode off into a herd of wild antelope. An orgy of shots rang out until eventually the two men, sated by all the loading and firing, rode among the slain animals delivering a finishing shot here and there.

'Cut out only the livers,' ordered Captain Gird. 'Tonight we'll celebrate those five paintings I did of the blue wildebeest.'

21

'And who here isn't family?' Ingi heard in Yearsonend. She felt increasingly free to visit and chat. But she picked up most of her stories from the barman, Look Deep, and the stationmaster, and at the general store. They came out skewed and stained with prejudice, but she could cobble together a narrative from the rough material and still she knew there was more to discover, much more. And since her visit to Mayor Moloi in his office, his daughter Princess Moloi had also been more forthcoming with her whispered snippets to Ingi in the Drostdy kitchen.

If you put your finger on Yearsonend's communal family tree, Ingi realised, you found what you'd probably find in any isolated community: your finger could run from name to name, a tracery of lines, and you need never lift your finger because there is always, somewhere, an unbroken line to someone else.

Blood runs downhill, she'd heard; like water, it chooses the easiest route. And blood was not impeded by colour or prejudice; blood flowed most freely down the furrows of love. Blood was the real lightning water. 'This is probably the true Law of Bernoulli,' Mayor Moloi told Ingi, when they met by chance on the steps of the post office and she told him how surprised she'd been to hear from his daughter that Captain William Gird had had a daughter by Ensign Moloi's daughter, the man believed to have trekked inland with the gold from the Fourth Ship, towards this area, and who had come upon Titty X!am's nomadic family and fallen in love with her.

'Aha!' cried Moloi. 'The black ensign! The buccaneer!'

'Buccaneer?'

'Gold,' whispered Moloi, dramatically. 'Gold . . .' He leaned over her, leered, walked down the steps and drove off in his shiny Mercedes.

Alone in her room, Ingi began to draw a family tree. She managed to fill in a good many names, but in no time she had to go off to the kitchen to get more information from Princess Moloi. She drew lines, erased them, and drew them again. But finally she had intertwined the three families accurately. Now her finger could begin with General Taljaard and, through intermarriage and all sorts of kinks, she could find a way from Big Karel Bergh to Huguenot Viljee, slipping down from there to Granny Gwen Viljee, who married Redbeard Pistorius; thus confirming that Jonty Jack was descended from two people who were blood relations. To her surprise, she saw that she could move on, up the vertical lines, past Sara Bruin, back into the past, as far as Ensign Moloi and Titty X!am and then it was a short way down to Charming Swartebooi and Lost Cause Moloi and Granny Siela Pedi – 'Downhill all the way!' laughed Ingi and Princess Moloi, as they worked it all out in the kitchen.

'It's a blood tree!' cried Princess Moloi as she pointed to all the branches and roots on the diagram.

Ingi felt so dizzy she had to go and lie down. She'd also heard that Jonty Jack had often gone to visit Granny Siela Pedi in the time after he'd given her the bust of his grandfather. Granny Siela had told the young boy a great many stories: she had taught him, whispered Princess, how the people of Pedi model and fire clay; she told him about the spirits of the ancestors and about the tokoloshe and still today these things held him in their grip.

'And Lettie Pistorius and the Welfare?' asked Ingi.

She had heard that after the tea party and the shock of what happened at Blood Tree, Lettie Pistorius moved into what later became known as Eviction Road. It was 1944, several years before Grand Apartheid got into full swing and her coloured neighbours had to move out and Lettie found herself sitting in Yearsonend with pots of money at her disposal, a firm of attorneys a few doors away seeing to her affairs, and a young son who gave every indication that he would not become an attorney in the Pistorius tradition. She had time on her hands, and a lot of regrets too, people suspected, so she rolled up her sleeves to help the poor.

'Miss Lettie from the Welfare' – that's how people in Edenville referred to her in time to come. And Ingi heard, 'So although

Miss Lettie from the Welfare didn't carry buckets of gold to Edenville, she brought another kind of treasure: sympathy, fellow-feeling, help.'

And this in those difficult years. 'The countless impossibly heavy years.'

22

Maybe it's really the angel's ox-wagon: crouched with swaying wings, the feathered man with the radiant plumage rides the gold wagon. It always passes Yearsonend at dead of night, any moonless night when you smell dust or rain; when the stars shine bright above the little town; when the fires flicker low in Edenville and bodies press closer to one another, and the wind rises and lightning flashes against the night sky, so far away that you know that no more than a whiff of great rains will ever reach here.

The dogs barked, tugging at their chains, and the lone constable on duty came out of the police post and saw that he had forgotten to lower the flag at dusk. He felt uneasiness in the air. Was it just a sign of the times, or the great shift of the seasons? But it was only the passing of the angel perched on the gold wagon's black canopy. The angel grinned and his thigh muscles rippled as he rocked on the wagon, which bounced over stones and brushwood.

All sorts of things stirred in the streets of Yearsonend. Ingi felt them, restless in her bed. She threw back the sheet and stared up at the ceiling. In one way, the Staggering Merman didn't matter any more. Neither did the gold wagon. She felt as though she'd been sucked into the branches of what Princess Moloi called Yearsonend's Blood Tree, into the troubled history of this town with its simply laid-out streets and smallholdings. It was like Jonty's sculpture garden, she thought, as the images passed her mind's eye in single file, and she understood: in his own way Jonty was carving his people's history up there in his sculpture garden. Every totem or image was trying to tell a different story;

in the night winds and in the heat of the day the sculptures stood motionless, staring at each other, bound to one another over time and distance. And they had nowhere else to go: this was their preordained place.

Which story was the saddest? murmured Ingi. The story of Big Karel Bergh abandoning Lettie? Or the story of Granny Siela Pedi, ignored throughout her adult life by Attorney Pistorius, the redbeard who might have fathered Goodwill Moloi the First – as Look Deep had whispered over a beer – the mayor's father.

'The mayor? Pistorius blood?'

Ingi pictured the black Princess Moloi with her intricately braided hair and her blue eyes. She remembered the mayor's quiet persuasive voice telling the story of how Jonty Jack took a bust of his grandfather to Granny Siela Pedi. So Jonty Jack and Mayor Moloi were distant cousins, thought Ingi, and Lettie Pistorius was half-sister to the mayor's father! In this scheme of things, Granny Siela Pedi must have been pregnant when the black ox-wagon arrived in Yearsonend.

Would everyone know this? Were General Taljaard and the matron aware that they had one of the first Attorney Pistorius' descendants working in their kitchen? Would the current Attorney Pistorius-Terreblanche know he had a black cousin who stoked the woodstove in the Drostdy?

Was this why no one had set out with conviction to find the wagon with the gold? Was there too much to hide? Were there, even now in the new era, too many things that were irreconcilable because they'd open up the past, things as explosive as dynamite?

That was why Jonty had withdrawn, Ingi realised. He was free up there in Cave Gorge: he enjoyed a kind of immunity there. And yet when you thought of his work you realised he wasn't free. As with many artists, the freedom was an illusion because one work after another portrayed engagement. The wrestling with things one could never be free of, thought Ingi. In striving for freedom, you only compounded your imprisonment.

She thought back to Jonty's sculpture garden: the image made from black wood with a head that echoed the Xhosa carvings tourists buy at roadside stalls on the Wild Coast, and the golden mayoral chain Jonty had painted on the chest in a mocking caricature. And Ingi wondered about the sculpture: from a distance it looked like a cartoon of Moloi, but from close up you could see the sadness in the features and the look in the eyes.

One eye, she remembered, was blue. She'd wanted to ask Jonty about that, but he had the kite and he was nagging at her to run into the wind with him so the kite could fill and climb into the sky.

Could it be that they were all, in some strange way, tangled up with one another? she wondered. Is it because Mayor Moloi is part Pistorius that Pistorius Attorneys' offices were so supportive of his candidature? Support that white Yearsonenders found inexplicable.

Or did he, as a seasoned politician, have some kind of hold over the Pistoriuses? Was he walking around with this knowledge which they'd give anything to prevent him using? She drew in her breath uneasily: she was the outsider; she was the one who had to find out little by little; who had to puzzle and guess.

Ingi pushed open the sash window. The night was still but every now and then a wind sprang up as if from nowhere to disturb the trees. She looked up at the Milky Way; she never ceased to marvel at how bright the stars were out here.

Then she noticed something moving under one of the trees. It must be the wind stirring the dry leaves around the base, making the heavy branches sway. But then the wind dropped and Ingi made out a figure under the branches. She had to narrow her eyes to focus. She saw the framed portrait in Mayor Moloi's hands. She saw the old woman, bowed by age with years of heartbreak in her eyes. Granny Siela Pedi stood under the tree and looked straight at Ingi in the open window. She saw the young woman in the nightshirt, the nipples showing through the fabric like eyes on a tree; she saw the heavy braided hair, she saw the expectation and the fright, the reaching out and the wonder.

It was dark and neither woman moved. Then Ingi heard someone coming round the corner of the house. A figure hurried past – the woman without a face. She walked quickly with her head turned away from Ingi. She went to the old woman, who was holding out a hand to her. They linked hands and walked away through the trees towards the avenue. Ingi's hands were wet with sweat, clenched on the windowframe. But something in her had loosened: a tension. It was like a dream, she thought. I'm caught between dream and wakefulness; between the living and the dead.

I'm beginning to understand more clearly how things fit together. There's a beautiful, painful pattern. There's a terrible beauty in it all.

Ingi lay down again. With considerable surprise she heard a long, satisfied sigh leave her body. She dreamed of gold coins, a heap of them. They gleamed on the paving near the fountain in the Drostdy courtyard. She was standing with Mario Salviati near the pile of coins. He could see and speak. 'Look!' he cried. She reached out a hand towards the coins, but they melted into water and flowed between her fingers.

'Water!' cried Mario Salviati, in a lilting Italian accent.

'No,' Ingi heard herself answer that morning when Princess Moloi stood at her bedside with a mug of steaming coffee and two buttermilk rusks. 'Gold!'

.23

'Hang on, hang on! Hang on a minute!' Jonty Jack spluttered, as he and Ingi Friedländer splashed about in Lampak's Dam. It was a hot afternoon and he'd allowed himself to be led down there.

First she had arrived, flushed and dripping with perspiration, at his house in Cave Gorge. She flopped down and accepted a mug of dagga tea. They studied the Staggering Merman for a while and in no time Jonty was up again rubbing some corner or curve of the fish-man. 'Phew!' said Ingi repeatedly, as she gazed at the sculpture. 'Phew!'

Jonty showed her his latest attempt. It was still a rough log – one he'd sat wrestling with for ages – but a chrysalis-like figure had begun to take shape.

'I think it's a butterfly,' said Jonty Jack, 'with the wings still pressed tightly against its body as it emerges from the pupa – look here: can you see the feelers lying flat on the head? And there: the neck arched like an impala's . . .'

'An impala?' Ingi butted in.

'Yes, an antelope.'

'An antelope? But I thought it was a butterfly.'

He looked at her for a long time in astonishment. 'Yes, but it can also be a dragon,' he said eventually. 'Or a sputnik.'

'Oh, yes,' she said. Now she got it. And that was how the afternoon began: with misunderstandings, youthful innocence and teasing. Until she said, 'Let's go and take a dip in the famous Lampak's Dam. Have any grown-ups swum there since Irene Lampak's day?'

'Of course,' Jonty told her. 'I have, and so has Mario Salviati, with his compatriots.'

'Let's go, then.'

He ferreted around in his wardrobe and dug out a pair of old bathing trunks from another era – the time of flower-power – with long narrow legs and big daisies on the backside. Ingi hooted with laughter when she saw them and they raced down the gorge, with a bottle of white wine bouncing in her backpack.

At the dam – there was no one in sight – she stripped down to her knickers. Jonty stood there dumbfounded, out of his depth. He watched her plunge into the water with nipples erect in the afternoon breeze. Bashfully, he joined her.

And now he had to hedge because she fired endless, provoking questions at him: What did he know about the mayor's parents? Had he ever discussed the past with the young Attorney Pistorius, the freckled one? What did General Taljaard ask Jonty when they met?

She dived and splashed round him, spluttering and darting about. 'Where's the gold?'

'Wait! Hang on! Take it easy! Hell!' Jonty tried to back off laughing, but she was all over him and his hands were full of water and suddenly full of Ingi too, her youth and her teasing breasts in his hands, till he yelled out, 'Leave me alone!'

Upset, she swam to the other side of the dam and clung on to the wall by her elbows. 'Sorry,' she said, while Jonty Jack heaved himself out, feeling ridiculous in his hippie swimming trunks.

'Look, you're fine,' he growled at her, 'but you're just a little too inquisitive.'

'Me?' she asked, and he couldn't tell whether her surprise was genuine or faked.

She was like a piece of wood waiting to be carved, he thought, as he wrapped a towel self-consciously round the beginnings of a paunch. You study it and you think you see something lurking in there, something you can release with a chisel. But then all at once you realise: you'd only seen wood, nothing more.

There was so much more that you'd missed. Yes, you are the blind one, he told himself.

Part Three

Mannequin's Plume

I

'All right, I'll tell you what little I know,' Jonty Jack said to Ingi, but she got the feeling he was just appeasing her. She knew, as he talked, that he wasn't sharing everything with her.

They were sitting under a rock ledge overlooking his sculpture garden. She was amazed afresh at the extraordinary colours and shapes in this gallery that no one ever saw. I must start painting again, she thought, as he turned to her, repeating, 'I don't know much, but there are people here in Yearsonend who know the odd thing. If you can ever get them all together, and each one adds his little piece of the puzzle, maybe you'll be able to patch together some sort of answer.'

'But it's impossible that nobody knows exactly what happened to the gold!'

'That's what everyone thought in the years after the Boer War. Those were the years when my grandfather Meerlust got even richer – particularly from ostrich farming – and Pistorius established a flourishing practice. Then people used to say, "These two men know the secret, they just don't want to admit it, and they're biding their time until one day they'll suddenly fetch the gold." But it never happened. Then they both died.'

'And your grandfather never said anything?'

'Grandpa Meerlust?' Jonty laughed. 'Of course he said a lot: he flourished his plumed hat and swaggered about on his ivory leg and he enlarged his homestead and bought more land and never missed an opportunity to refer to the gold. He even yapped on in the fashion houses of Europe about the black ox-wagon buried here with its load of gold.'

'So it is buried?'

'Everyone believed so. But Meerlust really didn't have a clue where the gold was – they realised that when his original male ostrich died in the winter frost and, for sentimental reasons, he asked the taxidermist to stuff it. When the man opened the ostrich's gizzard, he found more than ordinary stones and pieces of glass ground smooth with stomach acid: there were three golden coins too and you could see at once they were Kruger pounds.

'The taxidermist sent for Meerlust, and there was a hell of a commotion. Both my grandfathers – Meerlust and Pistorius – were there and just about the whole town, everyone speculating about which grazing-run the ostrich had been in when he ate the coins – until somebody reminded them that Meerlust put the bird out to stud (at a price) all over the district, and further afield. The ostrich could have eaten the coins almost anywhere, so it was impractical to start digging.'

'Is this why you sometimes use gold in your statues – touches here and there?'

'Kitsch?' he asked.

'No, oh, no. It works superbly. And it's only little touches.'

'Maybe I have also been infected by the obsession. Maybe I can't shake it off either.'

'And Lorenzo Devil Slap?'

He got up quickly, dusting off his backside. 'I don't know anything about him. Only gossip. Don't pay any attention to what you hear. Come, I've got to get going with the cow piss. See how dry that wood looks? This sun!'

'Wait!' She followed him, but he was already striding down the slope. He felt he'd said too much, she realised. She'd have to let it drop for now.

'Jonty! Do you think I should start painting again?'

He looked round at her. 'Inspired by all the nattering down in town?'

She took his elbow. 'Wait!'

He stopped and they balanced themselves on the steep slope. She stood squarely in front of him. 'I saw an angel.'

He looked at her and a smile crept slowly over his face. 'Watch out for that angel!'

'Do you know him?'

Laughing, with long, dusty strides, he ran down into the black stone landscape where his sculptures stood. 'He's the only one who knows where the gold is.'

'Do you know him?' she called after him, but he was already down with the sculptures that stood like totems among the stones. He picked up the bucket he'd put down there earlier. He turned to her as she caught up with him. 'The more questions you ask, the more the angel will avoid you, and the more wary he'll become.' She looked into his eyes, which were suddenly serious. 'That's why I live up here in the mountain. Up here, unlike you people at the gallery or at the university, I don't have to ask too many questions about the angel. I just take him as I find him. And that's why he . . .' He started walking away again, but she'd seen that he was grinning. 'That's why he has tea with me.'

'What?' She ran after him.

He laughed, and she had to trot to keep up with him. 'Every Tuesday morning at eleven the feather man and I have tea together.'

'But, Jonty!' She stopped, hands on her hips, unsure whether he was teasing her or not.

He turned to her, serious again. 'The angel visits you when you've moved beyond questions. That's what's exhausting everyone, Ingi: questions. Leave it all alone and he'll appear on your doorstep.'

'Or bring you a Staggering Merman.' She squared up to him. Don't underestimate me, she thought, and looked him in the eye. 'He brings it so suddenly and generously that you think it comes from somewhere else, so that you can't believe you made it yourself with your own hands, so that you always feel you don't have the right to do with it as you wish.' She stood with her feet planted wide apart in front of him, the little backpack on her back, her chin thrust forward and her fists on her hips.

Suddenly he turned away. 'I paint cow piss. This is me, Jonty Jack. Go and tell that to your museum people.' He walked away, then turned again, shaking the brush at her. 'Cow *piss*!' he emphasised, and then he was off among his sculptures, leaving her alone with the dogs, who rubbed their heavy bodies against her consolingly. She heard him shout once again: 'Cow piss – in the foyer of the Houses of Parliament!'

2

Big Karel Bergh, son of Meerlust Bergh and the Indonesian model Irene Lampak, was born clutching a gold nugget in his little red fists against his little wet chest, as Yearsonenders loved to recall when the memories of those years were summoned up.

No, it wasn't a myth. They all swore to it, the midwives who cut the umbilical cord, while the beautiful woman lay with her knees still apart reciting hymns of praise in a strange tongue, and Meerlust lit his cigar under a palm tree outside: covered with blood and slime, yes, but still a gold nugget. Shaped like a haemorrhoid or a polyp, the doctor noted, quite organic – except it was gold.

The nugget was put in a bottle of liquid, as though it had once been a living organ and, now that it was dead, needed formalin to preserve it from decay. There was talk about wombgold from inside the beautiful model, and pretty soon after that they referred to the Lampak-wombgold that Karel Thin Air was born clutching to his infant chest like a life-belt as he set sail on the oceans of life.

While he was still in his mother's womb, the child already knew, people said, that gold can keep you afloat, that keeping your head above water in this country depends on what you have in your hand – not necessarily on what is in your own heart, but what you can impress on the hearts of your friends and foes.

It was cynical, Ingi realised as she questioned everyone she could, but it was the image woven about the Berghs: their obsessive reaching for and clinging to gold and water and feathers.

She understood Jonty better now, up there in his little house in Cave Gorge, and the way he lost his temper when demands were made on him. Jonty wanted to turn his back on worldly things, Ingi realised, he wanted to live in the company of his arums and his logs, chisels and mallets – and, it seemed, the angel on Tuesday mornings. He displayed his art only to the wind and weather: 'The sun will be my critic,' he was fond of saying.

Big Karel had been born more than ten years before the black ox-wagon came to Yearsonend and the gold nugget was a portent of what lay ahead. The matron told Ingi this as they sat at the breakfast table talking about Meerlust Bergh, the matron's grandfather on her mother's side. 'And the covetousness of the years to come,' whispered the matron, as she and Ingi leaned close to each other over the table while they waited for the general to join them for breakfast.

Everything that lay ahead, the great hushed-up scandal about gold and a Boer commando, gold and the young Italians, gold and ostrich feathers, gold and water – all of this was predicted by the nugget clenched in those tiny fists, the nugget that didn't float as human flesh would in the formalin but dropped to the bottom of the bottle with a ping and stayed there, glittering, mocking, like the eye of the devil.

'Like the eye of the devil!' The matron sat back, her eyes like saucers, after she had imparted this piece of information to Ingi. This was the longest conversation that she had ever had with Ingi and she looked exhausted – partly, Ingi realised, because a certain betrayal of the general lay in her words.

At that moment he came out of his room carrying a new map. The position of Van Riebeeck's Fourth Ship, the one carrying the money, had now been fixed beyond all doubt, he said, pointing out the longitude and latitude. 'There,' he showed Ingi, the matron, and Alexander, who looked on with his head at the general's elbow, 'there she lies, belly bulging with gold. And porcelain for the castle Van Riebeeck would have to build, and all sorts of other things. What other treasures were destined for the new settlement? How will we ever know what lies buried beneath the tides?'

Later, after they'd finished their eggs and lamb chops, it was the general himself who went to fetch the formalin bottle with the Lampak-wombgold from the safe next to the study, to show Ingi. It was wrapped in a flannel cloth and mounted in a case that Meerlust had had made shortly after the baby's birth. If you stood the case upright, and swung the little door open, the general demonstrated, the bottle was held up by two silver clamps in the shape of ostrich plumes, and you could smell the faint odour of formalin, and there lay the gold nugget; gleaming and looking indeed just like the eye of the Evil One.

'How can it be possible?' Ingi exclaimed. 'In a newborn baby's fist!'

'The doctors reckoned that the model might have swallowed gold nuggets to smuggle them out of the country,' said the general, 'because she often travelled on Meerlust's behalf from Yearsonend to Cape Town, and then on to Paris, Amsterdam and London, using her beauty to sell the feather hats to the top fashion houses. People think she must have been smuggling gold the whole time, and then one nugget moved into her body and ended up in the womb, just as Meerlust Bergh impregnated her, Irene Lampak, the matron's grandmother, you know.'

'What is it worth?'

'As a reminder of what lies buried in the womb of the earth, it's worth far more than its market value.' The general leered and stirred his black coffee.

'And how did it end up in the Drostdy?'

'On the death of his mother, Lettie, Jonty Jack inherited everything, but he wanted nothing. He showed up here one day and handed over the little case with the bottle and said, "For what it's worth." He knew that I love gold.' The general grinned. 'The Bergh estate is administered by Attorney Pistorius' office – they keep the investments in order and make sure that the houses don't fall into disrepair. They have someone throw open the shutters every week to let the sun in, and they fumigate the places and put out cockroach poison and—'

'Which houses?'

'Karel Thin Air's. And Meerlust's Feather Palace. Haven't you been there yet?' The general was taken aback.

'No,' answered Ingi. 'So Jonty has another house ... two houses?'

The general laughed and gave her a sly look. 'I thought you were such great chums. Both involved in the arts and all.'

Ingi put her nose in the air. 'He's entitled to his privacy. He doesn't have to tell me everything.'

'Ask him to show you one day,' said the general. 'You'll be fascinated – Meerlust's Feather Palace, just over the railway line, and Karel's house on the edge of the smallholdings and Edenville. The In-Between House people used to call it.' He leaned closer to Ingi. 'Maybe you'll find the map for Gold Pit in one of the houses. They said it was rolled up in one of Meerlust's artificial legs. The leg was hollow and apparently he walked around with the map for years.'

'But why doesn't someone look for the map?' cried Ingi. 'And get it over and done with!'

'That's only one map,' sighed the general, breathing over Ingi as if he was talking into his ham-radio microphone. 'There's a second, and without it the first one means nothing. You see, Meerlust knew one part of the truth. But the other part of the truth was in the hands of that tight-arsed little Transvaler.'

'Field Cornet Pistorius.'

'Aha!' exclaimed the general. 'I see you've done your homework!' He laughed and snapped his fingers for more coffee. 'Yes, that little arsehole Redbeard. Little Finger Redbeard.' Again he leaned towards Ingi and she found that his meaty breath was not dissimilar to Alexander's. 'The cannibal,' said the general.

'Oh!' shrieked the matron, covering her face with her hands and fleeing from the room.

'Italian blood,' the general remarked laconically. 'And Catholic on top of it.'

3

By dawn of that terrible night, the black blindfolds that the black ox-wagon men had tied over one another's eyes had turned into a flock of black starlings that lived for years squabbling and mocking in the stand of reeds behind Meerlust's Feather Palace. On summer days they'd descend on the fig tree in the backyard at Pistorius Attorneys.

A starling, everyone in Yearsonend knew, is a bird with no honour. No one will ever use the starling as a symbol on his badge or family crest. The starling is quite different from the dove, which stands for peace, or the crane, which represents dignity, or the swallow, which symbolises the changing of the seasons, or the owl, which personifies wisdom. The starling is a bird of raucous vituperation, a boisterous gossipmonger; it flies in rackety black swarms, noisily descending on trees, devouring everything edible then flapping away again.

It was the Lord's retribution, the Yearsonenders said, that the starlings should remind them throughout their lives of what had happened that night on the Plains of Melancholy, out there at Gold Pit. 'Them', of course, meant Field Cornet Pistorius, Meerlust Bergh and their descendants. Everyone knows you can try to shoot those starlings with an airgun or catapult; but they just sit there unscathed, as though they aren't made of flesh and feather and sinew, just shreds of black night or mourning cloth.

The barman pointed out the blindfold birds to Ingi as the swarm passed over, making a noisy sweep over the town before returning to their reed bed for the night. 'The blindfold birds?' asked Ingi, but he shook his head and disappeared behind the partition to look deep into a bottle while the customers thought he was fetching a damp cloth or more ice, or picking lemons.

'This is all I know,' said Look Deep, 'and what I know comes from gossip and things I've heard. In a way,' and he leaned over to Ingi with his brandy breath, 'the people of this town are also just a bunch of starlings fighting and gossiping and shitting on each other's heads.' He grinned.

'I've realised,' Ingi tried to take advantage of his chatty mood, 'that people don't really want to talk about the past.'

He grinned again, buffing a glass with his white cloth. 'They're saving their breath for the day the gold comes to light. Everyone hopes to get a little. Even if it's only a few coins, it could change your life.'

'Oh?' Ingi thought for a minute and swilled the foamy dregs round in her glass. 'You mean people are actually still thinking about the gold? They really hope . . . ?'

'They think about it every single day of their lives. For them it's no longer just gold. It's been much more than gold for a long time now.'

'What is it, then?' asked Ingi.

But he shook his head and two young farmers pushed through the mesh door, their boots clumping over the floor. They smelt of sweat and sheep's wool and greeted Look Deep noisily. Ingi drained her glass, said goodbye to him, nodded at the two men and left.

She walked in the tracks of the black ox-wagon, and she didn't know that – yet again – it was trekking up the road she was on; and that Meerlust was waiting with the black field corner, Moloi; and that Redbeard Pistorius was looking up, narrowing his eyes because he could see a man with a wooden leg and a wide hat with a showy plume, but he could also vaguely make out another figure. Perhaps it was the sun in his eyes, he thought, but, no, it was definitely a young woman in strange clothes. He shook his head and thought: it was too much, more than a year out in the wind and the weather. And he looked at Ingi walking down the dusty road, and at Meerlust bowing with a flourish of his hat and he thought: Up to here, dear God, and no further.

That night, after his men had apologised to Meerlust as they tied his hands behind his back, loosely so he wouldn't be hurt, he galloped off in search of Siela Pedi, while the black ox-wagon creaked onwards. It had been arranged that once they'd covered enough distance and made enough turns to confuse Meerlust, one of the men would ride back to meet Pistorius when he returned from Siela Pedi. Then they'd catch up with the others again.

As he rode, Redbeard planned what he'd say to Siela. Over and over again he muttered excuses, pleas, explanations. He added verses from the Bible, he debated and quoted law books and old sayings, and shook his head, his beard glowing with regret and indignation and shame.

He rode into Yearsonend at two in the morning. He could hear the pack of dogs that followed the black ox-wagon ransacking the town: wild barking and yelping careered recklessly through the streets. He came upon the savaged remains of several town dogs. One was still alive and Pistorius stopped to cut its throat. Not many fowls or geese would survive tonight, he realised, but perhaps the pack's frantic meat-lust would be sated before they began on the sheep.

He easily found the place that would become known as Meerlust's Feather Palace during the ostrich feather days that still lay ahead. He sat on his horse in front of the quiet house with its white gable and experienced a sudden urge to pull his horse's head round and to be gone, back to the Transvaal, to the place he knew, to turn his back on all this and to forget all that had taken place.

Later in life he'd always think back to this moment, to this fifteen minutes of reflection and the emotions that went with it; he'd remember how he almost gave in to the impulse.

But a sign made him decide to stay: a shooting star, bursting across the black night sky. All he could hear was the dogs barking in the distance, and as he sat quietly on his horse, the star sparkled over the heavens like the plume of a huge ostrich feather.

And the passing of that ephemeral star-feather against the sky was a sign of permanency for Pistorius; he must stay in Yearsonend, he thought, he must make a life here, not decay like a feather, but embed himself permanently, like a rock. In any case, someone had to be the guardian of the gold. If it had to be him and the man with the wooden leg, then so be it.

He dug his heels into the horse's flanks and rode round the

house to the back door where he knocked softly after patting the scared yard dog, which was hiding from the baying pack. After a long time the door opened and a sleepy servant peered out.

'I'm looking for the woman who came with us – Siela.'

The woman stared at him drowsily. 'She's with Moloi.'

'And where is he?'

'Edenville. The house with two front doors.' She indicated the direction.

'Thank you.' He wanted to turn round, but then added, 'Don't tell anyone I was here.' He pointed a finger at her in warning and tapped his Mauser. 'If they ask who knocked, say it was a vagrant. Do you understand?'

She nodded and closed the door, startled and now wide awake.

He remounted, suddenly realising how late it was. Galloping into Edenville he found the house without any difficulty. The dwellings were huddled together, with fowl-runs leaning against them, and there were even a couple of grass huts, the kind that the Griquas wove in the north-west. Moloi's was the only house where a light shone. He knocked.

Field Cornet Moloi opened the door and Pistorius realised two things immediately: first it was obvious from the expression in his eyes that Moloi knew something about the wretched history of the commando and the woman Siela Pedi, and second, that Pistorius was on another man's patch.

The walls of the small house were painted green, and there was more and better furniture than Pistorius had expected. Siela Pedi was sitting at the table beside a guttering candle. She looked like someone who'd just unburdened herself, but perhaps it only seemed this way to Field Cornet Pistorius. For a moment the three eyed each other uneasily: the woman at the table with the flickering candle throwing her huge shadow on to the wall, the black field cornet poised, still holding the door handle, and Redbeard Pistorius, feeling like an intruder.

'Siela Pedi, I want to talk to you.'

'You can talk,' she answered, and he saw neither anger nor fear in her eyes. She just sat there, perhaps too exhausted to feel anything, too drained and too numbed by the horrors that had befallen her since her abduction.

'Can we talk alone?'

The house was small, and all three realised that the only privacy was outside. Moloi stood aside so Siela could pass. In the small hours the dark mountain lay ponderous against the night sky.

Moloi stayed inside and shut the door. The other two stood beside Pistorius' horse and Siela folded her arms.

'Siela, I think our trek group is going to lie low here for the time being.'

She nodded, but didn't say anything.

'We'll get you a place at Meerlust Bergh's house. In the outside kitchen—'

She looked up sharply. 'No!'

'I'm offering to find you a decent job and accommodation, and you—'

'I'm staying here.' She was determined.

'Siela . . .' He drew closer.

'Haven't you taken enough?'

'Siela, I . . .'

She looked him in the eye. 'I know that you took me out of sorrow and desperation the first time. And let me tell you: even though you started the thing, you always behaved more decently than the others. That – that – pack of dogs!'

'Siela.' The pack of hunting dogs bayed in the distance and a shot rang out. Someone was trying to chase the marauders away from his fowl-run: they could hear hens cackling, then a corrugated-iron door scraped shut.

'And I know,' she said quietly, turning away from him, 'that you developed a feeling on the long road.'

'A feeling?'

'Yes.' She still had her back to him. 'For this black girl.'

Field Cornet Pistorius stared at the back of her head. No, he thought, no, I feel nothing. I *cannot* feel anything, because I have other duties: I have another life ahead of me. I will have to finish this business, once and for all. It must end here, tonight.

'If you breathe one word,' he said, and his words struck like the lashes of a whip on her shoulders, 'about what happened on the trek, I'll shoot you like a dog and then I'll put a Kruger pound in your dead hand. I have the right summarily to execute anyone who robs the state coffers.' His eyes went up to the dark mountain. Lord, give me strength, he thought. 'And tell Moloi that goes for him too. I don't know what you told him but I can see that he knows something. Tell him that Redbeard will shoot him like a dog. And the second gold coin will go into his dead hand.'

Siela Pedi stood there while the man remounted and galloped away into the night. Then the door opened and Moloi led her gently inside. He could see that something terrible had happened to her, but he didn't know that it had been far worse than anything that had gone before.

He made her a mug of coffee while Pistorius raced madly over the plains.

A black horse streaked through Ingi Friedländer's dreams as she lay asleep in her bed in the Drostdy. She didn't know where the horse had come from or where it was going, she didn't recognise the horseman with his flaming red beard, but the hoofs thundered insistently in her dream and she woke drenched with sweat.

I was dreaming, she thought, a dream about horses and terror. Other animals too. A man and a woman, yes, and a love that dared not be called love, a twisted, deformed love. A war love – tragic, lost, compelled by circumstance and loneliness, broken by circumstance and, yes, loneliness again.

She got up restlessly and stood at the window with her arms folded. She looked into the night sky and saw a meteor shoot across the darkness then break up into a wide, sparkling shower. It looks like an ostrich plume, she thought. But it vanished as suddenly as it had appeared.

I'll still come to understand everything, Ingi thought, including my own involvement here. Why am I going to so much trouble? Why do I feel as if things that happened so many years ago are unfolding in front of me now, and that they have a special meaning for me as well as everyone around me? Do all these things haunt this place because they've never been talked through to a conclusion? Is it the unfinished past that so stubbornly inhabits the present? This town is glutted with strife and violence and greed, rotten with gossip and inbreeding, yet so much remains unsaid.

In these few streets and side roads with the surrounding farms and smallholdings, the same heat builds up under the same trees every day, the same doves croon in the trees, and the same stones lie baking in the sun. There's a feeling that everything has always been this way and will always stay this way, but under the apparent monotony, the energy of repressed memories and frustrations is simmering.

I must start to paint again, thought Ingi, as she dozed off. Her right foot jerked as she dreamed, and the horse felt the kick of Pistorius' heel in its flank. Pistorius had no difficulty in finding the place where he had left the wagon. His comrade lay sleeping with his hat over his eyes and his horse was hobbled close by.

'Khakis!' yelled Pistorius and the man farted in terror, but he was in the firing position as fast as lightning, his Mauser at the ready.

'Off the horse, Field Cornet!' he screamed, still half dreaming. 'They'll take you out, up there!'

Pistorius pulled his horse round and said coolly, 'Take me to the ox-wagon.'

As they rode into the night Pistorius kept an eye open for landmarks. Experience had taught him that the silhouette of a rocky hill memorised at night can look different in daylight, but he knew how to make a day picture out of a night image. He studied the trees, but he knew that trees die or are chopped down, so he turned to the stern rocks in the landscape and the centuries-old dry riverbeds and, far away, the crest of Mount Improbable.

They came to a halt on a hill above the black ox-wagon. Moonlight glinted off gun barrels and stirrups and the uneasy oxen's ghostly horns. Field Cornet Pistorius knew he was now running his thumb along the cutting edge of a blade.

When Ingi woke that morning and drew back her curtains, a swarm of rowdy black starlings flew over the Drostdy on their way to Attorney Pistorius' office. Graceless birds, she thought, and turned to her mirror to give her hair a hundred brushstrokes.

4

Shadows, shadows, Yearsonenders would say of Meerlust Bergh's Feather Palace, the house with the cellars and the turrets on the other side of the railway line. No, they weren't referring to the starlings that were sometimes frightened up out of the reed bed at dusk like scraps of mourning cloth, flapping round and round the house in the wind, as though they were waiting for someone to come out. They weren't referring to the big pools of shade under the oaks. They were referring, usually under their breath, to the fact that no one lived in the house or its grounds any more: there were only shadows.

Yes, the dead are long gone, but their shadows still go about their daily tasks. In the morning you can see a hasty shadow move across the yard to the well. You can't see the handle turn or the bucket go down into the depths, or hear the handle's complaining squeak, but you can see the shadow of someone working, and the shadow of a bucket, and of water splashing on to the dust from the full bucket on the way back to the house, though no drops hit the ground.

You can see the thin shadow of a trail of smoke from the kitchen chimney in the early morning as it crawls like a caterpillar over the roof, though no smoke can be seen or smelt. And then, once it is time for the day's work to begin, the shadow of a tall man falls across the front veranda, and the shadow of a hat with an ostrich plume whose shadow marks the wall. The feather floats down the stairs and crosses the garden, around to the stables where horse shadows stamp on the smooth-trodden earth in front of the stables, and the stable hands cringe as the big man moves towards them on his wooden leg.

And you can see the shadow of a horse with only one stirrup:

the other is fastened against the saddle because the man had to learn to ride with one leg. Nevertheless he is one of the district's best horsemen, and you can hear, if only in your imagination, the shadow horse thundering away. Then you see the shadow of steam against the walls of the grand old bathroom, of water running from the taps, and in the bedroom the shadow of a beautiful woman rising from her bed, the sheets slipping to the floor, the woman gliding across the walls. You see a gown folding to the floor into its own shadow, like something sinking into dark water, and you see the early-morning sun etch the woman against the wall as she rests her hand on the side of the bath and bends to stir the water.

You see the breasts swing forward and the slim neck that holds the head so high; and then, half-way down the road, the horse wheels round. The man hurries back up the veranda steps, and his shadow is now in the room with the shadow of the woman in the bath. You see him throw down his jacket – the jacket shadow floating down like a bird – and you see her rise from the bath, wet and steamy. You see his hat arc down to the floor, and you turn your eyes away from the shadows that now reach for one another, leisurely in their tenderness and longing.

You look away, because it is too painful to imagine the most beautiful moments of the dead, it is too poignant to think that they are gone, and that this man, whose need for the grand gesture Irene Lampak understood so well, will never stroke her face again, that she will never put her hand on his strong spine to find solace with him again.

'No, I never go there,' Jonty told Ingi, 'but if you're curious, I'll give you the front-door key. Just beware,' and his eyes twinkled wickedly. 'They say the shadows grab you by the elbows, haul you down the passage and sling you out on to the veranda so roughly that you tumble down the steps.'

'Ah!' Ingi shuddered and smoothed back her hair, which today was fastened up in a businesslike bun.

'I don't want to meddle with their lives.'

'Whose?'

'Grandfather Meerlust and Grandmother Irene.'

'What do you mean by that?'

'I mean they're carrying on with their lives in the old house. They still design their hats on the sheets of paper that you'll see clipped to the easels, and she still pins clothes on to the wooden torsos. Go and have a look, see for yourself. Little drops of blood from when she pricks her fingers still stain the wooden floors in front of the plaster of Paris models that stand around there. Go and have a look. The house is a museum of the style and aspirations of their times. But watch out.' He grinned at Ingi again. 'Apparently there's an ostrich with a belly full of Kruger coins who keeps guard. A big male, whose plumes are reserved exclusively for hats worn by the royalty of Europe. He's very jealous about what he guards. And he's got a temper like a wounded buffalo. He sneaks up on you . . .' Jonty leaned closer to Ingi and his voice gave her goosepimples. 'He creeps up on you, walking as silently as the dead.'

She laughed and smoothed her hair again. 'Oh, come on!' she said, as she always did when she felt a little nervous.

'The only one who still visits regularly is Gwen Pistorius, because—'

'The woman without a face!' Ingi cried, hugging herself.

'Yes. Gwen Pistorius was named after her grandmother, Gwen Viljee. They say that in Grandmother Irene Lampak's fashion sketches of Gwen Viljee she looks exactly like Gwen Pistorius. They're like twins, separated only by time. Gwen Viljee worked in Irene Lampak's studio, first as a seamstress, then as a bookkeeper, and then one day Irene and Meerlust noticed her profile, her hair and beautiful slim neck. So they took her on as a model for the feathered hats. Gwen often travelled with them to London, Paris, Milan. Grandma Irene was one of the leading milliners of her time.'

'And what was the woman without a face looking for at the old house?'

'Maybe she went to ask advice from Grandma Gwen,' Jonty answered.

'Oh, come on!' Ingi was sceptical: she'd heard other explanations about the woman without a face.

'It's true!'

'But why did she want advice? What happened to Gwen Pistorius?'

Jonty rubbed his eyes. 'Well, it's all just hearsay. You know how people in this town can gossip.'

'And?'

He stood up, smiling kindly. 'They say if she walks in the sun, her profile still casts a shadow. But you can only see it in her shadow. Her face has lost all its features.'

'What does it mean,' Ingi asked quietly, 'to lose your features?'

'I don't know,' said Jonty. 'How can we ever know?'

'I . . .' Ingi got up, suddenly cold.

'Let's go.' He started walking. 'I'll give you the key and you can go on your own.'

'No!' Her voice darted out like a frightened bird escaping from a cage.

'What's wrong?' He'd been on his way to the house to fetch the key, but now he stopped.

'I . . . I . . .' Ingi stammered.

'What?'

'I'm not much good with shadows.'

'You're a painter. You must go and look. Because unless you can work with shadows, you'll never be able to work with light.'

5

She decided to take Mario with her on her visit to the Feather Palace – the man whose eyes looked only inward, whose ears heard only his own thoughts; he who'd wrestled with the angel; the nurturer of parrots; the man with a stone grown into the palm of his left hand.

She also took her sketchbook and pencils, packed away deep in her bag – at the bottom. In Cape Town, in her cottage on the slopes of Devil's Peak, she'd finished packing for her trip to Yearsonend and had been ready to leave when something had made her pause at the door. Then she turned back, knowing that she was to drive into the Karoo with its unfettered winds, and she emptied the few pieces of clothing out of her backpack, and put the drawing materials in at the bottom, then replaced the clothes. It had been at least three years since she'd last sketched or painted because her work at the gallery and her interest in other artists had swallowed up her own inspiration.

Perhaps I should start by sketching, thought Ingi. Begin with the thin, spare lines, the humility of the pencil. The richness of oils can follow later – she'd be able to paint extravagant canvases one day, when she'd lost the self-conscious reserve of youth and could give free rein to the vigour that was surging inside her.

Or perhaps, she thought, perhaps I should start with the canvases I really aspired to: understated spaces with controlled colour and texture, implying restrained energy, which you only discover on careful examination. Canvases for people not driven to flit on to the next image, but prepared to linger, to return and look afresh. Perhaps later, thought Ingi, rubbing suntan lotion on her already tanned arms, maybe later.

She looked in the mirror and thought: You're something between an art pedlar and a detective, Ingi Friedländer. You may not get your Staggering Merman for the foyer of the Houses of Parliament, but there's always that wagonload of gold.

But Ingi was increasingly aware that Yearsonend had freed something in her. Yes, it was the awareness of her own patterns and textures. She could sculpt, she could sketch. Her curiosity about what had happened there was a curiosity about the multiplicity teeming in herself, she thought: everything that made her impossible, demanding – according to her family and friends – and everything that made her human, hungry, greedy for life.

Perhaps there's some deep secret in my life too, she thought, taking up the brush and punishing her hair, which she'd brushed earlier, with urgent strokes. Perhaps I'll always search for my own features like the woman without a face. With increasingly vigorous strokes of the brush she thought, I'll investigate this story and take from it whatever's important to me. I'll find my own gold – perhaps not the Kruger coins, but something worth so much more: my features, my vision.

She checked to make sure the key Jonty had given her was in her backpack – the heavy cast-iron key with its ostrich-feather motif. Then she sat on her bed and took stock: Am I prepared for what might lie ahead? The old house with its shutters, and the big trees and the silence? The shadows of the dead gliding across the ground like guinea-fowl?

She put down the brush firmly, swung the backpack over her shoulder and left her room. The general was in the passage, his compass in his hand.

'On your way again?' he asked. She could see that he'd slept badly. He was wearing his long johns, and a white vest under the unbuttoned tunic with the pips on the shoulders.

'I'm taking Mario Salviati with me.'

'Lucky old man.'

She couldn't ignore the mockery in his voice. 'He has to get out. He's fading away here.'

'Miss Friedländer,' said the general, 'we're all fading away, some of us more rapidly than others.'

'I'm in a hurry, General.' She tore herself away from his breath, and his eyes, his shadow falling over her. She hurried through the kitchen, where the matron was discussing the day's menu with the cook.

'Do you eat porcupine?' Matron Taljaard asked, as Ingi rushed past.

'Some other time, Matron!' she replied, and trotted to Dumb Eyetie, who was sitting at the fountain with his hand in the water while the koi fondled his fingers. She approached the old man carefully, standing still for a bit so that he could pick up her scent.

When he turned his head to her, she went up to him slowly. She remembered his mouth like a baby's on her breast. She took him by his left hand and drew him up. The two dogs, Alexander and Stella, joined them immediately and the parrots hopped, screeching, from one perch to the other in their cage. The peacocks shook their long tail feathers, so waterfalls of eyes spilled down from the grapevine.

But Ingi ignored all of it – and the general and the matron who were standing at the kitchen door, and the sighs of the woman without a face in her back room, sighs that gusted through the vines like wind.

She whistled to the two Great Danes, and led the old man out through the gate, laughing as she pulled him, running, after her through the irrigation spray. She smelt the scent of the roses and the herb gardens and the oak trees, and knew that he could smell them too. There was the cooing of doves, already warmed to laziness by the sun at that time of the morning, and she was aware of summer damming up in the trees.

The dogs were surprised to deviate from the usual route. They were accustomed to passing Little Hands first, then Lampak's Dam, then going to Eviction Road via Giraffe Corner. There they usually looked in on the general store, and walked past the schoolyard with all its smells, often returning to the dam for a joyous splash, with Ingi sometimes stripping off her T-shirt and jeans to join them and show off her bikini. They were also surprised by her haste and sense of purpose.

Dumb Eyetie's heart was beating fast from running under the sprinklers and from the tingle of water-drops and warm sun on his skin, the odour of Ingi's hair, her deodorant and sweat, and from the smell of wet dog, earth and roses. He knew he was allowing himself to be swept along, but he lost himself in the smells and the movement of their bodies. He felt the rhythm of her movements in her hand, sometimes pulling then relaxing, then tugging impatiently and teasing; her hip bumping against his, her fervour and youth; and he felt, in the vibration of her feet on the road next to his, her haste.

Motion, he knew, was the sixth sense – something those who could see and hear didn't understand. In moving your body and being aware of the things around you, you get a feeling of rhythm and space, of distance and limitation.

That's why he took such pleasure in this fragrant woman. He

had no idea who she was. He just felt her tugging at his hand and he remembered, through the fabric of her nightdress, her breast in his mouth and the soapy smell of her body. And she was seldom still, forever stroking or touching or observing.

As she walked beside him, Ingi couldn't forget what Jonty Jack had said: 'Unless you can work with shadows, you'll never be able to work with light.'

I'll have to confront my own shadows, she realised, before I can work with light again. And the man next to me, who sees only night and hears only silence? Is there still some difference in his life between noise and silence, shadow and light? Or is it all one to him? Has he gone beyond the point where the distinction matters?

She walked faster still and ignored the inquisitive workers on the smallholdings, who stared at her and the old man and the two dogs. They took a road she hadn't walked along before, which wasn't often used by anyone. Since the last rain, Ingi thought, no one had driven or walked there. It was a part of Yearsonend that people avoided through superstition and fear – so Jonty had warned her. And she could sense it then, and was glad she had with her the two dogs and Dumb Eyetie.

The winding driveway to Meerlust's house was lined with palms. Their leaves brushed against each other in the light breeze. Dumb Eyetie sensed the rustling of the leaves, for he walked closer to Ingi. When they rounded the last turn and Ingi looked at the imposing house with its verandas and shutters, she saw a flock of guinea-fowl, black as shadows, slipping into the long grass.

Other shadows, too, now receded around corners, slipped into cracks in the dilapidated garden wall, wrapped themselves around tree-trunks. The hair on the dogs' backs bristled and they rushed about barking, snapping at fresh air and smells too delicate for Ingi to pick up, but which made Dumb Eyetie lift his face.

The key weighed heavily in her hand when they stood on the veranda. She pushed open the front door and the coolness streamed out. She took Dumb Eyetie's elbow and whistled to the dogs. They followed her cautiously, sniff-sniffing at the threshold.

Then they went inside. In the hallway stood a grandfather clock with its hands at seven o'clock. There was a large mirror in a gilt frame. The mirror probably carries in its memory images of everyone who ever stood in front of it or walked past, Ingi thought. Irene Lampak's every gesture and movement, Meerlust Bergh's or little Karel's every doubting glance or confident gaze would be imprinted on it. For an image only appears to vanish in a mirror, just as a stone appears to disappear in a dam of water once it has broken the surface. As the stone lies waiting on the bottom, so what the mirror has seen also lies in its depth.

A large room led off the hallway – the Feather Studio, as it was known in times gone by. And there were the big designers' tables with fashion drawings in the elegant ink strokes of Meerlust and Irene Lampak still fastened to them. Ingi bent down and read, in ornate Gothic script, the words written next to one of the drawings: 'Irene, darling, read this and let me know what you think of it, it was written in haste . . .'

She had to bring her face close to the paper to decipher the faded ink: 'Autumn is almost upon us. Very soon we will feel a little uneasy in our light-as-air summer outfits. The sensible among us will already be looking at our wardrobes to see what can still be of use and what should be replaced with something new. It is indubitably a very serious and difficult time in our lives: the selection of a new wardrobe. The first photograph shows an elegant little hat, simply and tastefully trimmed with feathers. A short veil, leaving the mouth free, is . . .' And there the writing stopped. At the bottom was written: 'Remember: pay the stable hands on Friday.'

Ingi looked about her. Light beamed through the gaps in the closed shutters, and mannequins stood around her in the twilight. They wore hats, and the feathers on those faceless heads undulated gently in the breeze coming through the open front door. She looked at the plaster of Paris models, and the scattering of pins at the feet of one. She went over and bent to pick them up, but they were stuck to the floor – in rust or hardened dust, she couldn't tell.

Suddenly Ingi realised that Mario Salviati was no longer next to her. 'Mario!' she called, and the two dogs came running. She crossed the dim hallway and found him in another big room, where rows of hats in all shapes and sizes lay displayed on shelves. He sat cross-legged on the floor, stroking a long ostrich feather over his arm.

She went right up to him, and saw that he was so engrossed that he was unaware of her. Was she imagining it or was a smile playing around his lips? She bent closer and watched the feather move over the brown arm and then, when he turned his arm, across the softer paler skin, over the veins at his wrist and then the shell of the hand, over the stone, which had grown into the palm, before it tickled between his fingers.

She stood closer and her scent fell across him. He stopped and held out the feather. It was the first overture Dumb Eyetie had made to her. Until then, apparently involuntarily, he'd allowed himself to be carried along by her. She took the feather and began to tickle his face. She sat down next to him and brushed it across his nose and lips, his eyebrows and the crinkled eyelids.

All around them hats lay on shelves: each hat had a name, and labels like Ibis, Gigolo and Montpellier had been written neatly in calligraphic script under each one. Here, too, the feathers undulated like seaweed in an underwater swell.

Then the dogs became agitated. Ingi and Dumb Eyetie followed them on their search through the house. In the dining room the enormous table was set with wine glasses, plates, cutlery and napkins for a party of twenty-four. The mouthwatering aroma of freshly roasted leg of lamb wafted in. Ingi saw Dumb Eyetie lift his head and a thread of drool from Alexander's jaws fell to the floor. She listened incredulously to the clink of cutlery on china. Panicking, she took Dumb Eyetie's elbow and dragged him away, out of the room and down the passage.

The two dogs took to their heels as well, rushing ahead, skidding on the smooth floor. As they skated on Persian carpets, their great hindquarters crashed on to the wooden floor and then they all tumbled headlong out of the front door and down the steps.

After they'd rushed past, their images sank slowly into the mirror in the entrance hall, and they stopped to catch their breath in the sun on the lawn.

Still out of breath, Ingi gazed in astonishment at one corner of Mario Salviati's mouth. He seemed to have found his smile again.

6

Captain William Gird sat on a campstool under the oak in front of the Feather Palace. His horse was hobbled behind him, as was the mount of his guide Slingshot X!am. His drawing-table had been set up and the little bottles of paint had been neatly unpacked in rows. The smell of warm kikuyu grass wafted strongly up his nose. Slingshot X!am sat with his back against a tree-trunk and his hat over his face.

One might imagine he was dozing – Captain Gird certainly thought so – but Slingshot X!am had a small spy-hole in the top of his hat through which he observed the world. He looked with amusement at poor Captain Gird, who scratched his anus repeatedly, under the illusion that no one could see him. His pants were already daubed with numerous red and yellow fingerprints, but Slingshot X!am made no mention of this, although from the rear he reckoned his lord and master resembled a multi-coloured fighting cock.

That day they'd started by crawling around in the cave on Mount Improbable because Gird wanted to copy the blue ostrich. It was one of the strangest San paintings they'd ever come across – Slingshot X!am had led the captain there because he'd known about the painting. He'd been told as a child that it was the work of one of his forefathers.

Then they'd taken the horses to drink and ridden across to the Feather Palace. They hobbled their mounts there while Ingi Friedländer and Dumb Eyetie and the dogs were still walking to the house. As Ingi, heavy key in hand, hesitated on the veranda, Captain Gird decided to try to draw her and the dogs.

And that was what he was doing now, while Ingi and Dumb Eyetie were standing indecisively under the oaks after fleeing from the house, and the Great Danes ran around Gird, sniffing, and Alexander lifted his leg against the tree over where Slingshot X!am was sitting.

Captain Gird was a man who liked to draw animals, and he was also inclined to exaggerate a bit for the sake of the viewing public in England. So the giraffe was always a touch taller, the rhinoceros sometimes had four horns, and his study of an elephant with two trunks had become famous in London – and had also been purchased for the palace.

The drawing was presented as record of a species found between the Berg and Gariep rivers. And when Captain Gird drew people, whether he was copying Bushman paintings or creating portraits of Khoisan or Xhosas, he was also inclined to emphasise the women's breasts and buttocks, bulk out the men's muscles, make the spears longer and the genitalia larger.

And this was exactly what he did with Ingi. Her Florentine nose acquired Roman proportions, a great wind swept through her hair, her pretty lips became pouting red, and her little breasts, pressing so cheekily against her T-shirt, trumpeted forth her sensuality. The two dogs, Alexander and Stella, became monsters, standing almost as high as Ingi's shoulder. Dumb Eyetie was transformed into a hulking ape, an orang-utan looming over Ingi in blind, primitive lust.

I excel myself, thought Captain Gird, scratching his backside. Slingshot X!am looked on, grinning inside his hat. He already knew exactly where to lead the captain next, what should be brought to his notice and how to exploit his eager eye for the exotic.

Round the fire at night, he'd regale the captain with incredible stories about blue Bushmen and shipwrecks and runaway slaves and unknown kingdoms where gold was as common as gravel, and afterwards the poor captain would lie dreaming under his sheepskin rug and complain the next morning that his paint was running low, that they should ask a traveller going south to bring more coloured inks, and he'd bemoan the scarcity of paper, and the rainstorms that had destroyed some of his drawings.

Ingi was ashamed of her cowardly retreat from the Feather Palace. She realised that Dumb Eyetie knew exactly where they were – the old man would have recognised the rhythm of the steps, the feeling of the heavy door and the smell of the fabrics and ostrich feathers. It was familiar territory to him, so he'd found his own way to the hat room.

And the poor dogs – already so jittery from the matron's unpredictable behaviour and the groans of the invisible vanished wounded in the passages of the Drostdy, and the woman without a face and the visitations from the feathered man – they, too, gave in to panic and bolted when she had begun to run. Who could blame them?

Yet Ingi had the feeling that her shame hadn't been exposed only to the two Great Danes and the old Italian: someone else was watching her. She reckoned it must be Meerlust Bergh, who still wandered around here and now regarded her with a grin. She didn't know that she, the painter, was being painted into the landscape of this world by another painter; she didn't know that he was giving her the same robust energy with which he charged his drawings of antelope and predators; she didn't know that William Gird, her predecessor as artist, was painting a place for her in the landscape – a place that would make her a permanent inhabitant of Yearsonend.

7

A community with a surprising number of artists in its midst, thought Ingi, as she recalled Irene Lampak's beautifully shaped hats, and the gorgeous designs in the ornate strokes of Meerlust's pen, and the small, crouching hunters with bows and arrows and the game you'd see painted on the walls of the blocked cave, should it ever be dug open.

And then there was Jonty Jack with his Staggering Merman, who was supposed to have arisen miraculously out of the ground. And Mario Salviati, the sculptor of the statue of the Blessed Virgin Mary. And the explorer who sat down at what is now called Giraffe Corner and drew the sketch of the giraffe, which currently hangs in the palace in England. And even Karel Thin Air, with the stone channel that nowadays might be regarded as a work of art, cutting so beautifully and symmetrically through the landscape, winding so lyrically around hills, scaling so fiercely the spine of Mount Improbable . . .

Gradually she discovered more about that impressive couple, Meerlust and Irene, the man with the series of artificial legs that he could screw into place according to the occasion, and the woman who bathed in the dam on Sunday afternoons – causing such a sensation that people still spoke of it.

It seemed that by staying Ingi was attracting stories to her; she didn't need to make many enquiries now because each person she came across had something to tell her.

The storekeeper, a distant cousin of Jonty Jack, left his assistant to see to minor sales at the cash register while he leaned eagerly across the counter, pressing the tips of all ten fingers primly together, as if holding his tale carefully in the cage of knuckles, and told her about the man Meerlust who, against all good advice, began to farm ostriches. He had Huguenot blood, difficult and creative; he was a man who always wanted to travel further, hunt bigger game.

'Spectacular,' the storekeeper told Ingi, 'and a man with a nose for business.' He rubbed his thumb and index finger together and Ingi heard skin scrape against skin. 'A man like that decides to farm with ladies' fashions! Can you believe it? So improbable that the town threw up its hands in amazement.' The man bent closer to Ingi and pursed his lips. 'And disgust.' Triumphantly he straightened up and spaced his palms out wide on the counter. 'Fashion is about fads, the people said, and here at Yearsonend no one pays any attention to the whims of dressmakers. But that Meerlust was born for greater times. Ec-cen-tric.'

The man peaked his fingers again and Ingi watched a sunbeam slant into the dark shop making the flour motes glint. 'And not just the kind of fashions that could be sold in this shop. No, think big and act big – that was Meerlust Bergh. Paris, London, that class of operation.'

Ingi looked at his hands again. I could paint them, she thought, this little cathedral of old man's fingers, the dour, greedy eyes behind it, dusk and the labels on the tins of food behind him, the old cash register and the sunbeams rising up to the roof like tiny ladders.

'I—' she began, and felt suddenly as if she was about to confess a great secret.

'And the . . . Chinky wench,' the man continued, allowing his voice to drop just a fraction at the last two words and opening his eyes wide. He leaned on his elbows confidentially. 'A great beauty.' Triumphantly, as if at the climax of his story, he straightened and brushed his hands over his white apron as if wiping sweat from his palms.

'I—' Ingi started again.

'At first, when the people heard Meerlust was bringing a yellow woman home, oh, you should have heard them! But when they saw her! Shrank back in their shells like tortoises. For she had style. Look, our people didn't know what style was. To them, style meant a chestnut horse at a show. But Meerlust had said, "You'll see she has style." And when she arrived here, by God, she got out of the carriage that always stopped here, in front here, between the shop and Pistorius Attorneys, and when she put her foot out of the carriage, why, then you saw that thing Meerlust had spoken of. Style.'

'I—'

'With such a hat on her head, and just such an ostrich feather in the hat, and such long legs, and such a high bosom – I beg your pardon, Miss 'Länder, but to this day they talk about the woman's wasp waist, and such proud eyes looking down at the townsfolk from aloft. Supposed to be a descendant of eastern princes, and you could see it was true.'

Ingi drew a deep breath. 'Actually I came to ask if you perhaps have paint and brushes.' The words slipped out so rapidly that she scarcely heard them herself.

'Faint?'

'Paint!'

'Paint? Does the old general want to paint the Drostdy again? Only last year—'

'Painting paint. You know . . . er . . . artist's paint . . .'

The man plonked his open hands down on the counter again. 'Oh, like Jonty Jack!'

'Yes, exactly . . . I—'

'But he goes and buys his things in the city.'

'Yes, but it's . . . for me.'

The man's eyes opened wide again. 'Miss 'Länder! You paint too?'

'Yes.' Ingi sighed heavily. 'Yes, I'm also a painter.'

She watched the girl at the cash register, with one hand on the change, turn her head to them and listen, ears pricked. The smell of the shop took some getting used to, but once you became accustomed to the odd combination of flour, paraffin, sweets and tobacco it lured you back time after time.

'You're wanting paint and a brush?'

'Yes, if you could help me to order it from Cape Town. There's a train every day, isn't there? . . . Or the railway bus passes here on Wednesdays . . .'

'It'll only take a day, Missy,' he said. 'Then your equipment will be here. But I want first option on the picture. It must hang in here, over there.' She looked to where he was pointing: a dark section of wall, beneath rows of jam tins and boxes of washing powder.

'And what should I paint for you?' asked Ingi.

'Perhaps yourself, Missy?'

The man's body, with the rounded paunch pressing against the white apron, gave a skittish little twist at the hips, and Ingi saw something in his eyes she hadn't noticed before. Why, she couldn't tell, but she thought of a shiny lizard appearing suddenly on a stone, then slipping away as though it had never been there.

'Oh, yes?' She pushed the paper, with her order for oils, brushes and canvas, across to him. 'There's the phone number of the shop in Cape Town. Just add your profit and expenses. Please get exactly what's written there.'

Then she turned and fled from the shop. Outside she felt that everyone was looking at her. They must have heard me in there and now they're looking at me differently, thought Ingi. Now they know about this thing inside me that has to come out. And why does it bother me – why am I so ashamed of it?

She began bravely to walk down the street, glad in spite of her embarrassment to be without the dogs. When she went through the gate to take the path to Jonty Jack's little house in Cave Gorge, his telescope captured her in its lens.

Jonty bent low and adjusted the lens so that she was clearly and sharply defined as she walked along. With the way in which the lens distorted distance, her movements appeared strangely slow, yet certain too. She approached as if walking on a giant movie screen, and tossed back her hair and wiped the sweat from her forehead and swung her arms.

He turned round and looked at the freshly oiled Staggering Merman, glistening in the sun. She must have been to Meerlust's house already, he thought, and now she'd look at him, Jonty, differently, knowing about his money – old money – and the possibilities open to him: he could live in the homestead again, or sell it and travel far away, or buy a house on the slopes of Table Mountain with a sea view. She's approaching me differently now, he thought with satisfaction, as someone with choices.

The minute she saw him she waved and called, 'Today I want to hear all about Meerlust Bergh. I'm going to sit here until you've told me everything.' She laughed, and he raised his hands as if to ward her off.

'I'd rather go and fly my new kite.' He pointed to a bright yellow kite leaning against the wall.

'No.' She shook her head firmly. 'Today I must hear everything about Meerlust. What a house!' Then she gestured towards the sculpture. 'I see the Merman is shining like a live fish today. We must talk.'

He turned to his telescope. 'You've just taken twenty minutes to walk from here,' he indicated the front end of the telescope, 'to here,' and then the other end with the eyepiece. She started to say something, but he held up a finger. 'That's the route you covered, didn't you? From here to here?'

'No,' said Ingi. 'I walked along the path, from the gate to here. Surely you weren't watching me all the time?'

'I'm not joking,' Jonty continued. 'Listen again. As far as I'm concerned, you walked from here to here.' He gestured to the front and back ends of the telescope again. 'And as far as you're concerned, you walked along the path, from down at the gate, through under the trees, to here with me.'

'So what?' asked Ingi, uncertainly.

'That, Miss Friedländer, is your lesson for the day!'

'My lesson?' She laughed, and took a mock swing at him.

'Yes,' Jonty replied playfully. 'I want to teach you to be curious about the right things.'

'Is that so?'

'Yes – because which of your two journeys is the real one?'

8

'Let's begin with the angel,' Ingi said to Jonty, as they sat with mugs of tea, looking at the Staggering Merman.

'Like a totem,' said Jonty, gesturing at the sculpture. 'At night the angel comes and sits on the Staggering Merman. Look at those grey streaks of shit on the Merman's head. He sits there dozing, and when the sun rises he flies off.'

'Oh, you are an impossible man,' sighed Ingi. 'How can I ever get any sense out of you?'

'You got a lot today!' cried Jonty. 'A lesson on truth, a mug of tea and—'

'Here's the key to the Feather Palace.' She scrabbled in her backpack and gave him the heavy key. 'I can understand why you don't want to live there.'

'Too many shadows,' said Jonty. 'You trip over them. Here the wind blows everything clear each day, like a fresh breath, from up in the ravine, down to the town. Here, there are no memories, and that's most important.'

She took a sip of tea. 'Tell me about Meerlust and Irene now. The love story. That's what I want to hear. Not about the war or gold or feathers, but about their love.'

'Ah,' said Jonty and stretched out his legs in front of him. 'She was a princess and Meerlust loved her so passionately that it embarrassed the whole town. He'd walk around, his neck red with passion, picking flowers along the fences of the smallholdings and carrying them back to Irene Lampak in the Feather Palace. He showered her with gifts and employed violinists to play for her. He contracted artists to paint her and there are many old photos of her, taken by the top photographers in the fashion industry. He was quite a bit older than her – and, you know, it was a crazy business: an old rooster falls in love more desperately than anyone else. He glowed with love from top to toe, and people say that even his wooden leg was blood red with passion!

'Actually, Meerlust fell in love first with the world of fashion and clothing. And from that world, as if she'd been sent to him along a catwalk, Irene Lampak sashayed up to him. Through her he could adore the spirit of the times. Meerlust was besotted by his era and Irene Lampak personified it. Just look at the photos of her.'

Jonty poured more tea from the little tin kettle. Ingi noticed how delicately he handled the teaspoon with his heavy hands, those powerful sculptor's fingers.

'It was a love that, like many loves, flourished on contrasts. He was a man of the grand gesture; Irene was gentler, more cautious, almost secretive. He was of Africa, she from the East. He was also a European. Although his mother, Sara Bruin, had Moloi blood, Meerlust was a man who regarded himself as a European; a world-traveller and a Huguenot descendant on his father's side, Huguenot Viljee. The mother was incidental, mousy Sara Bruin, begotten by William Gird, the explorer . . .'

'And painter . . .'

'Exactly. Out of the union of William Gird and the daughter of Ensign Moloi, survivor of a shipwreck, and Titty X!am, the Bushman woman whose ancestors are said to have wintered in the cave up here, before heading for greener pastures.

'But Meerlust decided to be white, he could afford it. Right from the start he thought big, and when the ostriches arrived, his ship came in, so to speak.'

Ingi gave Jonty a sharp look. 'And the black ox-wagon?'

'The only loot my family ever got from that was grief.' Jonty's reply was so brusque it startled her. He reached out and touched her gently. 'I'm sorry.' He sighed. 'Yes, some nights, according to the people of Edenville, you can still see the black ox-wagon under way to the Murderers' Karoo. It never stops. There's a restlessness in gold and it never brings peace.'

'And the fashion houses?'

Jonty whistled softly. 'It's difficult to believe how the millinery business, which began so humbly, almost as a hobby, grew into a big business undertaking overnight. In those days a special train even came to Yearsonend to fetch hats and feathers. At times Meerlust and Irene were overseas more than they were here. People who know say they created the twenties' image – a whole era was created in the Feather Palace.'

'Here, in the middle of the Karoo.'

He laughed. 'Yes, here on the edge of the Murderers' Karoo.'

'And Meerlust's relationship with Irene? Tell me about their love.' She looked at him through her long lashes.

He laughed. 'You're luring me into stories.' He thought for a while. 'Yes, that's probably what it was: the attraction of different worlds. And the full-blooded days of the feather boom. People lived on champagne and parties. Farmers became million-aires overnight as the feathers were snatched up in Europe. And

Meerlust was in the midst of it: when the boom came, his infrastructure was in place and he was ready. He'd seen it coming. He was a genius in that respect. When he bought warehouses in Europe, people thought him mad. Nine months later every European fashion guru and clothing manufacturer was racing to those warehouses. I believe they sometimes broke down the doors. And here at the Feather Palace Meerlust and Irene sat and drew those beautiful, elegant, sometimes risqué lines that would define the era.'

'They were two artists, in fact.' Ingi brushed her hair out of her eyes.

He smiled. 'You're a romantic, Ingi. Yes, if you want to be kind, you could probably say so. You could make a case for them being more artists than rock-hard business people. For they were that too. Astute business people.'

'I believe they were artists.' Ingi spoke with conviction. 'I could feel it in that house.'

'Right, let's say they sometimes looked through the telescope, but they also often forgot about it.'

'The lesson continues!'

'No, the lesson of the day has been completed. And are you going to start painting again here at Yearsonend? Didn't you go to the shop?'

Ingi blushed. She was annoyed at the warmth that rose from her neck and coloured her cheeks. 'I hope so,' she said softly.

He looked straight at her. 'The wind clears your head, Ingi. Each time you come to my house, your eyes are brighter.'

'I don't ... know,' said Ingi, 'whether I'll still be able to paint. I ...'

'I feel that way every morning,' Jonty consoled her. 'Each morning I'm convinced I've lost it. And yet, when evening comes, I find I have achieved something. Never as perfect as the Staggering Merman, for that's not within my gifts. The merman sprang up from the ground to show me what I'll never be. Now I know, and I don't need to worry too much. I recognise my limitations.

The Staggering Merman freed me from striving to create a perfect image. Do you understand that?'

'Yes,' said Ingi, and thought: When will you be ready, Jonty, to acknowledge that the merman is the work of your own hands? Or, she wondered, had the Merman really grown from the earth, like a tree? 'You're lucky,' she said quietly. 'Most people spend their lives looking for their Staggering Merman. And you've got yours right here.'

'Granted to me,' said Jonty, getting up and going over to the kite. 'By the angel!' he called to her, grinning.

They launched the new yellow kite on the slopes of Mount Improbable, in a wind so clear and pure and against a horizon so blue and endless that Ingi didn't know whether it was the kite flying, or whether she, with the string in hand, was the one soaring in the blue.

Things are changing for me, she thought. And gulped a mouthful of Karoo wind.

9

Meerlust Bergh arrived in Amsterdam with a light suitcase, in which lay a suit, bow ties and a few smart shirts; a second, somewhat heavier suitcase, in which his ivory leg, a stinkwood leg and a blackwood leg with silver inlay were neatly packed in velvet compartments, and a third, which was so light for its size you might well have imagined it contained nothing but air.

It was this third case in particular that Meerlust watched over during the voyage from South Africa to Europe. He'd had it specially built, with tiny parallel filigree work for ventilation; a case covered with crocodile skin and lined with red velvet.

You might think he carried a musical instrument in it – perhaps a violin, or a trumpet. Because of this, people on the ship at first took him for a musician on his way to the concert halls of Europe: a flamboyant man with clothes of the best quality, and a handicap he had transformed from a humiliation into a fine ornament.

During his morning perambulation on the upper deck, and breakfast, Meerlust wore the dark stinkwood leg. He arrived at lunch with the silver-inlaid blackwood leg, and in the evening, in his elegant evening wear, it was the ivory leg with the carved symbols that drew attention.

Meerlust's leg, and the women's fascination with the way in which he had turned his disability into a flamboyant social asset, helped to develop his understanding that attraction and erotic fascination often centred on a deviation from the ordinary. He applied this insight to his designs: that single, daring divergence which caught the eye and, because of its incongruity, suddenly seemed so right, so exciting.

So he carried off his artificial leg in a manner that sometimes made other men feel a handicap like that might be an advantage – especially when the colourful hunting stories and tales of the monstrous lion that had caused his disability entered into the conversation.

Meerlust kept the light case with him wherever he went, and ensured that no sea spray reached it during the voyage. There was a living creature in it, his fellow passengers gossiped, and later, when they were better acquainted, they asked him playfully but cautiously, 'What do you carry in that crocodile-skin case?'

Meerlust smiled. 'A potential fortune,' he said. 'And I sleep with the case in my arms at night.' And then he'd invite them banteringly to further speculation, there in the dining saloon of the ship in the evening, when the orchestra continued to play long after dinner, and the men sat around him with cigars and Cognac, and the women watched him inquisitively and listened to his tales of Africa.

'Do you think it's the ash of a dear one that I'm going to scatter in a castle garden? Or do you think it's a Stradivarius, which I guard with my life? Or could it be a rare tropical animal, currently in hibernation, that will astound the zoologists in Europe?'

They shook their heads and laughed, and before the voyage ended – some had even tested the weight of the case – there was consensus that it was empty. 'Nothing at all?' Meerlust asked laughingly, late one evening, when he was sitting in a group playing cards as the ship crossed the Equator. 'Quite empty?'

But he never let on what he carried with him, and when he arrived in Amsterdam, one of his fellow passengers, a man of uncertain nationality who excelled at cards and claimed to be a *National Geographic* journalist who had to write an article on a voyage from Africa to Europe, tried in the hurly-burly on the gangway, among the streamers and balloons and milling crowds, to grab the case from Meerlust.

For a moment they wrestled, and Meerlust saw in the man's eyes an expression he would often encounter in the years ahead: a sort of covetous desire to take from him what he possessed at any cost; jealousy; contempt. For a moment four hands tugged at the case, then Meerlust trod on the man's foot with the sharp point of his stinkwood leg. He rested his full weight on the wooden leg and turned his hip slightly. When he heard bone crack, the man abandoned the attempt and limped off into the crowd. Meerlust watched him go and saw in him – with powerful foreknowledge – the epitome of all that would deter him, stand in his way, try to hold him back.

Meerlust checked in at an hotel, and cruised that afternoon on the horseshoe canals. What he didn't know was that the young model Irene Lampak, newly divorced from her husband, Anton Doubell, a Dutch civil servant in Indonesia, was unpacking her suitcase in the same hotel, in the room directly below his. She didn't feel strange in Amsterdam, because since her childhood her parents had made regular business trips to the Dutch capital and other great cities. But it was her first journey on her own, and with the same care with which she'd resolved to reject the advances of all men and focus on her career, she now unpacked her clothes.

Had she, at that moment, while unfolding a silk blouse, looked out of the window to her right, she would have seen the boat passing, the man stretched out comfortably in an easy chair on the deck, and also the wooden leg resting on a little bench, and she would have been interested in him immediately because he had a strong aura of originality – which Irene Lampak had always liked.

While Meerlust relaxed on the boat listening to the water lapping against the hull, Irene slid her hands over a blouse, then a dress. Carefully she took up a hat and settled it on her head. She looked in the mirror while Meerlust's boat slipped into a side-canal and out of sight of her hotel window, and she knew that she was happy.

They saw each other for the first time at breakfast the next morning. She was eating a boiled egg when she heard the odd footsteps on the wooden floor in the passage: a normal tread, and then a thud, a tread and a thud. She heard a voice and a clear, warm laugh, and the next minute Meerlust Bergh swept into the dining room, with the manager – already eating out of his hand – scurrying behind him. She recognised his Afrikaans because she knew Dutch, and realised at once that he came from Africa.

In his voice already, she imagined, she could hear something of the continent – the warmth and the exotic unpredictability. A hunter, she thought, or an aristocratic farmer. Or an explorer. An archaeologist, doing research deep in the forests?

Irene was young and romantic and she was ready for a liaison. Meerlust walked into her life on exactly the right day. She'd just arrived in Amsterdam, she'd broken free of a failed marriage and over-protective parents, and she'd come alone to a metropolis as a model, with promises of great things from fashion moguls. She was making a fresh start, with determination and a spirit of adventure that would always remain with her.

An important, self assured man, without the sly pretensions of Europeans. That was how she saw Meerlust, with his broad shoulders, his huge stature and the flash of silver on his artificial leg, as though he didn't wish to conceal his handicap but rather to emphasise it.

Meerlust had a cigar in his hand and a loose jacket hung from his shoulders. He didn't look at the delicious dishes with studied reserve, like the other guests, but bent over the food and voiced to the manager his delight with the delicacies. He took a large plate and heaped it with cold fish, prawns and meat, and sat down at a table in the corner. When he looked up, chewing, he looked straight into the dark eyes of Irene Lampak. It was a glance that would remain with him for the rest of his life.

Etiquette compelled both to avert their eyes immediately, but both knew by their accelerated pulse rates and a tingly numbness in the legs that this was love at first sight.

After breakfast Meerlust lounged in the foyer, smoking a cigar among the sofas and the table with newspapers and magazines arranged in front of a big window. He'd unfolded a newspaper, but kept a sharp watch on the stairway. The exquisite young beauty, he knew, would have to descend sooner or later.

And then she appeared, self-conscious and alert, a girl on her first visit to a great city on her own, with an elegance he'd seldom encountered before. In his imagination, he started to fashion garments for her body, as if he already knew every detail of each lovely limb. Textures, colours and cuts flashed through his mind and he draped them about her.

Under all the designs was the beautiful pale brown body of the woman he would learn later that day was Irene Lampak: junior model and previously a student of art, daughter of a well-known aristocratic merchant couple from Indonesia, survivor of an early, ill-considered marriage to a dreary civil servant.

When he heard her step on the stairs, he knew instinctively that it was she. He put down the newspaper and waited. When she appeared she also noticed him, but allowed her eyes to glide away as she handed in her key at the counter, right next to Meerlust's chair. When she walked out, she glanced at him again for a moment, but he seemed to be engrossed in the newspaper.

That day they wandered separately through the streets of Amsterdam. Both experienced the languid feeling of falling in love, that feeling of an unknown other, of instant fascination, of risk and daring.

When she returned to the hotel late in the afternoon, after appointments with clothing manufacturers and dress designers, there was a knock at her door. It was a waiter, who reported that another guest, an important gentleman from Africa, had enquired discreetly whether she would be prepared to accept a gift from him.

Irene stood at the door, hand on the knob, the waiter standing with raised eyebrows before her. She had to reach a decision quickly. Before her journey the decision had been so easy: she would avoid men, especially men who, like this one, moved quickly and used ploys like this waiter to create an illusion of discretion. But she had no choice. She had to give an affirmative answer.

In his room Meerlust waited anxiously for the waiter to return with Irene Lampak's reply. Should the answer be negative, he had decided to ignore her and respect her privacy.

At last there was a knock at his door and he flew to open it.

'Yes?' he asked the waiter.

'The lady is prepared to accept your gift.'

'Oh!' Meerlust was surprised.

'But she wishes to inform you that she is engaged and about to enter into a marriage.'

Meerlust considered for a moment. He had travelled far. Something had thrown him off balance. When he had seen the girl, all reason had fled. His business trip, so carefully planned around the contents of the crocodile-skin case, now seemed trivial. 'None the less,' he said. 'None the less.' Then he looked at the waiter. 'This is very important – have you a silver tray?'

For a minute the man was nonplussed. 'We have special trays,' he confirmed hesitantly, 'for special occasions.'

'Bring one. Silver or gold.'

Again Meerlust waited. He poured more Cognac and stood at the window. It was late afternoon and gulls hovered above the canal. Perhaps she'll have dinner with me tonight, he thought. That lovely woman and I in this beautiful city with its canals and lighted windows! Fifteen minutes later when the waiter knocked, Meerlust approved the splendid round tray he brought. It was silver. He stroked the cool metal, satisfied. He went over to the crocodile-skin case and opened it. Nothing else matters, he told himself. Forget your plans. What might happen now is of vital importance.

'Careful,' he told the waiter. 'And watch out for draughts. It's enormously valuable.'

When Irene Lampak opened her door to the waiter, the contents of Meerlust's case lay in all its extravagant splendour on the tray. Undulating gently as if it had a life of its own. The most beautiful feather she'd ever seen.

'Ostrich feather,' she whispered, and when she stroked her cheek with it, it felt like the hand, no, the breath of a new lover.

10

They were destined for each other. The fashion world's obsession with feathers from a variety of birds was at its height that year and, moreover, the Oriental influence pervaded the fashion industry, inspired by Russian ballets, which were popular in Amsterdam. The fashion moguls whom they visited with the crocodile-skin case to demonstrate the quality of Yearsonend feathers looked approvingly at the Oriental beauty on Meerlust's arm.

In particular, the hats interested Irene – not only the plain straw hats that were popular in summer but also the Parisian milliners' style she admired so much.

As if they were discussing each other's bodies, Meerlust and Irene wandered about over the next few days whispering, sifting through fabrics and making sketches, stroking their fingers through the feathers of terns and auks – birds which, from 1908, would be protected by royal decree in Holland because the interest in their feathers threatened them with extinction.

They bent over fabrics and exclaimed in delight, or felt the texture of dresses and blouses against their skin, or twirled ribbons between their fingers as if they were locks of each other's hair.

Meerlust spoke of the birds in his homeland, the golden bishops, pied kingfishers and guinea-fowl found in the riverbeds and in the trees at Yearsonend. But it was the ostrich feathers – the *pleureuses* – that most interested the fashion moguls they visited along the canals.

When Meerlust opened the leather case and displayed the amazing feather, their eyes glistened. Hundreds of birds, indicated Meerlust, with feathers like this, graze on my estate in Africa, at a place called Yearsonend. We can outstrip Paris if we co-operate, he told the Dutch. 'Look at what the French designers have achieved; we can outdo them. Look at what the French artists are doing with colour these days. Look at what the ballet is doing with Oriental colours. We can have enormous influence on the fashion industry!'

In the evening, by candlelight in expensive restaurants, he chatted quietly with Irene and told her about the structure and nature of the feather: the quill, which attaches to the wing, the shaft, bearing the barbs, and the ornate part, known as the flag. He talked of parrots having provided the clothing industry in France with feathers as early as the fourteenth century, and of ostrich feathers imported to Venice from Africa in the thirteenth century. And she told him of the beautiful pheasants of Indonesia.

Then he'd seduce her all over again with exotic names and places, telling her of the *plumassiers* of Kalver Street, Graven Street, Warmoes Street – businesses already active in the sixteenth century. He told of the great warehouses of Van der Sandt and Koie in Utrecht and argued that he should also acquire such warehouses, one in Cape Town and one in Europe – or even two. '*Plumes de fantaisie*,' he drawled, in the perfect French he'd learned from his father.

And without their realising it, they made plans together – for fans, for mittens of multi-coloured feathers – and they paged through fashion magazines. 'Did you know,' Meerlust told Irene, 'that when an Egyptian tomb was opened recently, among all the treasures in it they found a magnificent ostrich feather fan with an ivory handle, in perfect condition, as if it had been used yesterday?'

He told Irene of the incubators he was installing on his farm, which would double the production of chickens. 'To the species *Struthio camelus*, the ostrich,' he raised his champagne glass to hers, and when the glasses clinked, almost soundlessly, he bent across the table and, for the first time, placed a tender kiss on her cheek. She blushed, for some of the other guests in the restaurant had noticed, but Meerlust laughed his deep, rich laugh. 'Did you know the ostrich's knee is at the *back* of his leg?' he joked, helping her to relax. 'Oh, yes,' he told her, 'it was Pliny who first told the story of the ostrich burying its head in the sand when it's frightened.'

That evening, after they had spent a long time strolling through the streets until it seemed that everyone was asleep except them, Meerlust took Irene back to the hotel. He visited her in her room, and let his lips glide over her golden skin, over her stomach and her legs, her back and her neck. When day dawned and the canal outside her window shone silver, their plans were made: she would go back to Africa with him; they would enter into a partnership and start a business.

II

Mario Salviati lay in his little room and the tip of his tongue stroked the stone that had grown into his palm. He tasted the scents he had smelt over the last few hours; he already knew what the parrot food tasted like, how the aroma of the koi pond water tasted, how the hard sun tasted when he sat on the paving-stones, how Alexander's back tasted, and how different it was from Stella's.

Perhaps it wasn't just the last few hours. He knew – sometimes clearly and with conviction – that he'd lost his sense of time; sometimes he thought half an hour had passed, but then he realised that the smell of breakfast had been replaced by the lunch Princess Moloi had put into his hands. Then it amazed him that what felt to him like minutes had apparently been hours.

He knew it was early morning for he could smell toothpaste and bathwater. He got up slowly and groped for his clothes. He dressed and pushed open the door of his room. Alexander's wet snout was in his palm, and the dog's back against his hip.

He had dreamed, thought Mario Salviati, a dream that now surrounded him as if he were still in it. People thought he was blind, but he wasn't because at night the images came to him and he walked in a sighted world again. And now Karel Thin Air was with him, and they were both in the prime of life, but there were tears on Karel's cheeks, and Karel sat with the half-map that was found in the hollowed ivory leg after Meerlust Bergh's death: the map described in the will, the will dealt with by Pistorius Attorneys.

Meerlust's map only showed one part of the journey of the black ox-wagon that night when Meerlust and Field Cornet Pistorius had to decide about the golden millions of the state treasury. Another map must be in Pistorius' possession, in his safe, said Karel. But Pistorius kept denying this.

Mario Salviati stood lost in dreams, with his hand on Alexander's back, and he looked at Karel Bergh. He didn't smell the general, who emerged from the kitchen, stretched in the early sun and came walking towards him slowly, from downwind, obliquely across the paving-stones. General Taljaard came up very close to the Italian and listened with his head to one side, as if he could hear Salviati's thoughts, the rhythms of his dreams and memories. Something told the general that Mario Salviati was digging close to the most important vein in his memory: the vein of gold.

The general had a feeling for gold. He believed, rightly, that he could even perceive the scent of gold in someone's thoughts. 'One golden thought,' he liked to say, 'and I smell it, as if it were the sharp smell of tobacco or vinegar. I can also smell gold in dreams – for greed has an odour.'

Now the general was standing close to Mario Salviati and he sniffed the air. The Italian stood frozen like a statue and, indeed, he might have been carved from stone, with his sturdy, sun- and wind-weathered figure and expressionless face.

In the dream that was back with him, Karel Thin Air raced away from the dam after the lightning water had failed, and he, Mario Salviati, leaped on to a horse to follow his lord and master. He'd seen it coming: the consequences of vaulting ambition and obsessive dedication to a dream. He knew Karel would not be able to handle failure.

Mario took a deep breath, as if his breath was the rod of a wind pump reaching deep down to bring up water; his chest heaved and the general saw the throbbing of the little vein on the inside of his elbow.

The general approached, and saw how the old man began slowly to move. He followed Salviati, who shuffled past the koi pond and started to walk to the gate. The general was astonished, for Salviati seldom went near the gate; as though he feared that gateway to the outside world. It was only with Ingi Friedländer, and then with his hand firmly clasped to her upper arm, and his other hand on Alexander's back, that the general had ever seen him venture beyond the gateway.

Mario Salviati remembered the tremor as the lightning water recoiled from Mount Improbable, turned and swept back along the channel, which produced vibrations like a musical instrument. He couldn't call to Devil Slap to ask why he was following him: he could only dig his heels into the horse's flanks and try to catch up with the carriage before Big Karel did something irrevocable.

A dream, thought Mario, or reality? Since I have been unable to see, my dreams are as valid as the things that happened to me. Perhaps my dreams are more real than the things I've seen with my eyes and can still smell. In my dream I know that Big Karel's water was just as much of a madness as the general's lust for gold. In my dream I know . . .

Slowly Salviati's hand felt the gate. The general stayed just behind him, still downwind, watching, fascinated, as the old man sank to his knees and carefully felt the frame, the hinges and the handle, the key and the peephole in the gate. He saw how the old man brought his head to the handle and sniffed it as if trying to smell who had touched it last.

Salviati turned the key and began to sweat. Great damp patches broke out on his shoulders. The general watched him slowly push open the gate. The morning sun fell fully on Salviati's body and outside the general could see the trees, the guinea-fowl grazing in the lucerne field, and beyond, the first rocky ridges of the Murderers' Karoo.

Salviati, exposed to the outside world, stood there expressionless. The general noticed him move his head a little as he absorbed fragrances. Later the general sat on a chair waiting for the old man to move. An hour passed and the angle of the sun had so changed that the upper frame of the portal cast a shadow across the Italian's face.

Hours later they put down his lunch close to him, but he didn't stir. Alexander approached slyly and ate it in a couple of greedy gulps. The peacocks pushed past Dumb Eyetie and sauntered off into the open yard; the parrots, frustrated and unfed, climbed against the wire netting with their beaks and claws.

Later, the general went inside and carried on with his daily tasks. He sent messages on his radio, read faxes and studied maps. Covered with goosepimples, the matron followed the smell of cinnamon from room to room, unable to settle down to anything.

In her room, Ingi Friedländer unpacked the tubes of paint, the brushes and canvas on her unmade bed. She hadn't gone out for breakfast, but soaked long in a bath laced with fragrant oils, then brushed her hair with three hundred determined strokes, and looked at herself in the mirror for a long time.

Water, gold and feathers, she thought. In her mind images reached out to each other: a painting, perhaps, a canvas wanting to take shape? The tubes and brushes lay there, threatening; she couldn't imagine ever touching them. She studied her hands, her fingers.

Something in you has died, Ingi, she thought. Somewhere someone stole the vision from your head and went off with it, crumpled it up as if it were a paper bag and threw it away. What has become of you – your early dreams as an art student, the energy and rebellion you felt stirring in you, the decision to oppose and challenge everything that was ordinary and routine, to be new and fresh every day? And to paint! To paint as if it were the first morning! She sat with her head in her hands: you are wandering around here among the stories of the people of this place as if you're in search of your own story.

Outside, the scents of the wind and the angle of the sun on Dumb Eyetie's body changed. He stood there on the threshold, with a small step down in front of him, then the open yard, the curve of the driveway and the road running through the avenue of trees, with the rose bushes on each side and the heat haze dancing at the end of the road, beyond which even the eye could not see.

12

Just as Dumb Eyetie had stood at the open gateway, so Ingi stood near the statue of the Blessed Virgin Mary on Mount Improbable the next day. She had set up her easel, settled the three legs of her campstool in the stony ground, and her paint and her brushes were unpacked around her.

The canvas in front of her was out of place: it was the only defined space, angular, square, mounted like an accusation. Behind it the winds blew free and the Murderers' Karoo stretched on and on until it dissolved into the air. Lying down below, Yearsonend was no angular tidy scene, but looked more like a piece of patchwork: small houses and fields and roads and footpaths cobbled together at random – and behind it all, the crazy patterns of stories lying over the landscape like a multi-coloured canvas.

Ingi looked at the stones and plants at her feet: a multitude of textures and colours and shapes. In contrast the square canvas with its monochrome surface on the easel in front of her was like a hole into which she could jump. It framed nothing but her inability. After making a single brush-stroke on the canvas, she sat contemplating the streak of colour for a long time. A butterfly, she thought, fluttering in a vacuum. Or a leaf trembling in the wind. No, thought Ingi, it's the finger of a hand, a body, a whole tale yet to be told. What does the finger do? What does the finger think? What does the arm behind it look like? To whom does the body belong? What is his role in the story?

Ingi recalled how she'd waited for her paint and materials to arrive. They had come on the railway bus: on windless days the people of Yearsonend could hear the rumbling of the bus from a great distance, some said up to ten kilometres away. Or people quipped, 'If the wind is blowing in the right direction you can hear it leave Cape Town the day before, for there's nothing but silence between us here and the Boland.'

In the old days cannons had been mounted on high hills dotting the landscape, the hundreds of kilometres from Cape Town to here. When a sailing ship entered Cape Town harbour, the first cannon on Signal Hill behind Cape Town and the second on Kanonberg in the Tygerberg hills signalled its arrival. The cannon on Papegaaiberg outside Stellenbosch heard the firing of the Tygerberg cannon, and also fired. Further into the hinterland, beyond Franschhoek, the next cannon responded, and so, as though pounded out on a series of mighty drums, the news of the arrival of a ship spread inland.

And within hours, in those days a journey of many days, the cannon on Mount Improbable also fired its shot, and the farmers would begin to load their wagons with biltong and wool, sheep and goats, rendered copper and alluvial diamonds that they or their children had found in the dry riverbeds, and set out with the heavily loaded wagons to trade with travellers and sailors or the officials of the Dutch East India Company in the Cape Town harbour. All in the hope that the ship would still lie at anchor in the bay when they reached it; sometimes they were too late and had to barter their products with each other or bring them back home.

It was as though the firing of a cannon had announced the

journey of that railway bus, thought Ingi, because I knew exactly when it started off, when it would leave the Boland and enter the Karoo beyond the Hex River mountains and how it would take the long road across the plateau, the endless drive through wind and cicadas and silent stones. All the way to Yearsonend, with its particular textures of whitewashed walls and bougainvillaea, little houses with low verandas and flat roofs, gardens with orchards of stunted fruit trees, pruned back by generations, little gardens with flowering succulents, small lucerne fields with sheep and here and there a high-spirited horse.

All the way to her, where she stood waiting at the store with the others. There were quite a few people she knew, and they greeted her as if she were already part of their community. People no longer asked when she was going back to the city but commented on the weather, the hot sun, and the ford the bus had to negotiate on the final stretch instead. And people no longer asked her about the Staggering Merman and Jonty Jack – it was as though they'd accepted her presence now and let her be.

When the dust from the bus rose behind the trees, she moved forward eagerly, just like the others. There were several people with luggage – they were to travel further inland in the bus – and she stood looking at the old leather suitcases, the hat-boxes, the cake tins with sandwiches and hard-boiled eggs, the flasks with the aroma of coffee for the long journey, and she saw hands grasped and backs rubbed comfortingly.

The storekeeper asked her to sign for the materials, and said she could pay him later. His face was close to hers, too close. 'We can't wait to see the pictures, Miss 'Länder.'

Like a dog that's stolen a bone, thought Ingi, and fled to her room to unpack the paints. They smelt just as she'd hoped, evoking memories of her student days – but they took her back, too, to that time of choices, after graduation, when some of her peers kept at their painting and drawing, but because she'd doubted her talent, and because her parents had encouraged her to find a steady job, she'd accepted the gallery's offer of a post assisting with management and acquisitions for the National Collection.

It wasn't a thankless task, but you so lost yourself in other people's desires, their imaginations, their failures and successes, their jealousy and ambition, their gossip and cupidity, that you forgot that images also stirred in you, that your spirit also housed a little town like Yearsonend, full of memories, possibilities, textures, smells, incidents, dreams; full of life.

Ingi looked at the brush-stroke on the canvas again. It drifted there like a feather in the cosmos. No, she thought, oh, no. It isn't going to happen. It isn't coming to me; the timing isn't right . . .

When she hung her head and sat there with tears in her eyes, she didn't notice that the brush-stroke on the canvas began to move, to test its wings. The butterfly suddenly flew up, fluttered around her head, and sat lightly on her shoulder for a moment. Then it rose up again, and the wind, rushing as it always did over the spine of the mountain, snatched it up and raced into the valley with it, so that the splash of colour dived and soared and fluttered wildly, then disappeared somewhere between the trees and the lucerne.

When Ingi dried her eyes and looked up, the canvas in front of her was blank. Then I didn't start after all, she thought. I only imagined it. That first brush-stroke is still waiting. All the possibilities, like this canvas, are open.

Leaving everything there – the campstool, the easel and the paints – she wandered on up the mountain. She started to climb the rugged Cave Gorge, far behind Jonty's little house. Somewhere here, she knew, was the track leading to the cave. It was as though she was lured by the tales of the Bushmen who had once made their paintings on those rock walls.

At last she reached the overgrown road. It was evident that no vehicle had passed there in many years. Below her she saw Jonty's house, and further away Yearsonend. She could just distinguish the statue of the Blessed Virgin Mary, but her easel and stool had melted into the landscape.

It was hot up there, and Ingi breathed heavily. The wind had dropped, because she was around the curve of the mountain, and the cicadas shrilled deafeningly. The road levelled out on to something like a terrace, with a view in two directions. Then she saw the great heap of stones and the gash against the mountainside – just like a scar on a body, she thought – where the stones had become dislodged and tumbled down to block the entrance to the cave.

What Ingi didn't see was the angel, who was sitting on one of the big boulders in the shadow of a cliff. He sat with his wings relaxed but vibrating on his back, catching fleas in the downy feathers on his shoulder-blades. The sounds he made were like those of a fowl or a turkey, sitting in the summer shade, clucking gently to itself.

He watched her, observing the way she stroked the stones and smelt her hands; how she shook out her hair and held her head back to allow the sun to cascade over her cheeks as if it was water from a shower. He saw how she took off her little backpack and pulled out a tube of suntan lotion. The scent of the lotion, which she was rubbing on her face until her cheeks and forehead glistened, irritated him. He sneezed.

When she'd anointed her eyelids carefully – she had such fair skin – and opened her eyes and looked up, she gazed in surprise at the great shadow of a giant eagle or some other large bird sweeping over her and the flickering movements of the bird-man against the precipice, and she reminded herself to ask someone who would know – Jonty or the general – if there was a breeding pair of martial eagles up here.

Just to think, mused Ingi, that Jonty reckons his father, Karel Thin Air, along with his carriage and show horses, is still in the cave. She got up with difficulty, her joints stiff. I still have to carry that easel, the stool and the other stuff down the mountain, she thought. And all along the way, as she progressed from the gate to Cave Gorge and along the roads to the Drostdy, people would stop her and ask, 'Please, Miss, show us your picture.'

13

Karel Thin Air, born out of that first night of love in an Amsterdam hotel, was Meerlust and Irene's only son. His sister with the beautiful voice, Edit, who would fall for the Italian who couldn't speak, was born many years later.

Meerlust and Irene were proud of their son, their dream-child, who was always dressed like a prince in little sailor suits and tiny boots of the best leather. He was a young lad when the Anglo-Boer war broke out, and for the rest of his life he remembered the things that happened then.

Perhaps Karel's fascination with water had been sparked at Lampak's Dam, for on Sunday afternoons while the rest of Yearsonend slept, Irene put her little boy in his pushchair, and, accompanied by a servant's son who had to hold an ostrich-feather sunshade over little Karel, she strolled through the streets of Yearsonend to the dam.

As they walked, curtains twitched. The men of Yearsonend all secretly desired her – her mysterious grace, her Oriental silence, and her reserve that could suddenly thaw into warmth and a laugh as clear as a bell. Of course, they'd never acknowledge it to anyone – officially she was a coolie or a Chinky and off-limits. However, Meerlust's money and status, her beauty and refined manners led to a kind of acceptance: a precarious balance between friendliness and distance.

At the dam that was eventually named after her, Irene would peel off her clothes and display her bathing costume, for the benefit of the men of the town who had developed the habit of watching her with binoculars or telescopes poking through closed sitting-room curtains while their wives took a Sunday-afternoon snooze.

She floated luxuriously in the water – a dolphin – gazing up at the blue firmament over her, enjoying the sweetness of the freshly pumped windmill water, and watching her little boy gurgle with laughter in his pushchair. She sang the songs of her faraway country then went to lie stretched out on the grass.

Yearsonend was scandalised because the bathing costume showed more than was acceptable, and she flaunted herself openly – without a shred of modesty, it seemed – exposed to the gaze of any passer-by.

Irene was never invited into any white household in Yearsonend, and she and Meerlust had to turn to the city to socialise or travel to Europe or, once or twice, even America. As a result, they focused their attention on their children. They all dressed for dinner, as though guests were expected, and at weekends family meals were served in the grand dining room or outside under the oak trees. They put heart and soul into their work. Drawing on their own isolation, they sketched the melancholy of an era, at first sombre but later with an assertive, transgressive accent on femininity and passion.

Looking back on his childhood Karel remembered it as a time when he was told repeatedly to mind the pins scattered around the dressmaker's dummies; a time of helter-skelter ostrich rides with his father egging him on, laughing, and he clinging to the bird for dear life; a time of endless hats and dresses in countless shapes and forms; a time of comings and goings when foreign dealers were entertained like kings.

It was during their travels overseas in particular that he experienced his father's proclivity for the grand gesture: the expensive hotels, the distinguished guests entertained in fancy restaurants, the endless stories about life in Africa – stories in which Karel didn't recognise his home, his country, or the time he lived in, but stories that had the Europeans hanging on his father's lips while Irene enchanted them with her smile.

And all for the sake of business. As a child Karel never set eyes on the gold nugget he had been born holding. His parents kept it away from him, but he pieced together the story from snippets passed on to him by the servants: how Meerlust had the nugget washed and displayed shortly after his birth, as an omen of future prosperity, as a wonder of nature, as a message from the angels.

Field Cornet Pistorius' few visits to the house after the war stood out in Karel's memory too. Sometimes people addressed the man with the flaming beard as Field Cornet, and sometimes

– more frequently as time went by – as Attorney. Behind his back he was referred to as Redbeard, Red Peril or Pinky and other names.

In later life, Karel remembered one visit particularly clearly. It had been a Sunday and a large table was laid outside under the oaks for him, his parents and one visitor – his sister Edit was still in a pram. The visitor was a fashion mogul from Paris, a thin man who wore white suits with a flower in his buttonhole and refused to let meat pass his lips.

They'd finished the main course and the servants were bringing in the pudding and custard, pouring the dessert wine and offering cigars, when Attorney Pistorius came up the driveway. The red beard glowed in the distance. 'Like a turkey with inflamed wattles,' Meerlust growled, but nevertheless got up graciously, folded his napkin and went across the lawn to welcome the attorney, who was perspiring after his walk in the summer heat. Meerlust greeted him and led him to the table with a generous sweep of the arm. A chair had been placed ready for him between the Parisian fashion mogul and Irene, who, although she knew the story about him and Siela Pedi, smiled at him graciously.

The three men chatted about this and that, and sipped dessert wine. Eventually Irene withdrew, apparently responding to a wink from Meerlust, taking baby Edit with her. Karel stayed behind, playing at the men's feet, and watched as the servants cleared the table, shut the front door, and closed the shutters against the sun, and the dogs went to lie in the shade under the oaks.

He must have fallen asleep because when he looked up next, two empty wine bottles stood on the table and another lay on the grass. The shadows had shifted and now lay long over the lawn. He sat up slowly and there, under the oaks, stood Meerlust and Pistorius, back to back, each holding a pistol. The barrels pointed skywards. The Frenchman, slightly unsteady on his feet, stood near them. Marking time with his walking-stick, he began to count in French, and at every number the men moved forward a step. Karel was too drowsy to call out, and he glanced towards the house. The front door opened and Irene appeared with the baby on her hip. She cried out when she saw what was going on, but it was on the count of ten, just as the men swung round. Their attention – somewhat blunted by the alcohol – was now divided between the Frenchman's loud '*Dix!*', Irene's cry and the difficulty of executing a neat heel-turn on the lush lawn.

Neither was an accomplished duellist, but the Frenchman had persuaded them to settle their differences in this way – the most elegant and dignified solution, he explained. And when the shots rang out they both stood bemused, each holding his smoking pistol. It was the French fashion mogul who collapsed with a surprised expression on his face and a bloodstain like a second rose on his lapel.

Karel remembered sitting on the grass and the Frenchman's face hitting the lawn a little way from him, still wearing that startled expression.

Shortly afterwards, with Irene kneeling beside him, the man breathed his last. When Irene stood up and glared furiously at Meerlust and Pistorius, her hands were covered with blood.

The report made to the police and the magistrate was framed in correct legal terminology from Pistorius' lips, and it told of a guinea-fowl shoot that went wrong: a Frenchman who didn't know the protocols of a shoot and had run in front of the guns in his excitement. In addition, it was impossible to establish whose bullet had struck the Frenchman. Weeks later, a servant found the second bullet lodged in one of the shutters, right near the front door where Irene had stood with the baby.

'Pistols at a guinea-fowl shoot?' asked the magistrate, but it was during the difficult years after the war with Britain and the victim was some eccentric European, and Meerlust and Pistorius were citizens without whom Yearsonend couldn't manage at that stage. The magistrate closed the file, but the townsfolk kept their eyes open. That was a phrase Karel Thin Air would hear often in years to come.

14

'The townsfolk watch Jonty Jack with the same eyes that once watched his father, Karel Thin Air, and before that his grandfather Meerlust. Jonty Jack is watched especially closely because his father was a Bergh and his mother a Pistorius – two families whom you could say confronted each other over smoking pistols with the black ox-wagon between them. Ha!'

Look Deep the barman fanned away the cigarette smoke between him and Ingi and glared at the three men smoking in the corner of the pub. He leaned over towards Ingi, who sat with a beer in front of her. 'Jonty's the one who knows where the gold is, mark my words. And he's clever enough to keep quiet about it. Gold means nothing to him. Can you imagine what'll happen the day that gold comes to light? It'll cause a bigger stampede than when they marked out the mining claims in the old Transvaal . . .'

It's about more than gold now, as you've so often remarked yourself, Ingi wanted to say. Gold was a metaphor for something that was lost for ever and could never be recovered. Gold Pit didn't exist on the landscape or on any map. It could be anywhere; it was everywhere.

But she held her tongue and took another swig of beer. I'm looking for it on my canvas, it occurred to her suddenly. In that framed no man's land on the easel. My Gold Pit.

'Another?'

'Why not?' Ingi sipped her third beer. It was hot outside.

'And I hear from old Piet in the shop that you're also painting pictures these days, Missy.'

'You don't want to believe everything our friend Piet says.' She looked at the barman testily.

'Hey! He's an honest trader!'

Ingi laughed. What the hell? she thought. For them it was just pictures like the fishing boats over there on the calendar. I can just own up and that'll be the end of it. 'Yes, I paint too.'

'What sort of things?' he asked.

Ingi gazed into her beer. Then she said mischievously, 'Water, gold and feathers.'

Look Deep chortled. 'You're a real Yearsonender now, Missy!'

'I'm learning, I'm learning,' said Ingi. 'But tell me a bit more about the townsfolk's attitude to . . .' she searched for words '. . . the Berghs' coloured blood.'

'Oh, the dirty blood.'

'I didn't say that.' Her anger flared; she was ready to get up and march out, but he stopped her.

'Sorry, Missy. Forgive me. People just talk like that round here.'

'Yes, but not in front of me. I don't like it.'

'Sorry again. Have another beer?'

'I haven't even drunk half of this one yet.'

'One on the house?' he grovelled.

'All right, keep it in the fridge for me. And mind your language.'

'Sorry, sorry, sorry.'

'All right, now tell me.'

Look Deep sighed. 'Look, from Jonty Jack to Matron Taljaard, through Irene Lampak and Meerlust Bergh, who was the son of Little Sara Bruin, a descendant of William Gird and the daughter of Ensign Moloi and Titty X!am, there's coloured blood in all of them.'

'And how do people feel about that?'

'There are things you can say and things you can't say,' Look Deep's eyes glinted, 'but the way Meerlust and his son Karel Thin Air chased big things came from feeling brown in a white town.'

Ingi drank deeply of her beer. 'That's sad,' she said.

'That's the Karoo.'

'No,' she argued, 'it's not the Karoo. The Karoo isn't all this chasing after water or gold or feathers or white skins. It's rock. Rock that knows nothing of discrimination or dislike. Rock that tolerates and endures. For countless years. Years on end if you like. There's the Karoo out there. Look there: the hills, unchanging, asking nothing of you. Not there in the corner . . . those . . . those blind . . . louts who inherited farms and now . . .'

She reined herself in, surprised by her own emotion. 'I'm Jewish.' She sighed, as though that explained everything.

'And on my father's side I'm Karoo-Italian,' confessed the barman. He raised his shoulders as if to say, We both know what that means. 'So are you going to rather paint rock, Missy?' he asked, after a while.

Surprised, she looked up into Look Deep's brandy breath. 'Yes. Yes,' she said, half bewildered. 'I'm going to paint rock.'

And she pushed away her beer and hurried out of the pub. 'Miss 'Länder!' Look Deep called after her, holding up her half-empty glass. But she was already out in the street, having whistled up the dogs who'd lain sleeping in the shade on the veranda. She strode off in the direction of the Drostdy. Stones, she thought. Of course! It was obvious. Fat, rounded forms. Feminine stones, angular strata, cliffs: stone!

She went in through the gateway and almost walked into Matron Taljaard, who was standing there shaking like a leaf. 'Still enjoying your lodgings?' squeaked the matron, caught in the act of standing downwind and watching her father as he sat at the fishpond with his hand in the water so the koi could caress him with its fin.

Ingi, emboldened by the beer and her sudden inspiration about stone, asked straight out, 'Why don't you go and sit next to him and touch him? There he is. He's waiting for you. He is your father, after all.'

The matron drew a shuddering breath. 'Gold Pit.' The words escaped with her breath. She thrust her hands into her apron pockets and fled into the house.

Ingi stood there with her hands on her hips. 'You are all gold-fucked!' she shouted, making the servants peer nervously through the kitchen window; the parrots screeched excitedly and the peacocks took to the air with a whir of wings and a swish of their huge tail feathers. The koi, swerving quickly away from his hand, warned Dumb Eyetie that something was afoot. He smelt the peacock feathers and the warm bodies stirring round him, and the parrots, who vented small worm-like droppings when they were startled. He rose to his feet and turned to Ingi.

'Do you hear me?' she shouted at him, but he stood there like a statue, not moving a muscle. She came up to him, put her arms round him and rested her head on his shoulder. She knew the servants were watching her and that they'd call the general and the matron now, but she didn't care. She was aware that the dogs were staring at them in perplexity and that everything was suddenly quiet in the courtyard. But she didn't care. 'Hold me tight,' she murmured, but her words were no more than breath on his cheek.

15

Meerlust's ostriches were of the finest pedigree and he had collected them personally in Africa. He loved recounting the story of his expedition to North Africa, when he set off in search of the perfect ostrich feather, accompanied by two other South Africans: a zoologist and a veterinarian.

They prepared their safari on the quiet. They had to think of malaria, gun licences, unknown fevers and snakebite serum. They told family and friends they were going on a scouting trip to the continent's markets, while they secretly packed huge crates of equipment for an expedition into Africa. Luckily Meerlust was an experienced big-game hunter.

Months ahead, the men began to train because they had no idea what kind of ordeal lay before them. Meerlust had a special bicycle constructed with his artificial limb attached to a custom-made pedal. With his coat-tails flying and a peculiar rhythm caused by a good limb moving in tandem with a wobbly one, he was seen pedalling round the dusty roads of Yearsonend for weeks – always a man to throw himself heart and soul into a new project. It became something of a curiosity. In the early morning, when

Yearsonenders were still sitting on their verandas drinking their first cup of coffee and pondering over the day that lay ahead, Meerlust would whiz past with his jacket flapping and the spokes whirring; every day a new false leg welded man and machine together.

Every second day he climbed Mount Improbable, right up as far as the lookout point where Dumb Eyetie would erect the statue of the Blessed Virgin Mary many years later. Wherever he could find water deep enough he swam too, with the short leg slipping along like a white fish beside the kicking one.

Once a week the zoologist, who was also a snake expert, drove over from the Great Springs Agricultural College in his little Ford and injected a tiny bit of snake venom into Meerlust's backside. The first dose made Meerlust feel so under the weather that he couldn't even ride his bike, but the second week his system coped better. In the fourth week the dose was increased and by the time the group stood on the quayside, ready to embark, Meerlust and the others were immune to snake venom – or so the man from Great Springs promised.

Meerlust also sent for an old Indian from the city, a diviner of stars, to teach him how to read the heavens and how to calculate direction and distance from the orbiting of the constellations. While he was about it, the man gazed deeply into Meerlust's horoscope and predicted that the journey would be successful, and that they would return with a golden feather – a feather related to the feather that lay buried with a pharaoh in his sarcophagus under a pyramid, a feather fit to grace the forehead of a prince, or the shoulder of a queen.

Satisfied, Meerlust studied maps and drew up lists of words in foreign languages – words for ostrich, water, doctor, herb and poison, sun, crocodile, lion, pain, blindness and fever, flour, bread and woman; words for God and devil, spirit and salve, boils and cramps, compass and knife, sword and spear and arrow, moon and syphilis, camel and donkey, honey and salt, umbrella and blanket – oh, yes, also for loneliness and fear, desolation and bereavement. Meerlust knew what kind of provisions life might demand of you.

He learned the words by heart in all the languages, and until the day he died, according to the Yearsonenders, Meerlust could order the necessities of life in several languages. And all his life he believed that if a snake bit him, he could bite it back and the snake would die while he stood by on his wooden leg, laughing. 'As poisonous as Satan himself.'

The three men sailed to England then took a boat to Nigeria. They travelled on a slow steam-driven riverboat up the Niger, a stretch of water as broad as a lucerne field, as slow and resolute as time, as deep as the night. Meerlust sat on a deckchair in the bow watching the people who circled the boat in their dugouts, begging for coins. Over and over again, Meerlust showed them an ostrich feather, but they fell about laughing and begged for more money.

In time, weeks later, the river narrowed. They had to travel on a smaller boat, rowed laboriously by a team of black men. They'd all lost weight and at night Meerlust shivered. By the time this tributary petered out in a dry part of the country, they'd reached a railway station and headed on northwards in the weekly train crowded with goats and fowls and splendid chieftains surrounded by quiet women.

Word had gone ahead of them and wherever they stopped in this region someone was waiting for them at the station or a shop with a dead ostrich or a handful of feathers. Eagerly, Meerlust examined the feathers then shook his head, disappointed. On the whole, the feathers were no better than you'd get from the wild ostriches that occupied the Karoo's dry riverbeds.

Eventually they set off on foot with pack mules towards the north-west, into French Sudan. They had to think differently here, because the desert made demands different from those of the tropics. The people here were different too: wrapped in white linen, riding on camels, always watching from a far ridge. And the feathers they were shown were even mangier. But there, deep in the desert, among rocks and sand, they discovered the flock of noble ostriches they'd sought and to which the stars had led them. The feathers were thick and luxuriant, the birds tough and strong. It was a triumphant moment, after months of hardship.

It took another two months to get back to Cape Town with six blindfolded ostriches – two males and four females. In accordance with the agreement, Meerlust took one breeding pair and the remainder went to Great Springs. No one knew how it happened but all the Great Springs birds died shortly after arrival. Meerlust's pair bred successfully and, within a few years, his feathers were renowned as the best.

Great Springs chose to remain blind, the people gossiped, but over here in Yearsonend we keep our eyes open, we know how to see.

The years that lay ahead brought great prosperity to Meerlust Bergh. Sometimes he could hardly believe it himself. The world opened up for him: London, Paris, Amsterdam, and Milan. He developed his own artistic talent. And his business acumen. But it couldn't last, and he knew it.

Anxious times dawned for the feather industry. During the Anglo-Boer war, at the turn of the century, the ostrich farms did well: British soldiers, sad and homesick, bought feathers to send home to their families in England. Lords came out to deliver pep talks to the British troops in preparation for the horrors of their encounters with the Boer guerrillas, who galloped out of the hills, fired on the columns of British soldiers, then melted back into the landscape. The wives of these lords wore the extravagant feathers in their hats and created a huge demand in the British Isles.

But in the years after that war, the fashion industry started developing other interests. A campaign was launched in the Netherlands to save birds from extinction and this made the fashion industry cautious about the use of all feathers – even though ostriches weren't royal game, the industry began to look to other materials.

Then one black week the bottom fell out of the ostrich market and the value of ostriches blew away overnight like dust on the plains, and many farmers in feather palaces in and around the Karoo lost everything. The huge houses with their wide verandas, their intricate cast-iron curlicues, their roof spires and endless chandeliered rooms seemed suddenly to caricature humanity's arrogance and greed.

From the time of the Africa expedition, Meerlust Bergh's feathers in Yearsonend, far from the other feather palaces, were known for being strong and extraordinarily thick with a double layer of fronds. When ordinary ones fetched little, Meerlust's pedigree feathers were still in great demand.

But even these magnificent feathers weren't enough when the market faltered. The First World War destabilised the world and the time for lavish finery was over: young men were dying in tens of thousands in muddy trenches. On top of that the motor-car became widely available, and ladies found plumed hats and ostrich-feather fans difficult to manage in the open-topped runabouts of the day.

Meerlust was already an old man and his son Karel was as vigorous as his father had been in his twenties when the 1914 crash took place. Millionaires lost everything overnight; the great warehouses storing thousands of feathers for export to Europe became sad curiosities: people stared bemused at the high-quality sorted and classified feathers destined to grace gala occasions in Milan, the boulevards of Paris, the walkways of Kensington Gardens, and cruises on the Rhine.

Day after day, month after month Meerlust and Irene sat at their drawing-tables, half-heartedly trying to design hats with smaller, stiffer feathers, but even in England legislation had been passed to prevent the extinction of the world's bird population. It was as though Meerlust's pen, which had found such a natural outlet for his grand gestures in the line of an exquisite ostrich feather, could not trace the reduced scale and more understated designs of the new era.

With time Irene lost interest in fashion, and the studio at the Feather Palace began to feel like a museum, with pins still sprinkled on the floor, plaster mannequins with staring eyes and lengths of fabric draped over their shoulders, tape-measures with insects crawling up them, and feathers that swayed gently in the wind when you opened the door and peered in to see why it was so quiet inside.

16

At New Year, Ingi heard, Meerlust and Irene Lampak liked to send a fresh ostrich egg to each of their most important business associates in Yearsonend. Irene would decorate each egg with a painting of a model, or a beautiful dress or a scene from her homeland, Indonesia.

Meerlust had a penchant for opera and in later years she liked to decorate the eggs with scenes from Verdi's operas – Meerlust's favourites. It was a wonderful gift to receive: a woven basket with a decorated egg from the Feather Palace. There was always a special request that the egg should be eaten, not saved because of its decorated shell.

One year when the headmaster of Karel's old school received an egg he and his wife decided to save the shell by blowing out the contents and scrambling them. They were amazed to discover after they'd carefully drilled little holes at each end and blown out the contents that something was left in the shell.

A New Year's egg from Meerlust and Irene was always a status symbol and a school inspector, members of the school committee, and the most senior teachers were all present at the breakfast table, along with servants standing at the ready with pans to cook the egg. Then something rattled inside the shell.

Painstakingly, and after consulting with his intrigued guests, the headmaster enlarged the hole at one end of the shell, regretfully beheading an opera singer in the process. Out of the shell, still slimy and yellow with egg-yolk, plopped a gold Kruger pound.

The guests gasped.

What she could take as true and what she had to discount, Ingi never knew. Coins were discovered in eggs, and a general outlived generations. Some people never grew old in life, and others never died in memory. Jonty, too, spun yarns, joint in hand, speculating about his father, maybe forgetting more than he remembered, lost in the quicksands of the past.

What happened next, Jonty told Ingi, was one of the most significant things in his father Karel Thin Air's life. Karel was a young man at the time, accustomed to the good life, and, in spite of his Oriental features, accepted as one of the town's fine young men, thanks to his polished manners and his father's wealth.

At that time – before Grand Apartheid struck – it was easier to allow this kind of thing. Meerlust was the town's richest man – that is, if you excluded the speculation about Pistorius' bank balance. When Karel was a boy, the other children had given him a hard time, but later things improved.

And that morning Karel was up in the mountain with the young men of the town: they'd climbed Mount Improbable on New Year's Eve with rucksacks and provisions so that they could watch the New Year dawning from the peak. It was always a wonderful experience and over the years it had become something of a tradition: the red dawn opening like a flower over the monochrome landscape. As they came down the mountain at eleven o'clock, scarcely having slept and hoping for a hearty breakfast at the Feather Palace, then to take a dip in Lampak's Dam, the headmaster and his wife were already on the way to the Feather Palace to tell Meerlust and Irene the fabulous story of the gold coin in the egg, thus sparking – in subsequent weeks – renewed searches of the runs where the ostriches grazed, but all to no avail.

Karel and his friends carried their rucksacks under the oak trees, startling the flock of guinea-fowl that lived there and reaching the driveway of the Feather Palace at the same time as the procession of cars, in a jolly New Year mood, sporting balloons and ribbons. The young men jumped on to the bumpers and running-boards and the cavalcade proceeded up the driveway, laughing and hooting.

When they came round the corner that circled the lawn under the oaks, they found Meerlust Bergh on the veranda. Then the group saw something that, it was said, not even Meerlust's wife, let alone his family or friends, had ever seen: Meerlust, his hair tousled from sleep evidently having just woken, stood there on his one leg, without his artificial limb; when he saw them approaching, he began to hop inside, panicky, ridiculous.

Karel would never forget the sight of his father, in a dressing-gown but more exposed than he would have been naked, his shoulders heaving like a wild animal about to jump a fence but unable to, his body bending and straightening as he tried to evade the townsfolk, that New Year's morning when the feather market collapsed.

No one knew what had happened in Karel's absence that New Year's Eve. But while townsfolk set off fireworks, watching the stars explode in the night sky over the Karoo and the town dogs barked hysterically because, on top of everything else, it was full moon, while Karel and his companions basked shirtless in the balmy moonlight at the top of Mount Improbable and looked out over the wide landscape baptised with silver, something happened between Meerlust and Irene Lampak.

When Karel and the visitors arrived at the Feather Palace, Irene was gone. The smart black Ford was also gone, but Meerlust just shook his head when he was asked about her disappearance. Irene Lampak was never seen again, and Karel grew up with memories of a mother with soft hands, a taste for beautiful things, and an eye for fabrics and textures.

'Yes, the Yearsonenders said the magistrate had closed the file,' Jonty told Ingi, 'but people kept their eyes open. God never sleeps.

'Now you might understand better,' Jonty told Ingi, 'why my father couldn't face the scandal when the flashwater refused him. And why he disappeared. His mother had done it to him, and when he suffered his great disappointment, he did it to himself.'

Yes, thought Ingi, we recycle the things that hurt us most, because for some reason we need to feel the pain again. Perhaps because we feel that a return visit might take the sting out? Or break the spell? Or because we bind ourselves to our parents by repeating their mistakes? Is it a form of homage or love?

'That's why the history of a place like Yearsonend keeps on repeating itself,' Ingi told Jonty. 'People have to revisit their old wounds over and over again, like a murderer compelled to return to the scene of his crime. Nothing is ever completed; we're confined like the concentric rings in a tree-trunk.'

'Karel stood there,' Jonty spoke of his father as though he were a stranger, 'before his old headmaster, the townsfolk, the white youths with whom he'd struggled, successfully, to build relationships, and he felt as though he were naked: he felt like the half-breed, the coolie bastard, the Chinaman – words he'd heard from his playmates' mouths ever since he was a little boy, until he managed to forge friendships with some of them.'

Ingi and Jonty climbed up to the cave that had been closed off by a rockfall, and then higher, until they stood above the scar left by the rocks that had fallen to block the cave mouth.

'People thought that the lightning water that came over the mountain there, and the rain that fell that day, breaking a long drought, caused the rockslide.' Jonty pointed out how the cliff they were standing on seemed to anchor itself to the mountainside, but a ledge of the precipice below them was the one that had been dislodged and slid down to block the cave.

'It's extraordinary that the mountain could remain undisturbed for so many years,' murmured Ingi, 'and suddenly part of it gives way . . .'

Jonty took a pebble and threw it into the wind. 'Some people say you should never throw a stone – no matter how small – down a mountain.' They watched the pebble bounce from rock to rock then disappear into the bush. 'Even a stone as small as that may dislodge a slightly bigger one that rolls against an even bigger one and so on until it causes a major rockfall that might cost someone his life.'

'Here comes the train,' said Ingi. From this distance it looked like a scene from Toyland: the millipede creeping along dragging the column of steam behind it.

'When are you going back?' asked Jonty.

'Back?' Ingi was startled by the surprise in her own voice. 'Oh.'

'What do you mean, oh?'

'No, I . . . I—'

'You know,' Jonty teased, but she sensed his seriousness, 'you ask everyone so many questions, but you almost fall off the mountain when I make one simple enquiry.'

'I . . . I mean, I . . .'

'Look.' Jonty came round to face her. 'The question is simple. How long are you going to stay here, Ingi?'

Ingi sighed and shrugged. 'You know why I'm here, Jonty.'

He laughed. 'That hasn't been your reason for staying for ages.'

'That's true,' she conceded.

'Right, so what's your answer?'

She knew him well enough by now to recognise the edge that came into his voice when things weren't going his way. She also knew that she shouldn't see too much of Jonty. He was always glad – even elated – to see her; she knew he regarded her as a fellow artist and valued her company; he also liked expounding his own wisdom to her. His infatuation with her was a thing of the past – so she thought, anyway. But more than an hour in her company, and Jonty started to feel hemmed in.

Then he'd lure her out for a mountain walk, or get her to help him fly a kite, or invite her to come and spruce up his sculpture garden. And even then he didn't want her to linger. He soon felt constricted, as though his freedom was under threat. He had lived alone for too long – or perhaps this wildness and fear of intimacy was the reason for his solitary life.

'And when are you going away?' she countered.

'Me?'

'Yes, you, Jonty.'

'I've been away already.'

His answer was straightforward. And he made it clear that it closed the conversation as far as he was concerned. He brushed off his hands, because he had been fidgeting with pebbles and soil, feeling the texture and weighing the pebbles as though they were materials with which he planned to work.

Ingi felt slightly irritated as she always did when someone pried too much. 'But why do you stay here in your little house? You live in Yearsonend, but at the same time you don't.'

He began to walk away. 'If you want to be an artist, don't lose touch with your roots,' he growled. 'You must live close to the material that is given to you. It's your nourishment. But you must also distance yourself from your origins. If you can maintain this tension, then you might be able to liberate the figure you want to carve. Or complete the canvas you want to paint.'

His last sentence struck her like a lash. She knew it was aimed at her. Silent and angry, they went down the mountain, stumbling over rocks, past the sealed cave, and then lower, until eventually she left him and his surly silence, and went her own way. A detour took her to the Cave Gorge path and she struck out for home. She battled to open the concertina gate and her finger started to bleed. She put it in her mouth, tasting the salt of her own blood.

You drew blood again, Jonty, you bastard, thought Ingi.

17

'You know, I'm convinced that someone – or maybe everyone – knows where the gold is,' Ingi said to Mario Salviati. It was deep in the night and she was gently stroking his face and arms. 'I've got a feeling that the Yearsonenders could easily find the Kruger gold if they just put their heads together. But for some reason it just doesn't happen. Everything degenerates into gossip and back-stabbing.'

She wore a light nightgown and she'd added perfumed oil to her bathwater. She had to wait a long time for the Drostdy to settle down. Eventually Matron had turned off the fountain and even the plopping noises made by the fish catching mosquitoes on the surface of the water had stopped.

The parrots still squawked now and then in their dreams but the wind that had stirred restlessly through the vine leaves had dropped. Alexander had uttered what Ingi now recognised as his final late-night sigh before he sank like a stone into a deep sleep, the moment when he lay flat and stretched out his enormous body like a calf somewhere on the Drostdy's cool wooden floors – a different place every night in his search for respite from the heat.

But she had to wait a long time for the matron's endless string of Hail Marys to come to an end, and the general's mumbling to fall silent.

In the end she dozed off. When she woke again, she felt driven by the need to talk to someone, and crept from her room down the passages, into the courtyard, where she was suddenly bathed in moonlight, as though she'd stepped into water; she slipped over the ceramic tiles and pushed open Dumb Eyetie's door.

She still didn't understand her feelings for him. Is he really no more than a mirror for me? she wondered. Because increasingly she felt that she was confronting herself, or aspects of herself, in all the characters of Yearsonend. In Jonty's fervent resistance to the birthplace he was still so bonded to; in Irene Lampak, who had left when her life there became untenable; in Meerlust Bergh, with his grand flamboyant gestures; in Matron Taljaard, with her fear of the angel, the general and her father, and her fear of the secret of Gold Pit.

And perhaps, Ingi thought, as she pushed open the door and the rhythm of the old man's breathing changed and she realised he could smell her and the candle, perhaps I see too much of myself in Mario Salviati, the man imprisoned within himself: the Italian in solitary confinement, without ears and eyes, words or facial expression.

When she came in the old man had pushed himself up against his pillow. He wore only pyjama trousers and his chest was still strong and well-shaped despite his years. The white chest hairs grew up to his neck. He had large nipples, she noted, almost rudely large, and his hands spread brown and broad on the bed as he pushed himself up.

He waited for her expressionlessly and as she stretched out on the single bed beside him, he moved over for her. She lay with her head on his shoulder for a little while, and then she began to massage him gently as she talked, making sure that her breath fell on to his skin so he knew she was talking.

'I'm certain,' said Ingi, 'that you know where the gold is. And I know the general keeps you imprisoned here because he also suspects you know where the gold is. But I can tell that people are afraid to start looking in earnest, because they're afraid of the consequences of finding it.'

He'd dropped off to sleep but she shook him awake. He must be there, even if he couldn't hear. Tonight someone had to listen to her. And his deafness and blindness created a safe zone in which she could say what she liked.

'Mario,' said Ingi, 'I come from a place where caresses like this,' and she fluttered her fingertips over his stomach, 'are feared. I come from a place where, over the years, my vision and hearing, my daring and excitement have almost been taken away from me. And when I saw you, I recognised so much of myself.'

He began to snore lightly and Ingi looked at the meagre possessions in his small room. There was a crucifix against the wall, a figure of the Virgin Mary on the windowsill, old chisels and a mallet with a handle shiny from use laid out on a table; there was an array of twigs and pebbles and animal bones; and there was a pile of old books in the corner – who would ever read them? – and hooks on the wall where he hung his clothes. She saw a soldier's uniform and a trowel, a compass and a photograph of the Duomo in Florence. Apart from that there was only the ceiling fan, which had replaced a light because he didn't need light, bare walls, the narrow bed, a single easy chair and an old shotgun propped in the corner.

Everything was smooth, burnished from much handling; perhaps she imagined that in the flickering candlelight, but it looked as though he picked up each item, felt it all over then set it down again dozens of times a day. There wasn't a speck of dust in the room and the door to the bathroom stood ajar so she could see the washing that hung over the bath.

'And do you know, Mario, in a way you've made me believe in

my own senses again, in smell and touch, feel and taste? You gave that back to me, Mario – perhaps these are your senses, which I've seized; perhaps I'm the one who stole them from you. Mario?'

But outside on the patio the vine leaves stirred gently in the moonlight, the parrots dozed on their perches, and the woman without a face sat in her back room, motionless before the mirror in the lamplight. She saw nothing but she anticipated, she yearned, she waited.

18

In the years following Irene's disappearance, Meerlust Bergh invited the general over to the Feather Palace with increasing regularity. Their parties and capacity for alcohol became legendary in Yearsonend.

Setbacks and humiliation in a world that had turned its back on his beautiful feathers, and then the disappearance of his even more beautiful wife, drove Meerlust to seek consolation in the bottle, the gun, the pack of playing cards, the fortune-teller's crystal ball, the sangoma's bones. And the general's visions and dreams.

Day after day the two sat at the card table in the Drostdy or in the study at the Feather Palace and large sums of money changed hands, backwards and forwards, in a never-ending cycle: the same money between the two of them, like sea-bamboo swaying back and forth in the tide.

And always, with characteristic swagger, plans were hatched. Most of the legends wove themselves around the plan to seize the coins after waylaying the ghostly black ox-wagon, which still plied its agonised way across the landscape. This called for intricate planning, the two men decided late one night, Cognac in hand. 'We would first need to talk to that dust-farter, Redbeard Pretorius,' said Meerlust, as he took off the stinkwood leg and strapped on the ivory one.

'He isn't a field cornet's backside,' General Taljaard embroidered. 'What did he actually achieve? The Honourable President, may his soul rest in peace and dignity, entrusted to him a portion of the old republic's gold reserves, the gold that was to have helped build up the nation after the war, and what did he do? He misbehaved with a black maid from Pedi, meddled with the right hands of five dead boys, ate one of the little fingers, earning himself eternal damnation, then buried the gold and lost the map! Not even the greenest little English corporal could get so much wrong in a single career as a soldier. Truly an achievement! And now? Now he gets richer every day with the whole town's dirty linen locked in his safe. Thinks that a regular afternoon stroll and bowing his head there at the Little Hands monument will win him absolution. No, bloody hell, let's see some action, come, where's the car? Let's go and wake the bugger!'

And so they sallied forth in full cry, tipsily going over their plans while Meerlust's car stalled once or twice, then ran off the driveway into the garden so they had to reverse again, before spluttering and roaring through the quiet pre-dawn streets of Yearsonend.

As they drove, they set dogs barking and here and there a light flickered on behind a bedroom curtain, because it was unheard of for a vehicle to be driving through the streets at that time of night. With youthful exuberance Meerlust did a few wheel-spins around Lampak's Dam, and only missed driving into the Little Hands monument by a hair's breadth, which made them both collapse with laughter, and the general fired a shot into the air that echoed back from Mount Improbable.

The Pistorius's genteel house was situated near the practice in Eviction Road and, as if they'd been expected, there was a light on over the veranda when they drove up the drive and skidded over two rosebushes before the car shuddered to a halt with its bumper against the steps.

Attorney Pistorius stood on the veranda in his dressing-gown, holding up a lantern. He had a gun under his arm and a nightcap on his head. He must have been roused by the commotion. The engine died, shuddering, and the two men looked at Redbeard.

'Hey, you jingo lawyer, where's the republican gold?' shouted the general.

'Field Cornet, unlock your safe, my boy,' Meerlust bellowed. He remembered the night of the black blindfolds; it was time for revenge.

Pistorius had expected this confrontation for years, and he'd prepared his arguments carefully. But he'd never anticipated that the confrontation would be with two drunk men. His clever arguments would fall on deaf ears. He had no defence apart from the slender advantage of sobriety.

'Where's your map?' roared the general. 'Come, get it out, my little field cornet from the Transvaal.'

'General,' answered Pistorius, 'I must remind you that the tragic war is long over, and that I am no longer your subordinate. We are both ordinary citizens.'

'You're a dust-farter. It's a rank from which there is no promotion.' The hood of the car was down and, with these words, the general tried to get out, but didn't quite succeed. 'Veteran dust-farter!'

'Pistorius!' growled Meerlust. 'We swore a blood oath that night. Now it's your turn to keep your side of the bargain.'

'I am not the one with blood on my hands,' said Pistorius. 'And I warn you, keep your voices down. The whole neighbourhood can hear you.'

'Gold! Gold!' shouted the general. 'Let the wretched buggers hear! Gold! It's music to the ears. Gold! Gold!'

'Blood on my hands?' Meerlust attempted to climb the steps, but the car was in the way. 'Blood?'

'Yes, blood.'

Meerlust aimed a finger at Pistorius. 'Are you trying to say that you didn't fire as well? Do I remember wrongly, you little, you little – you—'

'I fired in my capacity as a commissioned officer of the Zuid Afrikaansche Republic's Kruger guard. You,' and Pistorius pointed his gun at Meerlust, 'were a Cape rebel with no military status. You are not a trained officer, you and your kaffir field cornet, that Moloi, you both—'

'And you? You weren't even an officer's arsehole, man. Where's that wagon now? Hey? Where's the wagon? I'm asking you. Shame on you!'

The general winked at Meerlust. The Cognac had finally got the better of him. Lethargy overcame him: he had to sleep. 'Oh, leave the tight-arse alone, man. He's not worth it. We know all about him. Auction attorney. Convict's friend. Yellow-belly. Let's get out of here.'

Meerlust turned away, but not before snarling at Pistorius, 'You spied from behind your blindfold, you little – little—'

Meerlust had never been one for strong language, after years of studied elegance, and, even now, loosened up by alcohol, he couldn't bring himself to swear at the field cornet.

'Dust-farter!' shouted the general, before his head fell on to his chest and he passed out.

And now the two men – Pistorius and Meerlust – stood facing each other. The silence stretched out between them.

'You know where the gold is,' Meerlust hissed, suddenly sober. It was as if the general's collapse had brought him to his senses.

'And I am convinced that you know, Meerlust.' Pistorius lowered his gun. 'Gold coins in ostrich eggs, your son born with a gold nugget in his hands, all those fashion houses overseas.'

'Are you saying I'm a thief?'

'I'm saying I think you know, and you've been living off the gold reserves for years.' Pistorius propped himself against the veranda railing. 'And lots of other people in town think the same.'

'Where's your map?'

'You know what happened. During the fight that Van Rooyen . . . when Taljaard and his men . . .'

'Rubbish.'

'Do you think I'd sit here with the map and not do anything with it?' Pistorius pointed his gun at Meerlust again, as if he wanted to force an answer out of him. 'Do you think I'd keep the map locked in my safe? Do you think I'm mad?'

'Yes, I do. And,' sneered Meerlust, 'lots of people in town think the same.' He shook a finger at Pistorius. 'That safe of yours—'

'I won't listen to such avaricious gossip.'

'They don't trust you,' said Meerlust. 'You're an outsider.'

'They all come and lodge their wills with me. I do their income tax returns. I defend them in court. They stream in.'

'But they don't trust you. They pay you for your services. With money. But no trust. Haven't you noticed?'

Meerlust knew his words had hit home hard. The Pistoriuses did everything in their power to be seen as leading members of the community: they sat on every imaginable committee; they organised bazaars and visiting speakers; they collected money for good causes and initiated prayer days for rain and better wool prices.

'And you, Meerlust, you know what they say about you?'

'I brought fame and fortune to Yearsonend, Pistorius.'

'But they say you're a half-caste and you always will be.'

Meerlust lunged forward but missed the first veranda step and fell over the bonnet of the car. Pistorius watched scornfully as he tried to regain his balance on his ivory leg, which kept slipping out from under him on the garden path.

Then he turned and slammed the door furiously. The light on the veranda was extinguished.

Meerlust shoved the car into reverse and deliberately drove over another seven of Mrs Pistorius's rosebushes. Then he drove slowly to the Pistorius Attorneys practice in Eviction Road where he let the engine idle, climbed out, hobbled painfully to the door, and urinated on the veranda. Then he felt ashamed. I have debased myself, he thought, and in his drunken state, as grief washed over him in waves, he saw the soft face of Irene Lampak, he saw her hands modelling and creating, he remembered her voice, the swish of her dress through the house, their evenings together on the veranda.

Meerlust drove back to the Feather Palace and left the car by the front door. He went inside to sleep, leaving the front door open so that he'd hear when the general, who lay slouched over in the passenger seat, awoke.

The sun was shining brightly by the time the two men stirred. Servants were surprised when they reported for work and found the general snoring in the still idling car, which had almost burned itself dry, and Meerlust fully dressed and spreadeagled in one of the guest rooms. He hadn't been able to face the bedroom he'd shared with Irene.

By the time they awoke, two baths had been drawn, scrambled egg, bacon and orange juice were ready, and, over breakfast, still bleary-eyed, they were able to try to unravel the events of the previous night, then continue bragging. When breakfast was over with, they fell to discussing the ghost wagon again.

They must ambush it, they decided, using fire to force it to a halt – people who are trapped in the hereafter must be afraid of *something*. Fire, yes, that should do the trick. That was the general's idea, and they were excited. The general remembered the horrors of fire. 'It's your best weapon in any war,' he said. 'Flames.' And he remembered the smouldering farmhouses, the fleeing people, the scorched earth and flocks of charred sheep, almost comical bundles, legs up in the air.

He remembered the pack of stray dogs running from farm to farm; the flames that grasped a train at one end then sprang from carriage to carriage while the wounded screamed and horses bucked, until the ammunition wagon finally exploded in a spectacular shower of stars.

The alcohol came out again – first, cold beer to restore their strength, then the expensive whiskies and brandies that Meerlust stocked.

How do you ambush a ghost wagon? This question had occupied the two men for weeks. First and foremost they had no idea when the wagon would appear: neither of them had seen the black ox-wagon rolling across the ghost plains with his own eyes, but there were enough Yearsonenders who swore by the apparition.

In the days that followed, they rode from farm to farm on the

Plains of Melancholy, calling at remote homesteads to ask about the ghost wagon's routine, and ascertaining that it was only to be seen on moonless nights, travelling from south-west to north-east. A group of horsemen accompanied it, along with a slender young woman with wavy hair. It was said that she was the mother of the boy whose hand was not buried along with the other children's – she was searching for the little hand, to honour her child and bring him to rest. Or was it another wandering soul? Who would ever know?

But she was the one to watch out for, they heard, because if you saw the wagon approaching and you went too close to it, it was not the horsemen who lifted their Mausers but that woman who aimed at you with a Lee Metford, and it was only then you noticed that she didn't have a face; and on top of this, a bullet from a ghost gun burned a hole through you that would never heal.

A war with so much pain and suffering, the people told Meerlust and the general, could never be laid to rest. And they brought out their stories and yellowed photographs and old letters, and sat and cried next to Meerlust and the general – cried for the dead and loved ones, cried over loss and betrayal.

'Gold,' said the general, as they rode away from one of these farms. 'Gold heals.'

'What am I mixed up in?' murmured Meerlust, because he saw that the general, unlike him, had no eye for sorrow. The general saw things differently, in a way that Meerlust didn't understand. Meerlust had suspected this during the war, but in his limited involvement as a Cape rebel he had never been directly confronted with it.

But now he saw it, and what he saw he didn't like. And yet he was caught up in it, dragged along because of his sorrow and longing.

Irene! his whole being screamed.

But out there on the rocky plains there was no one to hear him.

Only the angel, drifting invisible over Mount Improbable's highest peak, banked slightly, as if he'd heard something that upset him.

Then, dreaming and free, he sailed on.

19

At long last, they had their plans wrapped up. A load of sulphur was to be carted along, in case the angel appeared – apparently some kind of monster with an unbelievable wingspan and glistening feathers and, some said, a beak that could rip out your large intestine in one strike.

It was said, especially by farm-workers in the Murderers' Karoo, that the angel travelled with the black ox-wagon; that he'd even frightened off the tokoloshe, that he gave off the smell of cinnamon when he was angry or afraid, just as a polecat sprays urine at times of anxiety or danger.

The only talisman against him, the people said, was burning sulphur: the smell of hell sent even the angelman running. He was probably a fallen general from the Boer War, a hero who'd returned to earth; or maybe a sea captain whose ship had beached – maybe the Fourth Ship? – and who had then wandered inland growing wings to survive, and a beak for catching food, and feathers against the cold.

Laden with tents, compasses, flares, cans of petrol, everything you could think of, Meerlust and the general set off early one morning in two motor cars, which had been specially adapted, at considerable cost, for overland travel. Bubbling in Meerlust's blood was the memory of half-forgotten safaris, of the long expedition to bring the pair of ostriches to Yearsonend.

And war-lust was reawakened in the general: he remembered early-morning parades, the smell of freshly polished boots, the sweat of young men on commando and the sound of creaking saddles beneath restless riders. He reminded himself of the excitement of daybreak and danger, and later the smell of blood and the sound of sighs. There was also the guilty gratitude that you'd survived, as you carried the groaning wounded back to the Drostdy and laid them out in the broad, cool passageways and on the dining-room floor, and the silence as you carried the bodies to the lime-filled grave and tipped them into the earth with a short prayer.

For Meerlust the expedition was a way to forget. During those last days before Irene Lampak's disappearance, they'd argued endlessly. She had felt she'd exhausted the possibilities in Yearsonend. The caprices of fashion had turned against them; nobody was interested in her drawings or designs any more. The fashion magazines wanted other illustrators, to show new directions, usher in a new era. The fashion houses wanted to follow different designs: new, younger designers would dream up patterns and outfits now.

The flow of telegrams and letters dwindled; she looked around her, suddenly aware of the endless plains encircling her – she, who'd grown up in tropical Indonesia, now surrounded by stone and sun and winds that whispered of the transience of life and the insolubility of sorrows.

Come, she had said to Meerlust, come with me, with our available capital we can establish ourselves in Amsterdam, or somewhere in Italy, in a villa by the sea, or in the South of France, and you'll learn to love the heat and the stone there.

Look at what's growing in this country, she warned Meerlust: a nationalism with whiteness at its heart. We are brown: I am from the East, you have mixed ancestry. Soon your money won't be enough to buy yourself a place here. You'll be squeezed out, and so will I. We may have to flee eventually, because the whites won't allow us our wealth. There's no place for us in this country. And when the blacks take power – and that will happen, as sure as that mountain is there – they'll do all the things the whites did. It will be repeated. That's life, a cycle, and there is nothing new under the sun.

But he'd refused – he was of this landscape and the landscape was of him. He didn't see his earthly possessions as something that could be transposed to another continent. No, they were an intimate part of the earth that he knew; he had cultivated them and fetched them from the depths of Africa; they were born of this, and his way of life was a way of paying homage to the riches that this dry, hard land could yield and tolerate.

Irene would never understand it. She'd already emigrated from one marriage into another, from one continent to another, and then, after they had fallen in love, into a third. Africa had never really been hers: she'd enjoyed the climate, but had shut herself up in her studio, working hard, living for the times when they could celebrate the fruits of their labour in the cities of Europe. He could count on one hand the number of times she had been to the general store or run an errand in Yearsonend. And then, on Sunday afternoons, the ritual transgression of everything that the townspeople considered respectable: walking down to Lampak's Dam and swimming in a bathing costume ten years ahead of the local fashion. And with a body like hers!

How he'd pleaded with her not to provoke the local people! You always warn me, he'd said, that we're different and destined to be defeated by this difference, but look at what you do! You tease them – it's almost as if you challenge them deliberately! Can't you understand these people? If there's one thing they can't abide, the thing that causes them the most anxiety, it's difference. And you treat their deepest fear as though it's nothing.

Just wait, she'd said, these whites will learn when one day *they* will be branded as different. Then you'll see a thing or two.

'And when will that be?'

'Everything that you do,' she'd said, 'comes back to you. Autumn finds itself again, three seasons later.'

One moment, she effaced herself, the next she was an exhibitionist. She's an artist, Meerlust consoled himself: she wants to be private so that she can create, but she also needs to challenge the boundaries of convention in public to confirm her creative space – and this is the origin of her Sunday swimming expeditions.

It was harmless, really, but still . . . The dam was named after her, and the town began to gossip about the old men who spied on her lustfully and then the Monday after were all the more cruel, given to lashing out at anyone who was brown or black.

Racism has more to do with eroticism than with anything else, she told Meerlust that night: the desire for difference, and the guilt it brings with it. And because you believe you deserve to be punished, you mete it out to another.

During this last discussion she'd told him that she sometimes found his stump repulsive. Although he never allowed himself to be seen without an artificial limb strapped on, once or twice she'd seen the flapping motion of that red stump and the absurd see-saw of his body when he tried to manage on only one leg. And there were the raised welts on his thigh, where the lion had scratched him, he said, and the scar in his groin that ran up over his belly. He'd known she was lying, he'd known she spoke against her own love and better judgement. But she had to leave him, the time had come, that much was obvious.

And in the end he didn't know and would never know why Irene left. She was never a fair-weather person; she remained stoic through thick and thin, but when the fashion houses began to turn away, her life changed. She had to get back to Europe quickly, he thought, to try to re-establish herself in a new arena.

With these thoughts, and a car loaded with sulphur and guns, telescopes and flares, Meerlust drove on, watching the general in the vehicle behind him in the rear-view mirror. The old man was wearing gaiters and a row of pips on his shoulder; he was full of boastfulness and couldn't be diverted from the themes of women and war, blood and longing.

Gold, Meerlust realised, had a different meaning for everyone.

They drove over old farm roads, swung up rutted tracks and later bounced over stones and low bushes. They were in the area north-east of Yearsonend: the Plains of Melancholy, the beginning of the Murderers' Karoo.

The black ox-wagon had been last seen there, and there they set up camp in a narrow dry riverbed, parking the cars in such a way that they could suspend a piece of tarpaulin between them. They lit a fire and hauled out the whisky. Later, bored, they used the empty bottle for target practice then fell asleep without feeling the sun as it moved across their bodies.

When they awoke, their arms and one side of their faces were burnt blood red. Eventually it grew dark and the sulphur was set out in half kegs spaced at regular intervals on the plain. A fuse joined them and ran as far as the two cars, which were camouflaged with thorn-tree branches.

For eight nights they lay in wait for the ox-wagon. During the day they slept, and drank, and shot at targets and told stories, speculated about wars and women, about riches and the comings and goings of prosperity.

On the ninth night a great wind blew across the plains. There was a new moon and lightning veined the night sky, so far away that they couldn't hear the sound. But it was as if one side of the earth had exploded in electricity, lighting up their faces and the cars, their guns and the plains around them.

When they heard a distant rumbling, it was the general who, with his war experience, knelt down and put his ear to the dry riverbed. 'Horses,' he said. 'A big commando.' But suddenly he sprang up, yelling, 'Water!' In a panic, he began to scrape together the things around them. Meerlust also realised what was happening: it had rained far away and the sandy water course, which had started to tremble under their feet, was the conduit for a wall of water now rushing down on them.

As a child he'd often seen flash floods in the Karoo: one moment there was a dry water course, then a wall of water, several metres high, and the next moment a swirling river that swept tree stumps and dead animals along with it. Then suddenly everything was over, the water seeped away, and there was only the clean, open smell of mud and wet, washed earth.

They had trouble starting the cars, and forgot to take down the tarpaulin so that it tore in two as they pulled away. Eventually everything was up on the bank. And when the water came down, churning, as though it were a living thing, an animal suddenly charging past, they were on high ground out of harm's way.

Meanwhile, the sulphur had got soaked and a piece of the fuse had been washed away. Two days later they came across the woman without a face wandering on the plains. She just shook her head and wouldn't speak. All that she did, when they encountered her, was to take hold of their right hands, turn them over and inspect them. With a sigh she dropped them. She never did speak, and they took her back to Yearsonend to stay in a back room at the Drostdy until she felt better.

'Indeed,' said the general, 'she is a woman of many secrets.'

20

'Nothing exists before you name it,' said Jonty to Ingi, as they sat drinking a pot of reconciliatory coffee in front of his house. 'It's like a painting: it's absent until you paint it. And so it is with everything: it only exists once you verbalise it and call it by name. Then it's plain to see.'

'What I really want to know,' said Ingi, 'if you don't mind' – she was more cautious of Jonty since their skirmish – 'is what became of Meerlust and Irene in later years.'

Jonty sighed and put down his mug.

'Meerlust went to hunt in Malawi and got eaten by a hippopotamus. Only his ivory leg returned, by train, months later, smeared with blood and caked with dried mud and reeds, along with the death certificate. Many people – my father included – thought he hadn't died, that it was all a fabrication. He had gone to Europe, and to the East, the people said, to search for his lost love, my grandmother Irene. He had a lot of money in the banks in Europe, the gossip went, and he was alive somewhere and, like the general who forever yearns for gold, he's still searching for Irene Lampak. People said that an old man with grey hair down to his shoulders, and an artificial leg made of gold, had been seen in the most expensive hotels in Europe, sitting in the reception areas and waiting, behind an opened newspaper, for Irene Lampak to appear: older now, but still just as beautiful.

'Who knows whether or not this is true? But my father went to look for him a couple of times, and there's been speculation that my mother, Field Cornet Pistorius' daughter Lettie, went to meet Meerlust in Europe during her difficult times with my father – and to discuss the state of affairs between the Berghs and the Pistoriuses. Apparently people saw her walking with an old man in Kensington Gardens when she was pregnant with me. Whether or not it was Grandfather Meerlust, I don't know. But I prefer to believe that he ended up in the belly of a hippopotamus, in the reeds of Lake Malawi or Lake Nyasa as it was known in those days.'

Irene blew the steam off her coffee. 'And Irene Lampak?'

'My father went to look for her but he never found her. She was apparently in America – married to a stinking rich film maker. A Hollywood tycoon.'

'Was she an actress?'

'There were years when my parents went to see every new film shown in Cape Town in the hope that they'd come across her. My father went to see some films two or three times, to check that she hadn't appeared in the background as an extra. But she never showed up on the silver screen. The Pistoriuses spread the rumour that she ran a feather-duster shop in the worst part of Rotterdam, but that's not true either.'

'So that's the end of the feather history?'

Jonty nodded. 'Yes. Officially. But, as you know, things are never that neatly finished off.'

'I think . . . I think . . .' mused Ingi.

'Yes?' asked Jonty.

'I think . . .' she paused '. . . that Meerlust and Irene met up in Amsterdam and that they did live together again.'

'You don't want to put a frame around the painting and finish off the story?'

'No,' Ingi answered.

So Meerlust sent his ivory leg, with his half of the map, which might lead the treasure hunters to Gold Pit, with a few splatters of sheep's blood and a false death certificate, to Yearsonend. It's a long overland journey to Mombasa, from where he took a ship to Rotterdam, visited his bank in Amsterdam, reinvested the money he had hoarded there in various carefully considered investments, set up house in an apartment near the Rembrandt Square, and began his search for Irene Lampak.

He became a legend in the fashion houses he visited, a wandering chapter of fashion history. He was honoured everywhere he went and they listened to his story sympathetically. The newest fashions were shown to him: the drawings and the designs. Once again he breathed in the smell of fabric and the models' soft skin, felt their naked shoulders brush against his palm when he draped the fabric over them. It filled him with a terrible longing for Irene, but the new young designers comforted him by showing him how her designs, with subtle changes, lived on in the fashion of the time.

At night he wandered along beside the canals and dined every evening at the Herengracht where he'd spent that first night with Irene. The hotel smelt the same. He booked into their room for a night and watched the same silver water rippling outside the window, the same gulls hovering over the canal, the same trees etched against the grey sky with their black winter branches.

Each time someone entered the dining room Meerlust looked up. Once there was a graceful, older eastern lady; he wanted to jump up and go to her, but at that moment he dropped his napkin on to his plate and knocked over his glass of wine. But it was a stranger, elegant and attractive, with diamonds at her throat. Meerlust apologised to the waiter: he'd made a fool of himself.

He did find Irene, in a second-hand clothes shop in the Jordaan while he was wandering among the stands where old coats and tattered boas and jackets and hats were displayed. He found her in the half-light, in the depths of the shop: she was standing in front of a mirror and trying on a hat with an ostrich feather – a hat she might have designed herself.

He walked up to her, with the slight limp that had come with the years. His grey hair, combed back, hung down to the shoulders of his black coat. He carried a walking-stick with a silver knob and they looked at one another in the mirror.

'Irene.' His voice trembled.

But she walked into the mirror and suddenly all he saw was his own reflection: an old man, bordering on senility, a regular in the prostitutes' quarter.

Ingi sighed and her head flopped forward. Jonty was chiselling away at a piece of a wood. The splinters flew through the air and she smelt the wood and his sweat.

'Why do you work in the sun?' she asked.

'Sometimes it's a human necessity. I'm burning off my sins.'

'What are you making?'

'A thing,' said Jonty.

She stood up purposefully. 'And I'm going to paint now,' she said. 'It's time.' She swung her backpack on to her shoulders. 'Thanks for the coffee.'

And she walked down the Cave Gorge path, through the trees, with the smell of the warm earth in her nostrils, and with the sound of cicadas around her.

For the first time since she had arrived in Yearsonend – in fact, for the first time since her student years – there was that itchy excitement near her heart that she recognised as inspiration.

I'm starting to see things the way they are, she thought.

Part Four

Palm Stone

I

The quiet one: Edit Bergh. As quiet as a stone. Wherever Ingi went, people lowered their voices when they mentioned Meerlust's daughter, the sister of Big Karel. As quiet as a shadow, the Yearsonenders said, and so remote that the Berghs' great dramas played out as if she didn't exist.

Ingi remembered the photo of Mario Salviati and Edit in the stone cottage, the awkward limbs, the vagueness around her face, as if there the light were somehow troubled when the photo was taken. And she also remembered, unwillingly, the arias – somewhere between dream and wind – she'd heard during her first nights in Yearsonend.

Now Ingi studied a photo of Edit, the matron's mother. The photograph hung above the Drostdy sideboard where there was always a bowl of fresh fruit, and a candle that the matron lit at unpredictable times. What had the young Mario Salviati seen in this woman? Ingi wondered. Is there something in me that reminds him of her? Or am I completely different?

'Can I see more photos of Edit?' Ingi asked the matron, who went to dig in her room and came back with old black photo-albums, bulging with pictures. They sat on the sofa and Ingi flapped open the pages on her lap, while the matron clucked at her shoulder, pointing with a shaky finger. 'There's my mother at my first communion, look!' said the matron. 'I was dressed as the bride of Christ, barely six years old. Look at the little dress. Isn't that too sweet?' And next to her, standing to attention in his khaki shirt, a young Mario Salviati, his face carved into an uncomfortable silence, his feet splayed out in the big boots worn with short socks. His shorts were too small for him.

Ingi burst out laughing. 'Did your father come to your first mass like this?'

'Oh, oh, oh,' sighed the matron, and fluttered her eyelids,

'Father Mario rarely wore anything else. And look, there in his left hand, the stone.' Ingi could see it clearly in the hand that hung at his side.

'Had the stone already grown into his palm then?' asked Ingi, and said to herself, No, no, it doesn't look like it. No, look, he's still holding it with his fingers.

'Only later,' said the matron, 'when he went blind, the stone grew in.'

'How did he go blind?' asked Ingi, and her fingertips caressed a picture of Salviati standing at the stone furrow, trowel in hand, unaware of the camera.

She was surprised when the matron drew in her breath and whispered nervously, 'Gold Pit . . .'

'No,' protested Ingi, when the matron started to get up. 'Don't worry, don't worry, I'm not going to pry . . . Please, sit down . . . Look, is this you as well— ?'

'My mother saw visions,' whispered the matron, 'sent to her by the Holy Mother. Angels . . .' she whispered, and goosepimples came up across her arms.

'And where did your parents meet?'

'Mother Edit was at the station when the Italian prisoners of war arrived that day. She was the teacher at the little Catholic school in Edenville and the magistrate, in a fit of generosity, decided to let her school choir sing a welcoming song for the Italians, who were bound to be Catholic. That's where they saw each other for the first time. She sang the solo. He couldn't hear anything, he only saw her. And later, while Lettie Pistorius was away, she took food to Karel and Father Mario while they were building the channel. She was older than my father.'

'Older?'

'Yes. I think her love for him was the love of a Catholic mother for a son.'

'And are you at peace with that?'

'The ways are unfathomable.'

'And tell me,' Ingi probed gently, 'did she approach him, or did he come looking for her?'

Matron Taljaard smiled and rubbed her knee shyly. 'Now you're really cross-questioning me.'

'Sorry,' said Ingi, 'but I just wondered what kind of relationship they had.'

'She went to fetch him,' said the matron, 'one night, when it was raining, when they had to dynamite through rock to honour Bernoulli's Law. Everybody was gone – the blacks had gone home for Easter, Karel was in his house, nice and warm, everybody was peaceful, and poor Father lay alone in penury in the little tent he always erected at the head of the lightning water channel, as it crept over the plains. He always pitched his tent near where they were digging. My mother went to fetch him that night, after a visitation, and she brought him in . . .'

'Visitation?'

'Yes, the Mother of Jesus visited her. And gave her guidance.'

'What guidance did she give?'

The matron smiled, a little shyly. 'Well, who knows exactly . . . but not long after, after the water finally came, they were married. And Father didn't want to drop the stone, not even on their wedding night.' The matron giggled. 'Can you imagine? Stone in hand . . .'

Ingi laughed, surprised by the matron's levity. 'Yes, it's funny,' she said.

They paged on through the album. There were shots showing teams of workers with picks, the rocky outcrops of the Plains of Melancholy in the background. There were huge boulders with straps around them and teams of oxen straining to tow them away. There were sticks of dynamite, laid out on the ground, exhibited as if they were trophies. And there was the small tent with Mario Salviati sitting cross-legged in front of it, his hat beside him, his forehead white as snow, and his arms tanned and muscular.

'And his eyes?' Ingi urged softly, while the grandfather clock tick-tocked close by, Stella's elbow thumped rhythmically on the wooden floor as she scratched her ear, the servants' voices murmured from behind distant closed doors, and the musty smell of old photographs rose into their nostrils.

Ingi watched goosepimples creep over the matron's arms again. The woman glanced nervously over her shoulder, then said quietly, 'A terrible thing happened, a sin in the eyes of our Holy Mother, the Blessed Virgin. At Gold Pit . . .'

She stopped, breathing rapidly. Ingi waited, aware of the matron's warm body against hers, the quivering hands holding the pages with hers, and she realised that she was close to a secret, she was on the lip of the chasm.

'Yes?' she asked softly, but this last prompt was a mistake: it brought the matron to her senses.

'No!' The matron gave a little shriek, swallowed convulsively and snapped the album shut. In her eyes, Ingi saw something that she didn't want to see: madness, complete madness. But so repressed and controlled within the rhythms of the Drostdy that it was mostly imperceptible.

'Gold Pit.' The syllables dripped from the matron's lips, and Ingi thought, As slowly as a stalactite grows, the story is coming to me. Drop by drop.

When she looked up, General Taljaard stood in the doorway.

'What are you doing with him?' Ingi demanded. 'You promised he could come and sit down for supper, but nothing came of it. You could help him escape from his prison; these days there is help for people who—'

'He's in a deep darkness,' said the general, and his voice filled the room. It was as though a black cloth would shroud the events, for ever.

But Ingi decided to resist it.

'Oh, Mother of all Holy Ones, mercy . . .' muttered the matron.

'He's strong for his age! He has good years ahead of him!' Ingi was on her feet now.

The general grinned. He took a box of matches from his pocket. He struck one and kept the flame in the air. Ingi could smell it. The matron sat twitching beside Ingi, her hands in her lap, her eyes down.

'But he cringes away from a plain old match,' said the general. 'You . . . you— !'

Ingi marched out of the room. She had to step over Stella, who stumbled to her feet bewildered, and push past the general. She looked over her shoulder at the matron, who was weeping now. 'He's your father!' she snapped at her. 'Your own father!'

Alexander came bounding up, hoping for a walk, but she shoved him away and went to Mario Salviati's room.

Even before she opened the door, she knew.

The room was empty.

2

The channel was generally regarded as Karel Bergh's achievement, Yearsonenders who knew better pointed out after his disappearance, but in reality it was thanks to the efforts of that deaf and dumb fellow, rescued from the Plains of Melancholy by a girl who was supposed to become a nun but was apparently scared off by the Order of Silence, and had taken up teaching instead – Edit Bergh, the girl who played in the shadows at the Feather Palace or, when visitors came, hid behind the plaster models in the studio.

This was the version of the story they told Ingi Friedländer: Karel Bergh was the one who secured the funds for the lightning water channel and did the research, but Mario Salviati was the executor of the plans, the stonecutter, the genius who could apply Bernoulli's mathematical law to the gradient of the land, the smoothness of the stone, the resistance of the wind and the weight of the water. To Salviati, they said, mathematics was more than just numbers.

The deaf and dumb one, Ingi was told, had only three people in his life: Karel Bergh, with whom he had a peculiar relationship of trust, forged when Karel gave him a chance to prove himself at the station on that first day; Edit, his wife, who didn't mind that he couldn't speak, because in some way it was a penance for her after she decided at the eleventh hour that she could not take the vow of perpetual silence required by the Order of Silence, and then, of course, that other disabled Italian, the troublemaker and hot-cheek, Lorenzo Devil Slap, butler to the Pistoriuses and patient caretaker of Field Cornet Pistorius in the days after the first stroke when his greedy hand began to curl inward.

The matron, according to gossip, was strange because when she was a baby her mother, Edit, often tried to quieten her by holding a hand over her mouth when she cried, or by draping a cloth over her little bed, or by closing as many doors as she could between the infant and her parents or, more than once, by locking the child in a cupboard.

Of course, Mario Salviati had no way of knowing all this – to him there was always only silence. But it was the quietest house in town, people said, that little cottage close to the concertina gate that opened up to Cave Gorge.

Mario had built the little house out of stone and thatched the reed roof with his own hands. The wind was the only thing audible there, with the reticent Edit, who would always feel guilty about the Church, and Dumb Eyetie on his bench in front of his house in the sun, and the strange baby, with wide, quiet eyes and goosepimples all over her little body when you spoke to her, as if she was seeing a ghost or a tokoloshe or an angel.

Dumb Eyetie's friendship with Devil Slap was also consummated in silences and unfinished business. The two families they served – the Berghs and the Pistoriuses – eyed each other over smoking pistols, as the saying goes. They were the two prisoners of war who carried the signs of the devil: a red slap and deaf-muteness.

But one difference was whispered more and more often to Ingi: Salviati had been initiated into the secrets of . . . and then people would hesitate, look around, and lower their voices.

'Gold Pit,' they sighed, on an exhaled breath.

And furthermore, 'Devil Slap was outside,' they said mysteriously.

'Outside?' asked Ingi.

'Yes, the lightning water channel was about much more than just water. It was also about gold.'

To think that I've had to live here all this time, thought Ingi, before hearing this.

3

While Mario Salviati went down on his hands and knees to feel his way over the threshold of the gateway, almost nothing moved in Yearsonend. In her back room the woman without a face sat at her mirror remembering how the camp nurse had come and cut the stiff hand off her emaciated little boy. She always thought that the body laid out there on the bed looked just like that of a lamb which had died during the drought, with the thin shoulder-blades, the sunken stomach, the limbs absurdly angular. The camp nurse wrapped a bandage around the blunt wrist, added the little hand to the others that already lay curing in the bucket of salt, gave the mother a hug and left the tent.

Outside the veld smelt of fire, and rumours of commandos surrendering fluttered like washing on the line.

Later that afternoon thunderclouds banked up on the horizon, and seven more wagons came, loaded with women and children and the few pillowcases of things they had been able to bring with them. When it began to rain, the buckets of salt with the hands were smuggled out of the camp and hung with the sewage buckets on the refuse wagon.

The woman rolled her child in slaked lime, and a white cloud rose when his body flopped in with the others, the mutilated arm poker-stiff in the air, as if he was reaching for the last of the daylight.

Mario Salviati felt his way through the gateway on all fours. The earth was cool under his palms, as it was still early morning. Ingi lay in bed, dreaming of a lover, someone who listened to and cherished her, who understood her vacillations and her moods. 'You're worth your weight in gold,' she mumbled to him in her dreams, but when he kissed her, his mouth tasted as bitter as aloes and she awoke with a fright and turned over, her legs tangled in the sheet, and stared at the window where the morning light was already visible.

I'm going to paint today, she thought; I'm going to set up my canvas and get my paints ready and nothing and nobody will stand in the way of that: today is the day I'll start. Then she dozed off again, content in the peaceful dawn, the dew-fresh coolness perfumed by the smell of cultivated fields as the guinea-fowl started to chatter and ventured into the fields with their scuttling chicks.

Outside, Mario straightened carefully. The morning was clear of odours; the air was surprisingly pure. I'm alone, he thought; nobody is stirring here. But it was at times like these, when the wind was emptied of the smell of human activity, that he felt most blind and most deaf. There was so little to go on, only memory, only shards of remembrance.

He started to walk slowly, suddenly self-conscious. How would he look to someone watching him from the house? An old man treading comically high as if he expected a step at his feet, with his one hand stretched out as if he feared a wall looming, with his nose held up like a dog's, his face tilted in concentration.

Step by step he shuffled down the lane. He had taken off his shoes, and walked barefoot so that he could feel the texture of the ground. He knew he was wandering off the road when the smooth powdery dust, as cool and silky as water, gave way to gravel and twigs under his feet.

Suddenly fear gripped him, as he imagined General Taljaard spying on him from the Drostdy: the old man was taking his time to put on his shirt because there was no need for haste. The general probably thought, That Italian is moving as slowly as an earwig. Mario Salviati imagined the general's binoculars on his face, he thought of how the old soldier scanned his features to read his thoughts. He lifted his nose to see if he could pick up the odour of burning matches, but there was only the smell of earth and the fields.

Then he forced himself to forget the general and concentrate on the sensations on the soles of his feet. He remembered this lane, and he imagined that it still looked much the same: yes, this was where he'd walked with Lorenzo Devil Slap, years ago, with the energy and appetite of youth, during one of their days of discovery at Yearsonend. Here were the gnarled old trees and the irrigation furrow, the sluice gates waiting for water, lizards basking in the sun on the stonework.

While they were walking together, he and the limping man with the red cheek, they could have discussed everything that had happened to them if he, Mario, hadn't been deaf and dumb. Mario realised in those years that Lorenzo thought life owed them a lot, and maybe there was some truth in that. They were far from home, at the mercy of a strange community; their loved ones had no doubt forgotten them; they were begrudged their religious faith, some of them had been wounded in the war. Life owed them some recompense.

It wasn't his way of thinking. But he could see it in Lorenzo's manner. Lorenzo had his eye on the Pistorius daughter, and described with hand signals exactly what he was going to do to her. And then, with thumb and index finger, he made a signal that everyone understands, rubbing his thumb against his bent index finger, saying: Money.

Mario cursed the dark, quiet room he lived in. When this mood came upon him, he started to shake and sweat. It was rage, he knew. Fury that destiny should have picked him to be born not only without sound and words, but also to be a man who, that day when the water refused, saw something no man's eyes should ever have witnessed.

He knew how to cope with these seizures: first came the anxiety, the grip on the ribcage, as if a wild cat crouched there: who is watching me, who is standing near me, without my knowing it? Who is laughing close to me, or holding a raised knife, ready to drive it into my jugular?

Then the smells that flooded over him like waves: his own anxious sweat, the smell of his own skin. He thought: You smell the insides of your own nose; you see the insides of your own eyes; you only have the inside sounds. And then came the second fear, rolling over him like a wave: the general, with the match, wanted to burn his nose clean from the inside, the general wanted to take away his sense of smell. The general wanted to burn him clean, so that smell, too, would be lost, and then the general was going to cut out his tongue, so that he could no longer taste, then cut off his fingertips, one by one, carefully binding the stumps to stop bleeding and prevent infection.

And then, Mario Salviati knew, all gateways to the outside would be closed; then the winds, the subtle shift in odours, the subtle blends of smells, would also be gone. And if the general saw that you were trying to reach the things around you with blind feet, he'd also scorch the soles, make you walk over burning coals. He would take everything from you; he would lock you up in a soundless, odourless, surfaceless room, just you and your memories, the colours and smells as tangled as weeds, colour and odour and touch that would flow into one in a kaleidoscope of madness. God help me, thought Mario Salviati, and sank down on to the road, falling into shrubs that scratched and pierced him. Holy Mary, Mother of the Homeless and the Suffering, have mercy on me!

And that was where Ingi Friedländer found him. Her perfume walked ahead of her; he smelt her coming, and he concentrated on composing his twisted face before she saw him; he had trained himself to show nothing – the mask of stone, he had decided long ago. Learn from stone: the faceless expression of eternity.

He smelt her anxious approach, the alarm that preceded her like the Great Danes. They sniffed his tracks, tracks that zigzagged because, without realising it, he had staggered like a drunkard down the driveway, buffeted by suspicions and memories. Ingi had sworn everyone in the kitchen to silence: 'If you tell General Taljaard or the matron that Dumb Eyetie is gone, I'll kill you . . .'

She called Alexander and Stella with the high whistle she'd taught them to recognise, and made them sniff at one of Salviati's shirts in his room. Then she slung on her backpack, with an extra bottle of water and sandwiches, and the grappa she'd bought at the Look Deep pub.

She went out through the gateway and wanted to cry when she saw the palm prints on the ground, the dragmarks of the knees, and then the coming upright and the footprints staggering off in the direction of the lane.

When she saw the tracks, she ran back to her room, where she rubbed perfume on her neck, in her armpits, at the back of her knees and on her wrists. He would smell her from far off. She had no idea what to expect. How would he be after his solo exodus, the first since his imprisonment had begun?

Oh, I understand so well, Mario, she thought, because how do we escape the jails we live in? How do you leave the parrot's cage – defiantly and maybe with more stupidity than courage? Or is the koi destined to swim for ever round and round in his fountain pool?

How do I paint myself out of this canvas? How do I let go and daub the things that I feel inside me across this painting?

She found him lying in a bush with froth at the corners of his mouth. His hands were pulled up like claws against his body and one foot bled. The dogs were all over him, joyfully pressing their snouts into his crotch and his armpits; they licked his face and his bleeding foot.

Ingi stood upwind and allowed her smells to flow over him. Then she knelt close to him, at his blind, deaf head, at his expressionless face, and held his head in her lap and caressed him while the dogs circled inquisitively round them and the sun moved slowly over the dust road and the bantams took refuge in the shade and labourers fanned out in the fields to dig their picks and spades into the earth.

4

'I wanted to paint today,' Ingi confessed to Look Deep Pitrelli. She had two beers under her belt and her backpack at her elbow on the bar counter. 'But then things went wrong and now here I sit.'

'Artists,' Look Deep shook his head, 'have a hard time. Always on their backs, painting the skies, like Michelangelo.'

Wearily, Ingi listened to the low voices of a party of drinkers at a corner table. Earlier, the general's Plymouth had followed her slowly and now it crawled past the pub every so often. The exhaust fumes had a distinctive smell that she'd recognise anywhere.

After finding Dumb Eyetie at the roadside, she'd soothed him slowly to calmness then taken him home. Their footprints recrossed his swaying tracks. He held on to her tightly: his hand was like a claw and his nails left deep marks on her inner arm. She led him slowly through the gateway, pausing there long enough to let him acclimatise to the smells, then took him to his room.

As she leaned over her beer now, she remembered helping him to his bed. She made him sit as she took off his shirt. Then she pushed him on to his back and unfastened his belt buckle. She wriggled off his trousers and went to draw a bath. At the bath she stripped off his underpants, helped him in and washed him.

She took her time sponging his chest and stomach, the genitals that responded to her touch, and she made him stand up so she could wash his buttocks and legs, then allowed him to get out, rubbed his body dry and led him back to his bed. She helped him into clean underpants, shirt and trousers and led him to the koi pond, where she made him sit down again.

Her breath burning in her throat, she hurried to her room, locked the door and fell back on her bed. It was like loving an animal, she thought: you can't speak to him, you can't even feel his gaze. It was like adoring a landscape; something that doesn't talk back in conventional terms, that makes no appeal to you, offers you no choices. Yes, that was it: the absence of any expression of desire, the silence of mere existence.

I can't love like this, thought Ingi. I need more: a tumble of sentences, flirtation, the subtle poetry of the eyebrows, the corners of the mouth and eyelids; the caress of the eyes and love-making with words. I need jealousy, selfishness, demands.

But I have to free him; I must help him to get out. There has to be a way. She tossed on her bed, fretting over her resolution to paint, agitated, sighing. Then she got up and took her backpack, pulled the door open and almost walked into the general, who was standing eavesdropping in the hall.

'Ah, Miss Friedländer, I hear you went to save Mr Salviati from his own stupidity!' The words were sneering, but contained a reprimand too.

'I have to pass, General. Excuse me . . .' He blocked her way for a moment, but then she pushed past and went out, down the lane, where her tracks once again crossed the others, and she walked until she reached the bar.

Well, who else could she talk to? At Pistorius Attorneys there was only the tense, insecure young man in his old-fashioned church suit, collating and updating the town's secrets; in the kitchen the servants milled about gossiping endlessly behind their dish cloths while in the sunroom the matron sat whispering about days gone by and visitations from the angel; in town everyone spied on her.

Her head dropped on to her arms.

'Miss 'Länder?'

Look Deep came out from behind the partition with that brandy smell on his breath again.

'I'm worried about Mario Salviati.'

'Ah, the deaf and dumb one.'

'Yes, it's easy to write him off as the deaf and dumb one. And that's that. But inside that body there's a human being, Look Deep, a man.'

Look Deep smirked. Yes, the stories had reached him from the Drostdy kitchen where the servants kept an eye on the court-yard and carried the news to Edenville at night, stories that were redispersed via the workers in the houses and businesses of Yearsonend: the young miss from Cape Town was all too concerned with the old Italian.

'The general keeps him like a dog.' Ingi rubbed her eyes. 'And you'd never think the matron was his daughter.'

Look Deep buffed a glass. 'Families have funny ways,' he said.

'But there has to be something . . . something . . . I tell myself . . .'

He poured Ingi another beer, looked at the little group in the corner then leaned over to her. 'We of Italian descent,' he said, 'have known for years that Mario Salviati is walking around with something the general wants.' He straightened up again, very pleased with himself, but there was a hint of anxiety in his eyes.

'What do you mean?' she asked, but there were new arrivals. She sat, frustrated, watching him serve them. 'What?' she asked, when he passed her fleetingly again later, but he avoided her eyes, shook his head, and moved off to take a bottle from the shelf.

She left her money on the counter and walked outside. The streets were quiet and hot; the day was coming to an end.

Back at the Drostdy, she went to Dumb Eyetie's room. He was lying on his back, asleep. She sat down beside him to think. Later when it was dark, Ingi woke him gently. When Princess Moloi rang a small bell in the courtyard to announce that supper was ready, Ingi appeared with Dumb Eyetie. He wore yet another clean shirt, and shoes, and his sleeves were rolled down to his brown hands. She led him into the kitchen, past the surprised servants, down the hall.

In his room the general's head jerked up and he stiffened. The matron was already seated at the dinner table and her hands started to flutter over the cutlery in front of her when Ingi led in the old man. Slowly Ingi drew him to the chair next to hers, pulled it out and let him sit down.

Princess Moloi stood in the door, awaiting the matron's instructions, but it was Ingi who asked, 'Please set a place for him.' Princess hesitated, but when the general came in and nodded to her, she scuttled away with this piece of news for the other servants and to fetch the cutlery.

The general sat down and bowed his head for the grace. The knife, fork, spoon and plate were put down quietly in front of Mario Salviati. The matron served, and nobody said a word. Ingi tied a napkin around Mario's neck, so that it hung down in front of his chest, and she put his spoon in his hand. She put his other hand lightly against the soup bowl's edge, and the stone that had grown into his palm clinked against the porcelain.

He ate, with soup trickling down his chin and dribbling on to the napkin. The general looked on, sneering, as Ingi began to weep. Mario accidentally put his hand in his soup bowl, which startled him so that the plate tipped into his lap, then fell to the floor. It smashed, soup splashing everywhere.

Ingi sat shaking next to him, the general smiled and the matron looked at her plate as if she hadn't noticed a thing. Then Mario stood up, pushed away Ingi's hand, walked around the table and out of the room. He walked by memory, because there had been times when he was welcomed at this table, when the general entertained him jovially and spoke with sign language, years ago.

He walked down the hall, a little unsure of the turn to the kitchen, then passed the servants, who shied away; he walked across the courtyard and into his room, where he closed the door and sat down in his chair, facing the door. No expression could be read on his face. He sat there until his nose told him that it was past midnight; then he lay down on his bed.

Maybe it was dream, maybe memory; maybe wishful thinking. He remembered how the lightning water came back and lifted him out of the dam; the swirling water that spun him round and round then threw him out and up for gasps of air, pulled him in again and smashed him around as if it wanted to punish him for thinking that he could harness the power of nature with a neat trowel and spirit level.

He remembered how he had landed on all fours in mud, and the sheet of frothing brown water that slipped past, and the far-off commotion on the plains; cars and people surging about and carrying things away; the tables and chairs, the blankets and picnic baskets.

And Karel's carriage, and the thing that he, Dumb Eyetie, realised immediately: if Karel wasn't stopped, he would never come back.

Then chasing after the carriage, with Lorenzo hot on his heels, and there, where the tracks swerved away, where the water ripped open a piece of earth at the foot of Mount Improbable, where the

363

retreating water made its strongest turn, there, oh, Holy Mary: six skeletons had been washed out, their clothes had rotted away, but strangely the black blindfolds were still intact round their skulls, over the holes where the eyes had once been; and each with a clean bullet hole in the skull, fired by someone who knew how to kill.

And clenched in each skeleton's bony hand: a golden pound.

While his horse hesitated there, Lorenzo Devil Slap caught up. Together they looked down at the skeletons that lay exposed, with pools of shiny water around them. Then Lorenzo leaped from his horse, shaking with greed, and seized hold of the first hand with a golden pound.

But the bone fingers were locked like a claw around it. Lorenzo had to snap off the hand at the wrist and break the dry tendons with a twist. Grinning, he twisted off all six hands and shoved them into his saddlebag, then galloped off while Mario Salviati stood there with the sure knowledge that things would never be the same again.

From the carriage tracks he could see that Karel had also passed here, and that he had stopped for a while. Yes, there were his footprints, and there he had stumbled down to the gully, and he'd stood like this, at each of the skeletons, and at one there were two round knee-marks beside the skull.

With his bare hands, Mario Salviati covered the skeletons with gravel and mud. He worked hard. It began to rain, and after a while the place looked as if only rainwater had disturbed its surface. There was no sign of the dead or of the carriage tracks.

But now he and Lorenzo Devil Slap knew more than the rest. The lightning water had revealed it to them, allowing them to see what there was to see. The only other witness was Karel Bergh, and he was never seen again: Thin Air became his name.

5

'Obliging Edit', the people called her, because Meerlust Bergh's daughter, who packed a basket every morning and afternoon, took the Catholic Church's mule and rode out to call on Dumb Eyetie at the lightning water channel diggings. From a long way off he could see her coming. He would lay down his trowel and wash his hands in a bucket of water; then his face and neck and feet. His white shirt always hung on a branch while he worked, and he'd put it on and wait for her.

They sat to one side on a rug, drinking sweet wine and eating bread and some of the fruit she'd brought. She was older than him, and the people often made fun of the fact. She was big, broad at the shoulders, with angular elbows and big feet. Her breasts hung huge and low and her nose was as rough as a man's.

But when she touched him, it was with tenderness and love. She'd never been much of a talker, and the relationship with the deaf-mute clearly suited her. It couldn't have been easy, the people said, to grow up there at the Feather Palace surrounded by all those perfect, flowing fashion drawings when, in your early teens, you'd realised that your body would never match those of the plaster mannequins; that you'd never be the kind of person for whom your parents designed. As a little girl Edit had stood in front of the mannequins sighing: If only I could look like that one day. But something warned her even then that it would never happen.

During visits to the fashion houses of Paris, Amsterdam and Milan she kept to herself. Her parents adored the long voyages in their luxurious cabin, and Karel was always dressed like a young prince at the side of the picture-perfect Irene Lampak. Edit kept to the cabin, or stayed in the hotel room, or went to visit cathedrals and sat before their altars for hours staring at the candles.

As Edit grew up, Irene Lampak went to a lot of trouble with her. One summer's day she took her daughter, paler-skinned than the rest of the family, into the studio and battled for three days with materials and scissors and measuring tapes and feathers. The Feather Palace servants reported on the whole commotion at Edenville – the poor girl still looked as clumsy as a calf, with her knobbly knees, rough elbows, and those heavy breasts already hanging on her like sacks of maize meal.

The turning-point came for Edit after days and nights of measuring and fitting and the mirror that mocked rather than reflecting. She went to her room, ashamed, and she took the mirror off her wall, carried it past the flabbergasted servants and threw it on to the rubbish heap. In its place, she hung a Catholic crucifix. In a house where the mirror was everything! The daughter of parents in an industry where the mirror was the great arbiter! That set tongues wagging.

But she could sing. Alone in Europe's great cathedrals she sat and watched the choirs that came to practise, and started to hum with them. Once, in Antwerp, she was even invited by an old priest to join the choir. The poor girl, he thought, sitting for three days here in the Cathedral of the Holy Mother; let me invite her to join us.

In Belgium's harbour city, Obliging Edit realised that her voice was her beauty – she who loved silence so much. Her voice was her exquisite back, her neck, the curve of her leg, her beautiful breasts and her high cheekbones, the fine line of her nose and forehead. The voice was a body to her, and the ears of others were her mirrors.

For a while Edit lived through the small choir of the Yearsonend Catholic Church. She lived apart in the Feather Palace, and never put a foot in the studios. While Karel Bergh lived it up in the golden years of the Feather Palace, Edit Bergh turned her back on what she regarded as worldly things, on the fickleness of fashion.

But then she saw something she shouldn't have seen, and that drove her to the Sisters of Silence. One night she couldn't sleep. It was a hot night in Yearsonend during one of the summers that it didn't rain. Clouds gathered far across the plains, but always stayed out there, as if an invisible hand pushed them away.

This was the life the farmers knew. Your whole life depended on water, and sat fat and heavy out there in the clouds that bulged over the plains, flowering like cauliflowers in the sky, as if you could put out your hand and pull them closer. You yearned for rain, but then the mass of clouds would break up and move away until only blinding light and dust devils were left on the plains.

It was on just such a night, with lightning playing in the cloud masses far to the north-east of Yearsonend, that Edit lay at an open window and watched the storm. She reckoned she was the only one awake. Later she felt thirsty, and got up to get a glass of water. Light was burning in Meerlust's study, and when she crept down the passage she saw him standing at a window. There was somebody outside on the veranda, and Meerlust slid up the sash window.

Edit shrank back in the shadows, and watched, although she knew she shouldn't. Her father put his hand outside and someone took it. Meerlust pulled the man in through the window. It was – Edit couldn't believe her eyes – Field Cornet Pistorius, in a black attorney suit with his flaming beard. The two men were not on speaking terms – Edit had grown up with that as a certainty – and she wanted to call out, to her mother, to Karel, her brother, that something was seriously wrong.

The two men didn't talk and moved quietly. First Meerlust poured them some sherry and they lit cigars. They sat looking at one another without speaking, puffing on their cigars and sipping their sherry. Edit sat cross-legged on the passage floor, behind the big grandfather clock, and peered through the slit of the door. The men sat staring at one another, and she wasn't sure what they wanted to do. But there was no mistaking the anger in their eyes, a powerless kind of anger that she didn't understand.

Then, as if it had been planned, they laid their cigars in the ashtrays, drained their glasses, and Meerlust started to unfasten his ivory leg. Edit gaped – she'd never seen her father without his leg, and now he sat with the stump comically over the edge of the chair and the ivory leg in his lap. Pistorius turned his hat over on his lap. Edit jumped when the attorney took a pocket-knife out of his trousers and flicked it open.

Pistorius carefully slit open the seam under the headband. Meerlust leaned forward, with his ivory leg in his lap, his eyes glued to the groove Pistorius was cutting. Pistorius took a piece of paper carefully from the crown of his hat. Edit leaned forward – there were words written on the document, but mostly there were lines and numbers . . . Yes, it was a map!

Then, map in hand, Pistorius looked at Meerlust expectantly. Meerlust gave the clasp on the ivory leg a firm twist. It didn't loosen, and he had to hop to a cupboard – Edit's eyes opened even wider – to take out a pair of pliers. He sat down again and unscrewed the fastening, pushed his fingers into the hollow and pulled out a rolled-up document.

It was also a map, and Meerlust and Pistorius looked at each other again wordlessly. Edit would never forget the hatred in their eyes. At the same time, they spread the maps open on the table between them. They pushed the documents together and bent over them. For a long time they sat like that, then hastily turned the maps round and pushed them together again, then turned them again, measuring and lining up. And suddenly they both jumped up, their hands darting like snakes into their jackets, and then they were aiming pistols at one another, still without saying a word. Edit recognised Meerlust's small silver Derringer. He always took the pistol on the sea voyages to Europe and kept it close at hand during late-night gambling sessions.

She watched how the two men glared at one another over the pistols, how the cigars smouldered in the ashtrays, and how Meerlust's short leg jerked, as if in spasm.

She jumped up and ran into the study to stop them. In a flash their pistols were aimed at her. What she could never forget, and maybe this was why she eventually sought salvation in silence and solitude, was that Pistorius lowered his pistol the moment he saw through his rage that it was Meerlust's daughter. But her father, Meerlust, kept his pistol aimed at her, with a shaking hand and fevered eye.

Pistorius walked over and pushed Meerlust's hand down then turned his back on father and daughter. Edit retreated slowly from the room. She realised something terrifying: her father could kill. And she also realised: He has done so already – and not only in war. She could see it in his eyes, and she ran out of the room with the images of Meerlust's guileless laughter around the card table, the swaggering way he walked into fashion shows, his big body on a wild horse. She fled, with these images of a man who would stop at nothing, away from the pair of them.

Down the hall, out of the kitchen, and around the house, to the lawn and trees where she often sat and hummed, even at night sometimes, when she woke up and thought about God's plans for her. And she saw them sitting there, waiting on the veranda steps: six men in black, with spades in their hands and black blindfolds over their eyes.

It was many years after the war, and it was said that the six men still sat waiting there some nights. Few people had seen them, and still fewer knew where their graves were. But Edit Bergh saw them that night, and she ran like the wind to the church, fumbled there in the dark for matches and candles, and at the altar at three o'clock in the morning she lit a candle: a flame for every lost soul.

For a long time she sat there thinking. She heard something behind her, a rustling and a movement; a swishing sound. She didn't turn round, because she thought – and hoped – it was her father come to seek forgiveness. A smell, something like cinnamon, wafted around her, and a breath fell on her shoulder.

6

'It's about tenderness for small things,' Jonty Jack told Ingi Friedländer. 'You have to be able to run your finger gently along the scorpion's back, and trust him. You have to, without being disgusted, lie on your stomach with a snail, bring your face close to him and lick his little body. You have to—'

Ingi shuddered. 'You're asking too much,' she said.

'And what do you want to create? Comforting art that lulls

people to sleep? No, you have to become one with all things. Share their whims; what threatens them also endangers you.'

She looked down, distressed. 'I'll never be able to do that.' She sighed.

Jonty asked quietly, 'What's stopping you?'

'There was a time . . .' she hesitated, and licked her upper lip, combed her fingers through her hair '. . . sometimes I think that . . .'

'Yes?'

'No, I . . .'

He looked at her expectantly.

Suddenly Ingi snapped, 'That's enough, Jonty! You're a sentimental old man! It's all – it's – You're talking like an old hippie from the sixties . . . you . . .' She stood up, threw her tin cup on the grass and looked at the Staggering Merman, who stood there wrapped in blankets and tied up with rope. 'And you don't even want to open that cave and see if your father is really inside it. You want me to confront my demons, but you . . .'

He looked at her calmly, but she saw his eyelid twitch.

'You sit here in your little town and you – you keep to yourself, but you're just like the rest . . . you . . .' She searched for words, gesturing.

He rubbed his face and put down his cup. 'So let's go, then,' he said softly.

'Let's go?'

'Yes.'

'Where?'

'Attorney Pistorius.'

'Why him?'

Jonty sighed and stretched himself. Suddenly he looked tired. You've asked a lot of me, Ingi Friedländer, he thought. My infatuation with you, like a fire in a hearth, and eventually the realisation of my limitations. He looked at her. 'Pistorius is the town council's attorney. That part of Mount Improbable is town property. It belongs to Yearsonend. We have to get permission before we can use dynamite there.'

'Dynamite?'

'How else do you think you're going to move the rocks? There are tons of rock there.'

'But—'

'So, yes, let's go,' he said quietly.

And Ingi swung her backpack over her shoulder. Still somewhat taken aback, she watched him slip on his shoes, pull a waistcoat over his T-shirt and put an old cap on.

'Come.'

They started to walk down the path. They didn't talk, but once, before they got to the concertina gate, he looked back.

'I'm going to stroke the scorpion's back,' said Jonty Jack.

7

It was in the days after the angel visited her in the little church that Obliging Edit decided to join the local Order of Silence. The order resided in a small building and a series of rooms behind the church – a handful of quiet women who were hardly ever spotted outside the church grounds. They followed their rituals conscientiously: prayers and cleaning duties, cooking and prayers, church services and more prayers. Penguins without tongues, the Yearsonenders called them, and Edit had always admired them.

With the scent of cinnamon still in her nostrils she visited her mother, Irene Lampak, in the studio. Irene was sketching beautiful fine lines – and the light in the studio was perfect. It was her favourite time of day to spend behind the drawing-table. Meerlust was busy outside with the feather plucking, and the smell of the meal the servants were preparing wafted in from the kitchen. Irene was surprised when the child appeared in the studio, having avoided it for years.

Maybe it was because the things Obliging Edit had to endure were too much for her. How do you digest the knowledge that your own father is capable of killing you? She had seen it in his eyes, and that night in the church she had to ask herself why Meerlust could do away with her but – her instinct told her – not with her brother, Karel, or her mother, Irene.

And she had to try to puzzle out what pact Meerlust and Pistorius had made. It was a pact of furious connection, she had seen that night. And nobody knew about it. In the days after that night their family often walked past the Pistoriuses', but the Berghs and Pistoriuses looked away from each other.

When she stood in the studio in front of her beautiful mother that day, she knew that nobody would believe her. And yet Obliging Edit, who had always imagined that she was alone in the world, was mistaken because it was at times like this that Irene Lampak could hardly bear to see how the business of the black ox-wagon was eating away at Meerlust.

In the years after he and Pistorius came back from the veld and informed everyone that the business about the gold was concluded once and for all, Meerlust was still a high-flyer in the fashion houses and the ostrich industry. But the gold was his consuming passion.

Irene would never know what happened with the black ox-wagon that night. But she knew that whatever had happened was leading to a kind of frenzy with which she would not be able to live forever, and she'd grasped this before Edit came to her that day.

And when her daughter told her that she wanted to renounce the spoken word for ever, in the service of the Lord our God, and to the honour of Mary and the saints, and that she wanted to live until she died behind the church at Hush-hush, as the people called the building and the row of rooms, Irene pulled her child close briefly then let her go, the awkward calf with the unlikely combination of body parts.

There was a great fuss when Obliging Edit 'went out to Hush-hush', as the saying went in those days. Meerlust insisted on a huge reception at the Feather Palace, and tables and chairs were set out under the trees before a small stage, decorated with lanterns. It was only right, thought a lot of people, because after all Meerlust was handing his daughter over to the Bridegroom, so why not have a wedding?

Almost all the important people in town were invited, except the Pistoriuses, and that evening Meerlust and Irene Lampak pulled out all the stops: roast sucking-pigs with apples in their mouths and legs of lamb lay glistening juicily on silver salvers, and the tables groaned under salads, side-dishes and puddings.

Meerlust took his vintage wines out of the cellar and Irene proved her exceptional talent, by making Edit a frock that was something between a bridal gown and an evening dress, and gave lines to her body that everyone knew didn't exist, a grace that everyone knew was Irene Lampak's invention.

As the highlight of the evening, Edit got up on to the stage to sing an aria, so that her beautiful voice could be heard for one last time before the Mother Superior of Hush-hush carried her off to a lifetime of silence.

'The nightingale will sing one last time,' Meerlust announced on stage, in his emerald bow-tie and his beautiful evening suit. Irene led Edit to the stage but even the dress couldn't conceal the girl's calf-like clumsiness as she went up to her father, who greeted her with a hug and a bouquet. The strangest thing, people said afterwards, was that the parents didn't look sad. An air of relief hung over the whole evening: the Feather Palace, people reckoned, was glad to be rid of its ugly duckling. Not only was she bad for business, but she ruined the atmosphere in a house and studio where there was only one aspiration: harmony of line, beauty of form.

Or, at least, that's what the cruellest tongues said in those days. Meerlust left the stage with a flourish and took his seat at the front next to Irene Lampak. The crowd looked expectantly at Edit, now clearly visible in the bright light of the oil lamps, one breast much bigger and lower than the other, one foot turned sideways as she stood there – and the angle of the elbow: wasn't the upper arm too long?

How Meerlust and Irene must have longed to take an eraser and redo that part of the sketch! Or take a pair of scissors and snip away the clumsiness!

But when Obliging Edit folded her hands in front of her, under her breasts, on her midriff, as if she wanted to lift her lungs, people leaned back in their chairs, and the most beautiful voice Yearsonend had ever heard floated over the tables, over the cultivated fields, down the dusty streets and over the plains.

It was as if an angel had possessed her, people whispered, as if she sang out against everything taken from her, against everyone who looked only at the surface and outward appearance. Edit Bergh gave, for a moment, a glimpse at the perfection of human creation.

And then, as if she'd given birth to something too big for her, she fainted, to be caught in the nick of time by a scurrying Mother Superior, flanked by three sisters from Hush-hush, and they carried her off with surprising strength. Like a fatted calf, people muttered; God, look how they're carrying her like a calf to the slaughter, the dress rucked up high on her thighs, one foot dragging over the grass, the eyes rolled as in death, and the tongue that, just a moment ago, formed those heavenly sounds lolling half out of her mouth. They carried her under the dark trees, and then there was the sound of mule's hoofs, and thus the sisters of Hush-hush left the wedding of the year, with Edit flopped over a saddle.

An orchestra stepped onstage and when Meerlust nodded started to play. He and Irene opened the dancing on a special floor that had been set up between two giant oaks, with burning torches all round it.

With the artificial leg going tap-tap, thump, tap-tap-thump-pa-thump! on the wooden stage, the two executed the slow movements of a passion-filled tango. It was the first time the Yearsonenders had seen Meerlust and Irene like that – so intimate! And would you believe it? That coolie woman could certainly dance! It was a time when people were uneasy about such conspicuous passion between people of different colours – he was half brown, well, actually almost white, you know, and she, uh, yes, was she yellow? they whispered behind their hands.

Of course, Irene had a whole rich life behind her in the salons of Indonesia and Europe, but the Yearsonenders knew nothing of that. Neither had they any notion of what Meerlust had got up to during all his travels. But for a short while that night they glimpsed the daring sophistication of a lifestyle they hadn't even dreamed existed.

In Hush-hush the nuns laid out their new sister on a table and combed the unconscious child's hair out of her face. Quietly, accustomed to working as a team without needing words, they took off her shoes and her watch, the earrings Irene had given her as a farewell gift. The string of pearls was unclasped and all the jewellery was put into a black velvet bag, ready to be sent back to the Feather Palace.

Then they unbuttoned her dress, the petticoat, and the bra. They watched as the breasts fell sideways, the one indeed much bigger than the other, and they pulled her knickers down and put her clothes into a bag for the poor. Then they started to wash her carefully, as if they wanted to sponge off everything worldly. As the faraway music wafted in over the trees, and now and then laughter from the Feather Palace party, they bent inquisitively over Obliging Edit's body: this new body; the newcomer.

8

Afterwards the Yearsonenders would tell the story over and over again, as if they wanted to taste it anew. And, of course, they added to it. There were omissions too, and forgotten details, but the scene flourished, albeit in several different versions: the story of the first Bergh in years to set foot on the property of a Pistorius.

Jonty Jack, in a sweaty T shirt with a hat on his head, his broad chest braving the staring eyes of town, came up Eviction Road. Even if they weren't blood family, he was still related to Dumb Eyetie, for both of them had strong, well-developed hands and leathery forearms. Jonty also had the same lizard-like quality from all the exposure to wind and sun, the quality of someone who worked with the elements, people always said.

And next to him, trotting to keep up, backpack clinging to her shoulders like a little monkey, her hands every so often pushing her hair out of her face, Ingi Friedländer. She seemed more surprised than curious, somewhat out of breath, taken aback by developments, the sudden fervour and the realisation that something was going to happen, at last.

And like motorbikes escorting an important cavalcade, scouting about and pushing the gawking onlookers back, Alexander and Stella, the calf-sized dogs from the Drostdy. People made way for the dogs, taking refuge on the general store's veranda. The storekeeper came out to join them, squinting in the bright light with his small-change hands and his stained apron.

The receptionist at Pistorius Attorneys looked up, her lips forming the stock question: 'Do you have an appointment?' But when the two dogs put their enormous heads on her desk and stared at her, and she saw Miss Friedländer from the Cape standing there, sweaty and flushed from the exertion, she knew that this was an unusual situation. And there, God forbid, too big for this little reception room with its genteel attorney furniture, stood Jonty Jack, all hairy arms and grubby body, completely out of place here, as if the room might burst open around him. With the smell of sweat and dogs in her nostrils, she exclaimed, 'He's not too busy today! He's not too busy today!'

By then Attorney Pistorius the Fourth – his father's surname Terreblanche had had to yield to tradition – already stood in his office door, his suit too small, his tie hanging askew and ballpoint marks on his shirt pocket. He stood there holding an open file and looking confused. 'Um . . .' he said. 'Um . . .'

Ingi stepped forward resolutely. 'We're sorry we didn't make an appointment . . . um . . .' Without intending to – she could have kicked herself – she echoed the attorney's bewilderment. 'Er . . . sorry about the dogs, but . . .'

Now it was Jonty's turn to step forward and he shook hands with Pistorius. The receptionist watched, wide-eyed: news was being made right here under her nose. She jumped up. 'Tea? Yes?'

Once they were sitting in the attorney's office and the two dogs had lain down – Alexander with his heavy head on a stack of files standing on the floor, Stella under a framed picture of a proud, young Field Cornet Pistorius in his uniform – Ingi looked at Jonty. The young attorney, his fingers fumbling with a ballpoint pen that clicked open and shut, looked at the sculptor with similar expectation.

'God . . . yes,' said Jonty, his hands moving as if he wanted to give form to something in the air, something he couldn't put into words.

'Look,' started Ingi.

'Um . . .' said the young Pistorius, but then the door opened to reveal the receptionist.

'I nipped over to the general store for a milk tart. Would you all like a little piece?'

Relieved, all three looked at her. 'Yes,' they said simultaneously.

Once the door was closed again, Jonty braced his elbows on the arms of his chair and compelled himself to say the difficult words: 'The cave must be opened.'

'The cave?' The attorney grabbed a file and whipped it open. He took a clean sheet of paper, but it slipped out of his hands because the ceiling fan was on. He caught it between his fingers but it stuck to his palm when he lifted his hand.

'Yes.'

A sigh escaped from Pistorius. Ingi looked at the freckled hands, the nails bitten to the quick. There was a wart on the index finger of his left hand, on the inside. It glowed red.

'The town council . . .' Ingi said to Jonty

'Oh, yes,' said Jonty, ruffling his red hair and absent-mindedly putting his hat back on. Alexander started to scratch his ear with his back leg and Pistorius had to get up in a hurry to rescue the files.

Then the door opened and the receptionist marched in triumphantly with a large tray. The milk tart took pride of place, supported by a plate with three sweet pastries, and gilt-edged floral plates with three silver forks.

She put down the tray on the side table then went back to her office to fetch the tea. The door to the reception room was open, and Ingi saw the two nosy bookkeepers peering at them.

'God, yes . . .' said Jonty, suddenly remembering his hat and taking it off again.

When Pistorius stood up, Stella growled at him.

'I'm sorry,' sighed Ingi, 'she's a little irritable. Maybe it's too warm in here. Could you switch on the air-conditioner?'

'Because you hold the bloody power over the cave,' Jonty blurted out, leaning forward. Pistorius dropped the piece of milk tart he'd been scooping on to a plate for Ingi. Alexander lifted his head and barked excitedly.

Jonty's explosion seemed to put Pistorius at ease: he was used to dealing with conflict, the courts were his bread and butter.

'That's strong language,' he said drily, passing the plate to Ingi with a freckled hand.

'Well, sorry,' stuttered Jonty, and touched his hair, 'I . . . look . . .'

Ingi sat forward, with the slice of tart quivering on her plate. 'We want to . . . Jonty wants to open . . . the cave, but the town council has to give permission. Right, Jonty?' She looked uncertainly at Jonty, who accepted the delicate plate and fork gingerly and held them at arm's length, as if they might bite him.

'Indeed,' said Pistorius, from where he presided over the tart, and Ingi could tell his mouth was watering, 'indeed it is town commonage. We sustain an eco-friendly policy for Mount Improbable. Um . . .'

'Fuck um!' It slipped out before Jonty could stop himself. Ingi and Pistorius both looked startled. Jonty sat there with the little fork in his rough hands and the hat on his knee. They could smell him: a mixture of sawdust, wood-oil and sweat, and something of the mountain smell too. Pines? Ferns from those wet ravines? Cow piss, thought Pistorius, it's unmistakable. The man smells of cow piss.

'Look,' said Pistorius, 'you . . .'

Irritated, Jonty dumped the little fork in the ashtray, and took the tart in his hand. It wobbled, and a piece broke off, but he caught it on his tongue.

'My father's in there,' said Jonty. 'Karel Thin Air, son of Meerlust.'

In the silence that followed, Pistorius' chair creaked as he sat down. He stood up again, to turn the fan up higher, and to pour more tea. He held the tray for Ingi, who could smell his aftershave, and some sort of perfume she couldn't identify. They sat eating their tart and drinking their tea in silence.

Then Pistorius put down his cup decisively. 'You are welcome to put forward an application to the town council. As you know, I am their legal adviser. If your grounds are that you believe your father's remains are buried there, I will support your application.'

The two men looked at each other, and suddenly Ingi felt that more was being played out here than she had suspected. But she shook off the thought when Jonty rubbed his nose, sniffed, and asked, 'Who baked the milk tart?'

'The aunty down there at Little Hands,' answered Pistorius, and suddenly all three stiffened. A taboo had been broken: Little Hands with all its connotations of gold and the strife between the Berghs and the Pistoriuses. Two families, remembered Ingi, who had stared at one another over smoking pistols.

Jonty rose. He put out his hand to Pistorius. 'I appreciate your support.'

'But look,' said Pistorius, waving at Jonty to sit down again, 'you can't just go in there with a bulldozer and dynamite. The town council's eco-committee will need to know exactly which method.'

'I'll be careful,' said Jonty, 'I'll let you know exactly how.'

'Maybe,' the attorney suggested, 'you should use the method that worked so well with the lightning water channel.'

'And what was that?' Ingi asked curiously.

'They made fires round big rocks, then threw cold water over them. The rocks split and it was easier to break them up.' Jonty rubbed his eyes, as if the idea wearied him.

Then Pistorius leaned forward. 'And you say Karel Thin Air . . . your father . . . . is there? I thought . . .'

Jonty shrugged. 'My father drove in there the day that the water refused him. He's been in there ever since.'

'And who else knows about this?' asked Pistorius.

'My mother knew, but only later,' answered Jonty. 'And Dumb Eyetie, Mario Salviati.'

'Mario Salviati?' asked Ingi and Pistorius simultaneously.

Jonty put his hat back on his head. 'Yes, and Lorenzo Devil Slap.'

Ingi was dumbstruck. They all looked at the field cornet's photo on the wall.

'Devil Slap?' Pistorius started to chew his thumbnail. Ingi was fascinated to see how a sliver came off between his teeth and she listened to it crack as he chewed it.

'Yes,' answered Jonty, matter-of-factly. 'Your great-grandfather Redbeard's minder.'

'Um . . .' said Attorney Freckleface Pistorius-Terreblanche, and a little piece of milk tart quivered at the corner of his mouth.

9

Swifter than the wind that slipped over the sloping spine of Mount Improbable, faster than Ingi's feet when she whistled to the dogs and trekked up to the dam after a hot day, yes, as quick as lightning, the news spread to every house in Yearsonend: it was in every business, every little shop, at the police station, in the pub, everywhere. Jonty Jack was going to dynamite the cave open to get to his father, Karel Bergh. The man had never really left, after all. He had driven his carriage in there and he'd been sitting in there all these years, can you actually . . .

While Ingi and Jonty and the two Great Danes – relieved to be out of Attorney Pistorius' stuffy office – ran through the wind with a big red kite that bit into the air and clung obstinately as if it wanted to tame the blue sky itself, old grievances and suspicions came to the fore in Yearsonend.

It was like a beehive when the lid is lifted slightly, and the bees crawl out and swarm with a vehemence that amazes you. Front gates squeaked open and closed, telephones rang and children were sent running from house to house with folded messages. The pub was suddenly a hive of activity and Look Deep Pitrelli was kept on the hop. His ears were pricked because he liked little Miss 'Länder, and he knew she'd be doing the rounds at any time now, leaning over her beer melancholically, with the beautiful somewhat melodramatic sorrow of youth, and he'd have new things to tell her: the gossip and speculation, the drunken accusations and curses he'd picked up.

In the meantime Look Deep received a phone call from the storekeeper, breathlessly reporting that with his own eyes he'd seen Jonty Jack arriving with the missy from Cape Town – the one who couldn't get going with that painting. And after they'd left the office they ran wildly up the street, then up into the gorge. 'Most probably,' breathed the storekeeper, slapping the flour from his apron, 'to go and smoke dagga up in Cave Gorge.'

'And how's business today?' asked Look Deep.

'Quiet. With you?'

'The whole world is thirsty now.'

'Perhaps I should come over for a quick one too.'

General Taljaard was notified by fax that the cave was going to be opened. He heard the machine stammer and lumbered up from his sweaty bed. He'd been asleep because the previous night there'd been reports of a find on the Mozambican coast. When the fax came out, he tore it off and bellowed, 'Matron!'

When the matron appeared, the general was pulling on his trousers.

'They're getting ahead of us!' he called, trying to put his bandolier over his chest. She had to use all her strength to force him down on to the bed again and calm him. Her eyes rolled as she whispered, 'The angel,' with her mouth close to the vein that was pounding like a worm at his right ear.

And that very same angel shuffled restlessly in his cleft in the rocks, rearranging his feathers, ruffling himself and settling comfortably on his nest of feathers and excrement, nuzzling in his armpit with his beak, picking fleas and dozing off again, snoring. He was waiting for the night, for the dark of the moon, for closure.

That evening shortly after sunset, there was no one around to see Irene Lampak's beautiful naked body slip with a sigh into the cold water of Lampak's Dam and swim round and round while the sickle moon peeped at her and the mountain crouched over her, huge and dark.

And Field Cornet Pistorius hobbled down to Little Hands, with his walking-stick and a small boy leading him, and he came and stood at the monument and bowed his head, while in Edenville Granny Siela Pedi sat crocheting with thick black-framed glasses on her nose and the Bible at her elbow. She could forgive, but would never forget, the red beard hovering over her.

And the woman without a face sat in her room, and rolled her pillow in a sheet, as if it was a child's body, and stood on the bed and dropped the pillow into the gap between her bed and the cupboard. She remembered the cloud of lime that rose up from the grave, and she looked at herself in the mirror: nothing, only blame.

Mario Salviati came upright and supported himself on his elbow. He remembered . . . he remembered.

10

'There is a third map, and both Jonty Jack and Freckleface Pistorius know this,' the general told Ingi. 'It was meant for me, but in the drama of that night it was lost.' He had come across her in the shade under the thickest part of the vine where she was sponging down the two Great Danes. Stella shook her wet body and the spray made the startled parrots clamber away in their cage. Alexander stood submissive, covered with white soapy foam.

Mario Salviati sat on the edge of the fountain, his hand on the koi fish, his nose tilted up, alert to the smell of soap, wet dogs, Ingi's perfume, and now the general.

Ingi's eyes flew up and her hand went to her mouth. 'You mean . . .'

'Right under your nose, they were negotiating about much more than Karel Thin Air's remains,' sneered the general. 'You thought it was about the laudable desire to give his father a decent burial, about preserving the mountain ecology, when they're both burning with gold fever. Nothing but a pair of pirates!'

Ingi hid her shock by turning her back on the general and rubbing the soap so vigorously into Alexander's back that he groaned softly.

'Ha!' said the general triumphantly. He turned and went inside again. As Ingi worked on with a hollow feeling in the pit of her stomach, he came back to stand at the kitchen door again. 'They probably reckon that the third map is in the cave with Karel Thin Air!'

Ingi took the hosepipe and turned it on full. She squirted the dogs with such a blast that they staggered from the onslaught. Then she turned off the tap and threw down the hosepipe angrily. She stumped barefoot back into the house, laced up her walking-boots – well worn-in here in Yearsonend – grabbed her backpack, and went out through the gateway, down under the oak trees, while the clean wet dogs tore around on the lawn, shaking themselves and snorting, gambolling boisterously, then bolted through the trees.

I can't bear all this, thought Ingi. Has Jonty Jack kept me on a string all this time, playing with me, maybe using me to fish out clues about Gold Pit in the hope that all the stories I told him over these past weeks would enable him to patch together a location, a story that made sense, a conclusion?

She didn't notice that Dumb Eyetie was limping after her, falteringly, like somebody who was chasing a fluttering butterfly, with one hand in front of him in the air, slapping at imagined obstacles, his direction a muddle of hit and miss, but following the slipstream of her smell. Lately she'd been using more perfume than usual, for his benefit, so he could sense her coming from afar, could place her.

But now, in fits and starts, he stumbled after her and the dogs' smell, one hand cold from stroking the koi in the pond, the other curled around his love stone, as the Yearsonenders called it, that palm stone, which he had picked up on arrival and kept in his shirt pocket all those days when he was laying the lightning water channel.

The labourers in the fields had grown accustomed to Ingi's walks and now always waved to her when she passed with her bouncing backpack, but today they were calling and gesticulating, trying to draw her attention to the man following her drunkenly. She turned round, surprised, then waited for him with her hands on her hips, watching the old man, who took three steps, hovered, sniffed, tilted his head sideways, then took four more quick steps, turned slightly, froze, sniffed, reversed, then ventured once again into the void.

She waited for him until eventually they faced each other across the open road. His nose moved as he sniffed, like one of the rock rabbits scenting the wind near the statue of the Blessed Virgin Mary on Mount Improbable.

She reached out a hand and touched his cheek gently, a touch as soft as a butterfly settling. Does he love me, Ingi wondered, this man who behaves so differently from all the other men I've known? He suckles me like a baby, until his anxious heartbeat subsides; he follows me like an old blind dog with that snuffling nose. But he hardly ever puts out his hand to me; he doesn't touch me; he demands nothing. Doesn't he know desire? Maybe in that dark, quiet cave he inhabits, there's nothing left of the ordinary things you associate with love and attraction.

She slipped her arm through his, putting her hand over the hand that clutched her elbow, and felt how cold his fingers were from the water. She whistled to the dogs and they set off again, slower now, less fiercely, but with the same resolve.

Actually, thought Ingi, Mario Salviati was making tremendous progress. Would he have left the house on his own like this a few weeks ago, or have followed her? It might seem a small gesture, but for him it probably involved incredible risk.

So I'm helping him after all, she thought, as they tackled the footpath to Cave Gorge, and the smell of earth and pine trees and shrubbery drifted up. I'm helping him to start exploring slowly, to trust the senses he still has.

When they walked up the last ridge and saw Jonty's little house, they found him standing on his ladder with the Staggering Merman, busy washing the sculpture with cow urine. He looked up, and as they approached he could see that something was wrong: the dogs were now droop-eared and they carried their heads low, sniffing the ground but keeping their eyes on him; Dumb Eyetie was left standing alone at the last slope on the path as Ingi rushed forward. Her cheeks were glowing and she started berating Jonty before she even reached him: 'You sat there making a fool of me in Freckleface's office, you both sat there talking about gold over my head, you . . . both of you . . .'

'Ingi! Ingi!' She only calmed down when the dogs were racing around them, barking so furiously that she and Jonty both feared they – especially the possessive Stella – were going to attack him. When she raised her head, her tear-stained face was taut with frustration.

'What are you talking about? What's wrong?' asked Jonty. He wiped his hands on his trousers. 'Just relax, now. Bring the old man over – look how he's standing there.'

Overwhelmed by the smell of agitation that wafted towards him, Mario Salviati stood with one hand stretched out in front of him, his nose tingling from the mingled scent of cow urine and Ingi's sweat and tears.

Ingi led him closer, wiping away her tears. They sat down, and Ingi started to explain. She watched Jonty closely, because she was on her guard – more than most other people, she knew – against betrayal. When she was finished, he remained seated.

'Let me say a few things,' Jonty started. 'The first is that the gold has always caused problems like this between people in Yearsonend. It has always roused suspicion. And anger.'

'I'm sorry that I—'

'And that's why I've always tried to avoid it.' Jonty drew a couple of deep breaths and rubbed his forearms. 'I was probably also afraid of what the gold would do to me. When you arrived here in Yearsonend, Ingi, I started thinking. Why do I stay in this little house on the outskirts of town? You asked that yourself.'

'I . . .' Ingi felt remorseful: she hadn't meant to force Jonty into confession today.

'Wait, let me finish. Lately I've realised that the gold is keeping me prisoner too. I sit here, just like the general, like Moloi, like the matron, Pistorius, Look Deep and everybody else . . . I'm also sitting here and waiting and waiting . . .'

'But nobody is doing anything.'

Jonty sighed. 'Everyone's afraid of the moment that the search will begin. We're afraid of what it will reveal in us.'

Ingi was quiet for a moment. Then she asked, 'But why didn't you tell me this?'

'I didn't quite know what I was saying when I said I was going to stroke the scorpion's back. It was only once we were in there with Freckleface Pistorius that I realised it was about much more than opening my father's cave. It's always been at the back of my mind . . . the gold . . . and even now . . . even now . . .'

'Why don't you all just leave it, forget about it all?'

'But this is what's always kept us together,' said Jonty quietly. 'It's the dream and the possibility that give meaning to Yearsonend.'

'Gold?'

'No.' Jonty shook his head. 'For years now it hasn't been about gold, the shiny stuff. For years now it's been about much more than that.' His eyes held Ingi's. 'Take Mario Salviati, for instance: once the gold is found, the general will let him go.' He looked down between his feet. 'We'd be able to leave the past where it belongs – with yesterday, with what is gone. I'd be able to sell the Feather Palace. And maybe pack my van and go somewhere . . . else . . .' He didn't finish his sentence but swept the air in front of his face with that familiar gesture, as though he wanted to catch a word like a fly, or perhaps swat away a thought. 'But in a strange way we're afraid of finding the gold, because then we'll only have the future. And we know there'll be a huge fight once we find it – we'll have to decide who gets what.'

Ingi put her arm around his shoulders. 'I'm sorry,' she whispered. 'But it nearly drove me crazy to think that you, of all people . . .' Her voice trailed off and she shook her head.

'Gold fever.' Jonty sighed. 'Exactly what I feared.'

I I

It was those who stood above it all, following events down the ages, who were in the best position to observe the turmoil that now entered the hearts and souls of Yearsonend. Captain Gird and Slingshot X!am came up what was now known as Eviction Road. Their hearts were uneasy, because the giraffe was nowhere to be seen.

The paint bottles glowed in the horse's saddlebag, and the young captain's fingers itched for the brush. He could already feel, almost tangibly, how the figures would grow under his fingers. Yes, especially the giraffe because it was time for this elegant animal, the mannequin of the veld, it was time to capture and in the process also confirm the cruelty of the making of a likeness: in creating you destroy at the same time.

The captain held his binoculars to his eyes and turned his body along with his head as he scanned the surroundings for a small head, two little horns and flicking ears showing over the treetops. Slingshot X!am stood upright in his stirrups and sniffed the air. The cicadas shrilled and the mountain was mercilessly hot. They had a long journey ahead: the captain still wanted to draw the porcupine, the antbear, the blue-headed lizard, the mountain zebra and the leopard; he still wanted to look up the tribes towards the south east and capture the chieftains on paper; he wanted to draw a map of his travels and to determine the position of the stars from here.

The captain had an endless number of projects, and Slingshot X!am only hoped they would be able to track down the giraffe today; that he would be drawn; that he would be killed, measured, written up and left behind, so they could continue.

He missed women, and he knew that somewhere they'd come across a group of nomadic Khoi again, and women would be given to them. Just as long as it happened soon, because he was also getting impatient with the captain who stood scratching his arse absentmindedly and never realised why the Khoi they met laughed at his multicoloured backside. 'The cock,' the Khoi called him. 'The cock that scratches then draws.'

But today something disturbed the natural rhythms. There was a hazy heat over everything. It's dust, thought Captain Gird, although you might have mistaken it for mist. It's dust: probably one of those huge herds of tens of thousands of springbok on the move many miles away, beyond the horizon, kicking up this enormous dustcloud.

The fine powder sifted down on them, while their horses stamped restlessly and they moved around the place where the giraffe was supposed to be. But there was nothing, and Captain Gird felt uneasy. At night he perused his drawings, and felt, always, that the collection was too meagre. He was never satisfied: this mighty landscape, these plains and the fabulous fauna and flora, the strange people . . . and look at this pathetic little bundle of drawings. How would he ever be able to encompass the landscape and bring home the enormity, the drama of it to the people in England?

That's why he started to add and amplify. Here a line that bulged too much; there a tint too sharp or pen-stroke too dramatic. Slingshot X!am suppressed a chuckle when he saw the lizard with two heads and the ostrich with the infinitely long neck. But he liked the women with the buttocks like cumulus clouds, and the breasts that hung like fruit.

'Unsaddle,' gestured Captain Gird.

'Here?'

'Unsaddle, I say.'

'The lion will come and grab us by the foot right here tonight.'

'We can't leave until the giraffe has been painted and measured.'

But it was not only Gird and his scout, X!am, who were unsettled by the feeling that something was amiss, incomplete. Granny Siela Pedi walked down Eviction Road and saw the women leaning inquisitively over garden gates and the children skipping in the street, making up new games about gold and riches.

She saw Mayor Moloi slip into Pistorius Attorneys after he'd looked quickly over his shoulder. It might be regular town business, of course, but that furtive glance over the shoulder betrayed him. And there was the Mercedes that was carelessly parked, with one wheel in the flowerbed in front of the attorney's office.

Granny Siela noticed the pub was full all day long; vehicles from faraway farms stood there bumper to bumper, snout to snout. When she walked past the bar, she heard the hubbub of voices; the boasting and bragging, the loud laughter and jeering.

She went slowly past Little Hands and leaned over to read the inscription. Then she turned in the direction of Lampak's Dam. The little boy – that wet, spluttering redhead – should be in the water, and Redbeard Pistorius should be there to one side, lost in thought. He should look up startled when he saw her, and seem to want to run away. But he'd have to stay, because he couldn't leave the child alone. She had to walk right up to him and there, where nobody could see them, put her hand to his cheek. His beard and skin would burn under her hand, the heat of his body, of him, which she didn't want to lose again.

But he wasn't there. She walked round the block once more and approached again, slowly, walking towards the dam, her ears pricked for the little boy's splashing. But there was nothing. The water lay still, the wind pump's rod sucked mockingly in and out, and bees swarmed at the end of the pipe, just like the farm trucks clustered in front of the pub.

Granny Siela couldn't understand what was going on. Where

was the field cornet? And the redheaded boy? Why do things go missing? Why is it here one moment, so clear and full of colour, and the next moment as if it had never been there?

Where was Irene Lampak's body that swam here, while the curtains stirred as the men in town adjusted their binoculars? Where was . . . Granny Siela turned around: the mountain was there, as always. And the sun, on its harsh, unrelenting course. All that passes, thought Granny Siela, is us – and it is our desire for those things we may not have that drives us, most of all.

Ingi came down the street, but didn't see Granny Siela; she didn't smell the horse sweat from Captain Gird and Slingshot X!am's restless expedition. She had gathered her hair into a bun and was wandering round and round. She criss-crossed the streets and walked past the crowded pub. For a while now she had not talked to anyone there because she could no longer endure the curiosity and avidness in the faces she came across.

Did I make all this happen? she wondered. Look there, Mayor Moloi's Mercedes is driving away from Pistorius Attorneys in a dustcloud again, and there, under a pepper tree on the corner, the general is slouched low in the Plymouth. From that vantage-point he could watch the veranda of the general store as well as Pistorius Attorneys' door.

Oh, yes, thought Ingi, they all want some of the loot. They've been waiting for years, watching one another, waiting for someone to make a move. But everyone was too scared to take the first step and come up with an idea. That it had to be me who set the wheels in motion!

She walked up and down the streets, in the quieter part of town, where the smallholdings were bigger and the irrigated lucerne fields ran out on to the plains of the Murderers' Karoo. She stopped at the cemetery and looked out over the graves. She lingered at gates, studying sluices and masonry furrows, at water tanks and stables, at all the signs of years of patient labour; at the steady forward push of generation after generation.

Still she couldn't work out exactly how things fitted together. Who knew what, and when? Ingi Friedländer, from the big city, didn't know where to turn. So it would be Mario Salviati to whom she turned in the days to come.

And she'd realise later: fate had chosen Dumb Eyetie Salviati, Obliging Edit and Lorenzo Devil Slap – the three most unlikely characters – to bear the knowledge of Gold Pit. In the evenings she led Mario Salviati to his bath and allowed him to sink slowly into the soapy foam, sponged him down and saw with satisfaction how he responded more and more to her touch.

She turned to Mario Salviati who, under her hands in the bath full of foam, held his breath, slowly stretched his body, then turned his face against her arm, letting his breath escape over the soft inside of her elbow.

12

Following his talk with Ingi, Jonty went for a walk. He wandered down Cave Gorge, shaking his flaming red hair loose over his shoulders. As he moved, the flame bounced over his shoulders. The Staggering Merman, he thought.

What really happened that morning? I remember that for days on end I had battled with that piece of wood. Eventually I dragged it round and dumped it behind the house. And dragged it back to the front the next day. Then I started at the foot, yes, I remember, the biggest chisel, the chisel that glides over an eye in the wood, the angel . . .

He shook his head irritably and spat at the side of the path. He pushed open the gate and walked through it. Ahead lay Eviction Road, where he and his mother had lived for many years. Too many things were avoided here, thought Jonty. I'm so used to thinking things away, to avoidance and silence, that my mind just can't get to grips with the Staggering Merman.

But still it is true that the sculpture was already finished that morning when I pushed open the door to find him standing there in the early-morning mist . . .

Some of the town dogs started to bark and curtains twitched as he strode down Eviction Road. His mother had encouraged him to develop his knack for sculpture, he remembered. Yet she never knew about the bust of his grandfather, the field cornet, which he had given to Granny Siela Pedi, or of the many afternoons when he slipped away to Edenville to listen to her stories. But Lettie had encouraged him to break away from the obligation to be a Pistorius.

'You're named after a poster on a street corner, you were born on a ship – go your own way,' she had often said to him. It was in those days that she accomplished great things with her welfare work for the poor in Edenville. They had been difficult years, Jonty recalled. His grandfather often spoke to him about responsibility, about calling and duty. About the advantages of the legal profession, the scales of justice. His grandfather looked on with bitter pity when Jonty fetched driftwood from the riverbed and carved figures from it. 'Artists can't help us in the war,' the old man grumbled into his red beard, 'and they won't help the Afrikaner govern this country properly either.'

And still there was a special bond between him and his grandfather. The old man told him stories about the north, about the old days, when hunting was unregulated, the landscape untamed. Sometimes, his grandfather spoke about the war – about his commando days and nights in the veld; how they blew up trains, scattered the columns of khakis, then disappeared into the veld again, the world's first guerrilla fighters.

What his grandfather didn't know was that Jonty immortalised each of those stories in a sculpture, in a secret clearing in Cave Gorge, close to the place where his house now stood. It was his first sculpture garden, but eventually these first sculptures disintegrated in the rain and wind – they were all made of unfired clay and old wood.

Jonty paused for a moment in front of the little house in Eviction Road. He could still see Lettie Pistorius sitting there under the low veranda roof, and he smelt the coolness of the shade. She sat on a wicker chair with a glass of water. Geraniums bloomed in pots at her elbow – geraniums from Meiring's Pass, where the plant first grew. The screen door behind her squeaked when the little boy with red hair came out and drank from his mother's glass. He was barefoot, and his hands were rougher than you'd expect for a child his size. It was obvious that he worked with them.

She reproached him lightly for drinking her water, and then he leaned over the veranda wall, his eyes taking in every detail: the tuft of grass at the corner post, the line of ants under the veranda step, the gravel in the garden path and the red bougainvillaea at the water tank. He looked at the roofs of the other houses, the blue sky and the tawny ridges in the distance.

Suddenly he turned around. 'Ma, where is Pa Karel?'

She nearly dropped the glass. It was a question that was never asked. Somehow Lettie had managed to stop her son asking it. She looked at him and shook her head. Jonty would never forget the expression in her eyes. In sculpture after sculpture he tried to capture something of that expression.

Now, as if he wanted to shake off these painful memories, he hoisted up his big body and leaped on to the front veranda of the general store. There were a few small groups of customers: people who went in, bought a packet of sugar, took their change, came to count it outside, relaxed for a while, deliberating, then went back inside to buy tobacco, only to come out again to decide on the next purchase. They looked up, startled, when the man in the vest suddenly jumped on to the veranda.

Jonty walked into the store. He had to squint as his eyes adjusted to the gloom. The storekeeper came forward. 'Jonty!' he exclaimed.

Jonty knew that by now the news would have reached him that the cave was going to be blasted open. Just look at him rubbing his hands! Flour dust formed a powdery cloud around them and a sunbeam slanting through the gloom made it dance lightly. Jonty gazed at it in such fascination that he heard only the last bit of what the storekeeper had to say: '. . . can imagine that a lot of equipment . . .' But then he lost the gist again. His eyes followed the sunbeam, almost tangible, which bored in through the window. 'Jonty?'

'Yes . . .' Jonty turned away and scrutinised the shelves. 'Dynamite,' he said. 'Do you still keep sticks of dynamite?'

'Oh!' The storekeeper started.

Jonty ruffled his red hair with his fingers. 'Do you have dynamite here or not?'

'Yes, but . . .'

Suddenly the general stood behind Jonty.

'Jonty Jack!' his voice thundered, and the storekeeper's hands clutched at his apron. He retreated to a safer haven behind the counter. General Taljaard shook Jonty's hand, looked pityingly at the storekeeper, and said, 'This shop only sells chewing tobacco and dried fish. Dynamite I can obtain for you through my contacts.'

Jonty shook his head. The general was in the sunbeam's direct line of fire. It bored into his chest, and Jonty thought of the carving in his sculpture garden: the straining torso with the single medallion on its chest, the face distorted by wind and weather, featureless, one leg and buttock naked and visible, the piece of flesh wrenched out of the buttock, the hand around something that might be a gun or a crossbow. The other hand . . .

'Why are you so far away in your own world again today, Jonty?' asked the general. He had driven here specially when he had received the phone message that Jonty Jack from Cave Gorge was on his way down. The whole town was aflutter now, and everyone was aware of Jonty's movements. The general had asked a few strategically positioned associates to ring him when Jonty or Ingi or Mayor Moloi or Freckleface Pistorius – yes, him too, even him – made any moves other than their ordinary comings and goings.

'Look, if little Freckleface just goes to the claims court, don't bother,' the general said, 'but if he makes for Edenville, and particularly if he seems to be headed for the dagga smoker's house up there in the gorge, or if the city girl arrives there . . . ring me immediately. The fat, I reckon, is in the fire.'

Now the general stood there with Jonty, the storekeeper retreated behind the counter and the customers gathered on the veranda. They were mostly residents of Edenville, and they, too, had heard about the blasting of the cave. They jostled each other eagerly at the door to get a better view, and stared inquisitively into the gloom.

'For dynamite you need a licence,' the storekeeper pronounced from behind the counter.

The general gestured angrily. 'I have all the licences you'll ever need. You know my people are blasting far and wide.' Jonty thought he could smell brandy on the general's breath; the old man was also a little unsteady on his feet.

Here we go, thought Jonty. First the situation forced Freckleface Pistorius and me to make an alliance, then Ingi and I clashed and now this old man who, standing on the brink of his Gold Pit, can't take the suspense without a drink.

Jonty turned on his heel, looked at the sunbeam, plucked at it as though he wanted to snap off a piece to take with him, and marched out of the shop in his heavy walking-boots. The storekeeper scuttled out from behind his counter. 'Wait!' He stretched out a hand. But the general grabbed his arm.

'Leave him. Can't you see he's completely out of it again?'

13

Sometimes, just sometimes, Mario Salviati took pity on Karel Thin Air's little redheaded boy. He couldn't do it openly because Lettie Pistorius, though a charitable worker to the core, had no time for Dumb Eyetie. He was too closely involved with those last days, with the collapse of the familiar world.

So when he came across little Jonty Jack, he only swung him on to his shoulders and took him up into the mountain when he was sure Lettie was busy in Edenville teaching women how to crochet or knit, or caring for babies. The townspeople never told Lettie about the little boy's excursions with the deaf and dumb one, because they knew how she felt about Salviati. They understood her feelings. But at the same time it was good to see the Italian entertaining his missing boss's son.

Jonty still remembered the way his body rose and fell while he sat on Mario Salviati's shoulders as they climbed steadily up Mount Improbable, with the Italian's powerful legs doing all the work. They had their tried and trusted route: first up Cave Gorge, where they stopped at the quarry that had been dug when good paving stones were needed for the lightning water channel.

There, Salviati picked up stones and gave them to the little boy to feel and weigh in his hands. He showed with his fingers how the grain of the stone should run, where the weak points were, then showed him with another stone how to strike a stone to split it in the right place.

Jonty had vivid memories of the shrilling of the cicadas in the quarry, the gunpowder smell of rocks as they broke, the sun baking down murderously on his shoulders, and the Italian against the rocky precipice, staring up at the blue sky above.

Then they walked on – again that rocking sensation – up through the gorge, past the clump of trees where the woman without a face was in the habit of wandering in years to come, and then they'd kneel at the trickling fountain behind the place where Jonty's house now stood. It was moist there, with ferns and a clump of arum lilies, and the Italian would open his old army knapsack and take out oranges and slivers of dried meat and rusks.

The next stage would take them higher, with the Italian sighing under Jonty as it became steeper. At the blocked cave the man would sit on a big boulder while the little boy played and clambered about. Mario Salviati sat stock-still, and the child studied the bare rock, the nakedness of scarred earth. The child would climb about for a while, then sit like the Italian, looking out quietly over the valley, lost in thought.

One day, as they were sitting there, Salviati took out a pocket-knife. He put it in Jonty's hand and closed the boy's fingers around it. Then he walked a little way off and stared out over the valley for a long while. That night Lettie saw the knife lying on Jonty's bedside table.

'Where did you get that?' She was visibly upset.

Jonty's first impulse was to say he got it from Uncle Eyetie, as the children called Dumb Eyetie, but then he changed his mind. 'I picked it up on the mountain.'

'Where, my boy?' His mother's urgency disturbed him.

'Near the blocked cave.'

Lettie stared at him as though she'd seen a ghost. Her lips slowly formed the word 'cave', but no sound came.

That night Jonty heard his mother wandering restlessly through the house. Afterwards, years later, he realised she'd put two and two together. She'd understood then, as he had subsequently, that the cave was Karel Thin Air's last resting place and that Dumb Eyetie wanted to tell Jonty.

But Jonty and Salviati's walks didn't end at the cave: the last outpost was at the statue of the Blessed Virgin Mary, which the little boy could see from a long way off as he rode on the stonecutter's shoulders. They came over the level ground, and there, bigger than you'd expect, with the wide Karoo as backdrop, stood the statue.

Jonty watched the Italian pull out weeds around the Mary statue's feet; he gathered up the bits of broken bottle left by hooligans after a picnic, and scratched dried bird droppings from the statue's head and shoulders.

They would linger for a while, then slowly make their way down the slope again, back to town, where they shook hands formally behind the general store, and then went their separate ways as if they didn't know each other from Adam, the little boy skipping along in his shorts, with his chapped feet and hands and the red head flashing in the sunlight, and the old man, with his strong Roman nose and his sturdy khaki-clad body, walking down the water furrows, as if he was inspecting, making sure that the flow and the gradient adhered to the law of his countryman, Bernoulli.

14

Obliging Edit sat under the pepper tree at Hush-hush. The sounds of the town were far away, like a flock of strange birds flying past in the distance: the excited shouts of schoolchildren at break, the calling of servants over garden gates, smallholders talking to their workers. To Edit, accustomed now to careful rustlings, bated breath and mute prayers at the feet of the Holy Virgin, each sound seemed to be the body of a bright bird; like a pied kingfisher above the town dam; like a saffron-yellow bishop bird in a reed bed; like the shrill-green sunbird that came fluttering to the bowl of sugar-water she always put on her windowsill at the Feather Palace.

Edit learned here that silence became a discipline; a conviction; a world; a universe: a god. She often came to sit here under the pepper tree, and listened to the bright flock of birds that was giving voice on the other side of the fence. Voices, she found, were things with bodies. Voices had warm breath that caressed your ears and made you human. So Obliging Edit sat there on the bench that had been named by the Mother Superior: Decision.

Decision had been made by the Mother Superior herself – she enjoyed carpentry and produced beautiful chairs in a tiny room next to the kitchen. She had placed Decision in the furthest corner of the garden at Hush-hush because she knew that from there you could hear the sounds of the World – with a capital letter – at their clearest.

And the bench was put there and called Decision because only the newest arrivals ever sat there: the novices who intended to take the vow of silence, but first had to go through a three-month trial period before the vow was finally taken and the Order of Silence entered.

It was the new ones like Obliging Edit who went to sit there of their own accord when the silences in the rooms and passages and chapel of Hush-hush started to buzz in their heads, and became a deafening roar, when they began to yearn for the caresses of a voice, or the sound of a laugh or a cry.

It was the young ones, who still spoke in their dreams at night, sometimes calling out loud, so that all the sisters woke with a start, slipping from their beds on to their knees to pray for God's guidance for the little sister who couldn't control herself in her dreams.

The penalty for talking in your sleep was extra cleaning duties, hours on your knees in front of the statue of Christ, and washing and ironing. Almost everyone committed this transgression sometimes, and it was only the Mother Superior and two or three of the oldest sisters who could go through season after season without even a mutter, tight-lipped by day, mouths hanging open in sleep with slack, dead tongues.

Edit began to dream at night: people stood in front of her talking, but she heard nothing. Mouths opened, tongues stirred, faces became impatient, frowned; the throats began to scream at her and the arteries bulged in the necks of furious talkers, but she heard nothing for she was behind a thick glass wall. She dreamed of a choir in which she sang: a hundred mouths rejoicing in song, with a conductor who swayed and gesticulated dramatically, but everything took place in silence.

Now she sat on Decision and listened to the schoolchildren squealing. She heard them tease and giggle and squabble, she wanted to seize the sounds – she who was so scared that people would mock her clumsiness – and pull the voices to her breast like warm rabbits. She wanted to caress them and take them with her to her silent little room with the bed, the white sheets, the two grey blankets, the small chest of drawers, the jug and washing basin, the little stoup of holy water on the wall, the crucifix, the statuette of Mary, the porcelain chamberpot under the bed, the shelf for her sandals, the shutter and the windowsill.

She wanted to display the sounds there and scatter them around like flowers; she wanted to make necklaces from peals of laughter and giggles, and she wanted to hang them around everyone's necks and give the Mother Superior a big warm sound to hold in her arms; something to hug and cuddle.

The new one is in the Gateway to Silence, thought the older sisters, and they kept an eye on her through their windows. They were curious about how she was going to deal with these feelings. They remembered their own anxieties and fears, when something that was so natural was taken away from you; when, as it were, you bound up your tongue in honour of God and His Grace, the Mother and Son, and all the saints, blessing their souls to the glory of God.

They watched as Obliging Edit turned her face towards the rowdy schoolchildren and how she lifted her ear, and they saw her lips start to move. They knew that, as they had done long ago, she was now listening to her own voice, quietly and in solitude, out there where she thought the Mother Superior couldn't hear her.

And they also knew that, in desperation, she had started to mimic other voices; that she was playing out a little drama. She would start acting out her family, whom she was not permitted to see during this stage; then her friends would find their voices in her dreams; and finally she would go as far as creating people – voices to populate her world.

And indeed Edit did act out Meerlust, with his dark voice, and Irene, her mother, with the lilting inflexions of her Oriental accent; and Karel, whose voice was so similar to his father's, and the servants . . .

Edit sat there with her back turned so that her face was hidden from Hush-hush, stuttering, gossiping and whispering.

Maybe, people said later, her love for Dumb Eyetie was Obliging Edit's penance, because when it came to it, she couldn't take the vow of silence. And, of course, you weren't gifted with such a voice just to stifle it. Her singing voice was all Edit had, and the sisters of Hush-hush insisted that she swallow it, and there were those dreams – no, nightmares – of mute choirs who performed one beautiful aria after the other in silence . . .

The weeks passed, one after another, and Edit felt as if she was going insane. One evening, so the story went, with all the doors closed and all the nuns on their knees in front of their beds, a voice like a nightingale's soared from Obliging Edit's room. It was the golden bird in her breast, people said afterwards, that had to get out. When the nuns ran to her room, Edit sat cross-legged on her bed in her white nightdress. Her face was lifted in ecstasy and she sang the most beautiful song – a song of praise to God and His wild, astonishing Creation; a song that had never been heard before and would never be heard again.

That was the swansong of Obliging Edit: with a face so radiant it was as though God Himself had bathed it in moonlight, she bade farewell to her chances of ever joining the order at Hush-hush in Yearsonend. The Mother Superior packed Edit's suitcase herself and, late though it was, escorted the shy, gawky child to the Feather Palace, holding her hand.

She hammered on the heavy front door. When Irene Lampak, with her beautiful hair hanging loose to her hips, opened it, the Mother Superior pushed the girl forward without a word. Then she turned and walked away.

A strange golden bird sat on a branch of the pepper tree at Hush-hush when the Mother Superior arrived home. She hurried to the altar, because the bird was of an unknown species. It had to be Edit's voice, she thought, mumbling her prayers. She was alarmed by her own anxious, whispering voice, dropped her head and prayed for forgiveness: miraculously, the dark forces could also take on the image of a golden nightingale. Vigilantly, she prayed, always vigilantly . . .

In the study at the Feather Palace Edit stuttered out an explanation. Her suitcase stood next to her, her mother sat beside her with a soft hand on her arm, and Meerlust, with the stinkwood leg hastily strapped on, a cigar and a glass of sherry in his hands, paced up and down. Edit battled to string sentences together in order, she forgot the verbs, and then suddenly she started singing as joyously as a bird: full, bubbly sounds that mystified and fascinated Meerlust and Irene and the sleepy Karel who had come to stand in the doorway.

Edit's jubilant mouth overflowed with sounds quite new to her family, as if she'd stored things in her breast that now came welling up, showering out to merge with operatic arias – spine-tingling arias that even woke the servants in their sleeping quarters and brought them to the front veranda, to stare in through the windows at the singing girl with one hand in her mother's and the other on her suitcase.

But Edit would always feel guilty. After all, she had meant to take the vow; she was already bound in holy matrimony as a Bride of Christ; there had been that huge party . . . But the thing in her breast was too big: it had to come out.

It was inevitable, Meerlust and Irene told each other. The girl had a talent and she – and we – tried to go against it; we wanted to deny the one thing that made her unique. You cannot deny a bird its song; you cannot cut off a peacock's tail feathers; you cannot deny a tree its fruit, because then, whispered Irene Lampak softly to Meerlust, you're going against creation.

'But Edit must go and sing internationally!' exclaimed Meerlust. But Edit didn't want to: something in her kicked obstreperously against her father's flights of high fancy. No, she shook her head, she would train the school choir, because it was the children's voices that had brought her to her senses as she had sat on the little bench. And she'd take the little church choir under her wing. She'd also perform, now and then, at weddings or receptions in Yearsonend, but nothing else. The golden bird of her talent lived in these trees around her, here in the shadow of Mount Improbable, Edit knew. It wasn't a bird that belonged in Europe.

And when the train arrived with the Italian prisoners of war, and Mario Salviati bent down to pick up his stone next to the railway line, and everyone realised that the man couldn't talk or hear, then, with her welcoming choir next to the pavilion full of townspeople, Edit felt something melt in her. That tension that had built up over the years; the question: would she always be alone?

When she saw Mario Salviati there with the stone, she knew that this was the man to whom she'd give all her love and devotion.

She couldn't give up her voice: she knew now that she worshipped sound. But she would serve him, the deaf-mute sent to her by God – as she fervently believed – and bring to him whatever he might desire: food and clothing, drink and love; her life.

Which she also gave for him, Mario Salviati, in the end. Without considering for a moment the irony that he would never be able to appreciate her most beautiful asset, because he was held captive in his cavern of silence.

15

Jonty Jack's camper-van was watched closely as it eased through the concertina gate and waited idling, door open, while Jonty closed the gate. He wore a purple vest but no hat today. Then the vehicle rattled over the stones before it swerved round Blood Tree and accelerated so hard that it backfired, setting the neighbourhood's dogs barking.

Blue smoke billowed from the back of the camper-van, and Jonty had one hairy arm hanging out of the window and a bottle of cold beer to his lips as he sped past Blood Tree. Heads turned and tongues wagged, because Jonty turned off to the left then right again, choosing the quietest road, but clearly heading in a specific direction, for the Feather Palace.

Everyone craned their necks to make sure that the miss from Cape Town wasn't sitting next to him, but he was on his own. In Yearsonend everybody was suddenly aware of Jonty Jack. Many of them hadn't realised that he was already known – even famous – outside town because of the Staggering Merman, and if they'd discovered this they'd have turned up their noses and felt somehow betrayed, left out.

The camper-van bounced over the railway line, rattling the chisels and logs that Jonty kept in the back, just in case. He crawled up the driveway, stopping once in the hot sun, as if he wanted to punish himself. I can't go any further, he thought, into this palace of shadows. I never could. Why should I now?

But he remembered Ingi's anger, he remembered his own remark:

'I'm going to stroke the scorpion's back.' Then he released the clutch again, took another swig of beer and swung round the turn in the driveway. The large trees and the white gable came into view, and the broad front veranda and the lawns and shrubs, wild and overgrown, with flocks of guinea-fowl darting away, and slinking off behind the trees, the cats – descendants of Meerlust's stable cats that he kept to thin out the rats.

Jonty parked under an oak on the lawn, leaving a good distance between himself and the front door. He turned off the ignition and opened another beer. He sat there in the shade and looked at the old homestead, and he listened to his camper-van ticking as it cooled down.

The Staggering Merman, rising miraculously out of the earth, Jonty argued with himself. The night before, I'd struggled yet again with a rotten log and a chisel that split the wood repeatedly; a chisel that wouldn't listen; a sculpture garden that stood mute and ugly among the rocks; the conviction that I'd never be able to create the perfect sculpture.

I drank too much that night, sitting right there on the ground next to the stubborn log, and it was very late when I crawled into my room, and lay down on my bed and listened to the night winds pushing over Mount Improbable. No, not pushing, because on nights like that the wind didn't push: the wind jerked and jolted and stumbled over the mountain and wrenched everything open, forcing its way into everything, tugging and irritating.

How I fell asleep, I don't know. But I slept deeply and with strange dreams: totems visited me – long poles with wings and eyes and red tongues hanging out. I tossed around on my bed and called out, but when I woke up, the wind had dropped and it was a glorious morning. The guinea-fowl chattered under the trees; arum lilies had opened overnight at my window; in spite of too much wine the night before and the dreams, I felt light and happy.

I made coffee, whistling while I planned how I was going to get the better of the log with a new chisel that understood the wood, systematically and steadily. Not so hasty and eager, not so frenetically: just gently, restrained; the power of holding your breath, of feeling your way right through . . .

And then I went out of the front door, which had been open all night as I was too drunk to close it, and there, glistening in the morning light, glorious with wings and fins and . . . God . . .

I made a fool of myself, Jonty realised now, rushing into a little town like Yearsonend that day, early morning, to tell everyone about the sculpture, shouting and babbling and rejoicing. Nobody understood, and nobody would ever understand.

And then somebody rang a newspaper in the city – probably that blabbermouth Look Deep. And the first journalist came: a scrawny, cynical little man, who had once wanted to be an artist.

One morning when Jonty got home after testing his new kite up on the mountain, he'd found the little man sniffing around the Staggering Merman, with a camera and a notebook. Jonty broke through the shrubbery and, seeing the man standing there, walked up to him and smacked the camera out of his hand with one blow.

That had been the start of the fuss. Because where did you find a sculptor who rejected publicity? It drove the arts media crazy. They came in droves, even television crews, but everyone halted on the Cave Gorge's path when Jonty bombarded them with bits of wood and stones.

He heard later from Ingi that a cynical theory was doing the rounds in the city that he knew exactly how to manipulate the media. He kept himself aloof, he rejected their attention, which they couldn't understand or endure. It was said, by some, that he was following a cunning plan. That one day he'd throw open his studio doors. But until then journalists competed for a first photograph, a first interview.

And even the politicians saw an opportunity. Here was something noble and unsullied: a real artist, averse to worldly ambition and money.

What they didn't know about, thought Jonty, in his camper-van under the tree, was my fear.

He remembered how Ingi had sat with him and said quietly,

'Admit that the Staggering Merman is the work of your own hand, Jonty. Grant yourself that. You chiselled him. He's yours. Acknowledge him.'

'No.' He shook his head. 'No.'

No. Jonty shook his head now in his camper-van. No. He opened another beer. And, yes, he thought back to the years in Eviction Road. He had been an almost fully grown boy when the laws had started to change and in the mornings when he stood in front of the mirror he became aware of his somewhat swarthy complexion. He wasn't as brown as some of his friends who lived in the cottages of Eviction Road with their parents and were informed that they had to leave, but he was almost as brown. With his red hair, the dark skin was freaky.

Was it to protect me, wondered Jonty, that Mother Lettie had stood up for the rights of those coloured families when the order came that they had to move out to Edenville? He remembered vaguely – beyond denial and forgetting – how his mother had gone one morning to plead with the headmaster. What had it been about? Had he been naughty? Had they wanted to move him out to another school with the other darker-skinned children?

Jonty opened the camper van door and did not close it, as if he wanted to be able to beat a hasty retreat if necessary. He walked around the Feather Palace, with the heavy front-door key burning in his trouser pocket – it had been lying on the front seat in the sun. He peered into the outside kitchen, saw the oven, the shiny floors, and the worktables. Then he wandered down to the wagon-shed where old Cape carts still stood, and smelt hay and horse manure, and saw rats' tracks in the dust at the stable door.

He went round to the front, and stood on the veranda with the key in his hand. Then he turned it, pushed open the door, and walked determinedly to Meerlust's study. He found the ivory leg in its velvet case on the shelf behind the desk. He unscrewed the heel. It took a great deal of effort, but his hands were stronger than Meerlust's had been, and it came off with the second twist. He took the rolled-up map out of the leg, screwed on the heel again and went outside. He locked the front door, jumped into the van, and roared across the lawn on to the driveway, sending gravel flying, bounced over the railway tracks and down William Gird Road, the complaining engine backfiring every so often.

General Taljaard and the matron, who had come to visit the store in their Plymouth, pointed to the camper-van and its cloud of dust. 'See how he runs. He's been running for years, he's still running.'

'Visitation!' shuddered the matron, daughter of Obliging Edit, in a shrill, inappropriate voice.

16

It was as if a snake was slithering down to Yearsonend, people said years later; that channel that chiselled relentlessly through the landscape, cut through hills, slithered around cliffs, and finally lifted its shiny head towards the impossible, Mount Improbable.

It was only Karel Thin Air and Dumb Eyetie's daring and madness – yes, what else but madness could have made such a project possible? – which drove the stone conduit up the mountain, and over it.

On the town side farmers, who didn't have much to do on their farms because of the drought, supplied teams of convicts to deepen the town dam and enlarge the wall. The irrigation furrows that led from the dam through the streets of Yearsonend, down to the smallholdings and into town gardens and orchards, were enlarged at the same time, but this had to be fine-tuned later under Dumb Eyetie's supervision, after the lightning water finally rumbled into the town dam. It developed into an irrigation system that served the whole valley, and Yearsonend became the most renowned agricultural town in the area. Olives and even sweet grapes were cultivated, palm trees were planted, and there were experiments with cotton and lucerne.

The blooming years, the Yearsonenders called them, and a light came into their eyes when they leaned closer to Ingi and talked with a mixture of melancholy and drama in their voices. Dumb Eyetie was blind by then, they told her, and he wandered on Obliging Edit's arm through the fields with his nose tasting the fruits of his labours. Often they'd sit at the town dam and she'd sing to him softly, while he sat with his fingertips on her throat feeling the vibrations of her voice. Edit never knew whether he understood anything of her music, but he always sat dead still, his nostrils flaring slightly as he kept his hand on her larynx.

Ingi listened with bated breath; she saw the two of them sitting there. She knew how they must have looked because of the photographs the matron had showed her, and she saw them before her as if she was with them.

At times like these, Ingi learned, at the dam, Edit would sing Italian arias to Mario, beautiful songs from his motherland and more popular Italian songs that she taught herself. She watched how his right leg found a rhythm and kept it while she sang; she felt his fingers softly on her throat, and when she sang high notes, his fingertips pressed quite urgently. Sometimes it felt as if he wanted to close her larynx and smother her; and the story did the rounds in town that a schoolboy saw Dumb Eyetie grab his wife by the throat at the town dam, one Saturday afternoon when everyone was snoozing, and strangle her until she made high-pitched sounds.

When she heard this rumour, Edit started to take him to church on Sundays, and when the congregation sang she put his hand on her throat, so that the congregation forgot their songbooks in wonder and, to add to the priest's suspicions, stopped singing, so that Edit's clear nightingale solo filled the church.

Maybe the churchgoers reckoned that Dumb Eyetie was attacking his wife once again, but when they saw the tenderness and devotion, the deaf-and-dumb blind man listening to the song in praise of the Lord, they took over as a choir from Edit, from shame over their own whisperings, and sang that morning so that even the priest had tears in his eyes and the sisters from Convent Hush-hush in their quiet chapel, on their knees in front of the cross, looked sidelong at each other.

Palm Stone

But nobody was with them, or in sight of them, as they relaxed on the wall of the town dam one afternoon and Edit hummed softly, with Dumb Eyetie's head resting on her lap and his hand resting lightly on her throat – a hand that turned in years to come to the vibrations of the koi fish for comfort. Edit didn't see Devil Slap Lorenzo, now paunchy from all the good food he prepared at the Pistorius's house, coming towards them.

Maybe he crept up on them, but suddenly he was there, with the red stain under his black hat, and his tie askew. Edit stood up when she saw him – wild and obviously deranged. Mario Salviati also started up, and stood with one hand in front of him, sniffing urgently like a dog. It was impossible to tell whether he recognised Devil Slap's smell or not, but when Devil Slap drew a pistol and aimed at Mario Salviati, quick as lightning Edit threw her body in front of her husband, with those awkward limbs, the breasts and hips revealing a purposefulness that the body had always lacked.

The bullet struck her in the throat, and the artery – and, yes, also the larynx – was wrenched out. The force of the shot flung her against Dumb Eyetie – the man for whom she sacrificed her life – and he fell with Edit on top of him. Devil Slap made off in alarm. Mario Salviati raised himself upright on an elbow and smelt the death-throes of his beloved. Edit was lying half over him, but he didn't push her away. Gently he held his hand to her lips and when he felt the breath cease, he felt all over her body and found the stickiness at her throat.

When help arrived, he was splashing madly around in the water like an otter, beside himself with grief, in and out, foaming in the muddy water, up and down, as if he was punishing himself; as if he wanted to drown himself.

It was after this incident, after Devil Slap had been caught and put on trial, at which he did not utter a single word, and was hanged without ever giving an explanation for his deed, that General Taljaard started to take an interest in Mario Salviati.

'But,' asked Ingi, 'didn't Devil Slap flee the country?' She had heard that he was deported, against his will, back to Italy.

'Against his will?' came the answer, with a laugh. 'No, he was hanged against his will!'

'Yes, he skipped the country,' claimed another.

'Oh, it's so long ago.' A third dismissed the question. 'People forget. Or make something up. As things go in these parts. You daren't trust history.'

Ingi sighed. 'And the general, then? Where does he fit in? Wasn't he there that night with the black ox-wagon loaded with gold?'

'It was a night of disorder,' said Look Deep. 'He feels cheated.'

'And the child?' Ingi asked, lost in myth and speculation. 'Matron?'

'She was still small when her mother died,' came the answer.

'The general took immediate interest,' said another.

Ingi fitted and matched the pieces; the puzzle started to take shape. Why the general's interest in Mario Salviati? He must have realised that something had happened between Mario and Devil Slap – employees of the Berghs and Pistoriuses respectively – that had led to blindness in the one and craziness in the other.

'And then?' asked Ingi.

17

Some nights you could go and sit out there on the dam wall and hear the songs of Obliging Edit, Ingi was told. Beautiful Italian songs about love and loss, about sadness and death.

But, she heard, nobody ever went to sit there and listen, because at the end of the last song there was a scream, a pistol shot, the sound of fleeing feet, and then the crazy splashing of somebody going berserk in the water, as if he was drowning. Don't go, Ingi was told, because maybe the bullet will hit you. Maybe one of the songs was meant for you and you'll be the one who dies.

She didn't tell anyone that soon after she arrived she'd heard the songs in the stone cottage that Dumb Eyetie had built with his own hands for his beloved Edit. That is my secret, she decided, because the songs never ended with a pistol shot. Maybe that was the place where Edit found peace.

Of all the love relationships that she heard of in Yearsonend, it was the one between Dumb Eyetie and Obliging Edit that intrigued her most. There was something diffuse and tragic in the love between Karel Thin Air and Lettie Pistorius, love swept off by water into oblivion. The passion between Meerlust Bergh and Irene Lampak glowed as dramatically as an amethyst couture gown on the body of a beautiful woman, as titillating as an ostrich feather, flamboyant in its greed and ambition, but just as doomed, eventually, as the caprice of an era, and as fashion. The unfulfilled feeling that Granny Siela held for Field Cornet Pistorius was as melancholy as the plains; his refusal to respond as mean and scanty as the grazing in a particularly dry year.

But the love between Edit and Mario! Unconditional, bigger than the two people whom fate had brought together. Was the key perhaps their imperfections? Was love born of desperation and incompleteness maybe the greatest love? Love that seeks a beloved who can change the lover's inadequacies into fulfilment and strength: this love grows into something grander than the selfishness and fleeting passions of ordinary relationships.

Ingi walked beside the orchards. The evening smells, here at dusk, were overwhelming. When the two dogs pushed through grass or lucerne, warm, moist aromas tickled her nostrils. Ripe peaches and apricots hung on the trees, and the lucerne was blue with blossom. Even now, at dusk, butterflies were still fluttering among the trees.

What would happen, wondered Ingi, if I walked up to the dam tonight, and waited there for Obliging Edit and Mario Salviati to get themselves settled, and for Edit to start singing? What would happen if I kept a watch for Lorenzo Devil Slap and confronted him even before Edit saw him; maybe throwing my body in the path of the bullet, to save her, the ugly nightingale?

But Ingi knew that she couldn't intervene; that events took their course and that stories completed themselves in their own time.

Life went on its tragic way; irrevocably, forcefully, as water flows along a channel. You couldn't stop it.

And she also knew that Mario Salviati never lifted his hand to her, Ingi, in tenderness because he still listened to the songs from Obliging Edit, and still loved her. Ingi stood still. How presumptuous I've been to try to compete with Obliging Edit! How could I, attracted as I am to men who flit around like that butterfly in the trees, who can never find a proper resting place, how dare I bring my tentative, conditional flirtations here to Yearsonend and pester that old man?

Overwhelmed by her sudden understanding of her own limitations in the face of the tragic story of Obliging Edit and Mario Salviati, Ingi stood in the trees, woeful amid the fragrance. The dogs came looking for her, sniffed anxiously at her hands and then went on. Their heavy paws thumped on the ground and their heavy bodies rustled through long grass until darkness fell and she realised that she had come to Yearsonend alone, and would have to leave alone.

18

And it was easier for her now: she was more distant in the days that followed – the preparations to open the cave, the town-council meeting where Freckleface Pistorius defended Jonty Jack's concern about the unfitting resting-place of his deceased father's remains, although each councillor only had gold on his mind; the general's increasing hastiness, the narrowed eyes through which he watched her over the breakfast table; the whole house smelling of cinnamon and the feathers that lay trampled into the sofa in the sitting room one morning, as if the bird man had nested there overnight, and the greyish droppings behind the dining-table, between the grandfather clock and the sideboard, excrement spiked with the undigested, white bones of small animals: the snouty skulls of rats, sparrows' wing bones.

In the pub, Look Deep Pitrelli eyed her keenly, and other drinkers turned to her: it was her presence that had brought things to a head. One way and another this little miss from Cape Town had got the ball rolling, and now Yearsonend was seething with barely suppressed anticipation.

The pub was packed every night, people crowded round the veranda of the general store, and in the late afternoon inquisitive folk who normally never set foot on the mountain hiked around on Mount Improbable, where they located the blocked cave and sat musing on the heavy boulders that lay scattered there, staring down at their little town, which suddenly looked quite different.

Ingi felt the changes, and they seemed to be edging her out. It was as though she had no part now in what was going on. She mused over her beer: I'm already missing it, the cultivated fields in the early morning, the peaceful donkey carts trundling along, the eternal loitering of customers on the veranda of the general store. And the mountain, with its fragrances and breezes, and Jonty's colourful kites riding in the wind against the threatening black cliffs.

'And what do you think, Miss? What's going to happen now?' asked Look Deep, as he wiped wet rings from the counter with his white cloth.

Ingi smiled. 'Well, Look Deep, I hear Freckleface Pistorius has suddenly found a map in his safe, apparently in a little wooden chest with a lost key, and Jonty, you probably know, went to fetch a second map from Meerlust Bergh's ivory leg in the Feather Palace. So, now for what the general calls the third map, the treasure map.' She smoothed her hair back off her forehead, and took another sip of beer. 'And then, I suppose, the gold.' She was surprised at the slight irony in her voice – even bitterness?

Look Deep leaned closer, years of brandy on his breath As always when he was sharing a secret, he spoke with a distinct Italian accent: 'And who will divide the gold? And how?' he asked, with a mischievous lilt.

Ingi echoed him, in a mocking whisper, her head low over her glass. 'And who will divide the gold? And how?' And she would have liked to add: This wasn't what I wanted, not this venal grubbing around after Kruger coins and gold bars and rights of ownership. No, I wanted something different, actually something very ordinary: I hoped you'd look your past in the eye and reconcile yourselves with it.

But now gold fever was running rampant. When Ingi turned, she saw that the drinkers' eyes gleamed yellow in the late-afternoon light that flooded the pub. Had anyone else noticed? But everyone just carried on as usual, laughing and drinking. Look Deep's eyes glowed like the eyes of an animal caught in the headlights of an oncoming car on a dark road.

Ingi retired outside into the twilight. She ran with her backpack bouncing between her shoulder-blades. Then she saw Jonty's camper-van. Even though it was already quite dark, he hadn't turned on the lights. He sat with his elbow sticking out, and a cap pulled low over his eyes. She thought he'd stop for her because there was no one else on the quiet William Gird Road.

But he drove past, as if he hadn't seen her, his eyes hidden under his cap, and it was only as he overtook her that she saw the van's sliding side door was open and that the feather-man was sprawled on the seat, with one foot hanging out and his huge wings half open and silvery in the dusk. The petrol reek of the van's old engine mingled with the smell of cinnamon and feathers.

Ingi ran back to her room in the Drostdy and started to pack. It didn't take long, but when it was done, she stared at her bag as though she was waking from a dream, then unpacked it again.

Too soon, she thought. As usual, you're trying to run away.

19

They were together on the train from Cape Town: Mario Salviati, against the window, his eyes on the rocky landscape of the Murderers' Karoo, and Lorenzo Devil Slap next to him, his glowing cheek furthest from Dumb Eyetie and his dead foot like a heavy brick on his leg.

As the prisoner-of-war train moved further and further away from Cape Town, the cleverest, fittest young men were stationed first. On the Boland platforms and later, as the train progressed, at Karoo stations, it was always others who were chosen for the large vineyards and later wheat and sheep farms. Dumb Eyetie held back because increasing quantities of stone in the landscape intrigued him. But Lorenzo Devil Slap tugged at the thong that joined them and pushed forward eagerly when the train stopped. But each time he was overlooked – with his ugly cheek and knotted foot.

Eventually he stood back with Dumb Eyetie. He was tired of the continual embarrassment, station after station, with children pointing at his face and squealing, others looking past him as if he didn't exist. It was then, so many people reckoned afterwards, that Devil Slap was led astray by bad ideas – the day when he sliced through the thong and cut himself loose from Mario Salviati.

In the years after their arrival at Yearsonend, fate seemed continually to throw them together. One couldn't help but compare the two deformed Italians, who were allocated to those arch-enemies, the Berghs and the Pistoriuses, and forged a kind of friendship without their employers forbidding it.

Of course, they were watched closely by the two families, and never dared to visit one another at home. They always met in the late afternoon at Blood Tree, then started to walk, wordless, investigating everything. They were giving this new continent, Africa, the chance to seep in through their skins. Each lost in his own thoughts, they walked; people got used to seeing them – 'the two blighted ones', as they called them.

When Dumb Eyetie first started work on the lightning water channel, Devil Slap enjoyed riding out on Saturdays and Sundays, when he wasn't on duty, to see how the conduit was coming on. In the beginning it was a good two to three hours on horseback before the smell of disturbed earth, dynamite smoke and wet cement reached him, and then he came to the head of the diggings, with Dumb Eyetie's Italian army tent erected under a tree, and the branch screen around the black workers' sleeping places a little way off.

Devil Slap liked lingering, and often stayed the night. He rolled out his mat under the stars, a little dizzy from the grappa they often drank on such occasions. For him, Devil Slap felt, things weren't working out as well as they had for Mario Salviati. While he, Devil Slap, made pasta and chivvied the servants to maintain Pistorius standards, and stood at the ready, with a cloth over his arm, behind the masticating family, Mario Salviati built his trench over the face of the earth, working in freedom with great creative energy; he was part of a tremendous undertaking, that was how Devil Slap saw it. It was a project for posterity. Something one could build on, not just an endless parade of plates of pasta . . .

And on top of it all, he'd lost his beloved Pistorius mistress: the family had finally drawn the line. And he had to watch how the generous-hearted Edit Bergh took pity on Dumb Eyetie, how she brought him things and cared for him. Lorenzo didn't regard her as pretty, he was not attracted to her at all, but he was jealous of the relationship that was developing. A Bergh, he thought, she was a Bergh: rich old family, people of the soil.

Lorenzo also watched how Mario handled stone; how lovingly he turned the rocks over to look at the grain, how he picked one up and weighed it, felt it on his palms, and how he measured it and made it fit miraculously into the wall of the channel as if it had slipped into a place that had always been waiting for it.

Then he thought about the kitchen with its oppressive steamy aromas, how he couldn't wash the stink of cooking fat and pasta sauce from his body at night; he thought of the plates and plates of food that disappeared down the Pistoriuses' insatiable gullets when they gathered sanctimoniously around the family table, often chewing in earnest silence, as though they were performing an onerous and noble task.

My years are going down those throats, Lorenzo brooded, and in the morning I also have to bend over their lavatories and clean up whatever the servants miss. All this while Mario Salviati laid stone after stone, took sightings through the theodolite, lifted his eyes to

Mount Improbable, and drew a line with a stick in the bare veld so that the workers knew where to sink in the first pickaxes.

They were friends, everybody thought – Mario too, probably – and the names Devil Slap and Dumb Eyetie were mentioned side by side in conversation. But Lorenzo was just biding his time. And that day when the lightning water refused, then surged back in a mighty wave with froth spilling over the walls of the channel, and Mario was thrown out on to the plains while Karel Bergh raced away, something – instinct? – made Lorenzo realise he had to stay close now, at all costs.

When Dumb Eyetie leaped on to a horse to chase his master, Lorenzo also grabbed a horse. Those at Washout who saw them galloping away suspected nothing out of the ordinary – after all, weren't those two Italians inseparable? Dumb Eyetie was chasing after Karel, and his friend, Lorenzo, was racing after him to lend a hand.

When they reached the skeletons with the blindfolded skulls, newly exposed by the water, they realised that Meerlust Bergh and Field Cornet Pistorius had somehow persuaded the six Boer fighters with the black ox-wagon to bury the gold then murdered them in cold blood. What they couldn't know was that Pistorius had done this out of bitter conviction and a sense of duty – to the old president, the state treasury and the rebuilding of the country after the war   while Meerlust had joined in from avarice

But there lay the skeletons with the golden coins in their hands, and Devil Slap lost his reason there and then: he grabbed what he could and galloped off, leaving Mario Salviati behind to cover the shame, to re-inter the skeletons under mud and gravel so that the transgressions of the past would remain secret, so that nothing could come in the way of Karel Bergh's scheme, so that everything could be kept ready for the water to come over the mountain after all.

Because Mario was convinced that their calculations were correct: the Law of Bernoulli couldn't lie, he knew. Friction made the first stream of water refuse; but then Karel had lost heart and charged off.

Both men who made off that day were wrong. Karel Bergh ran away too soon, fearing humiliation and disgrace, and Lorenzo Devil Slap grabbed too quickly, from lust for gold.

It was the patient Mario Salviati who did the right thing, he who was mindful of everything in his dead silent world. Over the years he had learned patience and endurance, because he worked with stone.

He let Devil Slap be, and as the rain bucketed down, he climbed further up the mountain, leading his horse, because he was convinced that the carriage couldn't have got very far. When he saw the cave, he knew. He tethered his horse and, rain streaming down his face, he walked slowly up to the mouth.

Inside sat Big Karel Bergh, as brown as his Oriental mother, on the driver's seat of his carriage. In his hand he held a document he'd found in the left hand of one of the skeletons. Unlike Lorenzo's experience with the right hands, which hadn't wanted to let go of the coins and had had to be snapped off at the wrists, the left hand easily gave up the rolled map, which was tied with a shoelace. The parchment was wonderfully preserved: like the black cloths, it had survived all those years underground with remarkable obduracy.

Karel saw Dumb Eyetie approaching. The two men looked at each other. The eyes of one were filled with the anguish of failure; the eyes of the other pleaded, Don't do anything foolish; our dream of stone has just begun. The water will not refuse: let's try again – you'll see.

The rain pelted down outside. The news had already reached Yearsonend that the water had refused, and everybody waited for the people to arrive back from Washout and fill in the details. Lettie Pistorius and the new-born Jonty Jack's ship was nosing its way into the Table Bay harbour.

Karel looked at Dumb Eyetie and gave him the map. The two men bowed over the third map, and then Karel Thin Air put out a hand to Mario Salviati to take it back.

He took the stone out of Mario's hand, lit a torch, calmed his horses and sat on the ground. He took out his pocket knife and slowly carved the precise directions to Gold Pit – the resting place of the blindfolded skeletons – on to Mario Salviati's beloved stroking stone.

When he was finished, he gave the stone back to Mario, who took it with his left hand. Karel closed Mario's fingers gently and firmly around the stone. He walked with the map to the carriage and took out a box of matches, then dug underneath the seat.

The fact that Mario couldn't speak probably played a big part in it. Because when Karel held out the stick of dynamite to Mario, there could be no debate. They looked at each other for a long time: the exiled Italian prisoner of war, and the man who feared that he was going to become a prisoner in his own country, in shame, in disgrace, through laws that, in his blood, he could feel coming.

Mario held the stone tightly in his left hand, walked out of the cave, waited until Karel got into the carriage, put his hat on his head and lit a cigar. Then, as a man with an intimate knowledge of rock and gravitational forces, he stuck the dynamite into exactly the right crevice in the rocks and lit the fuse, then fled through the rain to his horse and rushed at breakneck speed down the mountain.

20

Where Jonty Jack sat on the ledge overlooking his sculpture garden, he could see the road that went south from Yearsonend. He often sat there with his binoculars – once he'd even brought the telescope – and watched vehicles approach. Once, twice, maybe three times a day a little worm of dust appeared on the horizon. Bravely the bus or car progressed over the landscape, and slowly the puff of dust dissipated into a misty cloud that sifted out over the plains until there was no longer any trace of the traveller.

These days Jonty sat there often, driven by the fear that the outside world might hear about the opening of the cave. He paid close attention to every vehicle that approached. His experience with the journalists who came to enquire about the Staggering Merman, and Ingi's arrival, with the instruction to buy the sculpture, had resurrected his old anxieties about the outside world.

I sit here guarding the gates, he thought, with a bitter laugh, but I can't do anything about it. Now that everything is coming out into the open, now that we want to unearth it all, lay it bare, I seem to want to run away into the mountain. I want to throw the merman over my shoulder – if only I was strong enough! – and find a cave where I can hide.

And it was from here that he saw the Plymouth take the road out of town and head slowly over the plains towards the south. Under a thorn tree, approximately five kilometres out of town, the general pulled over. The motor car was the only speck of colour in the landscape, and Jonty adjusted the binoculars. To his surprise the Mercedes now drove out of town too, faster, more urgently. Moloi! thought Jonty. Would you believe it?

The Mercedes pulled up near the Plymouth. Jonty saw the two men get out. They were far away and small, and he couldn't make out their facial expressions. They stood there talking for a long time, waving their arms, gesturing animatedly, and later went to urinate side by side. After this they walked back to the cars, shook hands, and Moloi got into his.

He drove back to town, now apparently at ease. The general stood for a while at his car, then bent and took out a gun. He produced something that looked like a Coke can then paced a good fifty yards into the veld. He put down the can, walked back to the car, then suddenly turned and fired at it repeatedly. Jonty looked on, fascinated. With the sun reflecting on it, the can was a shiny insect darting about as the bullets slammed into it.

The sounds of the shots took a while to reach him. Continuous sharp, cracking reports. They made the small falcons flutter, and rock-rabbits dived into their rock fissures. The general seemed to have let off steam now. He left the twisted can where it lay, got into his car and raced at an incredible speed back to town – so fast that the Plymouth skidded round corners and Jonty feared it would leave the road.

When the cloud of dust had disappeared, he stood up and started to walk through his sculpture garden. He stood in front of the sculpture that had something of the general in it. He looked at the buttock with the bite wrenched out by shrapnel. He walked over to the sculpture of the angel: the one crippled, disappointed wing; the beak like an owl's; the paint strokes that made the faeces drip.

So you want to take the Staggering Merman, thought Jonty, and cordon him off with a little rope fence in a cold entrance hall with white light where people hurry past. How could I allow this? This is the sculpture that was given to me, how could I give him up as though he was not part of me?

And then, I know, you would summon the journalists with their cameras and questions, because you owned the merman, and you would want the world to know about your wondrous merman. You would want him to be honoured – not for what he is or what he represents, but because he is in your possession. It's yourselves that you want to see honoured.

He climbed up the slope and walked over the back of the mountain to his little house. It was late afternoon when he reached his house, took off his shirt and shoes, found a crowbar and a pickaxe, and started to work. The evening found him there, and he had to make a fire to see what he was doing. In the flames his sweaty upper body was grimed with dust. He anchored the merman with a series of ropes, so that when he'd loosened the base from the ground, the merman wouldn't topple. He opened the tarpaulin he kept in his camper van, and lowered the sculpture slowly on to it.

It wasn't the first time that he'd loaded a large statue like this singlehandedly into the camper-van. The set of pulleys worked well, and just before midnight the Staggering Merman, wrapped in smaller tarpaulins and blankets, was in the vehicle. The sculpture's muddy footpiece stuck out of the back and Jonty fastened the spotlight on to the roof, switched it on, and started to crawl slowly up the mountain.

Springhares scuttled through the spotlight's strong beam. An antelope appeared for a moment and stood, bewildered and blinded, so that Jonty had to stop, switch off the light and wait for it to go away. Jonty sat there under the stars for a while. Far below him he saw the few lights that were still burning in Yearsonend – the yellow ones at the railway station, the speck in front of the police station. Maybe the constable on duty had looked up and seen the spotlight here against the mountain and thought a bunch of hooligans was shooting steenbuck out of season. But he was alone on duty and wouldn't go to the trouble of ringing to wake his colleagues.

When he could drive no further, Jonty stopped. He took out the braces and slipped them through the loops he'd sewn on to a tarpaulin. He had dragged all his sculptures over the mountain to the sculpture garden with this sledge. The Staggering Merman was the biggest and most precious sculpture, and he was extra careful.

With the rope biting into his shoulder and hands, Jonty started the climb. Every so often he took a break, and made sure that the sculpture was still lying safely. Dawn was breaking with a red glow when he finally threw the rope off his shoulder, straightened, looked at the sculptures around him, and let out a huge sigh.

He walked back to the camper van, got out his backpack with food and water as well as a pickaxe and crowbar, and walked with wobbly legs and a stiff back, back to the sculpture garden, where he started to dig a hole. By late afternoon he was straining on his pulleys and rope again, and he anchored the Staggering Merman upright, where he belonged.

21

Because rain washed everything away, and because haste and hysteria erases the memory, Lorenzo Devil Slap could never find Gold Pit again. He didn't want to let on that he knew that Mario Salviati knew where it was, because that would immediately relegate him, Lorenzo, to the background. His big chance would be spoiled. So the great wait began.

For Karel Thin Air there was nothing more to wait for. After he'd raced away from Washout in his carriage, and seen his own body turn brown, he came upon the remains of the six Boer fighters and he knew they marked the place where the state treasury's coins were buried. Hastily, in the rain, he climbed out of the carriage and, starting with the skeletons, he paced it out: twenty paces to the gnarled tree that had stood there for generations; thirty paces east; turn right on your heel at the big overhanging rock, just before the steep slope; then another ten paces to the dried-up fountain, the crags where the cerval cat family always lived when he was a child; then back again, five paces west towards the six skeletons. So he determined Gold Pit's precise location.

Why Karel Thin Air didn't turn and race back to Washout with the news that he'd found the Kruger gold, nobody would ever know. Mario Salviati wrestled with this riddle for years and reflected: if Karel had returned he would have been able to offer gold instead of water to Yearsonend. And the only answer he could come up with was that Karel was already brown by then, and that he hadn't seen his way clear, given the way things were going in those days, to return to Yearsonend as a brown man. Apartheid lay ahead: it would be a new struggle for the Berghs. Karel must have sensed that the acceptance he'd bought with money and influence wouldn't last in the new era.

So he gave Salviati the directions to Gold Pit, leaving him to use the knowledge as he saw fit. And for Mario Salviati, who never let the stone out of his hand – not even when he was eating or sleeping – Devil Slap's behaviour was a sign of what might happen to Yearsonend when the gold was finally dug up.

Devil Slap began to stalk Mario; he became Mario's neurotic shadow. He couldn't speak to the man, he couldn't reason with him, but he appeared at unexpected times, shook Mario awake at night and bent drunkenly over him. Once he even marched him at gunpoint from the town dam to the mountain, but Mario hesitated at the point where the channel veered off up into the mountain, shrugged his shoulders and indicated to Devil Slap: Sorry, like you, I just can't find that place any more.

Devil Slap's jealousy of Mario Salviati deepened; he didn't tell anyone else about the six skeletons, because if he and Mario should find the gold, he wanted to keep it for himself. He spied on Mario from a distance and kept watch over his house at night. But Mario just went about his daily business, performing the tasks necessitated by the fiasco at Washout.

After the water refused he inspected the channel and organised the removal of the rocks and sand that had fallen in during the backwash. He opened the sluice gate again and had the satisfaction of watching the water surge tensely up the mountain, come to an apparent halt, but then, as if sucked over by the power of the downward slope ahead, quietly, with a sigh and an almost invisible movement, slip over to gush suddenly in full spate down the other side, speeding, like a hare before the dogs, to bring the town dam to foaming, churning life.

Dumb Eyetie began the important task of laying out an appropriate channel system below the town dam; cultivated fields had to be levelled properly; irrigation schedules had to be worked out. He worked like one possessed. Only he knew what he was working away – but no! Wait! Obliging Edit also realised that something had happened, on the day of her wedding with Mario Salviati, the stonecutter, the builder of the lightning water channel.

That day the Catholic church was filled to capacity – the town felt it owed a big debt of gratitude to Dumb Eyetie for his great work so the Calvinists walked the considerable distance to the Catholic church, where they looked cynically at the statues in the niches next to the altar and pinched their noses against the incense. Even the Mother Superior from Hush-hush had marshalled her mute penguins and covered the long distance of two hundred paces from the Hush-hush chapel to the church – a conciliatory token for Edit, but also a demonstration to her sisters: look how noisy, how messy it is in the world. Or maybe it was in honour of the man who really knew how it felt to live in absolute silence.

After the blessing of the rings, Obliging Edit gave her bouquet to her bridesmaid and stepped forward. She went to stand next to the priest, looked at the congregation, nodded at the pianist, and sang like a bird. Before her, his hands almost black from the sun, the palm-stone already starting to grow into the palm of his hand, stood Dumb Eyetie with hunched shoulders, ill at ease in a borrowed church suit that strained, almost bursting at the seams, over his bulky shoulders.

And while Edit sang, Devil Slap Lorenzo came in from outside. The priest and Edit were the only ones facing in Devil Slap's direction; the rest of the congregation had their backs to the rear of the church. While singing, Edit watched Devil Slap hold a golden coin high – one of those he'd wrenched from the bone hands. It was an intentional repetition of the scene years ago when the prisoners of war arrived at Yearsonend station and Mario Salviati held his stone above his head for everybody to see. But this gesture was meant just for Edit, sister of Karel Bergh. And while Edit looked at the gleaming coin, Devil Slap produced a pistol with his other hand and pressed the barrel against his temple.

The priest was entranced by the singing and kept his eyes closed. So Edit was the only one who saw Devil Slap, and watched him slink off again. She put two and two together, just as the audience did something totally unheard of in church: they burst into spontaneous applause.

She never let on to her husband that she knew – she intended only to live her life for him, and give it to him when the time came, like a pitcher of cold water after a hard day's work in the sun.

For Devil Slap the real frustration was only beginning. One morning he arrived with the pistol at the stone cottage that Mario had built for him and Obliging Edit, and marched Mario Salviati off to the mountain. Edit was at the little school that day, teaching the choir, and Mario had been alone at home. He was sitting in the sun in front of his house when Devil Slap suddenly appeared, pistol in hand. He saw that Devil Slap was crazed again: the man's warm cheek was red hot.

Devil Slap made Mario get up and walk ahead of him, through the concertina gate, up Cave Gorge and then to the left, to the statue of the Blessed Virgin Mary. There he made him sit and produced a bottle of grappa. With the barrel of his pistol he gestured: unscrew it. Mario obeyed.

'Drink.' Mario didn't hear the command, but caught the meaning, and took a sip. He realised that Devil Slap wanted to get him drunk, in the hope that he could then force the truth out of him. And he decided that there was only one option: drink the spirit and pass out. Which he did. The alcohol burned in his throat, and Devil Slap encouraged him with the pistol. But when the bottle was empty and a terrible fire was burning inside Mario, Devil Slap bent over him with the pistol's black eye, and everything turned hazy, then black, then light again, and Mary's stone arms were stretched out to him, and then the town below turned and the horizon revolved . . .

That wheeling skyline was the last thing Mario Salviati ever saw. Because while he lay unconscious on his back, stretched out beneath the statue of the Blessed Virgin Mary, Devil Slap crouched over him in a fury of frustration, yanked his limbs, forced open his eyelids and blew in his ear, but Mario was completely intoxicated. He was so far gone that his eyelids didn't even close properly over his eyes, and it was then that Devil Slap, overflowing with the acid of hate and envy that had brewed inside him over the years, apologised to the Mary statue behind him, opened his fly and urinated in Dumb Eyetie's half-open eyes.

And this was how the corrosive piss of the grappa-drinking Lorenzo Devil Slap deprived Dumb Eyetie of his sight. The next day he had to get down the mountain with the aid of the frenzied Obliging Edit, step by step, sometimes sliding on his backside, sometimes stumbling and rolling, shuffling and staggering.

To go and sit in front of the little cottage, on the bench, in the sun until the time of Edit's death at the dam, when the general took him under his wing, and until, years later, the smell of Ingi Friedländer fell over him like a soft shower of rain.

22

With hasty brushstrokes the captain captured the moment. Ingi came out of the clump of trees in Cave Gorge, up the path to where Jonty waited for her. He'd been standing at the telescope for more than a day now, watching for her to come.

The captain threw a testy glance over his shoulder at Slingshot X!am, who was trying to control the horses: they were extremely skittish these days. But then he turned his attention back to the canvas. There was Ingi Friedländer now, with flushed cheeks: look at the expectation as she comes over the knoll, then see how her face falls, how she turns pale, looks as though she's about to faint. Captain Gird knew he had to work faster because this was a seminal moment: see how worried Jonty Jack is, he rushes forward, and see how black the scar in the earth is where the merman was anchored . . . And what's that shadow suddenly falling over the scene?

The horses whinnied, Slingshot X!am had to rein in sharply, and Captain Gird stared. A shadow flapped and wheeled in the trees, sweeping through the branches on wings too big for an eagle. Captain Gird was torn between two scenes: the fascinating human drama in front of him, with Jonty Jack trying to calm the furious Ingi, and the birdlike thing – an undocumented species? – above and behind him.

Then one of the horses broke loose and made off into the bushes. Slingshot X!am had to go after it, and the captain cursed, because the horse toppled his drawing table and the little bottles fell to the ground. When he looked up again, after setting up his table, rearranging the bottles and replacing the sheet of paper stained with blue ink, Ingi was saying to Jonty, 'I'm sorry, Jonty, bitterly sorry. I'm really sorry I reacted like that. I don't know why . . .'

Jonty comforted her. He was high on the dagga tea again today: you could hear it in his speech. 'I am but a poor woodcutter, a carver seeking refuge from the world. God is my witness, I do not deserve this world's attention. And as for the merman! You know, he pulled himself out of the earth with a power that amazed me; he struggled out like a thing that had to be born . . .'

Ingi looked at him. She was still pale. 'Where is he, Jonty?' Jonty shook his head. Panic started to rise in her. 'What did you do with the Staggering Merman?'

'He's standing where he should be. He walked there by himself. The angel led him.'

'Where, Jonty?' And then she understood. 'In your sculpture garden?'

Jonty nodded, and Ingi sighed with relief. They stood there, facing one another, which gave the captain the opportunity to draw them more carefully: the young woman smoothing her hair nervously, and the older man, somewhat stooped and even more unkempt than usual. A red curl had escaped from his ponytail and hung over his cheek. It trembled when he spoke.

'Sit down, please sit down,' begged Jonty. He waited until Ingi had perched on a log, and went into the house. He came back with a mug of dagga tea for her. She thought back to her first visit to Jonty; the mug that he had given her; the butterflies, suddenly, in her stomach; the allure of thoughts that began to turn in a time and place of their own.

Slingshot X!am emerged from the trees with the two horses. He shook his head. 'Startled by a lizard,' he said. 'Or by the funny crane bird with the pink penis.'

When his drawing was finished, Captain Gird started to fold up his table. He put away the little bottles and let the drawing slide into the saddlebag. He took out a pouch of tobacco, gave a little to Slingshot, then filled his pipe. The two men stood there smoking and watching Ingi and Jonty. Two artists, thought Captain Gird, coming to an agreement. Jonty explaining and almost pleading, Ingi nodding after a while.

'I understand,' she said at last. 'And I apologise for my reaction. I think . . .' She hesitated and took another sip of tea. 'I think you're confronting me with my own struggle. Your choice highlights my own inadequacy.'

Jonty raised his mug in a toast: 'To the Staggering Merman who wouldn't let anyone mess with his mind.'

And Ingi raised her mug too: 'To our artists.'

To which Captain Gird, the intrepid explorer, raised his hat. Then he knocked out his pipe and stamped out the few remaining embers, scratched his backside, mounted his horse and waited for Slingshot X!am to do the same. Then he suggested to Slingshot, 'Let's go and find some women who understand the body's itch.'

What he didn't hear, because they were already pulling their horses round, was what Jonty whispered, his mouth close to Ingi's ear, 'All sorts of stories are doing the rounds about the woman without a face. You know who she is?' When she shook her head, he whispered, 'My mother, Lettie Pistorius.'

And Ingi suddenly felt so light-headed that she had to grab Jonty's elbow.

23

With every shuddering explosion of the dynamite it was as if something in him broke free; a rock or a stone from a cave roof plunged down in the dark and came to lie in him with a dead weight. Dumb Eyetie lay on his bed, on his stomach, with his face in his pillow. He knew the terrible tremor that dynamite sent through the earth. It shook your insides, your marrow. He remembered the bombs in the war, when everything juddered around you and inside you, when you looked surprised at your hands and feet and realised that you were still whole.

But something was happening to him that was similar to what had happened to Karel Thin Air in the cave. It was already so dark that you thought it couldn't get any darker, yet it grew blacker still; it closed in around you; you fell weightless, tumbling into a black hole: disembodied, light as a feather, but plunging downwards as irrevocably as stone.

Karel sat on his carriage, with the cigar in his mouth, the horses reined in firmly. He calmed them, and when the explosion came and the earth started to move and thunder and collapse and the light disappeared under dust and night, it was only years of training that made his show horses stay put, still standing there in harness. They tossed their heads and stamped anxiously but the carriage didn't budge; the dust made them snort but they felt him behind them, the tug of his hand on their bits.

When the last dust settled, Karel could only see his hand, with its shiny wedding ring, in the red glow of his cigar, and then he stood up, feeling his way. He stroked his horses and fumbled through the carriage chest to find two torches. Water was now streaming down from the roof of the cave, and the stalactites began to drip like open taps. The explosion that brought a rockslide down to block the mouth of the cave had disturbed other rock layers overhead.

He listened to the drops making music on the stalagmites that accepted them so eagerly, their shiny points even shinier in the light of the torches, glowing and grateful. They were silver, the droplets that fell from the stalactites, and over the black horses' backs, and over the roof of the carriage.

Karel went to sit on the carriage again. He lit a second cigar, and waited. Then he stood up again, restless, and looked at the map of Gold Pit. Ten paces, he remembered, but then a torpor came over him, a serenity. He sat and listened as the horses inhaled deeply then sighed. He saw their heads sway uneasily and he watched the torches burn.

When he no longer felt like smoking, or perhaps when the cigar died of its own accord in his mouth, he had no wish for the map either. He sat with the white parchment in his hand, and before the last torch flickered out, his breath failed, and he slept, twitching, shaky, spiralling down into the pit.

With each spasm, a finger or toe grew numb. Dumb Eyetie felt the veins in his head burst; but he felt no pain. There was no blindness to fear, because his darkness had already fallen; he lost no sound, because for him it had never existed. All he felt was the black become blacker, as he began to lose the last thing he still possessed: the sensation in his body. He lay with his face in the pillow and the pillow was wet under his cheeks. He could no longer move one of his arms or one of his legs. And there it was again: a deep spasm that made the bed shake.

He struggled to turn over, and felt that his trousers were wet at the crotch. I wet myself, he realised. Old dog. Humiliation. He struggled upright. Only half of his body worked and he shuffled to the corner where his chisels lay. He took a knife and went to sit on the bed. Slowly he cut away the skin that grew over the stone in his palm. The sour stink of old flesh and sweat pierced his nostrils, and then his sense of smell was suddenly gone. He toppled, almost lost his balance.

I'm going now, he realised, to an even darker place. God, Mary, Mother, I thought it was black where I was, but now I have only my right hand left. Only this sticks out of the cave's mouth. Only this reaches out above the foamy water. Doesn't anyone want to take it?

He was not aware of much more, but the servants cried out when he came limping over the paving and the parrots fled squawking deeper into their cage. Alexander and Stella, who had already crawled as far as possible into a corner because of the dynamite crumps, pressed even closer to each other. The servants watched Salviati stagger and almost fall against the fountain, then turn back and stumble in the direction of the kitchen.

He was now without smell, reliant purely on memory. He limped through the kitchen, and the startled servants retreated from the old man who, stinking of urine and dragging a strangely lame leg, disappeared down the hall.

He reached Ingi's room and pushed open the door at the moment that the last dust from the explosion settled, and those gathered there craned their necks and saw the black mouth of the cave, and behind that the awesome sight of the black carriage, the skeleton with the parchment in his hand – parchment on which the fireflies sat, glittering – and the horse skeletons, amazingly still upright in their harness.

Mario Salviati put his palm stone on Ingi's pillow, turned, and went to his bed to die.

24

At the cave everyone waited for Jonty Jack to climb over the boulders. It wasn't easy for him, Ingi saw. His jaw was white with the effort of controlling his emotions. Everyone was there: the general with his hooked nose, the matron muttering beside him, and Look Deep, with his ruddy face, and Freckleface Pistorius, and Mayor Moloi, and the whole town crowded on the clearing in front of the cave or gathered like rock-rabbits on the mountain slope, in positions with the best view.

Yearsonend lay below them, quiet and patient, and a swarm of locusts struggled up the dry riverbed. The Murderers' Karoo baked mercilessly under the blazing sun, and on the horizon sky and earth blurred together.

What would Jonty touch first? wondered Ingi. His father's hat, still on the skull, the skeleton's skull, or the bony shoulder? Jonty walked into the gloom, coughing from the dust in the unsettled air. The fireflies sparkled once, as if his arrival or their fright made them glow more intensely, then flew up from the document and disappeared, becoming drab little creatures in the daylight.

Jonty drew closer to the carriage, which was caught in stalactites and stalagmites, as if stone fingers held it. He reached out a hand – and a communal sigh was heard – toward the parchment in Karel Thin Air's grasp. When he touched it, it disintegrated into a little cloud of dust that wafted away and disappeared. Jonty rubbed his thumb and index fingers against one another in surprise. There was grey powder on his fingertips, as if he'd touched the ash of a dead fire. The priest made the sign of the cross, and went in to help Jonty, who was now trembling. But the irony didn't escape Ingi: the gesture that Jonty made, rubbing his thumb against his index finger, was the universal sign for earthly riches, for money.

25

It was the angel who mocked them all over town that night. He sprayed urine over the school, and over Hush-hush, and over the Feather Palace and the concertina gate; he flapped his gigantic wings in the gorge above Jonty's little house, so that Jonty thought a wind had come up to run away with his kites, and he went outside to make sure they were securely anchored. And the angel swooped with the sound of rushing wings low over the Drostdy trees and the matron lay trembling on her back and waited, her body anointed with oils and a black cloth bound over her eyes; and the general crouched over his ham-radio trying to find the cause of the hissing noise.

The angel walked down the dusty Eviction Road, stretched his wings wide and spun round in front of Pistorius Attorneys' offices, and his wings and feet left huge scuff marks, so that people would wonder and speculate the next day; and he bathed in Lampak's Dam, snorting and cavorting and spouting fountains of laughing water from his mouth.

26

Ingi sat up all night at the fountain, in the moonlight. The paving was cold beneath her, and she leaned against Alexander and Stella's big bodies and wiped her face on their backs.

The next day she packed her bag, said farewell where she could, hesitated in the Drostdy's kitchen and in front of Dumb Eyetie's room, popped into the pub for a last beer, and made a turn past the town dam. She hooked the empty trailer on to her Peugeot station wagon and drove to the concertina gate, where Jonty, as arranged, sat waiting. He had a cold beer and the doors of his camper van were open to catch the breeze.

He stood up as she approached. So much had happened between them, and now they didn't know what to say to each other.

'So you're on your way, Ingi Friedländer,' he said, and she saw the heartache in his eyes.

'Yes,' she answered, and embraced him. She held his red ponytail for a moment, and smelt sawdust and cowsheds and dagga tea, and was overwhelmed with sadness for the things that might have been, that almost were. He was the first to break the embrace.

'You loved the old man,' he said.

Ingi shrugged her shoulders. 'In my own way, yes,' she said softly. They stood looking at the stone cottage, and the pale road lying in the sun, and the old woman with the bucket walking in the heat haze along the route that she had to take over and over again every day.

'I've decided to leave the gallery,' Ingi said suddenly to Jonty. 'It's high time.'

He nodded. 'I knew you would.'

She looked at him. 'And you?'

He shrugged and made the familiar gesture in front of his face, as if he was chasing away a fly. She nodded. They parted without saying any more. Ingi drove past Mario and Edit's stone cottage, out of Yearsonend. She didn't look back, but concentrated on the dependable rumble of the Peugeot's engine under her hands on the wheel.

A fair distance from town, when she was alone and only Mount Improbable was visible, rising up above the plain, she pulled over and, without switching the engine off, got out, stood in the road and looked out over the vastness of the Murderers' Karoo. She saw a canvas stretched in front of her, and felt her hand move; she felt the stone landscape grow in her, she smelt the oils. And Ingi Friedländer thought: Now I will go and paint.

She took Mario Salviati's palm stone from her jeans pocket and, without looking at it properly, flung it as far as she could into the plains, among the other stones and the low shrubs.

Then she climbed back into her yellow Peugeot, and when she

434

came to a slight rise, she saw a herd of springboks prancing, those ballerina leaps. 'Mario Salviati,' she whispered to them, as they raced over the rocky plains, free, exuberant, fleet of foot and fired with the joy of being alive.

Glossary

assegai – a light, short stabbing spear used by Zulu warriors.

buchu – an indigenous plant, renowned for its healing properties.

dagga – South African vernacular for cannabis.

dominee – commonly-used term in both English and Afrikaans for a pastor of the Dutch Reformed Church.

Drostdy – official name for the building housing the court of the magistrate (or 'landdros') under Dutch rule.

fynbos – collective name for the group of shrubby plants indigenous to the Cape (especially the South West Cape). Literally 'fine bush', from the Dutch, referring to the narrow leaves.

kloof – ravine (originally a Dutch term now commonly used in South African English).

kudu – spiral-horned African antelope.

meerkat – swift burrow-dwelling creature of the mongoose family.

muti – African term for medicine or magic potion dispensed by a traditional healer.

pandoer – pandour; historical term for a Khoi soldier serving in a regiment under Dutch rule. The term 'pandoer' was also sometimes used by the Dutch as a nickname for the infantry.

rooibos – literally 'red bush'. A popular South African herbal tea brewed from an indigenous bush.

sangoma – traditional healer or 'witch doctor'.

sjambok – a tough whip of animal hide (originally a Dutch term now commonly used in South African English).

tokoloshe – evil spirit who appears in the form of a malevolent manikin, much feared in African tradition.

ZAR – Zuid Afrikaansche Republic; South African Republic.

Author's Acknowledgements

Erik van den Bergh of Working Group Kairos, Utrecht, in the Netherlands provided continuous support with research into numerous subjects over a long period of time. He also put me in contact with the Delft engineering company specialising in water affairs who were able to explain Bernoulli's Law in practical terms.

Paul Murray, Senior History Master at the Diocesan College ('Bishops') in Rondebosch (Cape Town), assisted with background research and accompanied me on an information-gathering trip to Florence. He also introduced me to South Africa's Italian community and told me the story of the channel-builder of Clanwilliam. This inspired the character of Karel Thin Air.

Hannes van Zyl of Tafelberg Publishers put me on the trail of Captain Sir William Cornwallis Harris and his book *Wild Sports of Southern Africa* (Struik, Cape Town, 1987). This was the inspiration for Captain Gird.

Wilma Stockenström told me about the Fourth Ship.

Information about the feather and fashion industries was obtained from Edmond Lefèvre's research report *Le Commerce et L'Industrie de la Plume pour Parure* (Paris, 1914).

The inspiration for Irene Lampak's fashion studio came from a Hague Gemeentesentrum publication, *125 Hoeden*, published in 1986 on the occasion of an exhibition of women's hats from the years between 1914 and 1940.

The Netherlands Kostuummuseum publication *Mode in prent 1550–1914*, by the Irish writer M. A. Ghering, published in 1988 in the Hague, provided visual stimulus.

Further inspiration was gleaned from J. M. Adriaans-Buij's 'Veren in den mode', which appeared in *Leer, bont en veren in samenhang met kleding*, a report published for Textile Day (18 November 1982) at the Netherlands Opelugmuseum, Arnhem.

The advertising copy on page 281 is quoted from a 1916 edition of the Dutch magazine *Panorama* under the headline 'Voor onze dames'.

Ideas for the character of Mario Salviati formed around a photograph of an Italian mason working at the Meiringspoort Pass. The image was published in the tourist guide *Meiringspoort – Scenic Gorge in the Swartberg* (by Helena Marincowitz, 1990). The caption to the picture reads: 'An unknown Italian, unable to communicate with his fellow-workers, laying stones in the retaining wall built at the time of the tarring of Meiringspoort'.

Jose Burman's account of the Thornton ostrich expedition to North Africa in her book *The Little Karoo* (Human & Rousseau, 1981) was of considerable assistance. My mother sent me the book years ago with the suggestion that I use the information in a novel. Together with a plaited leather belt given to my father by an unknown Italian prisoner of war who worked on our farm Doornbosch during the Second World War, the book provided seminal inspiration for this novel.

As far as the original manuscript is concerned, I'm grateful to my wife, Kaia, and my Dutch translator, Robert Dorsman, and my publishers Nèlleke de Jager and Charles Fryer also helped a great deal. This English language version is hugely indebted to Isobel Dixon, my agent, and Carole Welch, my publisher. I am very grateful for their sound advice, hard work and professionalism.

Translator's Acknowledgements

The translation is the product of collaboration: Etienne van Heerden and Isobel Dixon both spent a good deal of time working on the initial English draft to help create a translation with nuances that echo the original. As captain of the process, editor Carole Welch led the group with an awesome blend of professionalism and understanding. During the arduous months of origination, a circle of my friends and colleagues made an invaluable contribution in their communal role as sounding board and informal discussion panel. The lively creative debate put a spring into the work. Particular thanks and acknowledgements are due to Mariss Stevens and to Maretha Potgieter, who helped with initial interpretation of the Afrikaans in Parts Two and Four respectively.